image® COMICS PRESENTS

GLITTERBOMB

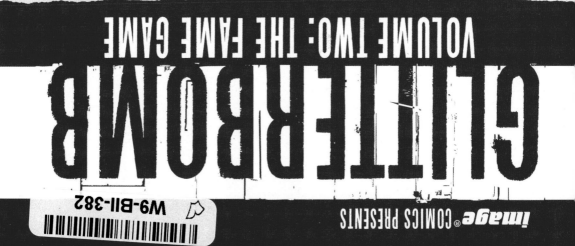

VOLUME TWO: THE FAME GAME

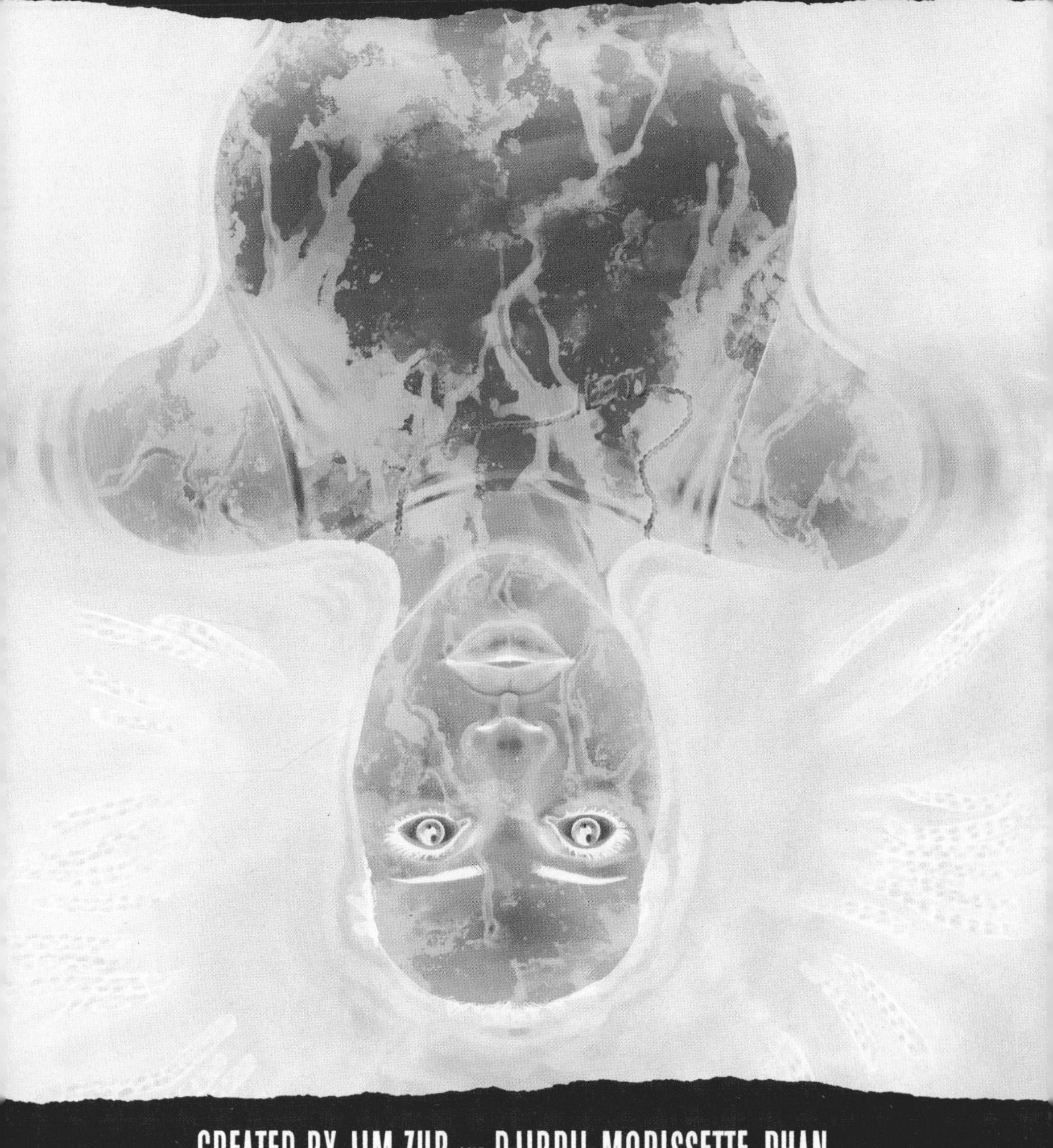

CREATED BY JIM ZUB AND DJIBRIL MORISSETTE-PHAN

GUTTERBOMB VOLUME 2: FAME GAME. ISBN: 978-1-5343-0490-1. First Printing, February 2018. Published by Image Comics, Inc. Office of publication: 2701 NW Vaughn St., Suite 780, Portland, OR, 97210. Copyright © 2018 Jim Zub. All rights reserved. Originally published in single magazine form as GUTTERBOMB: THE FAME GAME #1-4. "GUTTERBOMB," its logos, and the likenesses of all characters herein are trademarks of Jim Zub, unless otherwise noted. "Image" and the Image Comics logos are registered trademarks of Image Comics, Inc. No part of this publication may be reproduced or transmitted, in any form or by any means (except for short excerpts for journalistic or review purposes), without the express written permission of Jim Zub or Image Comics, Inc. All names, characters, events, and locales in this publication are entirely fictional. Any resemblance to actual persons (living or dead), events, or places, without satiric intent, is coincidental. PRINTED IN THE USA. For information regarding the CPSIA on this printed material call: 203-595-3636 and provide reference #RICH – 778300.
For international rights, contact: foreignlicensing@imagecomics.com.

STORY
JIM ZUB

LINE ART
DJIBRIL MORISSETTE-PHAN

COLOR ART
K. MICHAEL RUSSELL

COLOR FLATS
KJ PAGADAUN

LETTER ART
MARSHALL DILLON

BACK MATTER
HOLLY RAYCHELLE HUGHES

ALT COVERS
REBECA PUEBLA
SEAN IZAAKSE
VIVIAN NG
MIGUEL MERCADO

PROOFING
MELISSA GIFFORD
STACY KING

SPECIAL THANKS
BRIAH SKELLY

GRAPHIC/LOGO DESIGN
JIM ZUB

PART 1: PAIN PARADE

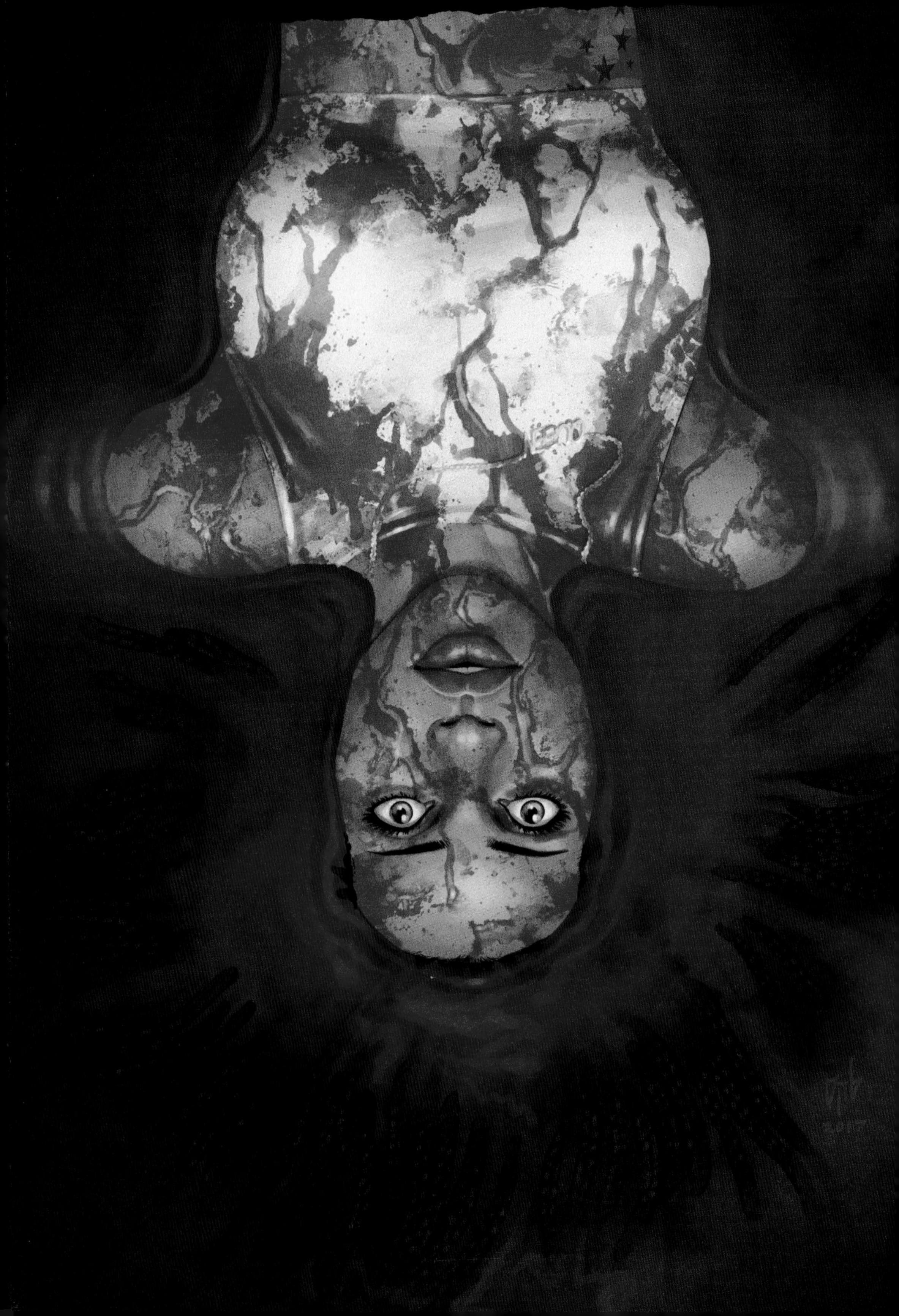

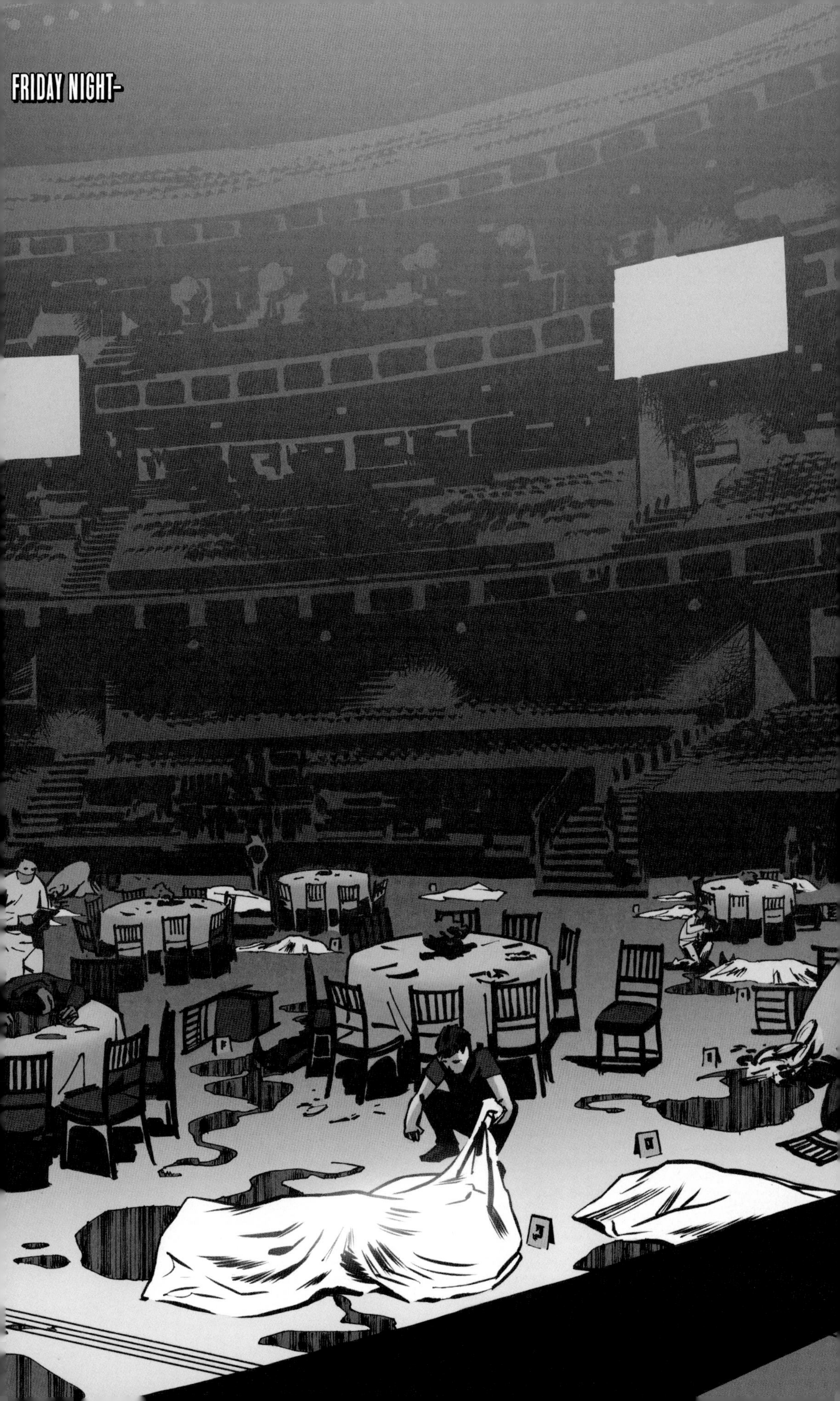
FRIDAY NIGHT-

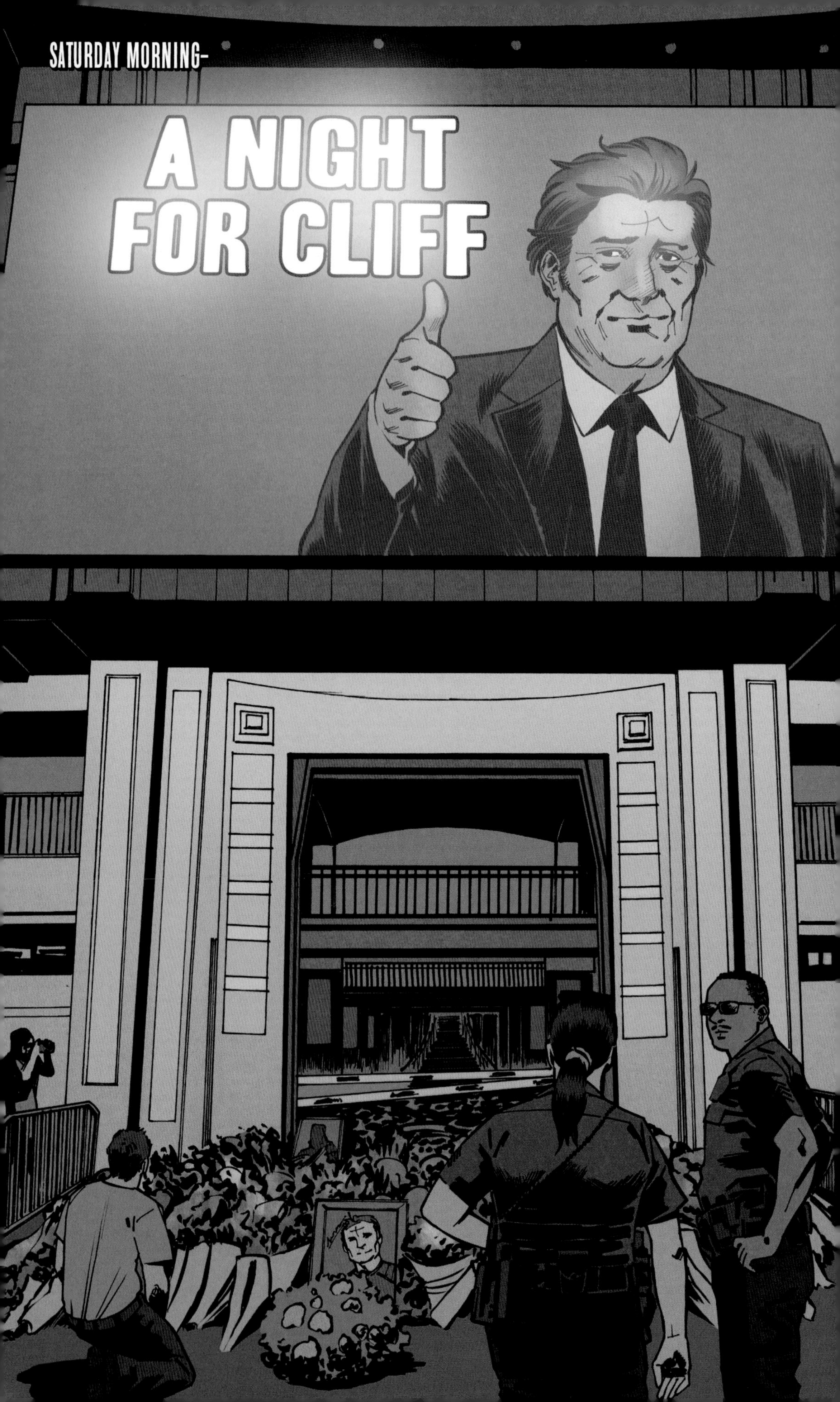
SATURDAY MORNING-
A NIGHT FOR CLIFF

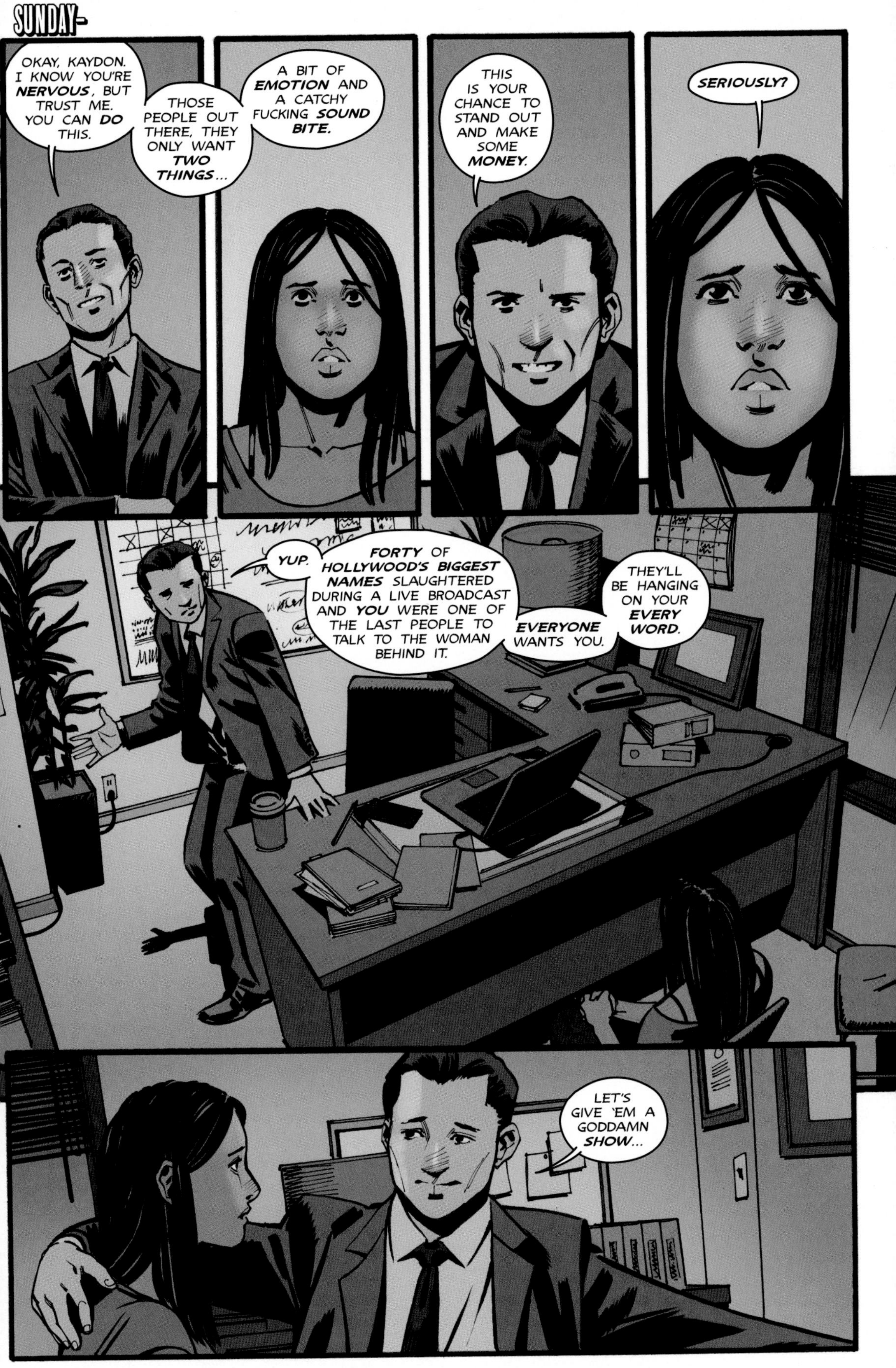
SUNDAY–
OKAY, KAYDON. I KNOW YOU'RE NERVOUS, BUT TRUST ME. YOU CAN DO THIS.
THOSE PEOPLE OUT THERE, THEY ONLY WANT TWO THINGS...
A BIT OF EMOTION AND A CATCHY FUCKING SOUND BITE.
THIS IS YOUR CHANCE TO STAND OUT AND MAKE SOME MONEY.
SERIOUSLY?
YUP.
FORTY OF HOLLYWOOD'S BIGGEST NAMES SLAUGHTERED DURING A LIVE BROADCAST AND YOU WERE ONE OF THE LAST PEOPLE TO TALK TO THE WOMAN BEHIND IT.
EVERYONE WANTS YOU.
THEY'LL BE HANGING ON YOUR EVERY WORD.
LET'S GIVE 'EM A GODDAMN SHOW...

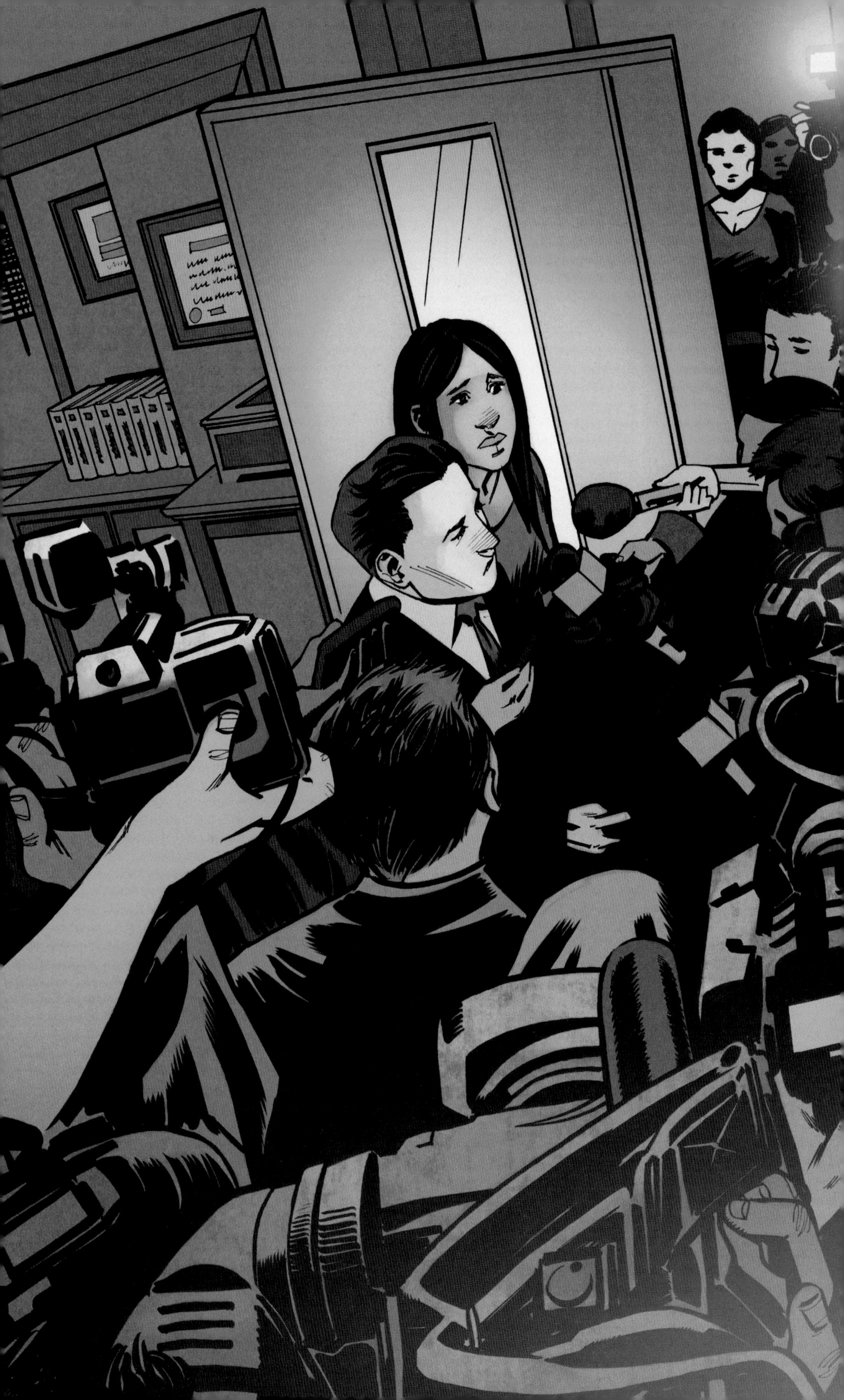

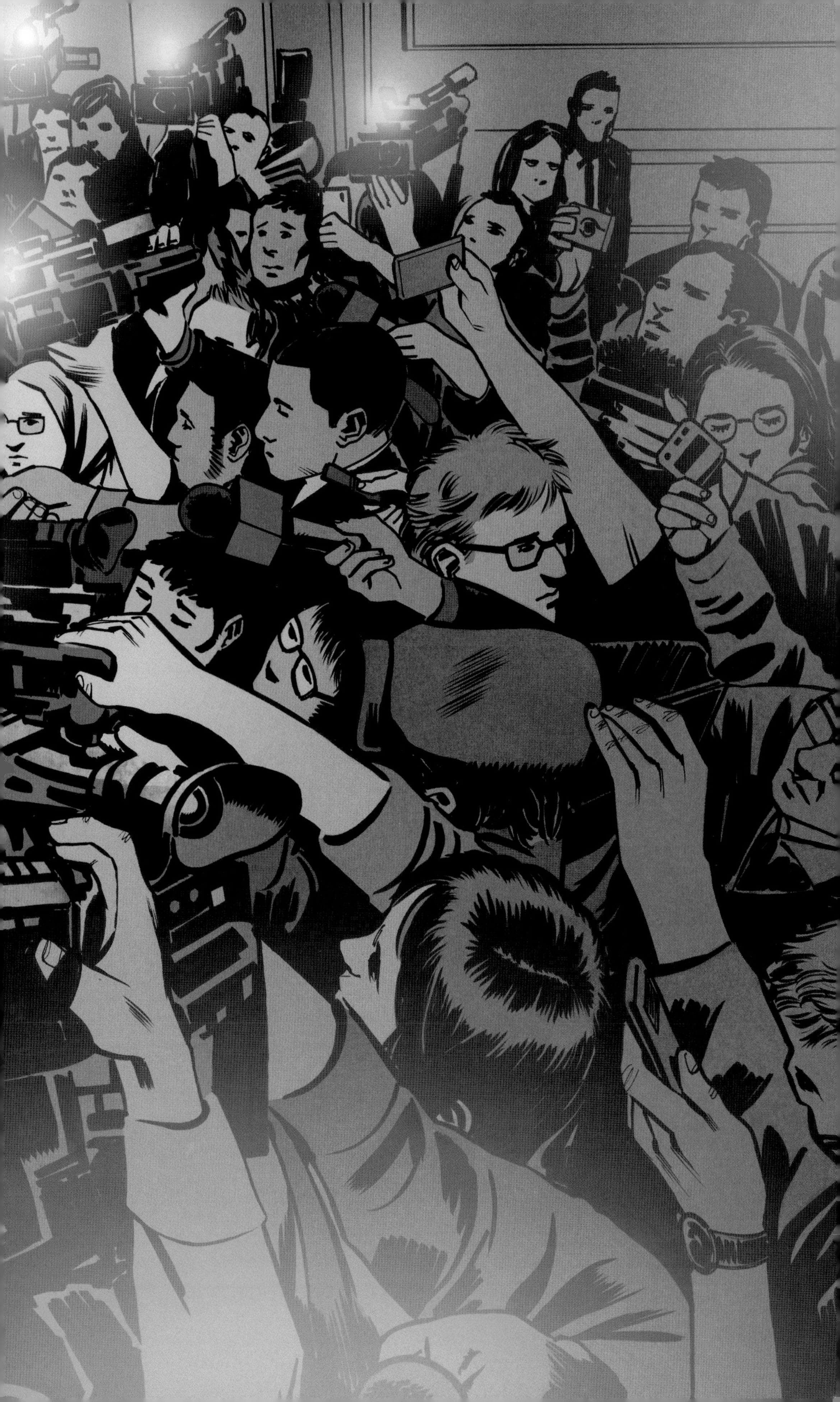

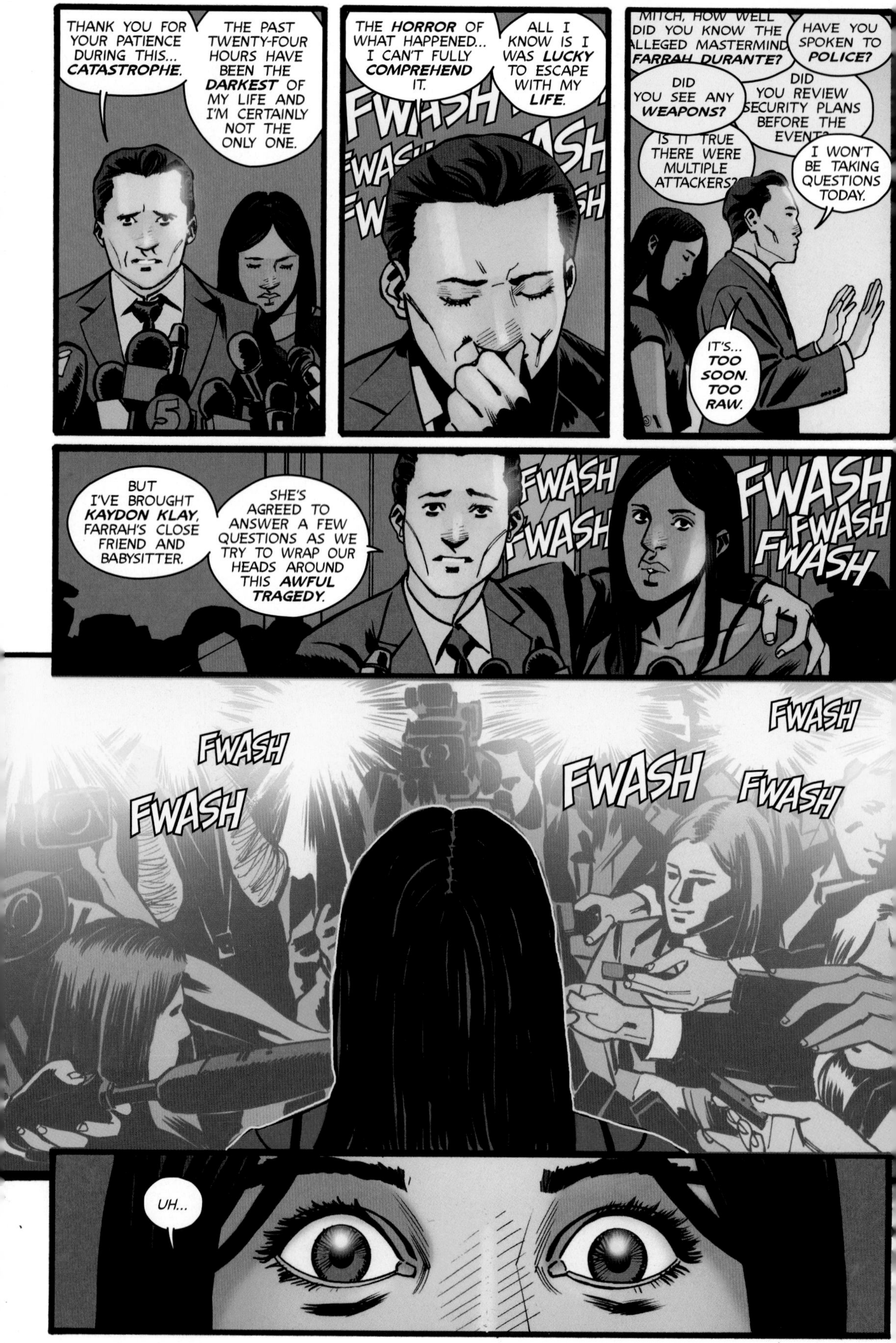

THANK YOU FOR YOUR PATIENCE DURING THIS... CATASTROPHE.
THE PAST TWENTY-FOUR HOURS HAVE BEEN THE DARKEST OF MY LIFE AND I'M CERTAINLY NOT THE ONLY ONE.
THE HORROR OF WHAT HAPPENED... I CAN'T FULLY COMPREHEND IT.
ALL I KNOW IS I WAS LUCKY TO ESCAPE WITH MY LIFE.
FWASH
MITCH, HOW WELL DID YOU KNOW THE ALLEGED MASTERMIND FARRAH DURANTE?
HAVE YOU SPOKEN TO POLICE?
DID YOU SEE ANY WEAPONS?
DID YOU REVIEW SECURITY PLANS BEFORE THE EVENT?
IS IT TRUE THERE WERE MULTIPLE ATTACKERS?
I WON'T BE TAKING QUESTIONS TODAY.
IT'S... TOO SOON. TOO RAW.
BUT I'VE BROUGHT KAYDON KLAY, FARRAH'S CLOSE FRIEND AND BABYSITTER.
SHE'S AGREED TO ANSWER A FEW QUESTIONS AS WE TRY TO WRAP OUR HEADS AROUND THIS AWFUL TRAGEDY.
FWASH
FWASH
FWASH
FWASH
FWASH
FWASH
FWASH
FWASH
FWASH
FWASH
UH...

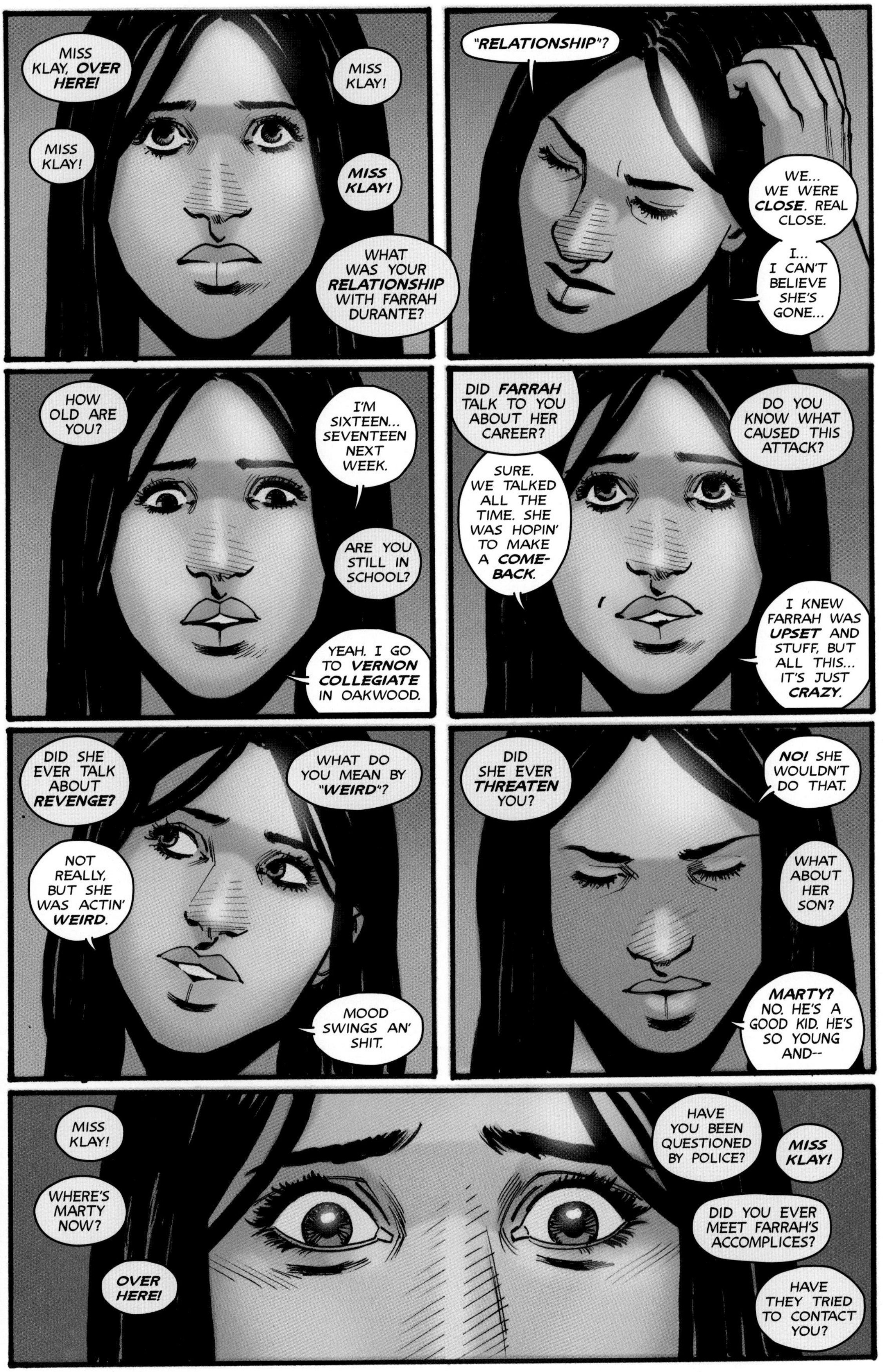
MISS KLAY, OVER HERE!
MISS KLAY!
MISS KLAY!
MISS KLAY!
WHAT WAS YOUR RELATIONSHIP WITH FARRAH DURANTE?
"RELATIONSHIP"?
WE... WE WERE CLOSE. REAL CLOSE.
I... I CAN'T BELIEVE SHE'S GONE...
HOW OLD ARE YOU?
I'M SIXTEEN... SEVENTEEN NEXT WEEK.
ARE YOU STILL IN SCHOOL?
YEAH. I GO TO VERNON COLLEGIATE IN OAKWOOD.
DID FARRAH TALK TO YOU ABOUT HER CAREER?
SURE. WE TALKED ALL THE TIME. SHE WAS HOPIN' TO MAKE A COME-BACK.
DO YOU KNOW WHAT CAUSED THIS ATTACK?
I KNEW FARRAH WAS UPSET AND STUFF, BUT ALL THIS... IT'S JUST CRAZY.
DID SHE EVER TALK ABOUT REVENGE?
NOT REALLY, BUT SHE WAS ACTIN' WEIRD.
WHAT DO YOU MEAN BY "WEIRD"?
MOOD SWINGS AN' SHIT.
DID SHE EVER THREATEN YOU?
NO! SHE WOULDN'T DO THAT.
WHAT ABOUT HER SON?
MARTY? NO. HE'S A GOOD KID. HE'S SO YOUNG AND--
MISS KLAY!
WHERE'S MARTY NOW?
OVER HERE!
HAVE YOU BEEN QUESTIONED BY POLICE?
MISS KLAY!
DID YOU EVER MEET FARRAH'S ACCOMPLICES?
HAVE THEY TRIED TO CONTACT YOU?

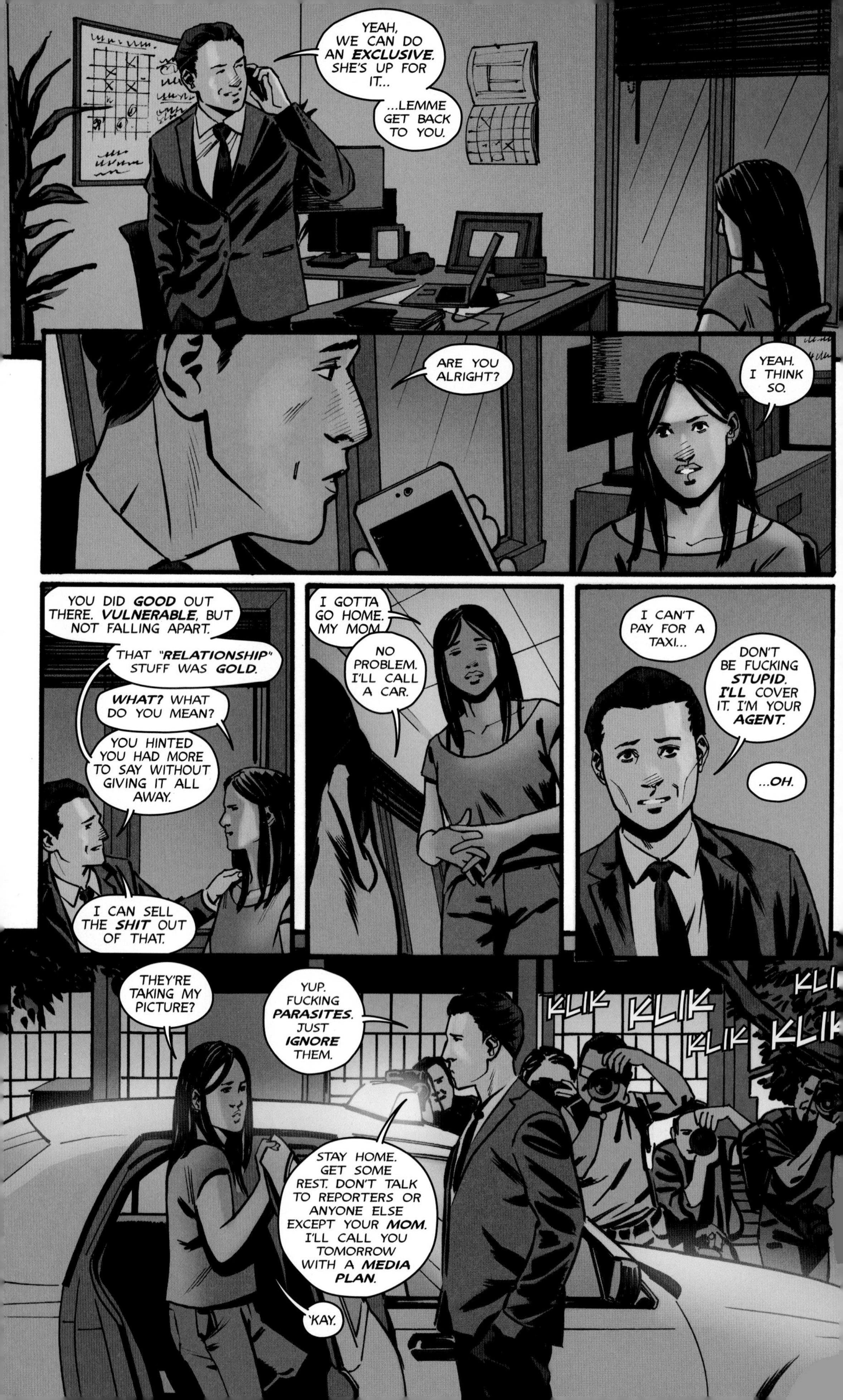
YEAH, WE CAN DO AN EXCLUSIVE. SHE'S UP FOR IT...
...LEMME GET BACK TO YOU.
ARE YOU ALRIGHT?
YEAH. I THINK SO.
YOU DID GOOD OUT THERE. VULNERABLE, BUT NOT FALLING APART.
THAT "RELATIONSHIP" STUFF WAS GOLD.
WHAT? WHAT DO YOU MEAN?
YOU HINTED YOU HAD MORE TO SAY WITHOUT GIVING IT ALL AWAY.
I CAN SELL THE SHIT OUT OF THAT.
I GOTTA GO HOME. MY MOM
NO PROBLEM. I'LL CALL A CAR.
I CAN'T PAY FOR A TAXI...
DON'T BE FUCKING STUPID. I'LL COVER IT. I'M YOUR AGENT.
...OH.
THEY'RE TAKING MY PICTURE?
YUP. FUCKING PARASITES. JUST IGNORE THEM.
KLIK KLIK KLIK KLIK KLIK
STAY HOME. GET SOME REST. DON'T TALK TO REPORTERS OR ANYONE ELSE EXCEPT YOUR MOM. I'LL CALL YOU TOMORROW WITH A MEDIA PLAN.
'KAY.

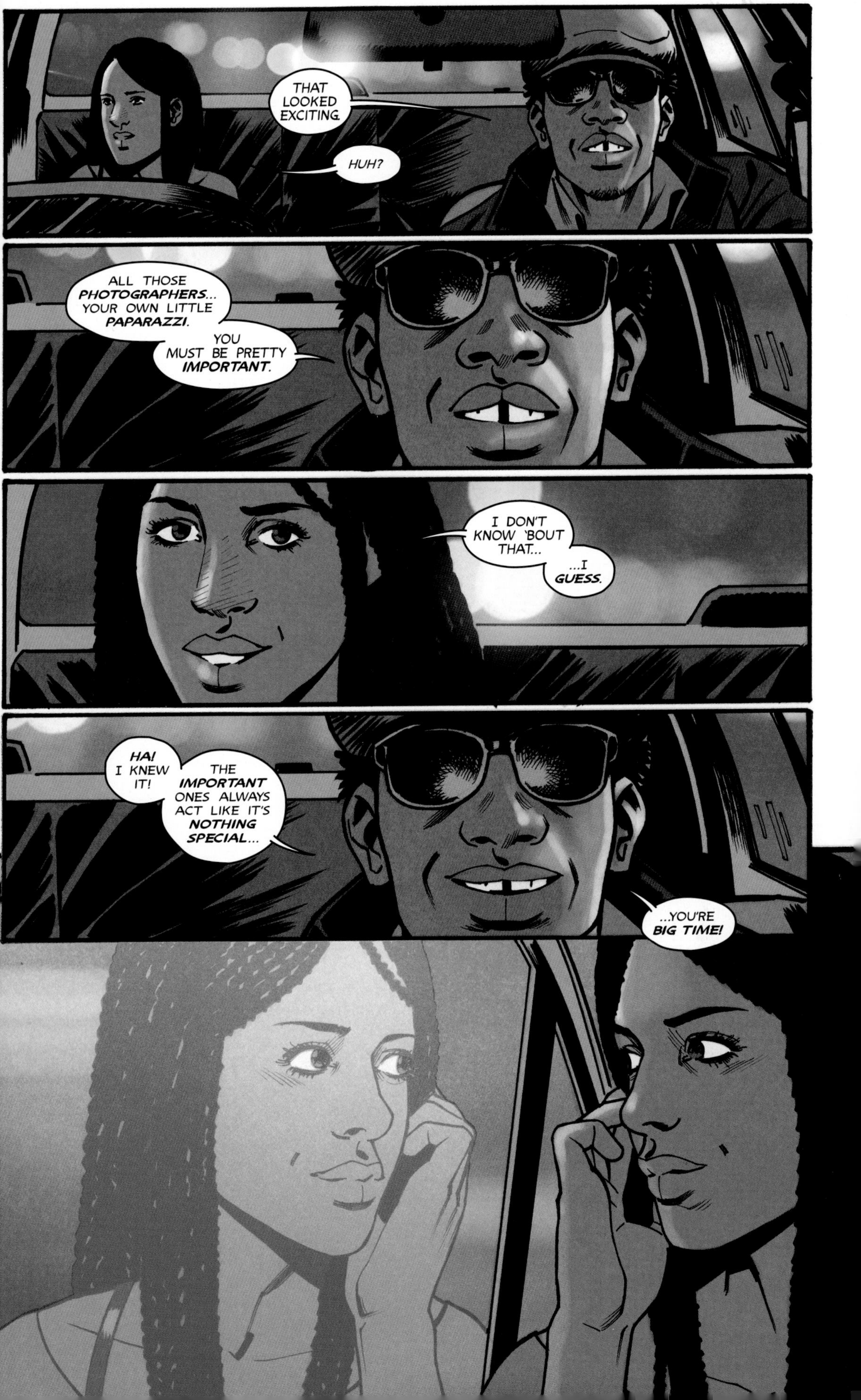
THAT LOOKED EXCITING.
HUH?
ALL THOSE PHOTOGRAPHERS... YOUR OWN LITTLE PAPARAZZI.
YOU MUST BE PRETTY IMPORTANT.
I DON'T KNOW 'BOUT THAT...
...I GUESS.
HA! I KNEW IT!
THE IMPORTANT ONES ALWAYS ACT LIKE IT'S NOTHING SPECIAL...
...YOU'RE BIG TIME!

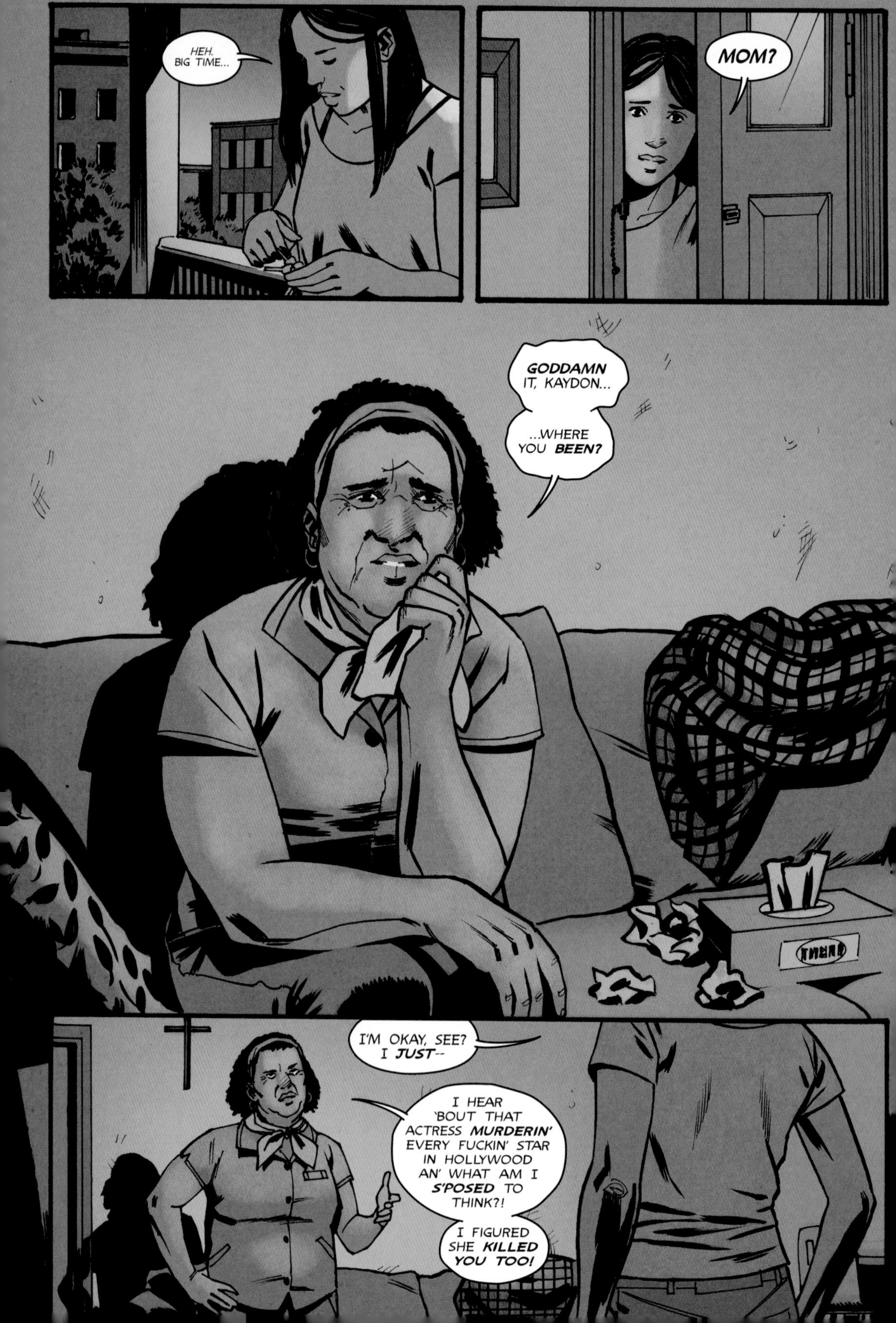
HEH. BIG TIME...
MOM?
GODDAMN IT, KAYDON...
...WHERE YOU BEEN?
I'M OKAY, SEE? I JUST--
I HEAR 'BOUT THAT ACTRESS MURDERIN' EVERY FUCKIN' STAR IN HOLLYWOOD AN' WHAT AM I S'POSED TO THINK?!
I FIGURED SHE KILLED YOU TOO!

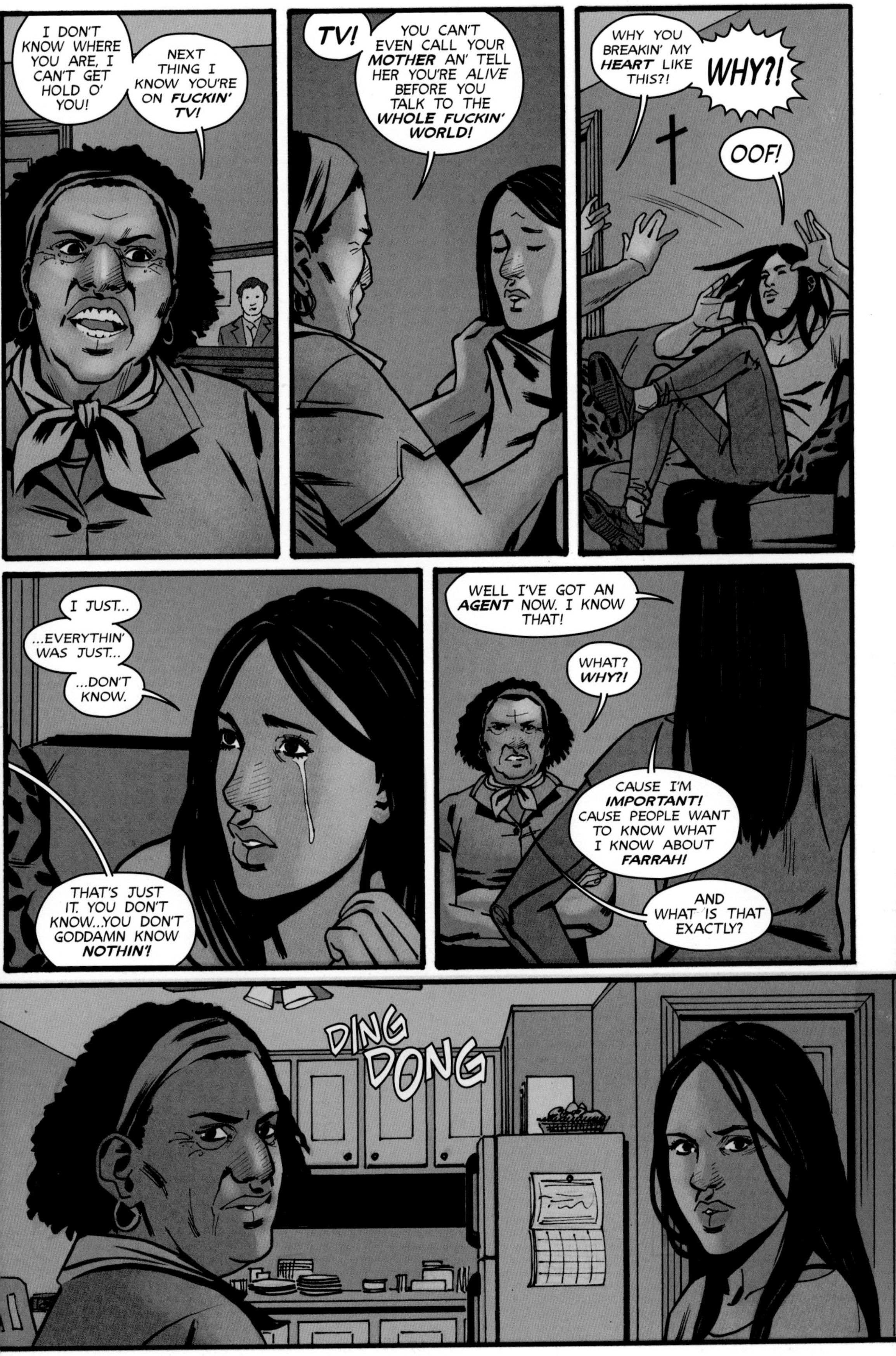

I DON'T KNOW WHERE YOU ARE, I CAN'T GET HOLD O' YOU!
NEXT THING I KNOW YOU'RE ON FUCKIN' TV!
TV!
YOU CAN'T EVEN CALL YOUR MOTHER AN' TELL HER YOU'RE ALIVE BEFORE YOU TALK TO THE WHOLE FUCKIN' WORLD!
WHY YOU BREAKIN' MY HEART LIKE THIS?!
WHY?!
OOF!
I JUST...
...EVERYTHIN' WAS JUST...
...DON'T KNOW.
THAT'S JUST IT. YOU DON'T KNOW...YOU DON'T GODDAMN KNOW NOTHIN'!
WELL I'VE GOT AN AGENT NOW. I KNOW THAT!
WHAT? WHY?!
CAUSE I'M IMPORTANT! CAUSE PEOPLE WANT TO KNOW WHAT I KNOW ABOUT FARRAH!
AND WHAT IS THAT EXACTLY?
DING DONG

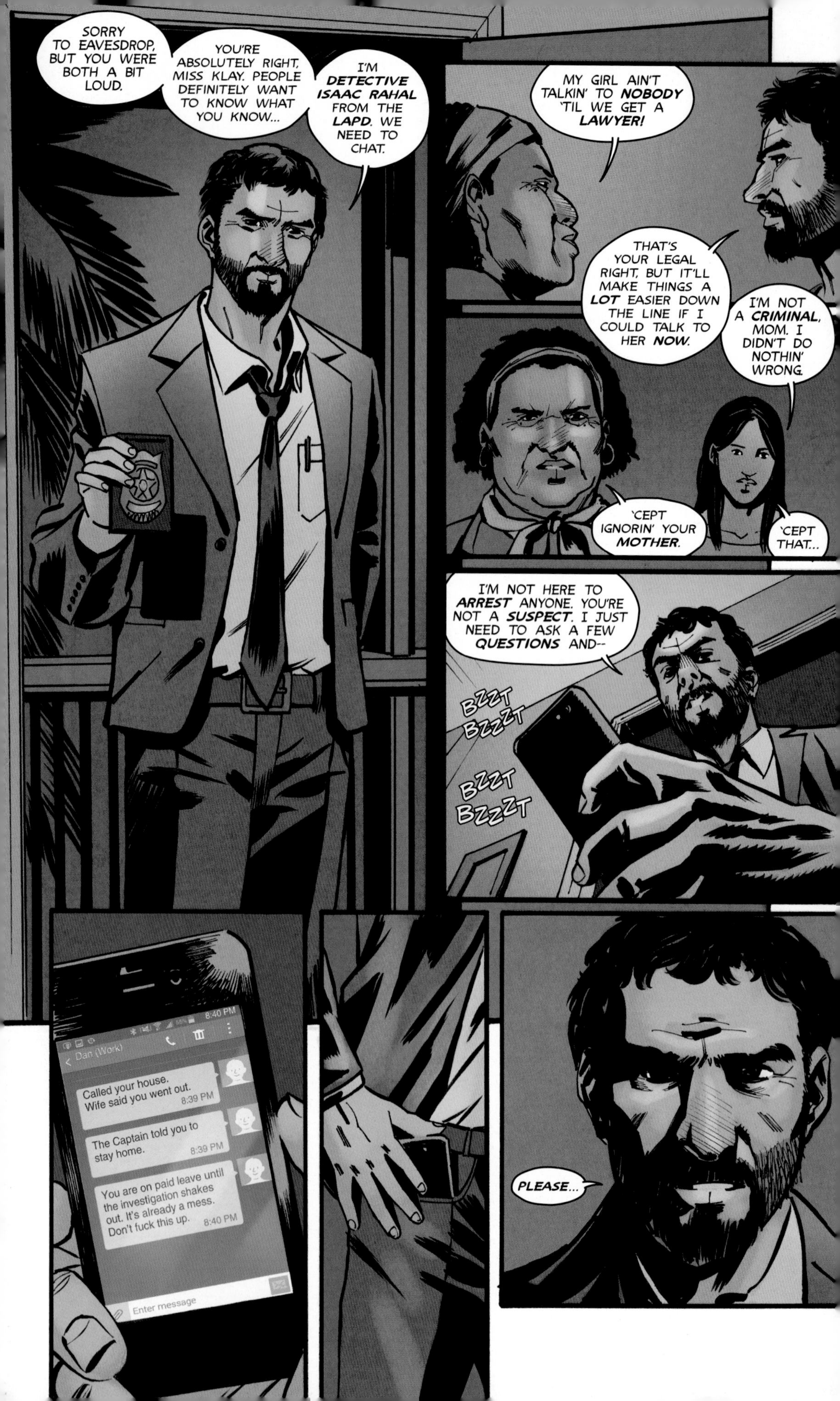
SORRY TO EAVESDROP, BUT YOU WERE BOTH A BIT LOUD.
YOU'RE ABSOLUTELY RIGHT, MISS KLAY. PEOPLE DEFINITELY WANT TO KNOW WHAT YOU KNOW...
I'M DETECTIVE ISAAC RAHAL FROM THE LAPD. WE NEED TO CHAT.
MY GIRL AIN'T TALKIN' TO NOBODY 'TIL WE GET A LAWYER!
THAT'S YOUR LEGAL RIGHT, BUT IT'LL MAKE THINGS A LOT EASIER DOWN THE LINE IF I COULD TALK TO HER NOW.
I'M NOT A CRIMINAL, MOM. I DIDN'T DO NOTHIN' WRONG.
'CEPT IGNORIN' YOUR MOTHER.
'CEPT THAT...
I'M NOT HERE TO ARREST ANYONE. YOU'RE NOT A SUSPECT. I JUST NEED TO ASK A FEW QUESTIONS AND--
BZZT BZZZT
BZZT BZZZT
8:40 PM
Dan (Work)
Called your house. Wife said you went out. 8:39 PM
The Captain told you to stay home. 8:39 PM
You are on paid leave until the investigation shakes out. It's already a mess. Don't fuck this up. 8:40 PM
Enter message
PLEASE...

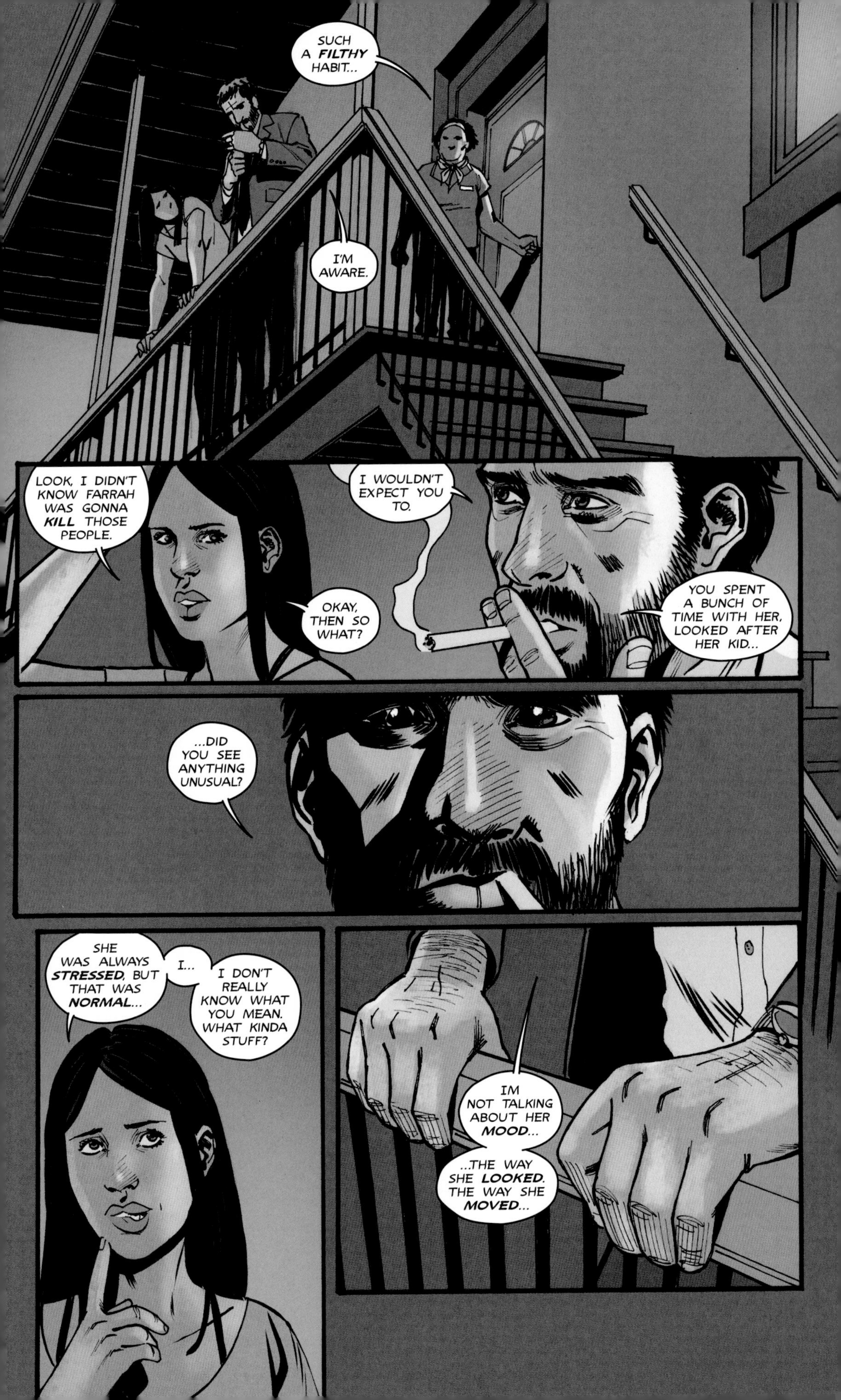
SUCH A FILTHY HABIT...
I'M AWARE.
LOOK, I DIDN'T KNOW FARRAH WAS GONNA KILL THOSE PEOPLE.
I WOULDN'T EXPECT YOU TO.
OKAY, THEN SO WHAT?
YOU SPENT A BUNCH OF TIME WITH HER, LOOKED AFTER HER KID...
...DID YOU SEE ANYTHING UNUSUAL?
SHE WAS ALWAYS STRESSED, BUT THAT WAS NORMAL...
I...
I DON'T REALLY KNOW WHAT YOU MEAN. WHAT KINDA STUFF?
I'M NOT TALKING ABOUT HER MOOD...
...THE WAY SHE LOOKED. THE WAY SHE MOVED...

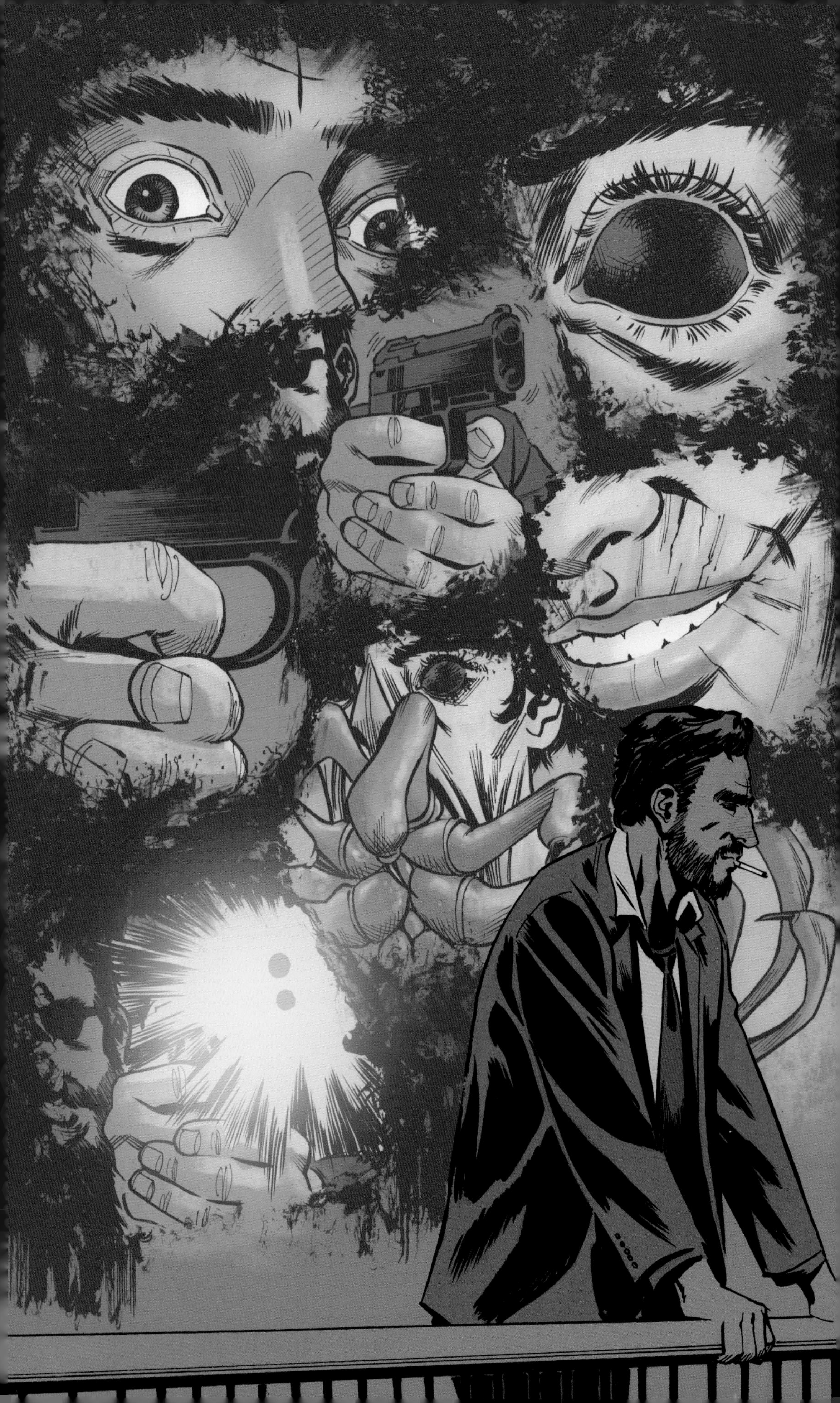

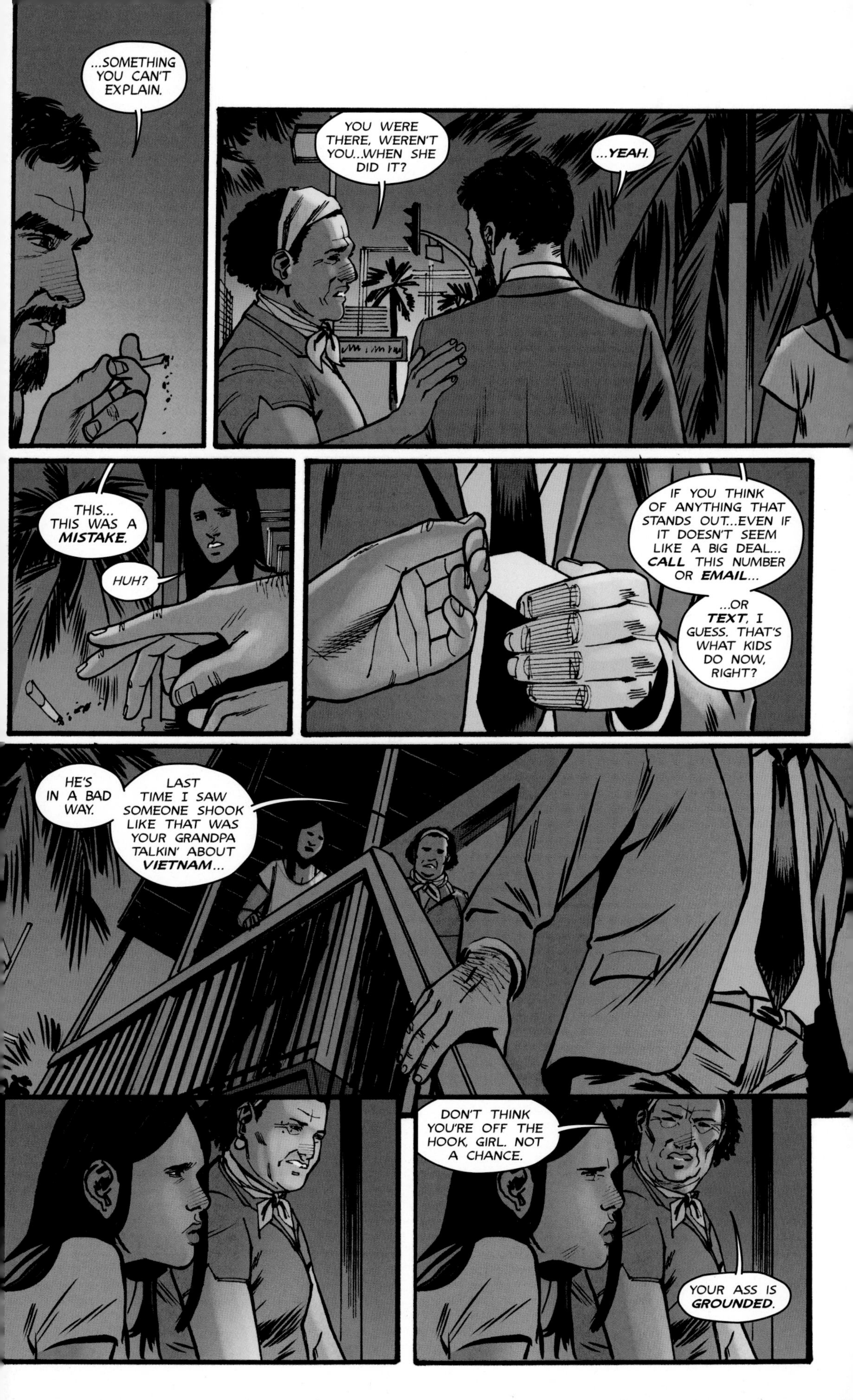
...SOMETHING YOU CAN'T EXPLAIN.
YOU WERE THERE, WEREN'T YOU...WHEN SHE DID IT?
...YEAH.
THIS... THIS WAS A MISTAKE.
HUH?
IF YOU THINK OF ANYTHING THAT STANDS OUT...EVEN IF IT DOESN'T SEEM LIKE A BIG DEAL... CALL THIS NUMBER OR EMAIL...
...OR TEXT, I GUESS. THAT'S WHAT KIDS DO NOW, RIGHT?
HE'S IN A BAD WAY.
LAST TIME I SAW SOMEONE SHOOK LIKE THAT WAS YOUR GRANDPA TALKIN' ABOUT VIETNAM...
DON'T THINK YOU'RE OFF THE HOOK, GIRL. NOT A CHANCE.
YOUR ASS IS GROUNDED.

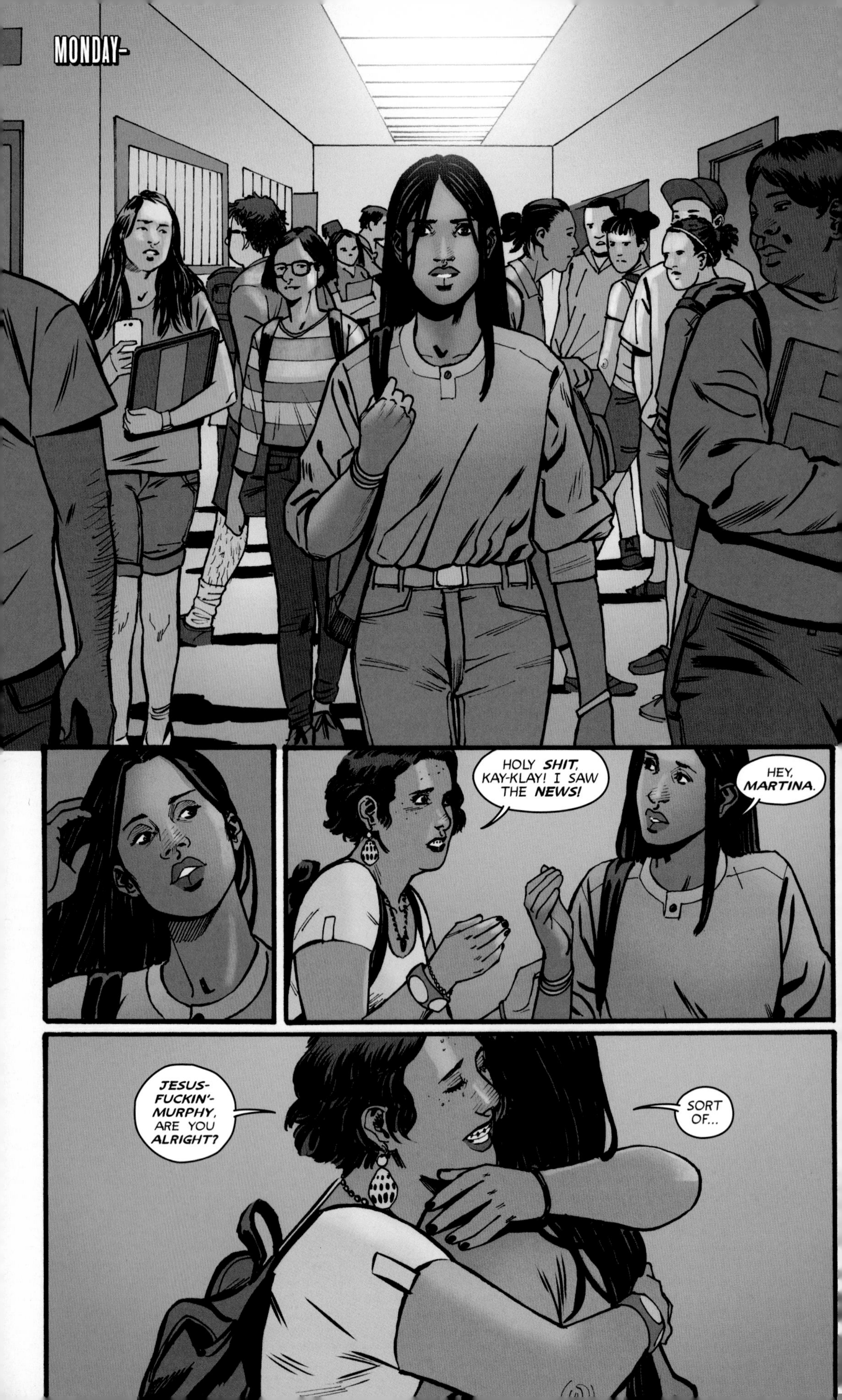
MONDAY-
HOLY SHIT, KAY-KLAY! I SAW THE NEWS!
HEY, MARTINA.
JESUS-FUCKIN'-MURPHY, ARE YOU ALRIGHT?
SORT OF...

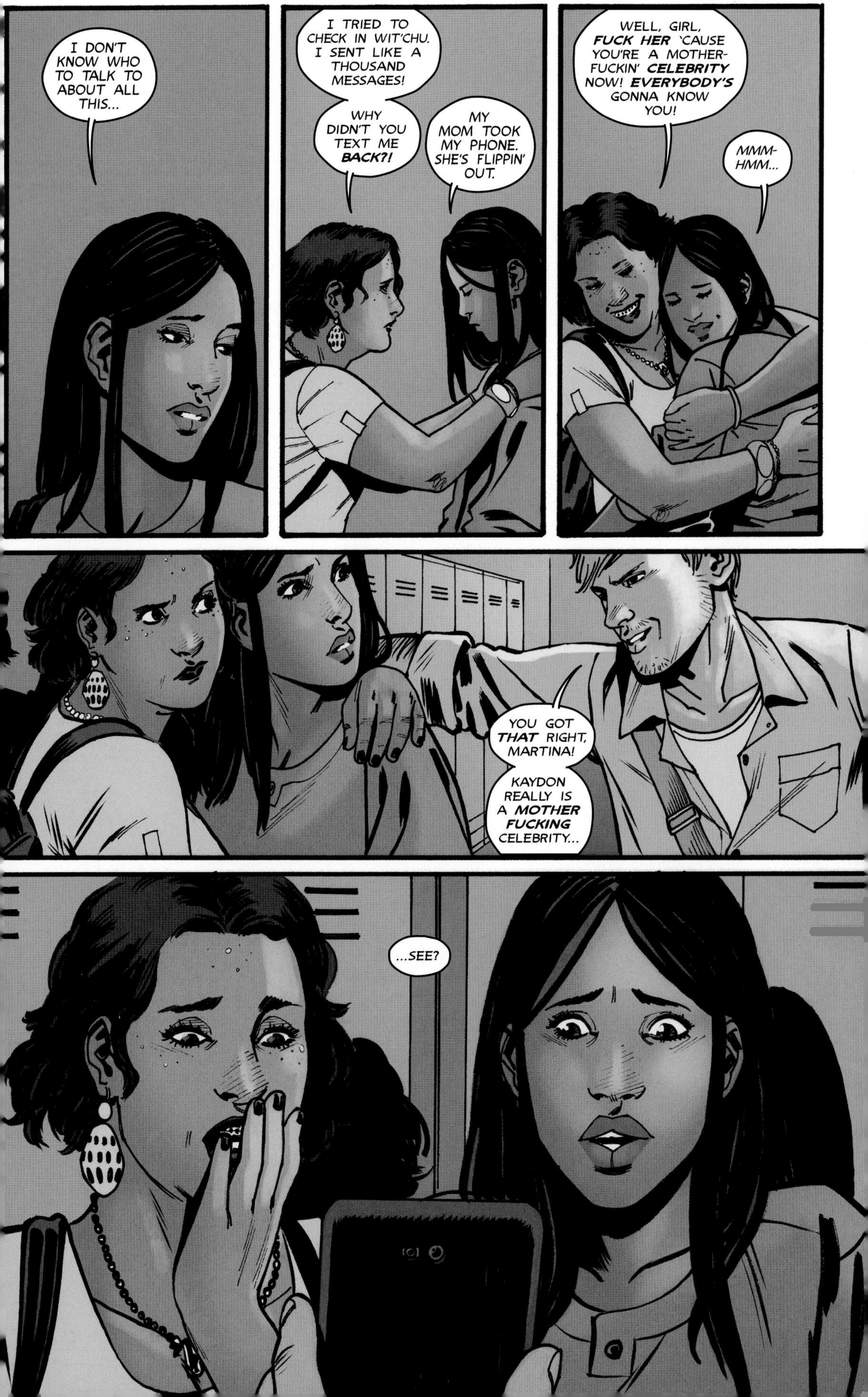
I DON'T KNOW WHO TO TALK TO ABOUT ALL THIS...
I TRIED TO CHECK IN WIT'CHU. I SENT LIKE A THOUSAND MESSAGES!
WHY DIDN'T YOU TEXT ME **BACK?!**
MY MOM TOOK MY PHONE. SHE'S FLIPPIN' OUT.
WELL, GIRL, **FUCK HER** 'CAUSE YOU'RE A MOTHER-FUCKIN' **CELEBRITY** NOW! **EVERYBODY'S** GONNA KNOW YOU!
MMM-HMM...
YOU GOT **THAT** RIGHT, MARTINA!
KAYDON REALLY IS A **MOTHER FUCKING** CELEBRITY...
...SEE?

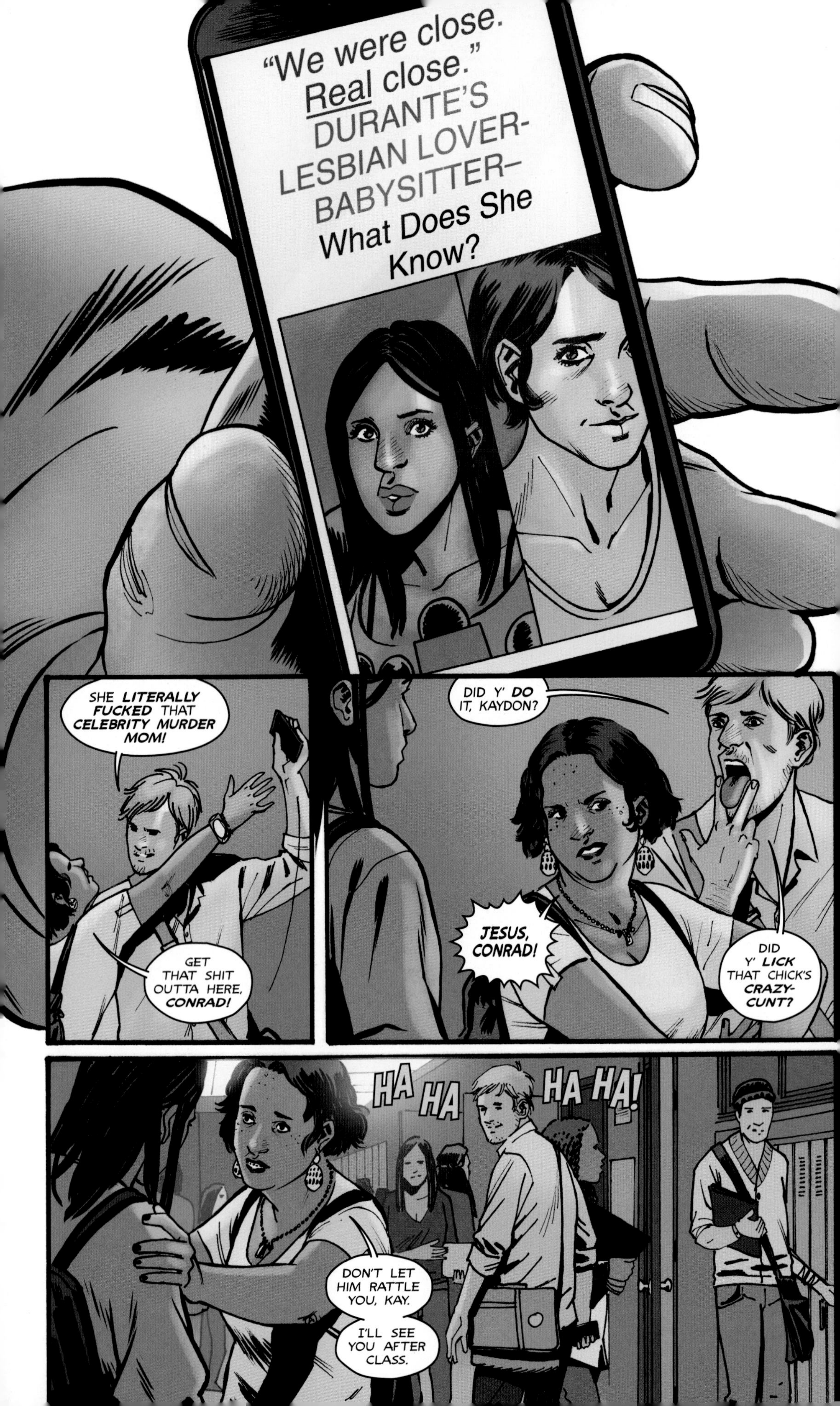

"We were close. Real close."
DURANTE'S DURANTE LESBIAN LOVER-BABYSITTER–
What Does She Know?
SHE LITERALLY FUCKED THAT CELEBRITY MURDER MOM!
GET THAT SHIT OUTTA HERE, CONRAD!
DID Y' DO IT, KAYDON?
JESUS, CONRAD!
DID Y' LICK THAT CHICK'S CRAZY-CUNT?
HA HA HA HA!
DON'T LET HIM RATTLE YOU, KAY.
I'LL SEE YOU AFTER CLASS.

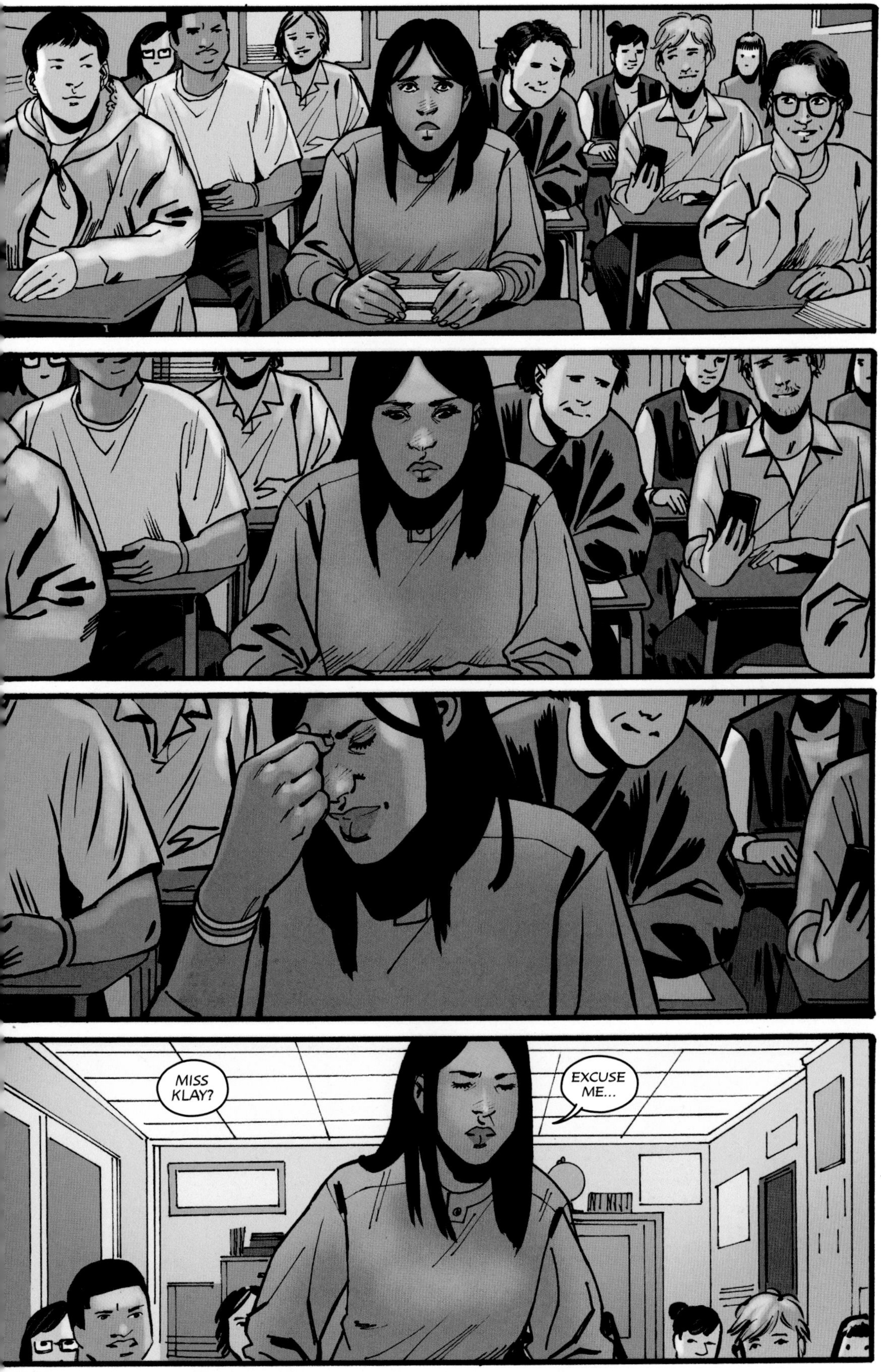
MISS KLAY?
EXCUSE ME...

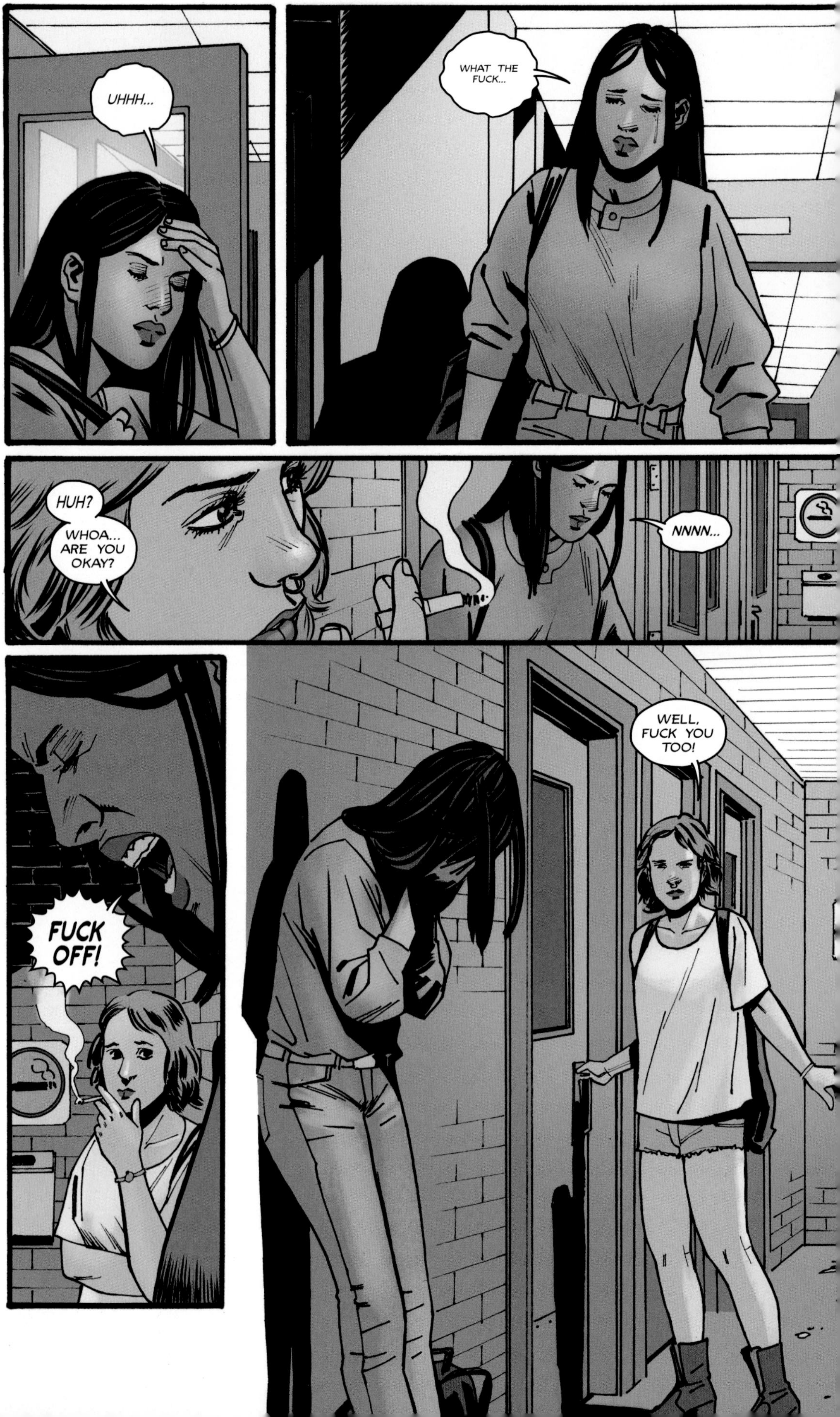
UHHH...
WHAT THE FUCK...
HUH?
WHOA... ARE YOU OKAY?
NNNN...
FUCK OFF!
WELL, FUCK YOU TOO!

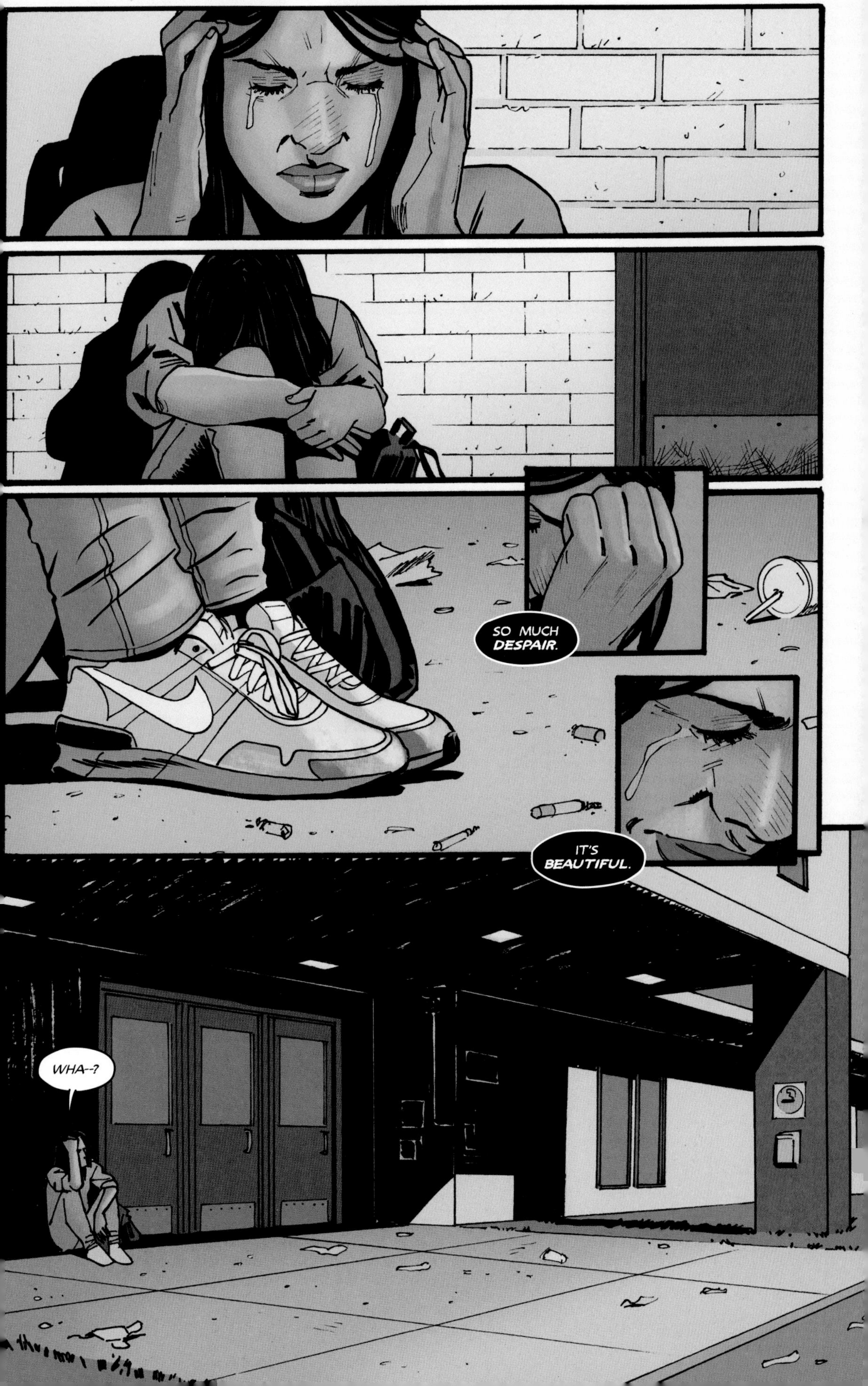
SO MUCH DESPAIR.
IT'S BEAUTIFUL.
WHA--?

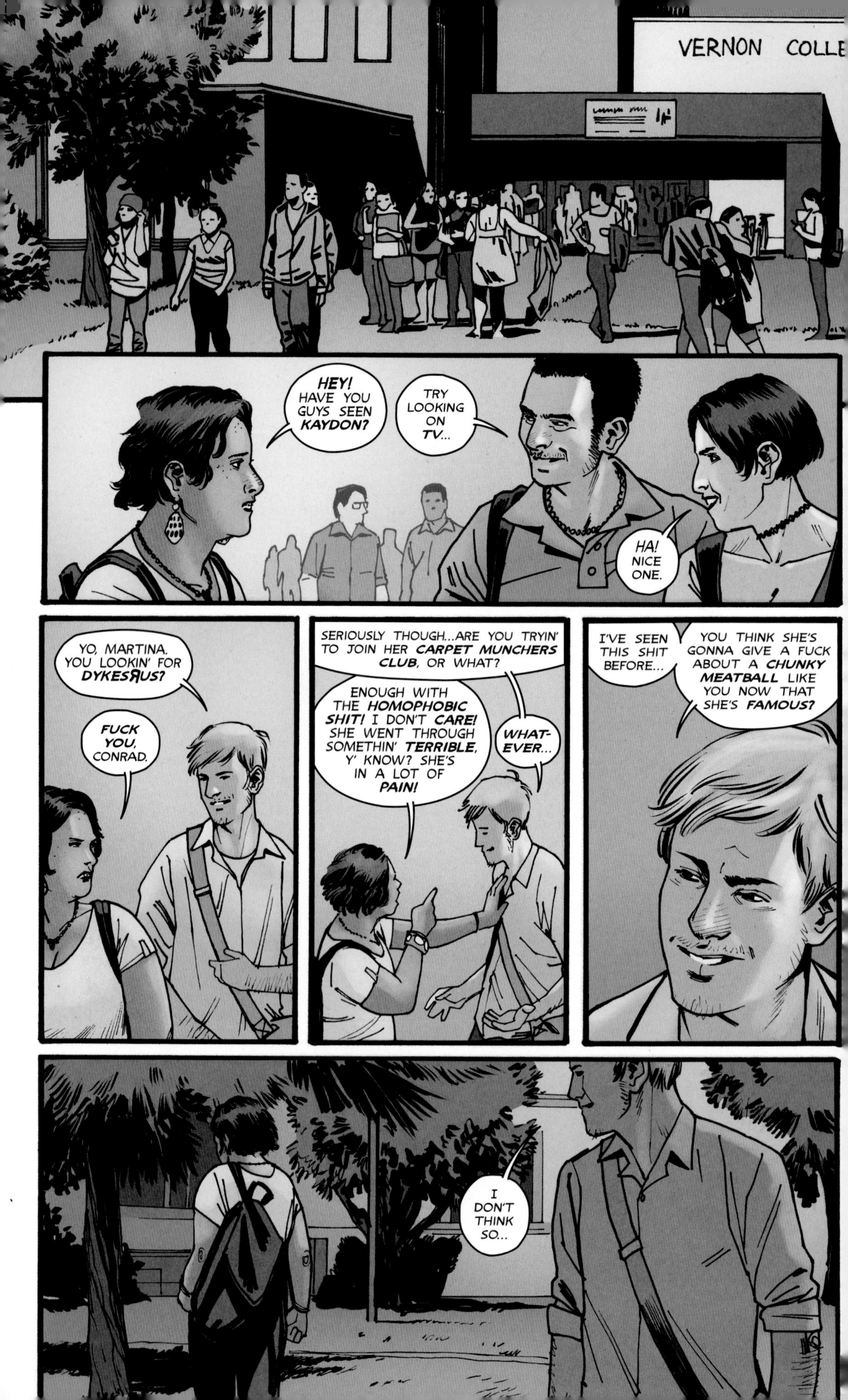

VERNON COLLE
HEY! HAVE YOU GUYS SEEN KAYDON?
TRY LOOKING ON TV...
HA! NICE ONE.
YO, MARTINA. YOU LOOKIN' FOR DYKESЯUS?
FUCK YOU, CONRAD.
SERIOUSLY THOUGH...ARE YOU TRYIN' TO JOIN HER CARPET MUNCHERS CLUB, OR WHAT?
ENOUGH WITH THE HOMOPHOBIC SHIT! I DON'T CARE! SHE WENT THROUGH SOMETHIN' TERRIBLE, Y' KNOW? SHE'S IN A LOT OF PAIN!
WHAT-EVER...
I'VE SEEN THIS SHIT BEFORE...
YOU THINK SHE'S GONNA GIVE A FUCK ABOUT A CHUNKY MEATBALL LIKE YOU NOW THAT SHE'S FAMOUS?
I DON'T THINK SO...

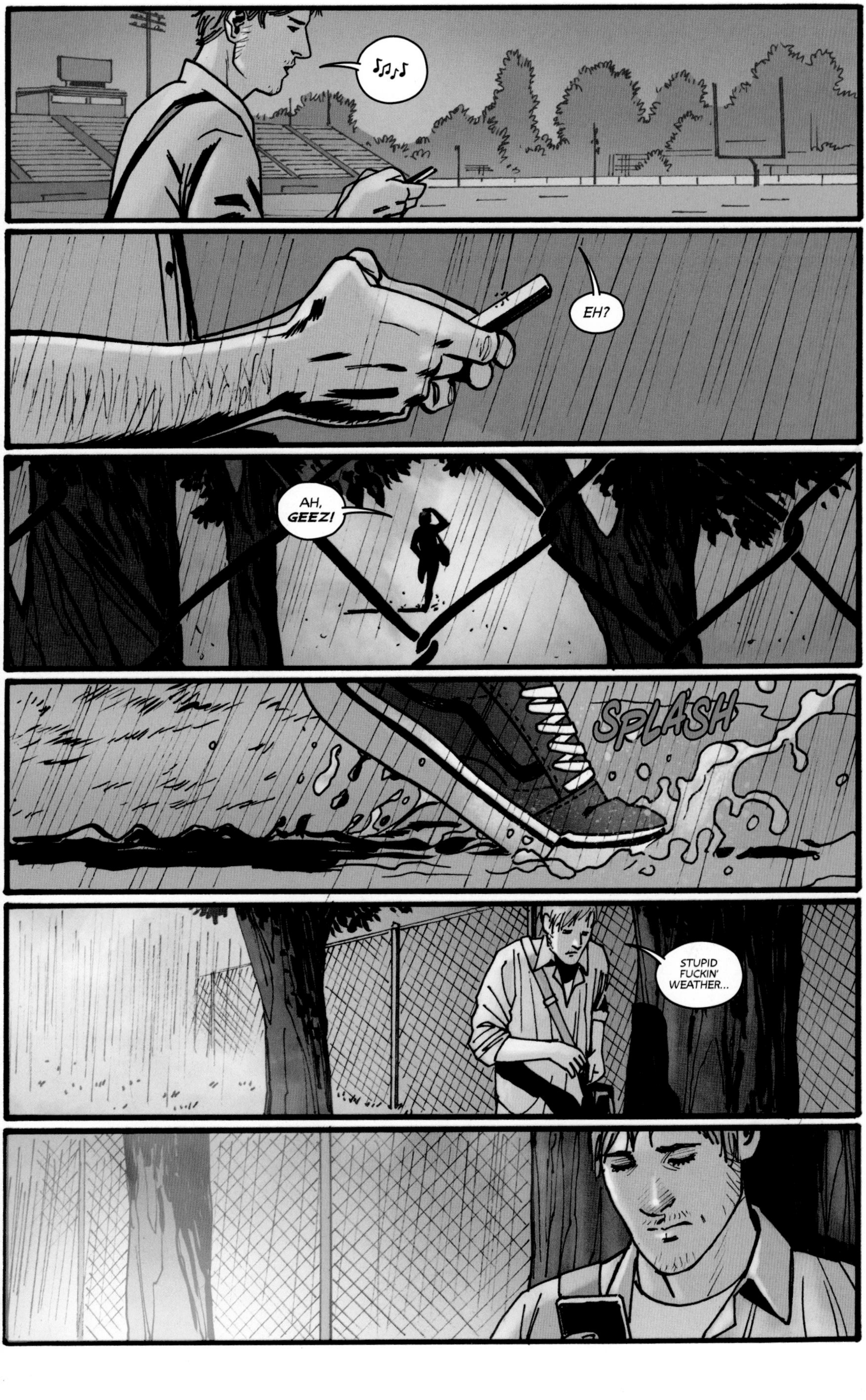
♪♫♪♪
EH?
AH, GEEZ!
SPLASH
STUPID FUCKIN' WEATHER...

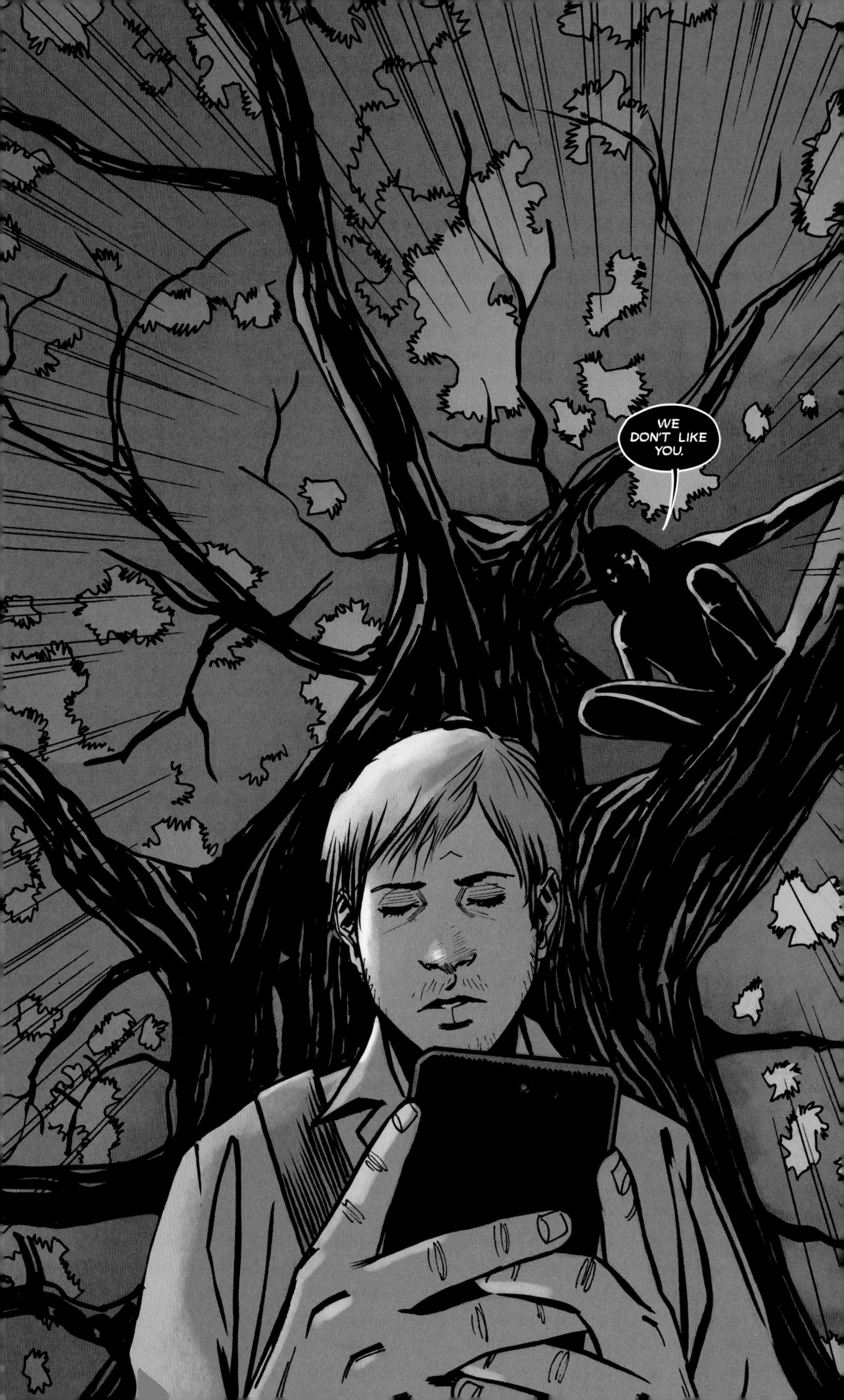
WE DON'T LIKE YOU.

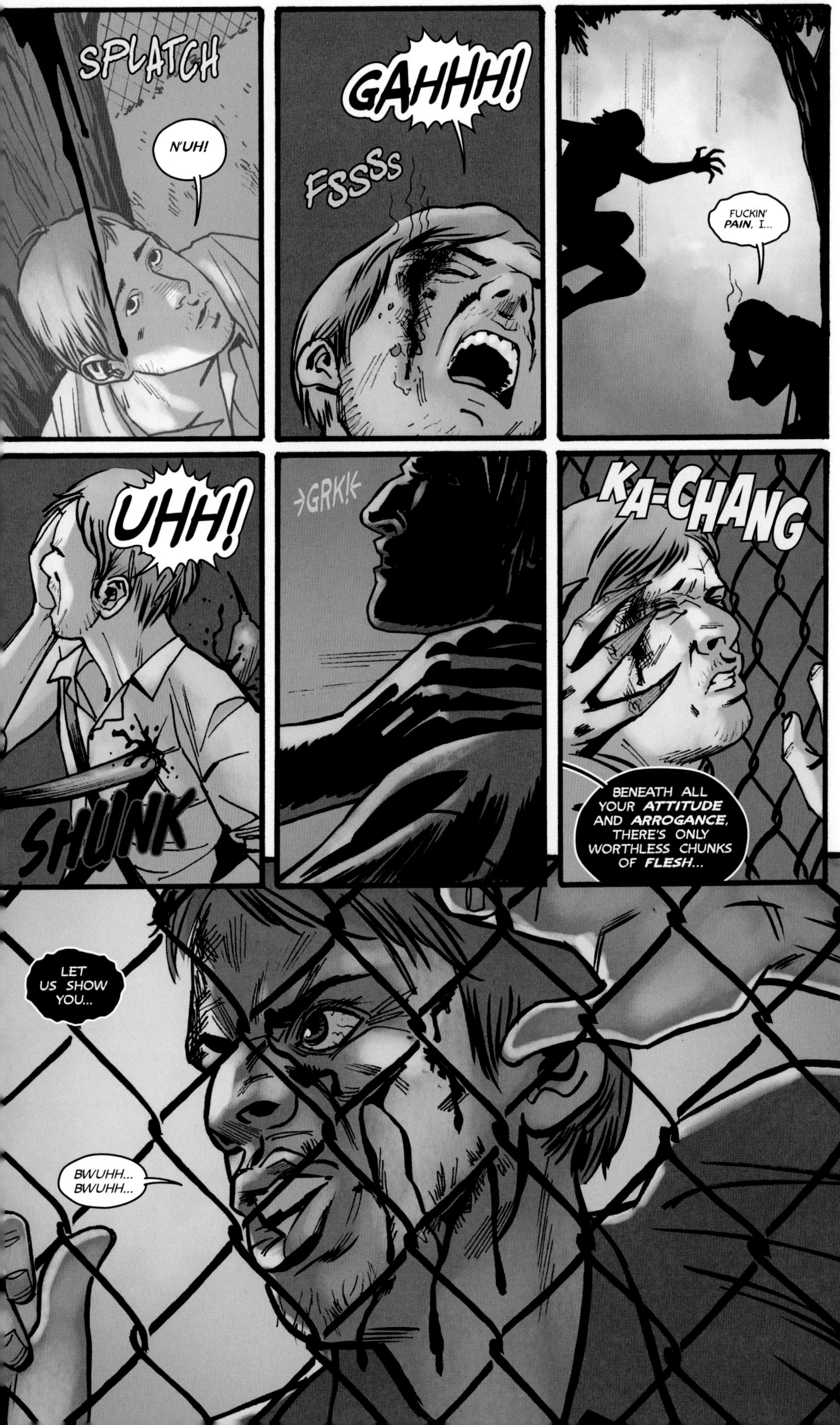
SPLATCH
N'UH!
GAHHH!
FSSSS
FUCKIN'
PAIN, I...
UHH!
SHUNK
GRK!
KA-CHANG
BENEATH ALL YOUR ATTITUDE AND ARROGANCE, THERE'S ONLY WORTHLESS CHUNKS OF FLESH...
LET US SHOW YOU...
BWUHH... BWUHH...

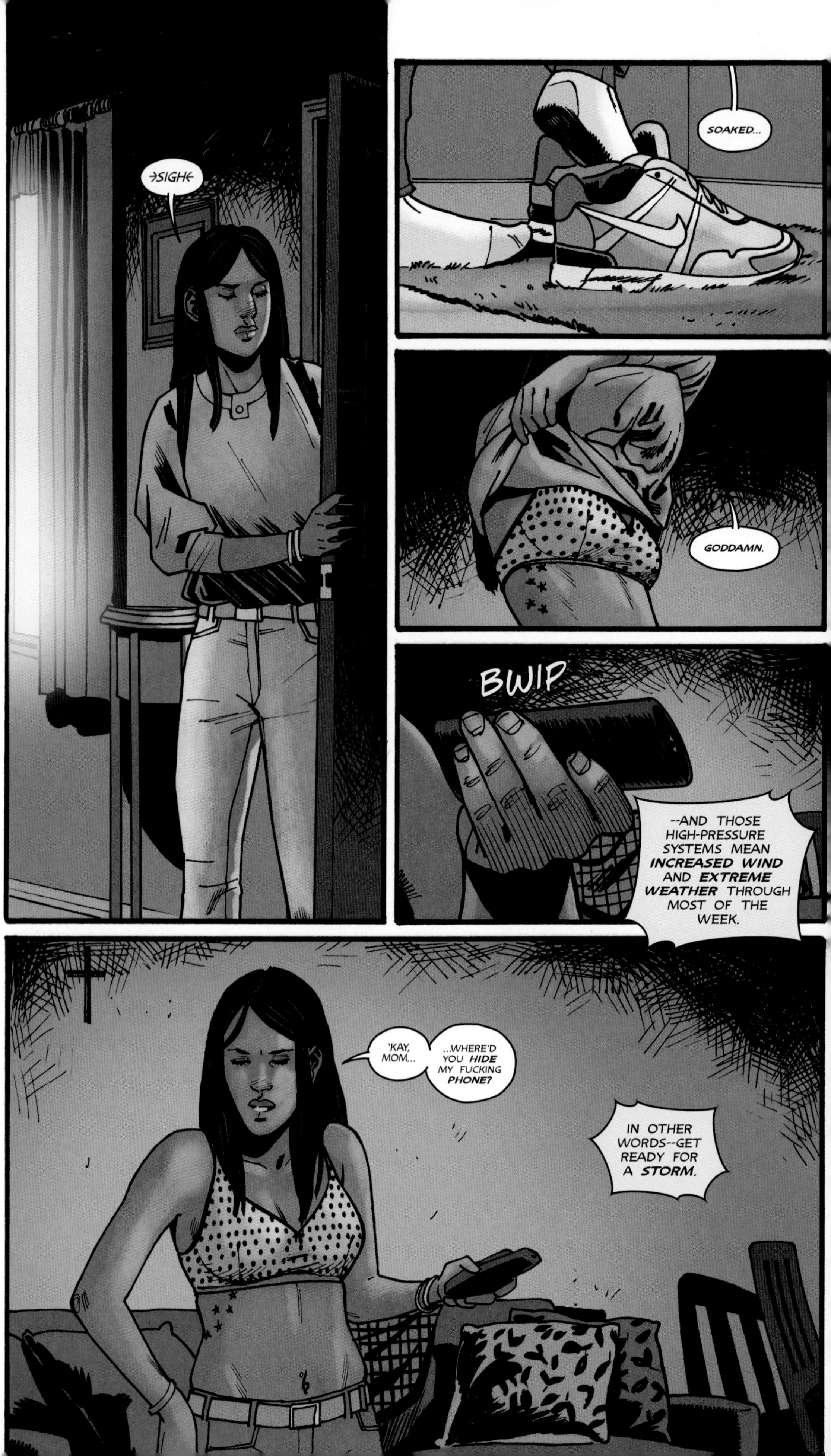

SIGH
SOAKED...
GODDAMN.
BWIP
--AND THOSE HIGH-PRESSURE SYSTEMS MEAN INCREASED WIND AND EXTREME WEATHER THROUGH MOST OF THE WEEK.
'KAY, MOM...
...WHERE'D YOU HIDE MY FUCKING PHONE?
IN OTHER WORDS--GET READY FOR A STORM.

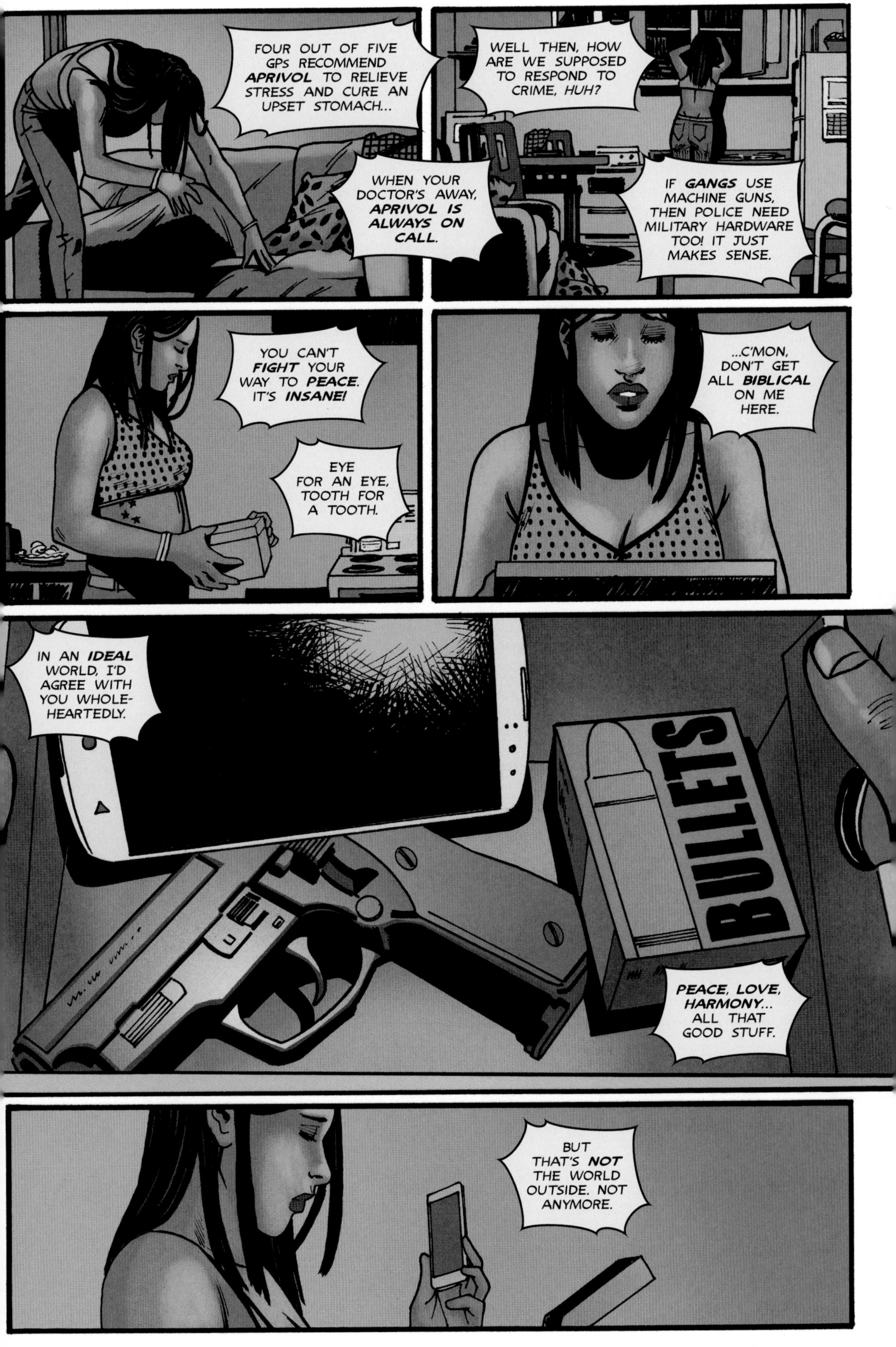
FOUR OUT OF FIVE GPs RECOMMEND APRIVOL TO RELIEVE STRESS AND CURE AN UPSET STOMACH...
WHEN YOUR DOCTOR'S AWAY, APRIVOL IS ALWAYS ON CALL.
WELL THEN, HOW ARE WE SUPPOSED TO RESPOND TO CRIME, HUH?
IF GANGS USE MACHINE GUNS, THEN POLICE NEED MILITARY HARDWARE TOO! IT JUST MAKES SENSE.
YOU CAN'T FIGHT YOUR WAY TO PEACE. IT'S INSANE!
EYE FOR AN EYE, TOOTH FOR A TOOTH.
...C'MON, DON'T GET ALL BIBLICAL ON ME HERE.
IN AN IDEAL WORLD, I'D AGREE WITH YOU WHOLE-HEARTEDLY.
BULLETS
PEACE, LOVE, HARMONY... ALL THAT GOOD STUFF.
BUT THAT'S NOT THE WORLD OUTSIDE. NOT ANYMORE.

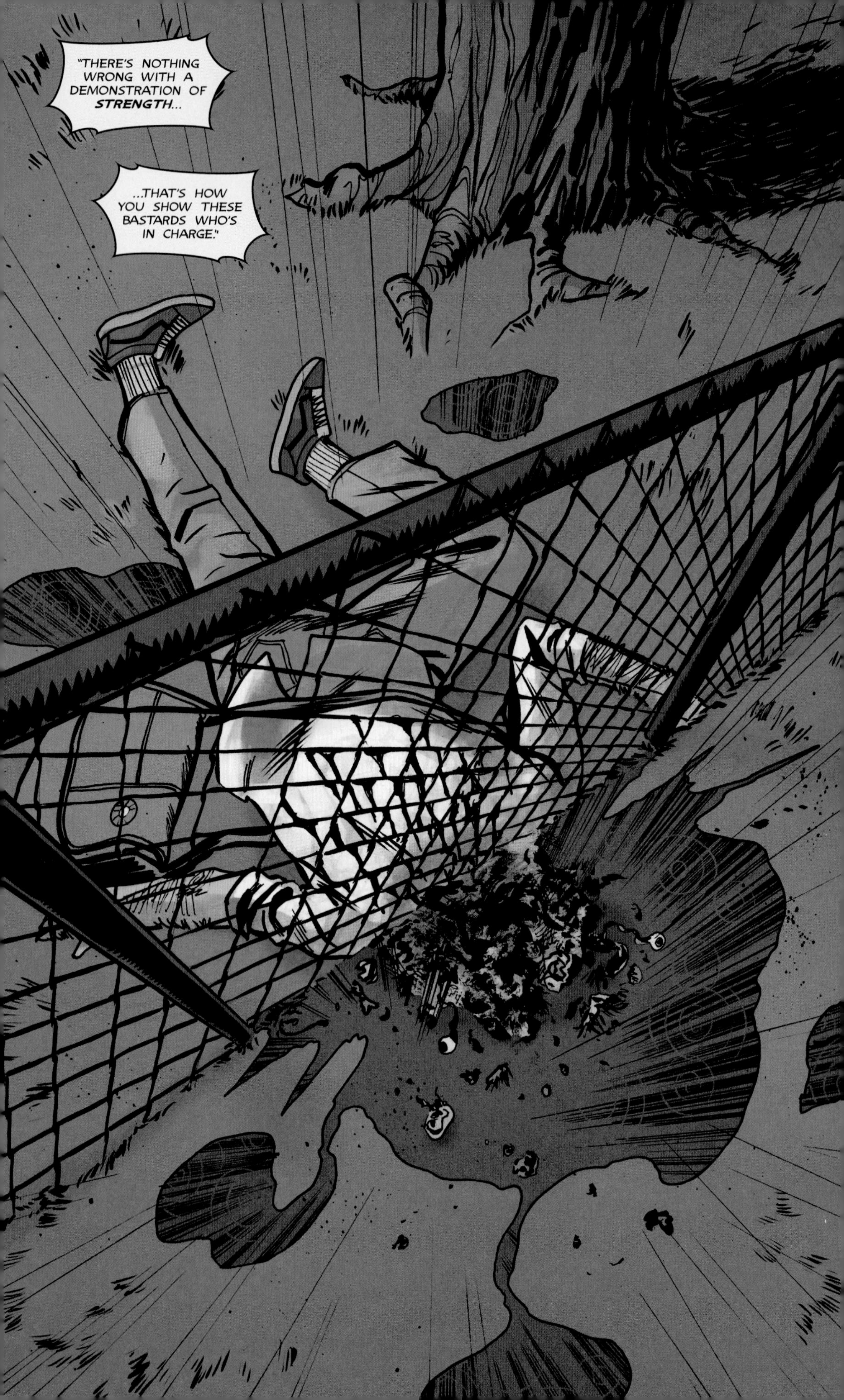
"THERE'S NOTHING WRONG WITH A DEMONSTRATION OF *STRENGTH*...
...THAT'S HOW YOU SHOW THESE BASTARDS WHO'S IN CHARGE."

PART 2: STATUS UPDATE

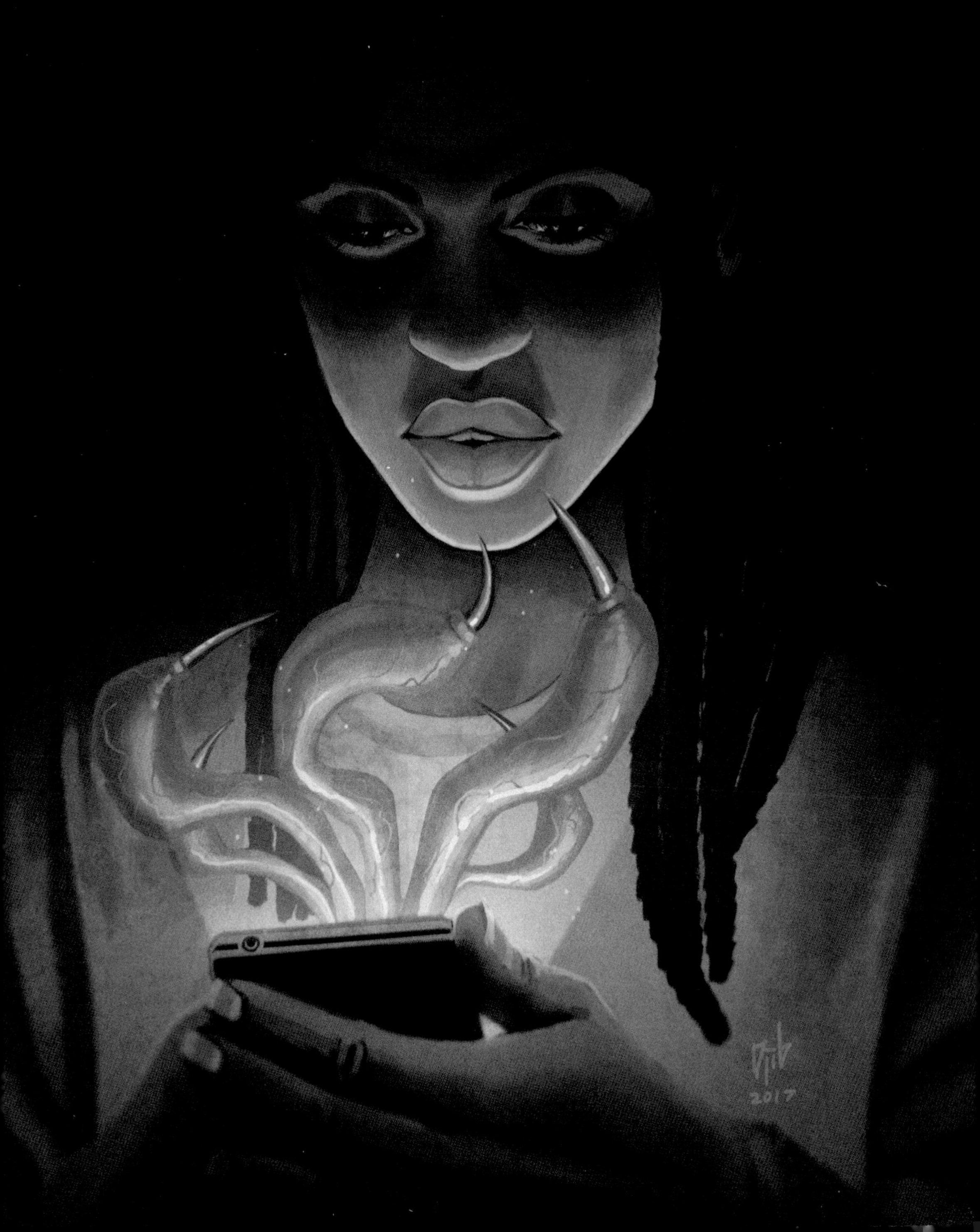

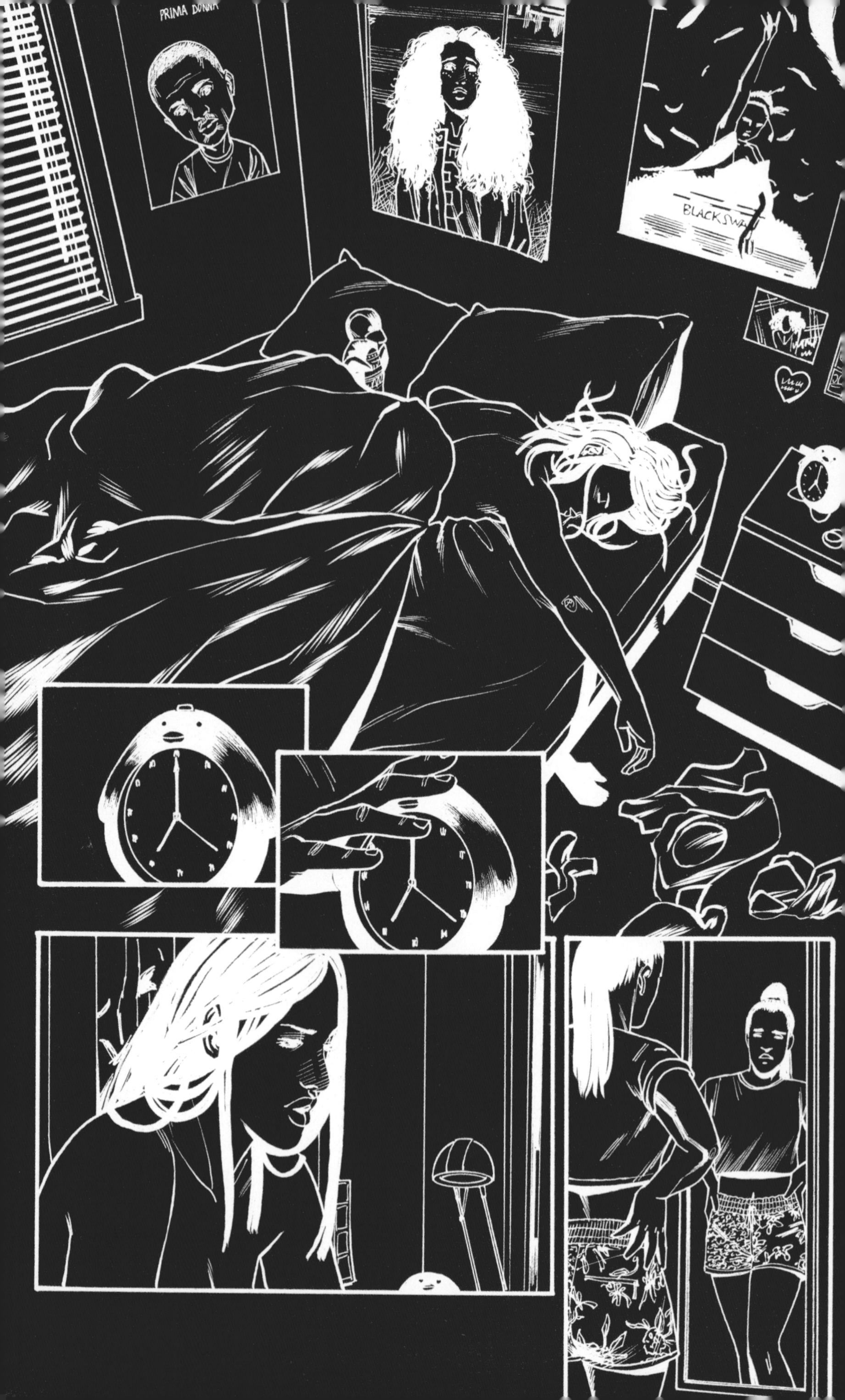
PRIMA DONNA

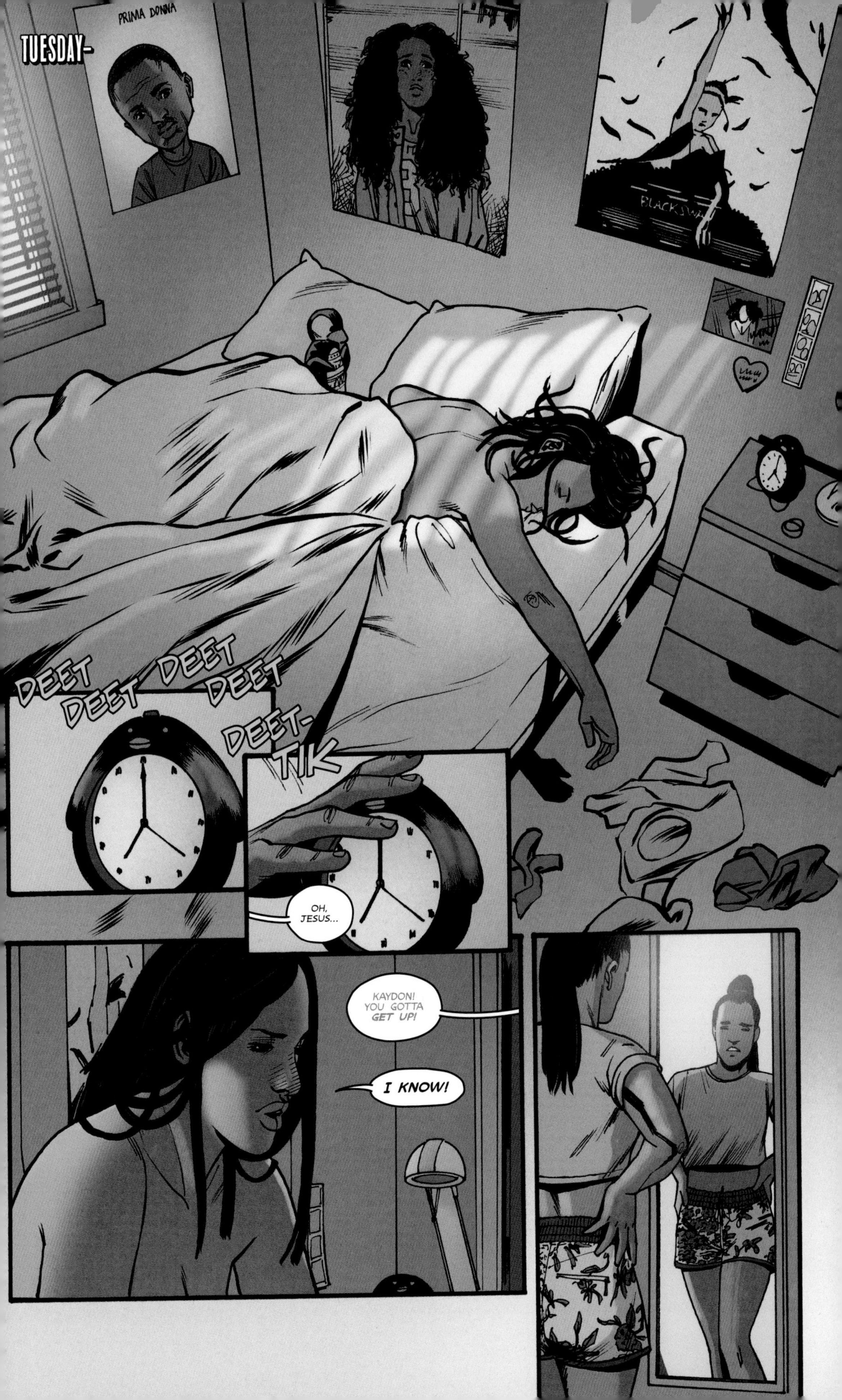
TUESDAY-
PRIMA DONNA
BLACKSWA
DEET DEET DEET DEET DEET-
TIK
OH, JESUS...
KAYDON! YOU GOTTA GET UP!
I KNOW!

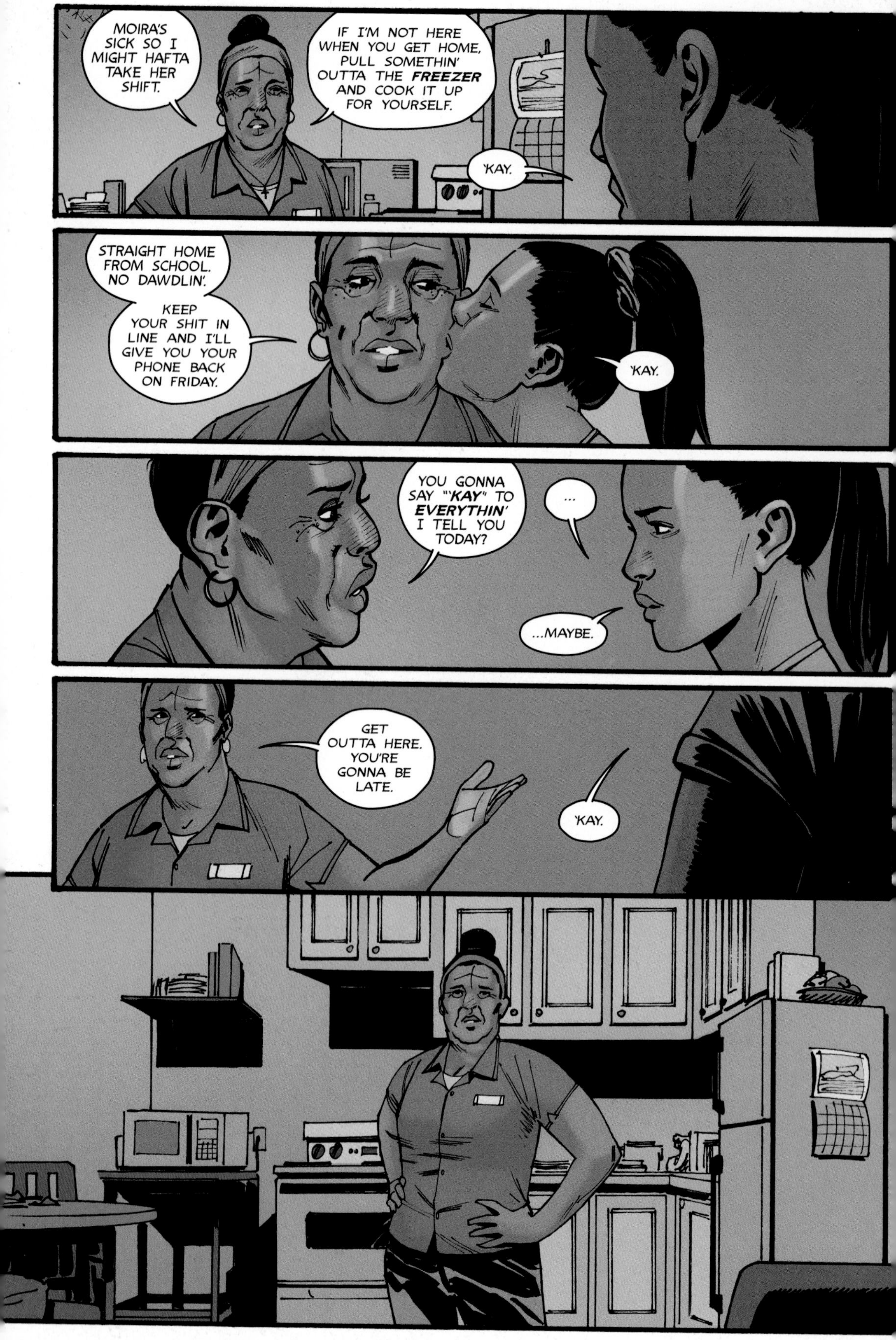
MOIRA'S SICK SO I MIGHT HAFTA TAKE HER SHIFT.
IF I'M NOT HERE WHEN YOU GET HOME, PULL SOMETHIN' OUTTA THE FREEZER AND COOK IT UP FOR YOURSELF.
'KAY.
STRAIGHT HOME FROM SCHOOL. NO DAWDLIN'.
KEEP YOUR SHIT IN LINE AND I'LL GIVE YOU YOUR PHONE BACK ON FRIDAY.
'KAY.
YOU GONNA SAY "'KAY" TO EVERYTHIN' I TELL YOU TODAY?
...
...MAYBE.
GET OUTTA HERE. YOU'RE GONNA BE LATE.
'KAY.

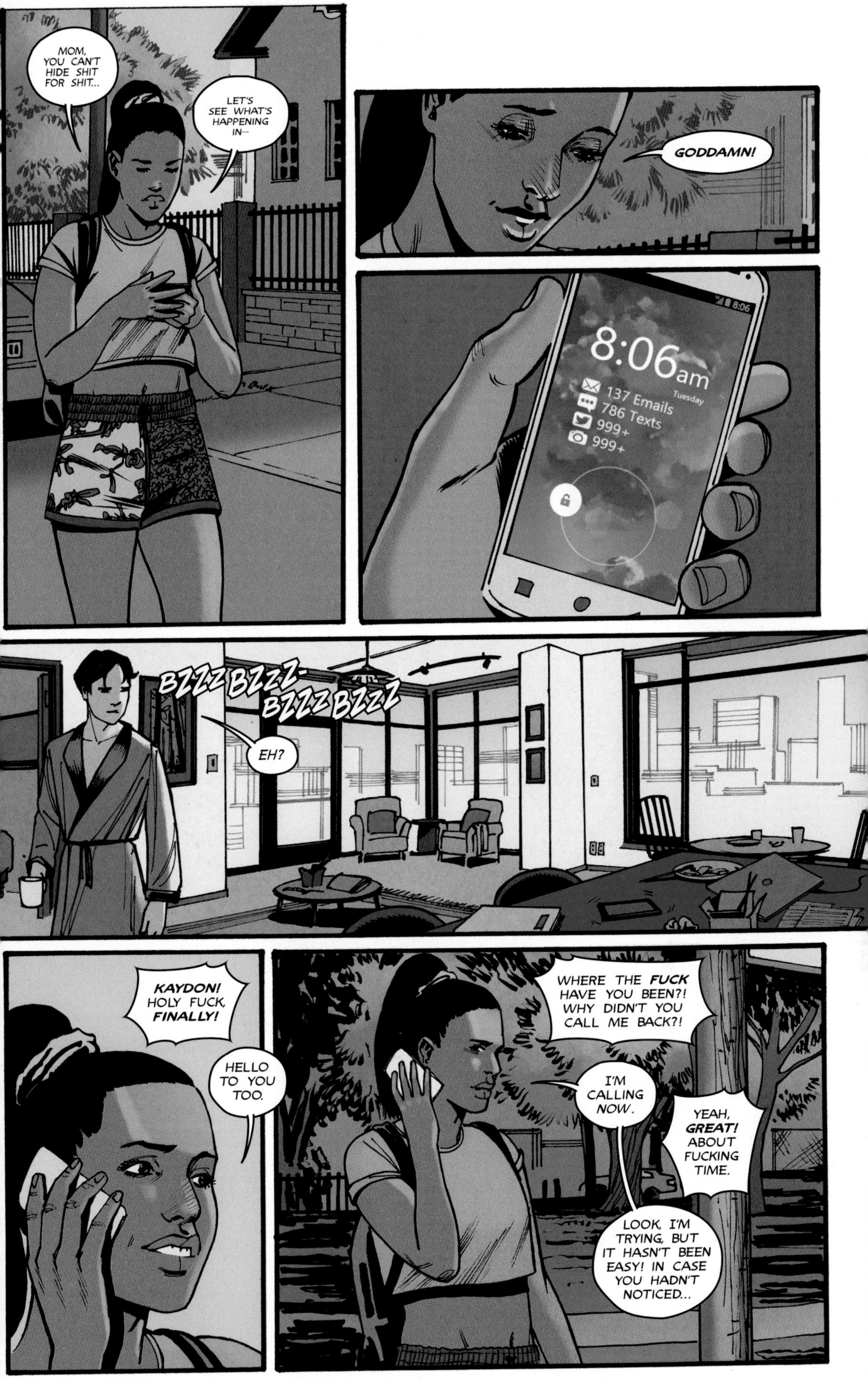
MOM, YOU CAN'T HIDE SHIT FOR SHIT...
LET'S SEE WHAT'S HAPPENING IN--
GODDAMN!
8:06
8:06am
Tuesday
137 Emails
786 Texts
999+
999+
BZZZ BZZZ-BZZZ BZZZ
EH?
KAYDON! HOLY FUCK, FINALLY!
HELLO TO YOU TOO.
WHERE THE FUCK HAVE YOU BEEN?! WHY DIDN'T YOU CALL ME BACK?!
I'M CALLING NOW.
YEAH, GREAT! ABOUT FUCKING TIME.
LOOK, I'M TRYING, BUT IT HASN'T BEEN EASY! IN CASE YOU HADN'T NOTICED...

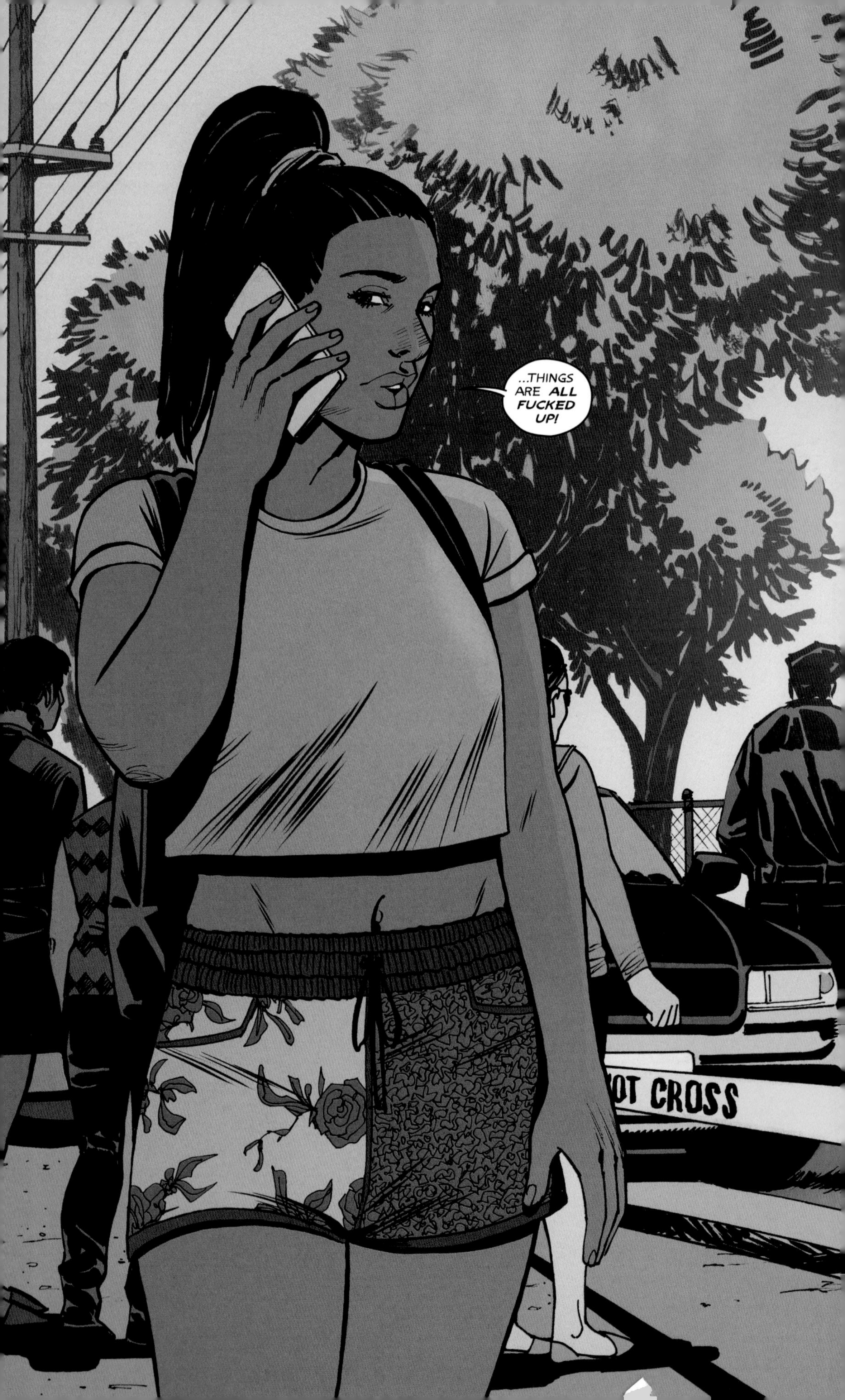
...THINGS ARE ALL FUCKED UP!
OT CROSS

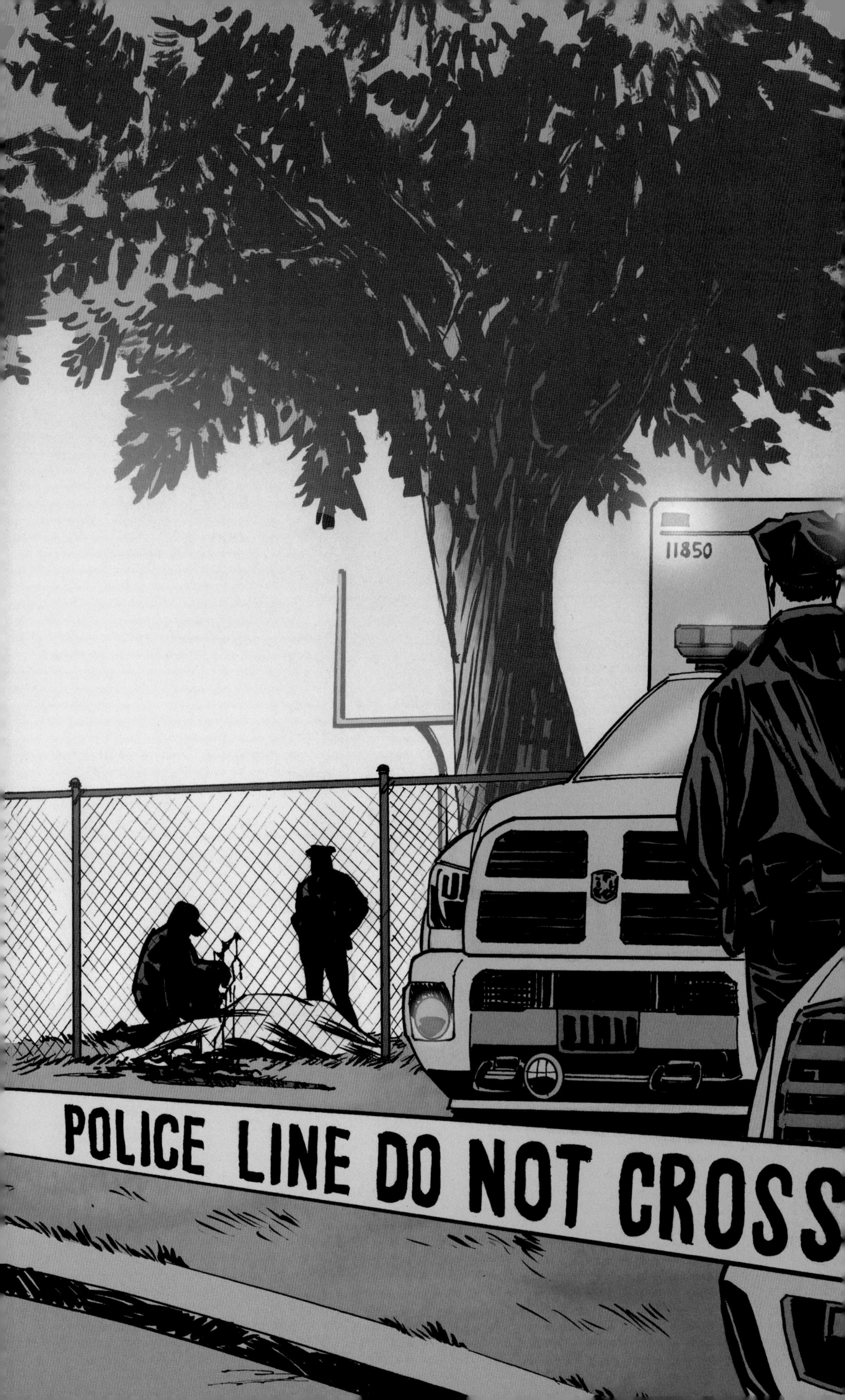
11850
POLICE LINE DO NOT CROSS

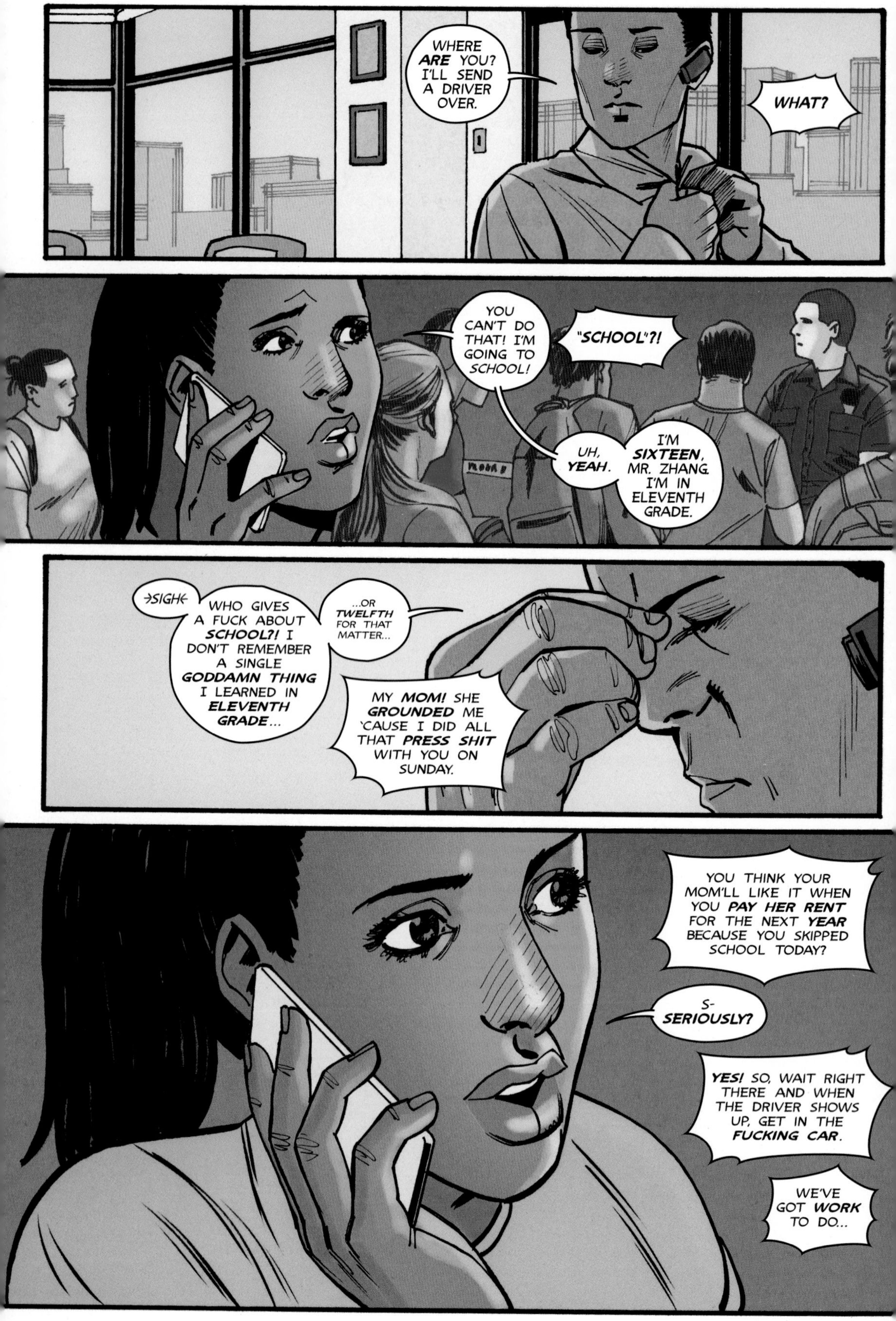

WHERE ARE YOU? I'LL SEND A DRIVER OVER.
WHAT?
YOU CAN'T DO THAT! I'M GOING TO SCHOOL!
"SCHOOL"?!
UH, YEAH.
I'M SIXTEEN, MR. ZHANG. I'M IN ELEVENTH GRADE.
>SIGH<
WHO GIVES A FUCK ABOUT SCHOOL?! I DON'T REMEMBER A SINGLE GODDAMN THING I LEARNED IN ELEVENTH GRADE...
...OR TWELFTH FOR THAT MATTER...
MY MOM! SHE GROUNDED ME 'CAUSE I DID ALL THAT PRESS SHIT WITH YOU ON SUNDAY.
YOU THINK YOUR MOM'LL LIKE IT WHEN YOU PAY HER RENT FOR THE NEXT YEAR BECAUSE YOU SKIPPED SCHOOL TODAY?
S- SERIOUSLY?
YES! SO, WAIT RIGHT THERE AND WHEN THE DRIVER SHOWS UP, GET IN THE FUCKING CAR.
WE'VE GOT WORK TO DO...

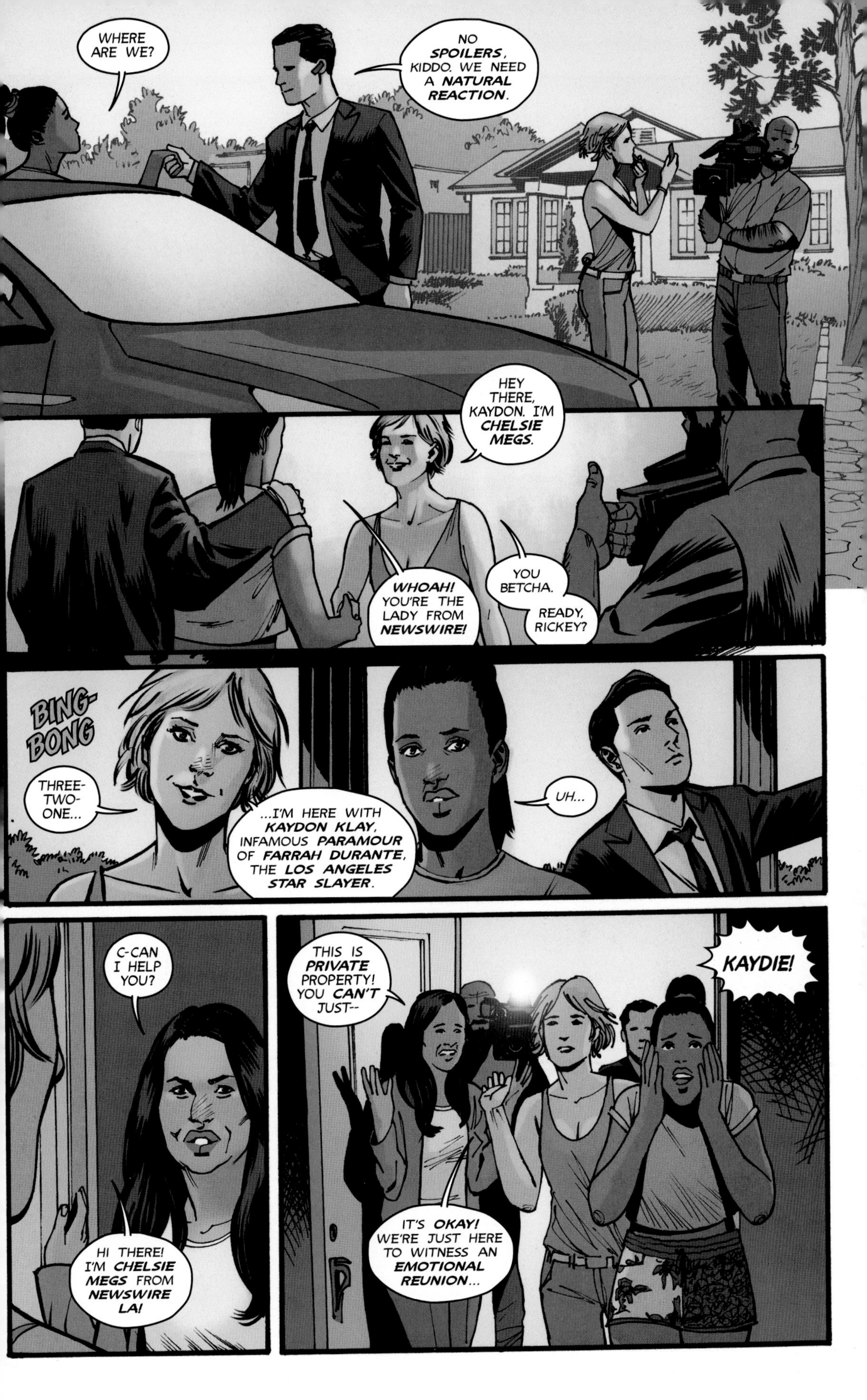
WHERE ARE WE?
NO SPOILERS, KIDDO. WE NEED A NATURAL REACTION.
HEY THERE, KAYDON. I'M CHELSIE MEGS.
WHOAH! YOU'RE THE LADY FROM NEWSWIRE!
YOU BETCHA.
READY, RICKEY?
BING-BONG
THREE-TWO-ONE...
...I'M HERE WITH KAYDON KLAY, INFAMOUS PARAMOUR OF FARRAH DURANTE, THE LOS ANGELES STAR SLAYER.
UH...
C-CAN I HELP YOU?
HI THERE! I'M CHELSIE MEGS FROM NEWSWIRE LA!
THIS IS PRIVATE PROPERTY! YOU CAN'T JUST--
IT'S OKAY! WE'RE JUST HERE TO WITNESS AN EMOTIONAL REUNION...
KAYDIE!

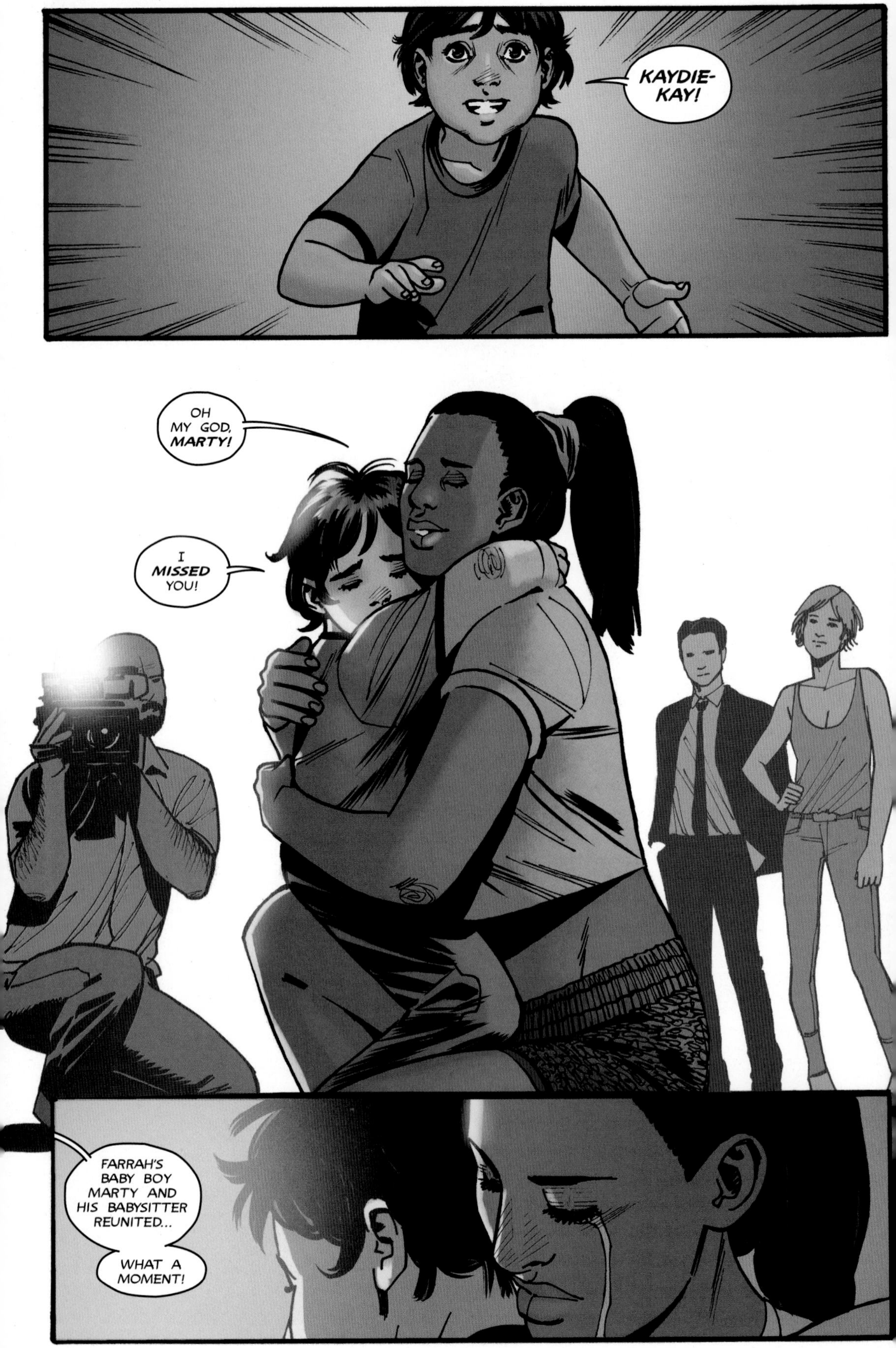
KAYDIE-KAY!
OH MY GOD, MARTY!
I MISSED YOU!
FARRAH'S BABY BOY MARTY AND HIS BABYSITTER REUNITED...
WHAT A MOMENT!

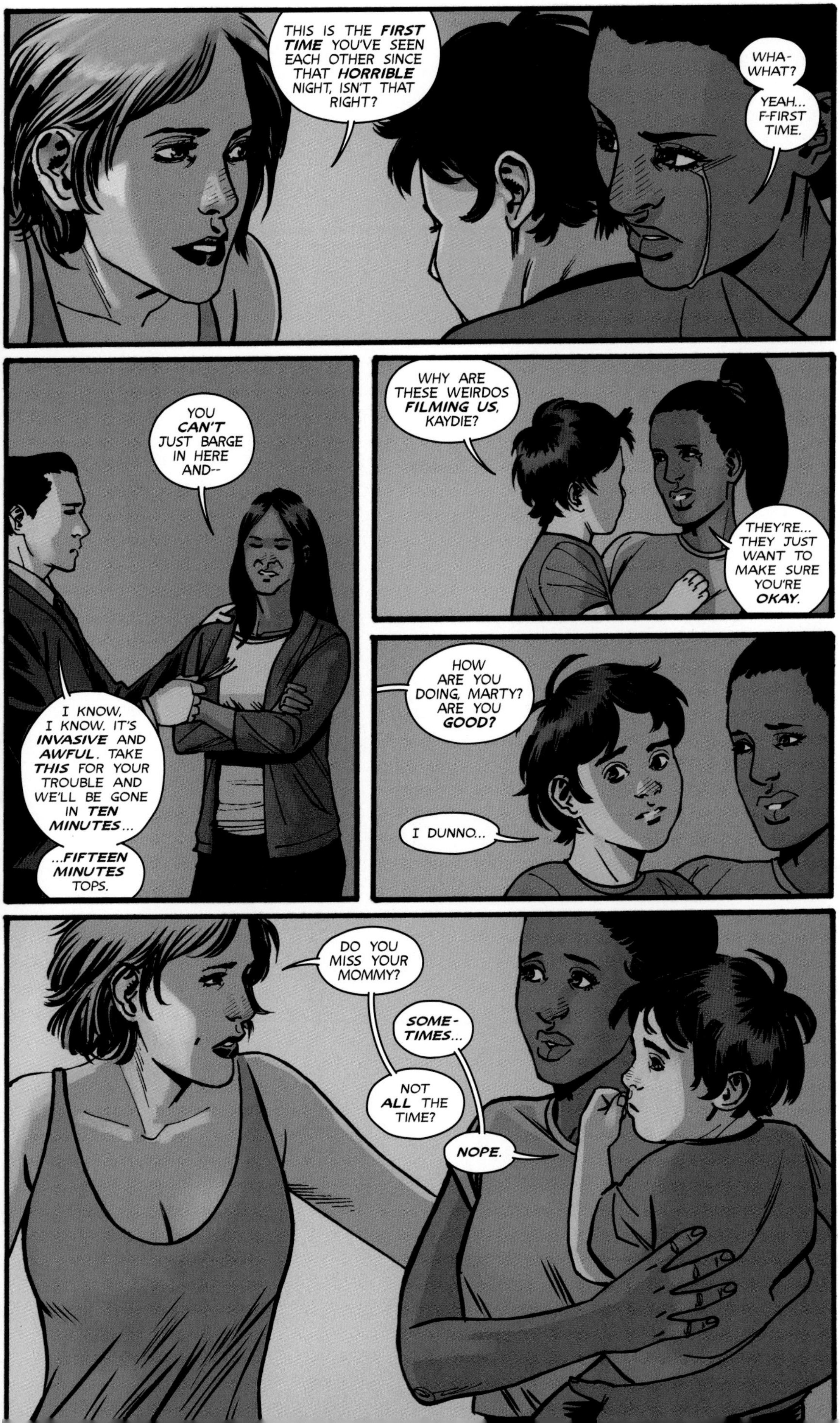
THIS IS THE **FIRST TIME** YOU'VE SEEN EACH OTHER SINCE THAT **HORRIBLE** NIGHT, ISN'T THAT RIGHT?
WHA- WHAT?
YEAH... F-FIRST TIME.
YOU **CAN'T** JUST BARGE IN HERE AND--
I KNOW, I KNOW. IT'S **INVASIVE** AND **AWFUL**. TAKE **THIS** FOR YOUR TROUBLE AND WE'LL BE GONE IN **TEN MINUTES**...
...**FIFTEEN MINUTES** TOPS.
WHY ARE THESE WEIRDOS **FILMING US**, KAYDIE?
THEY'RE... THEY JUST WANT TO MAKE SURE YOU'RE **OKAY**.
HOW ARE YOU DOING, MARTY? ARE YOU **GOOD?**
I DUNNO...
DO YOU MISS YOUR MOMMY?
SOME-TIMES...
NOT **ALL** THE TIME?
NOPE.

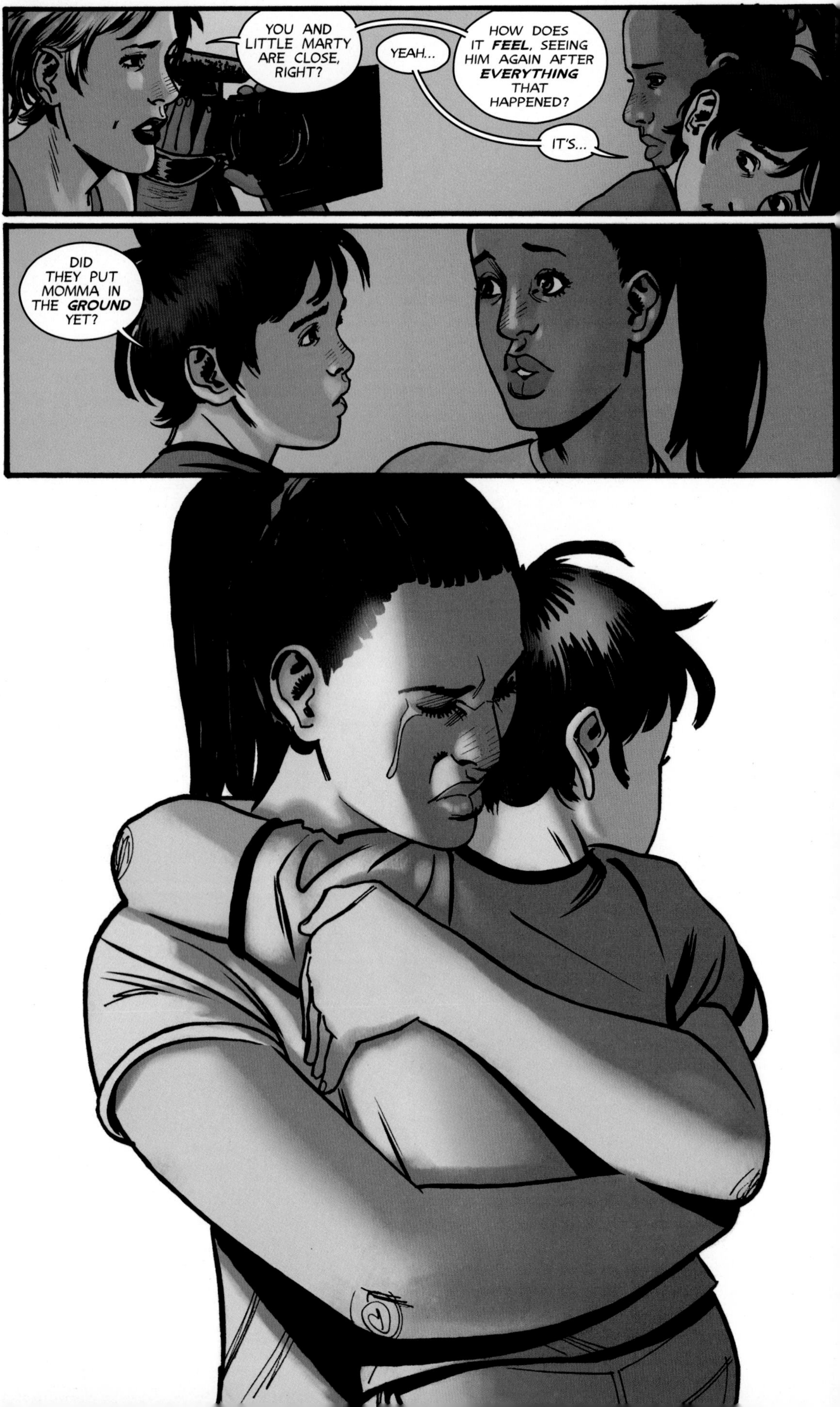

YOU AND LITTLE MARTY ARE CLOSE, RIGHT?
YEAH...
HOW DOES IT FEEL, SEEING HIM AGAIN AFTER EVERYTHING THAT HAPPENED?
IT'S...
DID THEY PUT MOMMA IN THE GROUND YET?

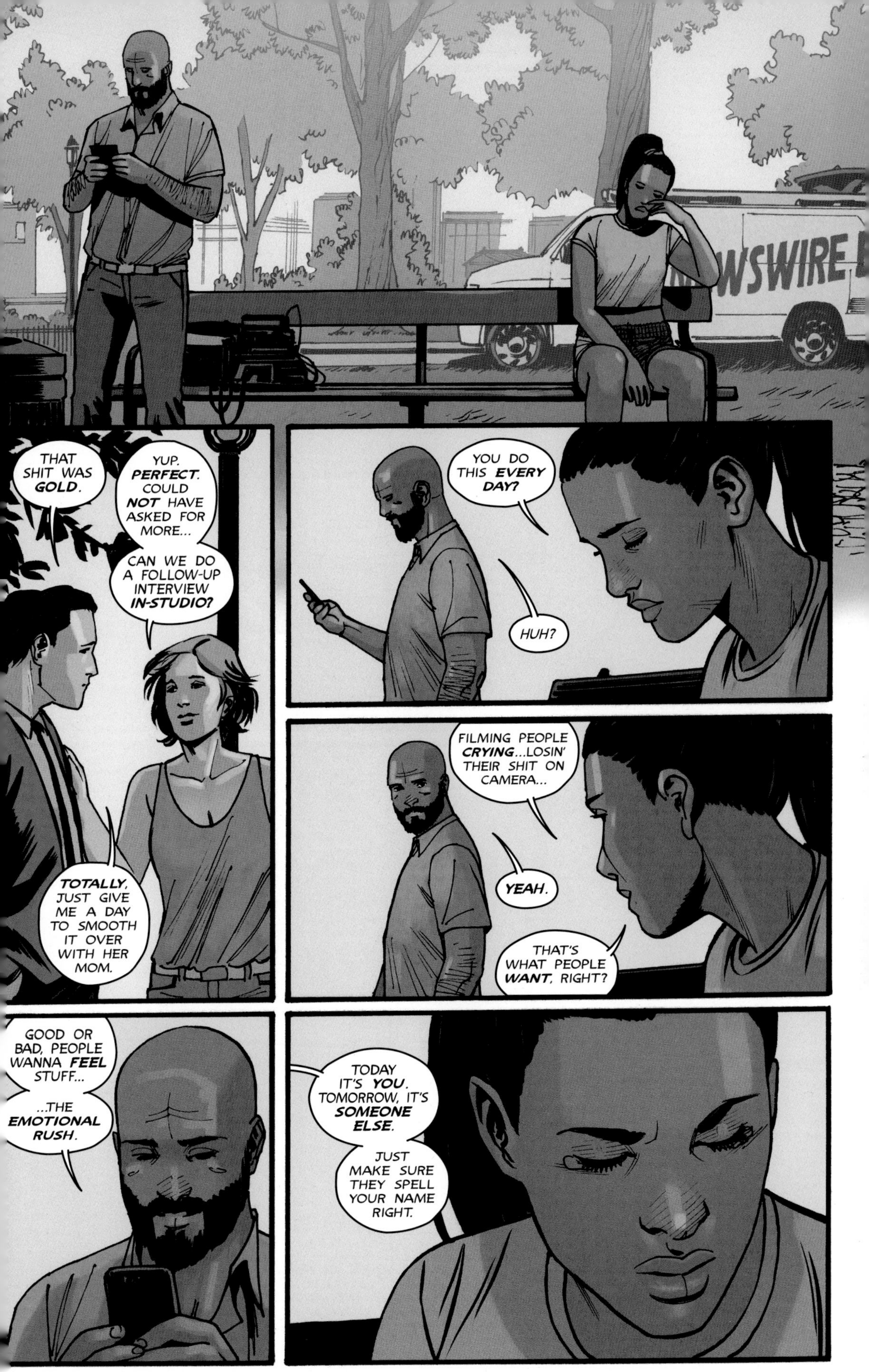
NEWSWIRE
THAT SHIT WAS **GOLD**.
YUP. **PERFECT**. COULD **NOT** HAVE ASKED FOR MORE...
CAN WE DO A FOLLOW-UP INTERVIEW **IN-STUDIO?**
TOTALLY, JUST GIVE ME A DAY TO SMOOTH IT OVER WITH HER MOM.
YOU DO THIS **EVERY DAY?**
HUH?
FILMING PEOPLE **CRYING**...LOSIN' THEIR SHIT ON CAMERA...
YEAH.
THAT'S WHAT PEOPLE **WANT**, RIGHT?
GOOD OR BAD, PEOPLE WANNA **FEEL** STUFF...
...THE **EMOTIONAL RUSH**.
TODAY IT'S **YOU**. TOMORROW, IT'S **SOMEONE ELSE**.
JUST MAKE SURE THEY SPELL YOUR NAME RIGHT.

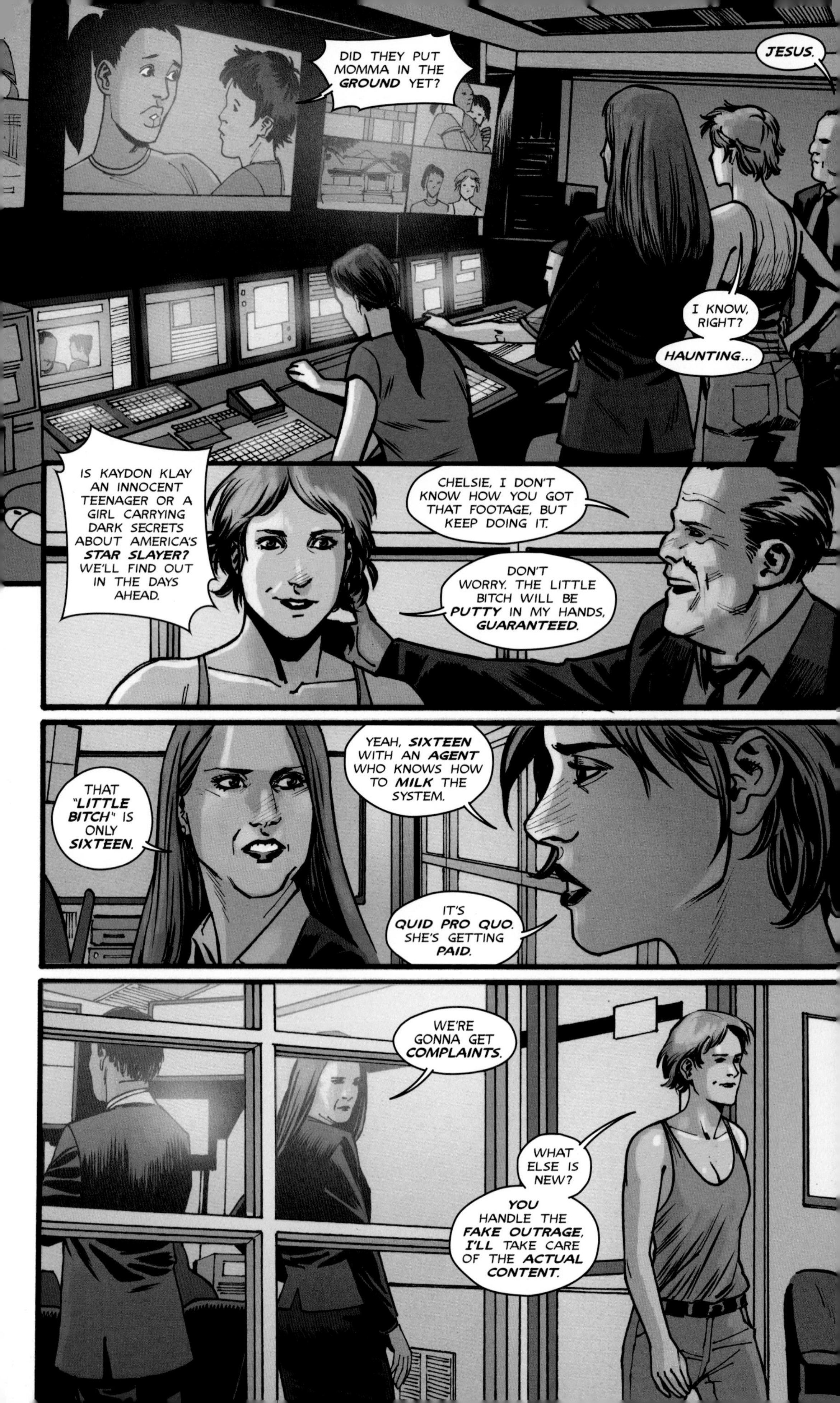
DID THEY PUT MOMMA IN THE GROUND YET?
JESUS.
I KNOW, RIGHT?
HAUNTING...
IS KAYDON KLAY AN INNOCENT TEENAGER OR A GIRL CARRYING DARK SECRETS ABOUT AMERICA'S STAR SLAYER? WE'LL FIND OUT IN THE DAYS AHEAD.
CHELSIE, I DON'T KNOW HOW YOU GOT THAT FOOTAGE, BUT KEEP DOING IT.
DON'T WORRY. THE LITTLE BITCH WILL BE PUTTY IN MY HANDS, GUARANTEED.
THAT "LITTLE BITCH" IS ONLY SIXTEEN.
YEAH, SIXTEEN WITH AN AGENT WHO KNOWS HOW TO MILK THE SYSTEM.
IT'S QUID PRO QUO. SHE'S GETTING PAID.
WE'RE GONNA GET COMPLAINTS.
WHAT ELSE IS NEW?
YOU HANDLE THE FAKE OUTRAGE, I'LL TAKE CARE OF THE ACTUAL CONTENT.

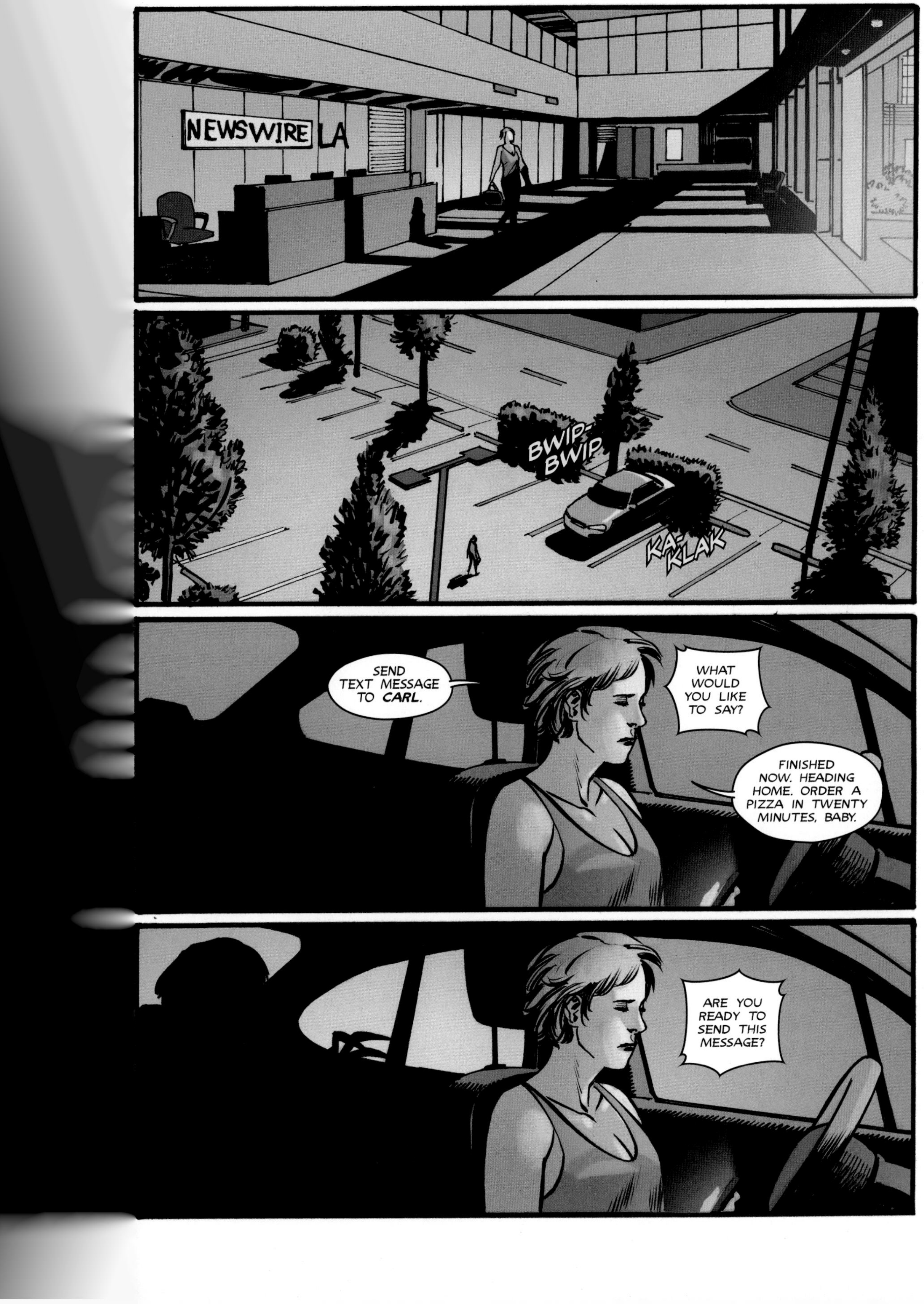
NEWSWIRE LA
BWIP-BWIP
KA-KLAK
SEND TEXT MESSAGE TO CARL.
WHAT WOULD YOU LIKE TO SAY?
FINISHED NOW. HEADING HOME. ORDER A PIZZA IN TWENTY MINUTES, BABY.
ARE YOU READY TO SEND THIS MESSAGE?

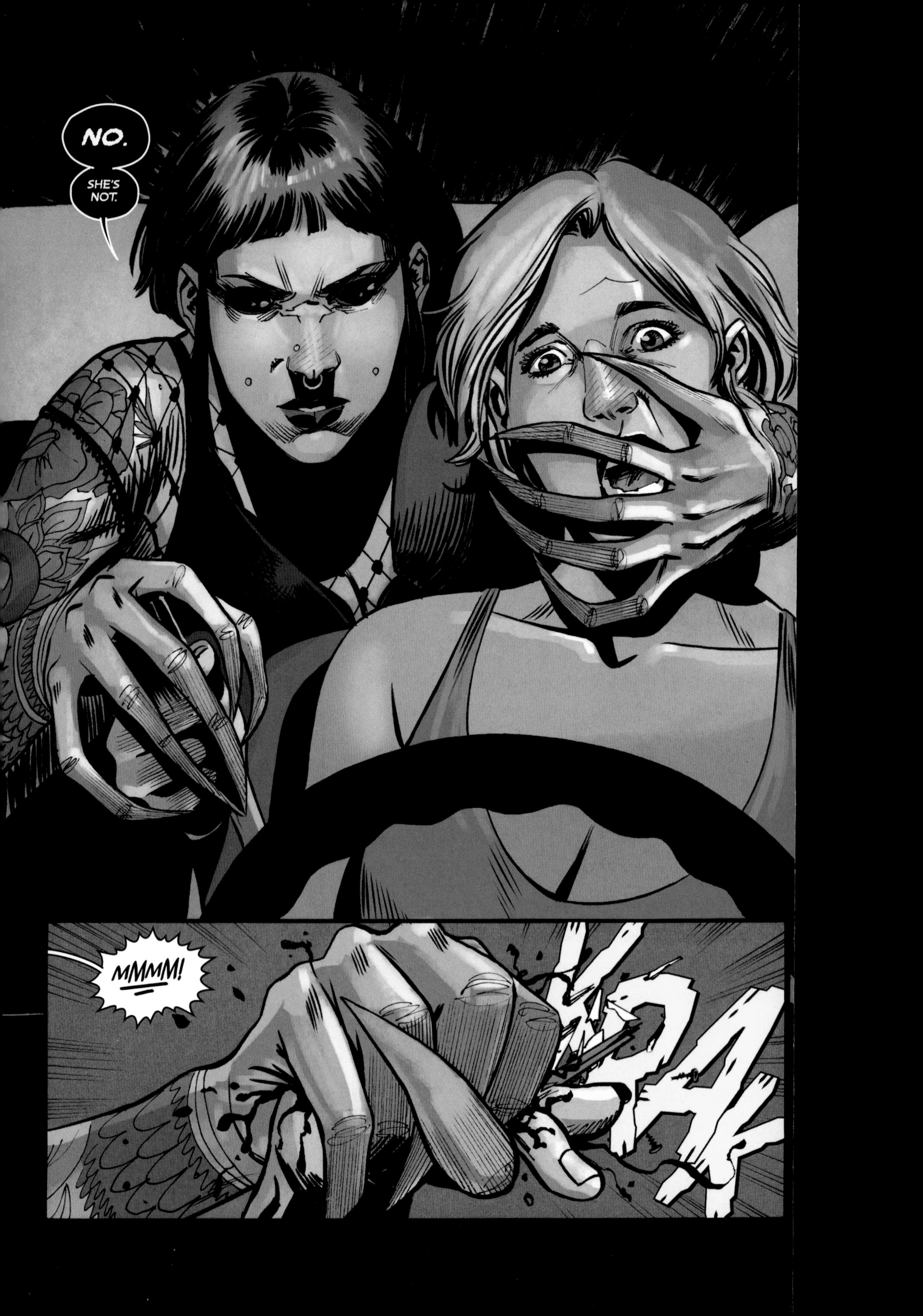
NO.
SHE'S NOT.
MMMM!

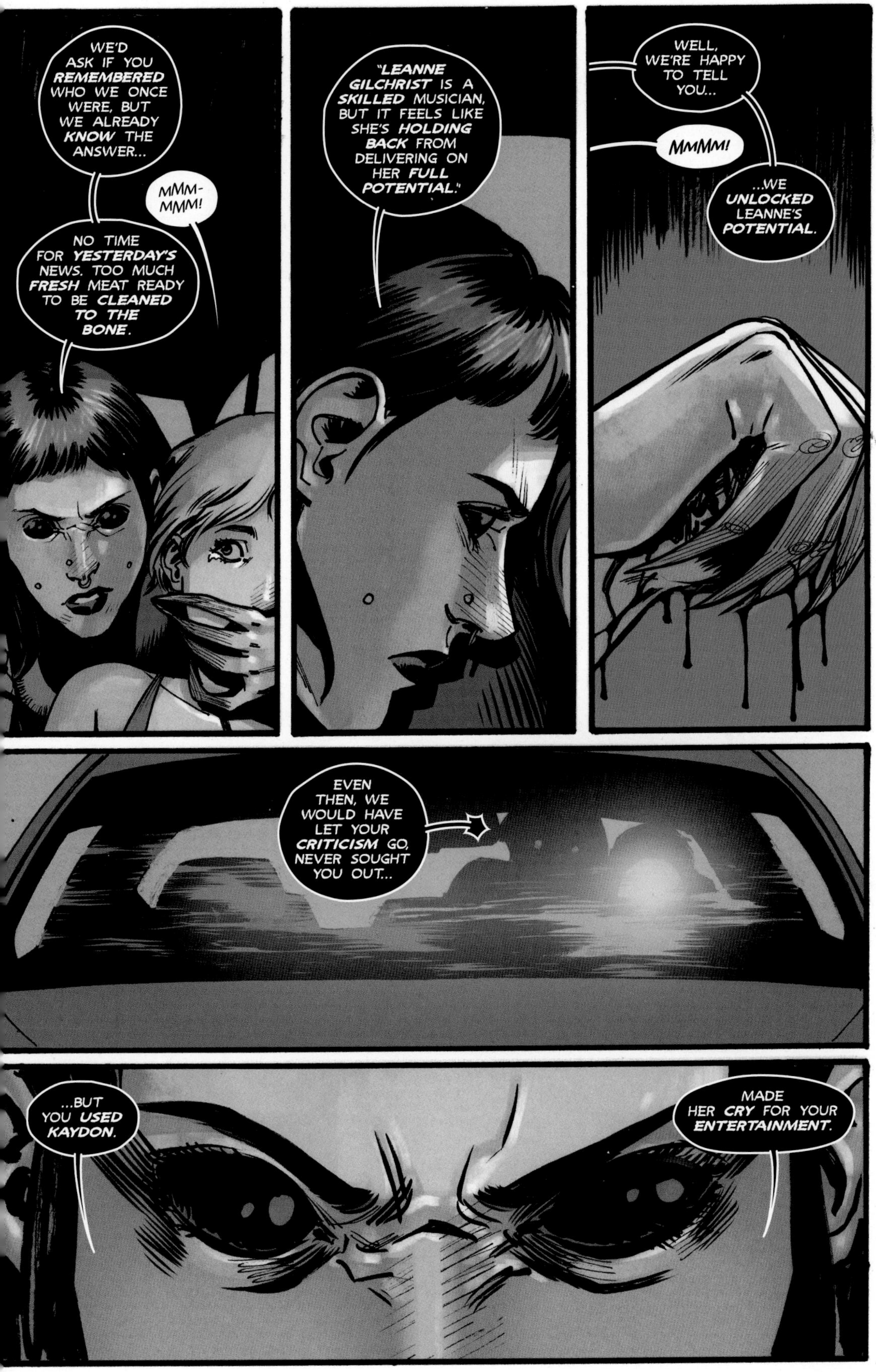
WE'D ASK IF YOU REMEMBERED WHO WE ONCE WERE, BUT WE ALREADY KNOW THE ANSWER...
NO TIME FOR YESTERDAY'S NEWS. TOO MUCH FRESH MEAT READY TO BE CLEANED TO THE BONE.
MMM-MMM!
"LEANNE GILCHRIST IS A SKILLED MUSICIAN, BUT IT FEELS LIKE SHE'S HOLDING BACK FROM DELIVERING ON HER FULL POTENTIAL."
WELL, WE'RE HAPPY TO TELL YOU...
MMMM!
...WE UNLOCKED LEANNE'S POTENTIAL.
EVEN THEN, WE WOULD HAVE LET YOUR CRITICISM GO, NEVER SOUGHT YOU OUT...
...BUT YOU USED KAYDON.
MADE HER CRY FOR YOUR ENTERTAINMENT.

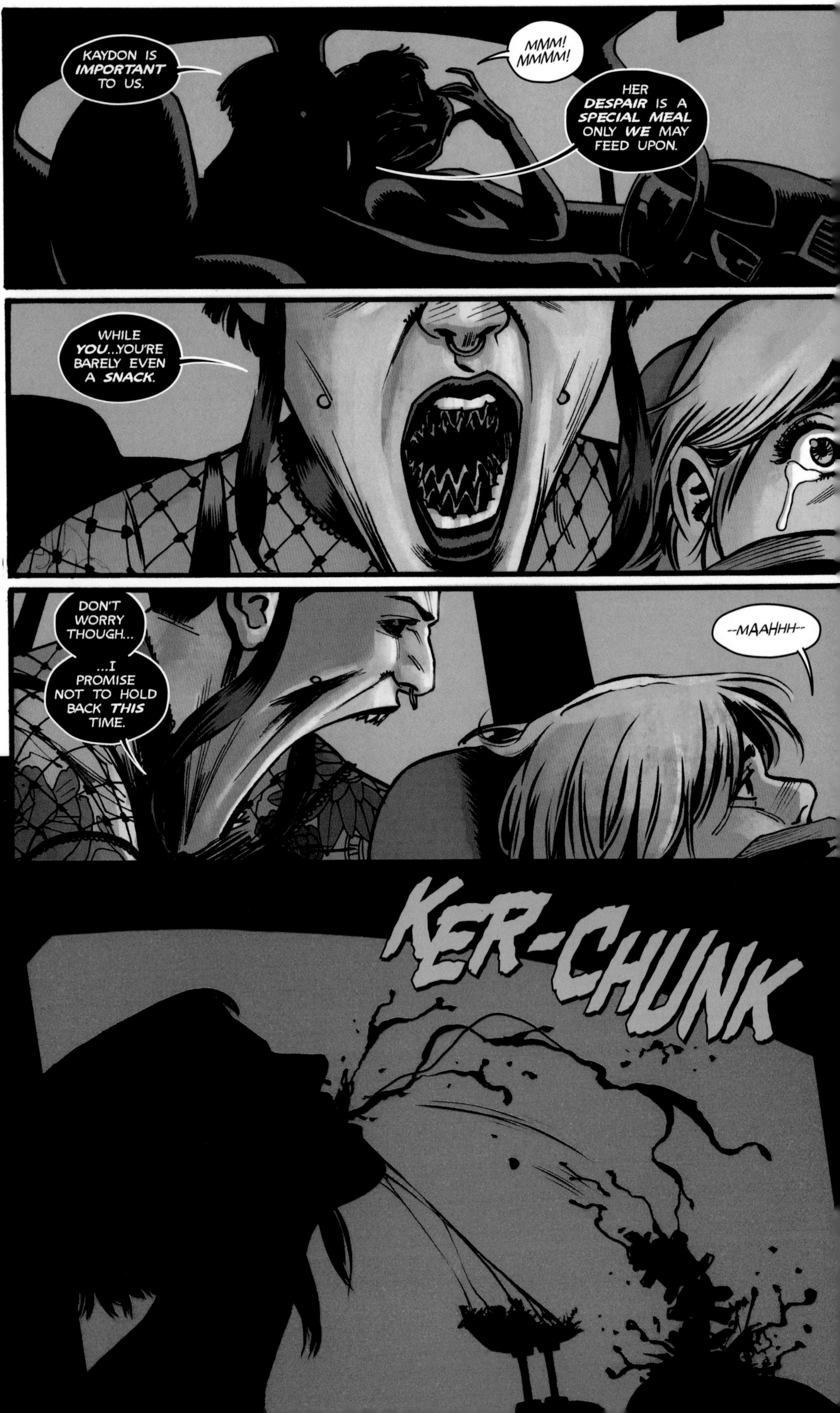
KAYDON IS IMPORTANT TO US.
MMM! MMMM!
HER DESPAIR IS A SPECIAL MEAL ONLY WE MAY FEED UPON.
WHILE YOU...YOU'RE BARELY EVEN A SNACK.
DON'T WORRY THOUGH...
...I PROMISE NOT TO HOLD BACK THIS TIME.
--MAAHHH--
KER-CHUNK

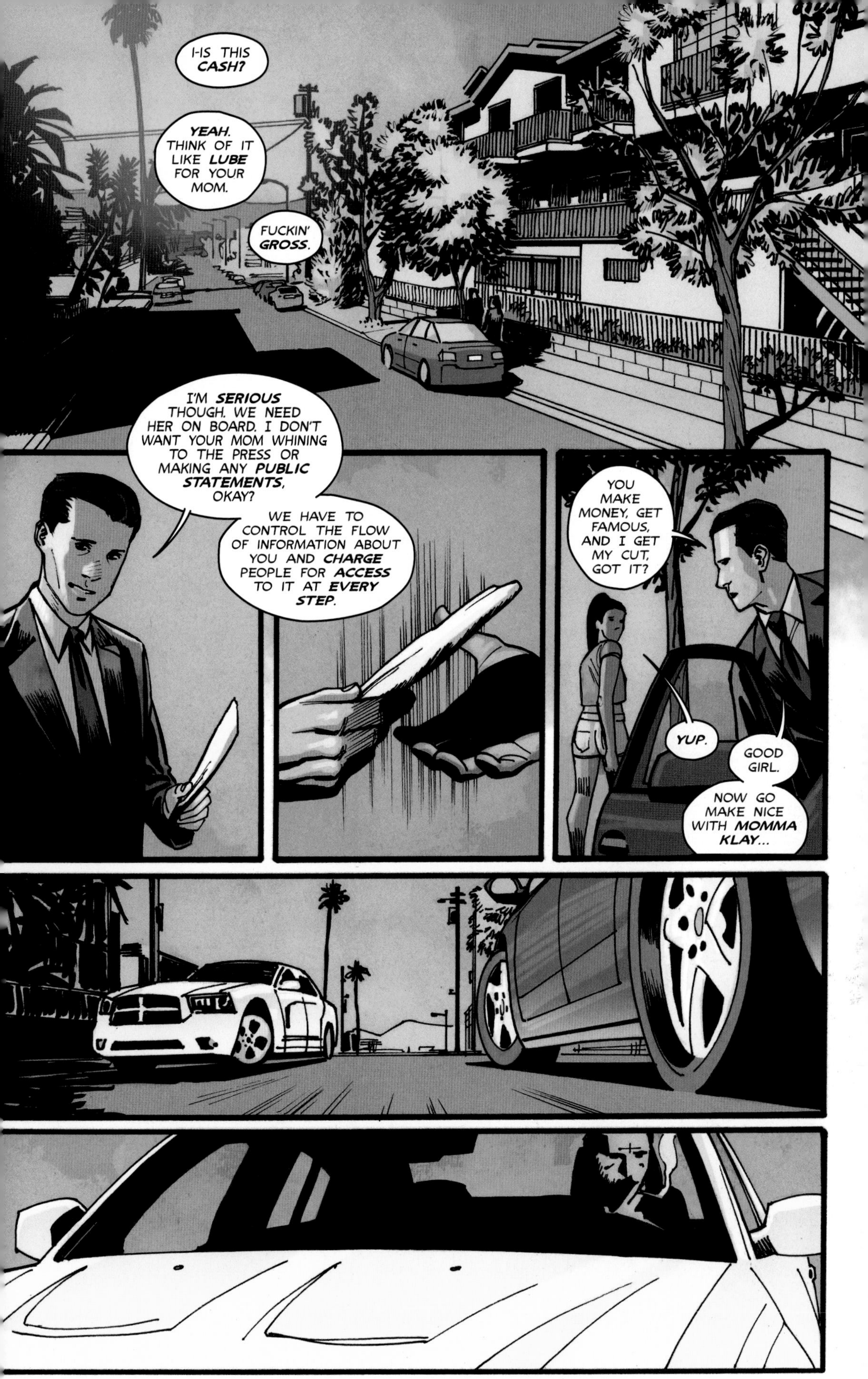

I-IS THIS CASH?
YEAH. THINK OF IT LIKE LUBE FOR YOUR MOM.
FUCKIN' GROSS.
I'M SERIOUS THOUGH. WE NEED HER ON BOARD. I DON'T WANT YOUR MOM WHINING TO THE PRESS OR MAKING ANY PUBLIC STATEMENTS, OKAY?
WE HAVE TO CONTROL THE FLOW OF INFORMATION ABOUT YOU AND CHARGE PEOPLE FOR ACCESS TO IT AT EVERY STEP.
YOU MAKE MONEY, GET FAMOUS, AND I GET MY CUT, GOT IT?
YUP.
GOOD GIRL.
NOW GO MAKE NICE WITH MOMMA KLAY...

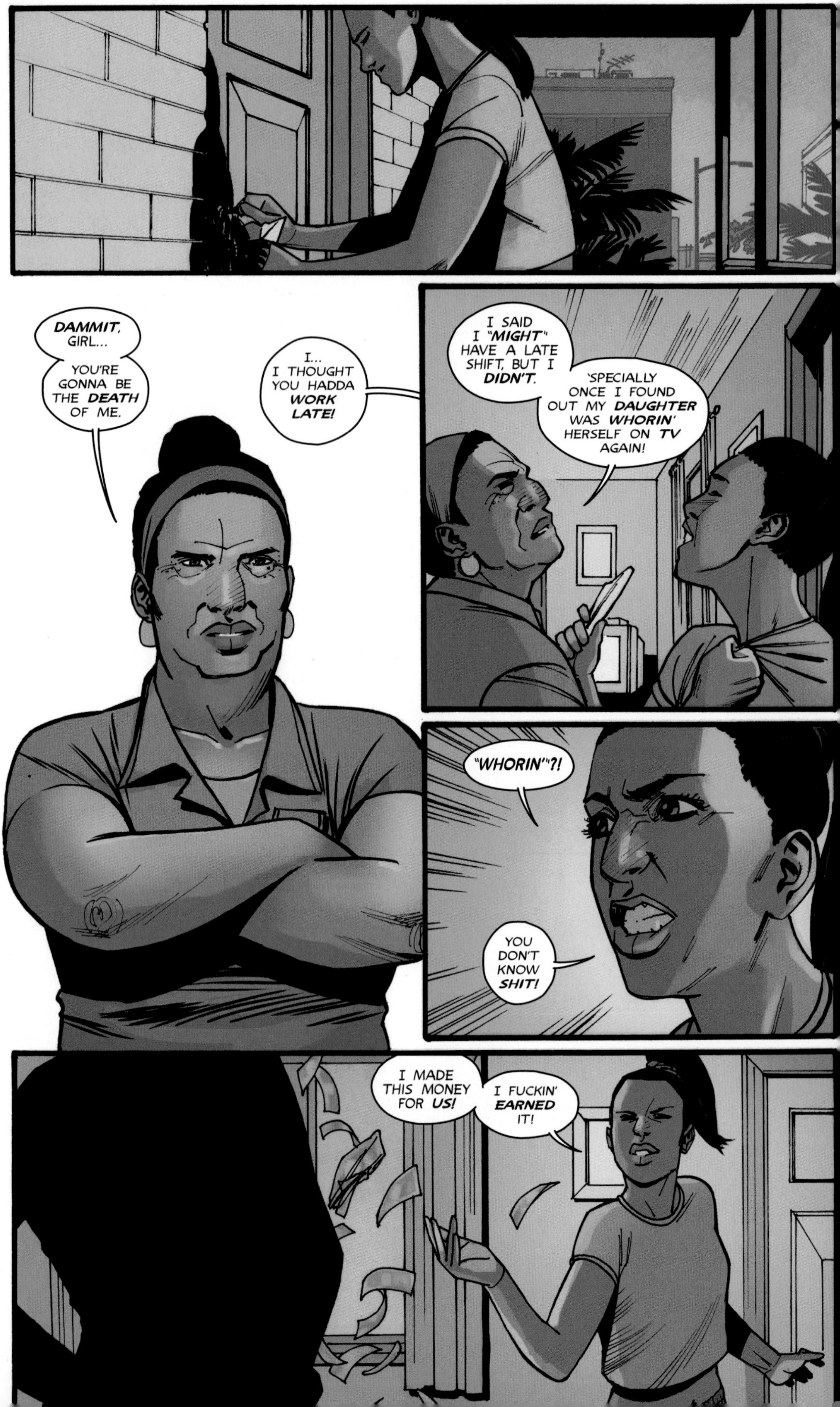

DAMMIT, GIRL...
YOU'RE GONNA BE THE DEATH OF ME.
I... I THOUGHT YOU HADDA WORK LATE!
I SAID I "MIGHT" HAVE A LATE SHIFT, BUT I DIDN'T.
'SPECIALLY ONCE I FOUND OUT MY DAUGHTER WAS WHORIN' HERSELF ON TV AGAIN!
"WHORIN'"?!
YOU DON'T KNOW SHIT!
I MADE THIS MONEY FOR US!
I FUCKIN' EARNED IT!

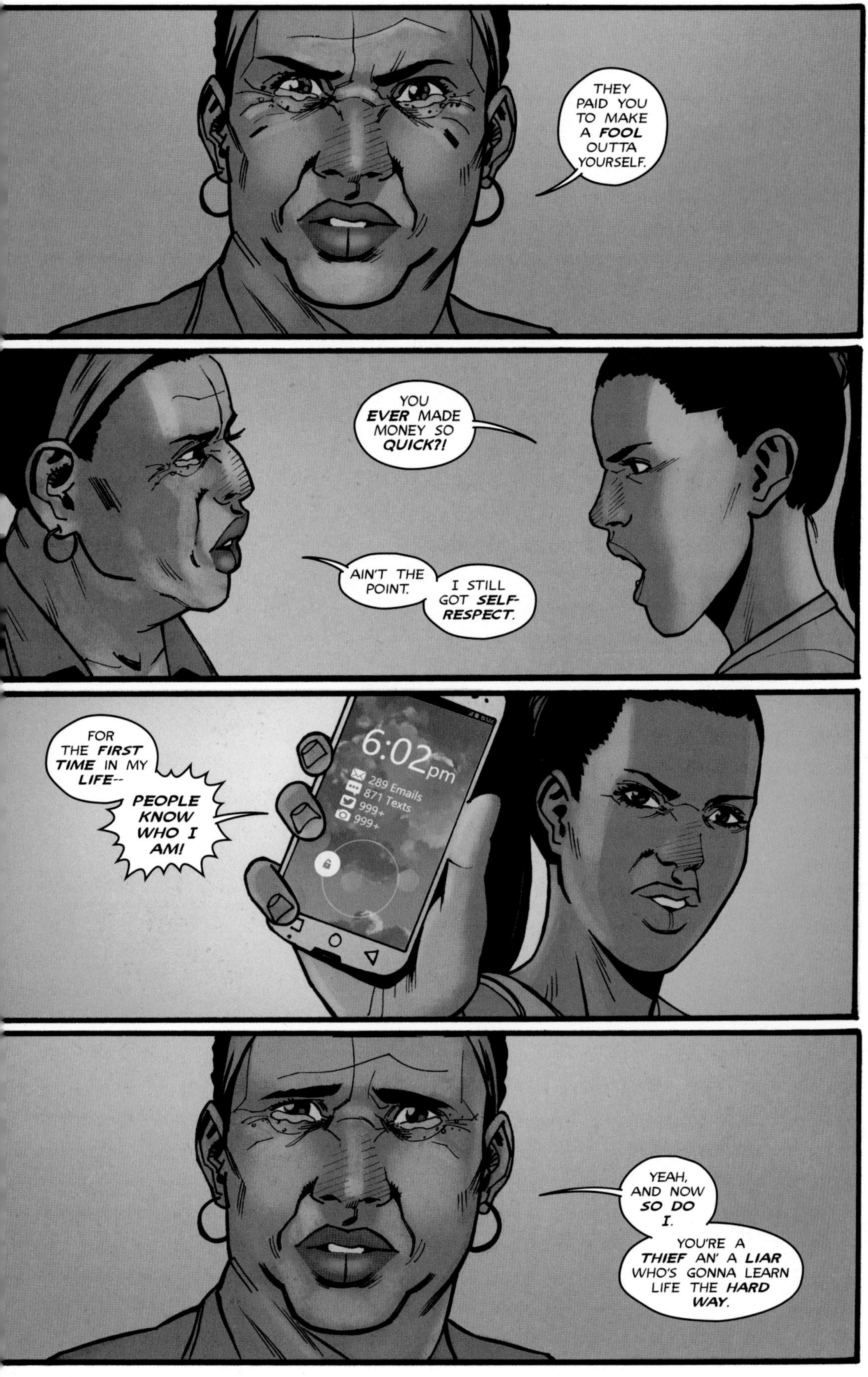
THEY PAID YOU TO MAKE A FOOL OUTTA YOURSELF.
YOU EVER MADE MONEY SO QUICK?!
AIN'T THE POINT.
I STILL GOT SELF-RESPECT.
FOR THE FIRST TIME IN MY LIFE--
PEOPLE KNOW WHO I AM!
6:02pm
289 Emails
871 Texts
999+
999+
YEAH, AND NOW SO DO I.
YOU'RE A THIEF AN' A LIAR WHO'S GONNA LEARN LIFE THE HARD WAY.

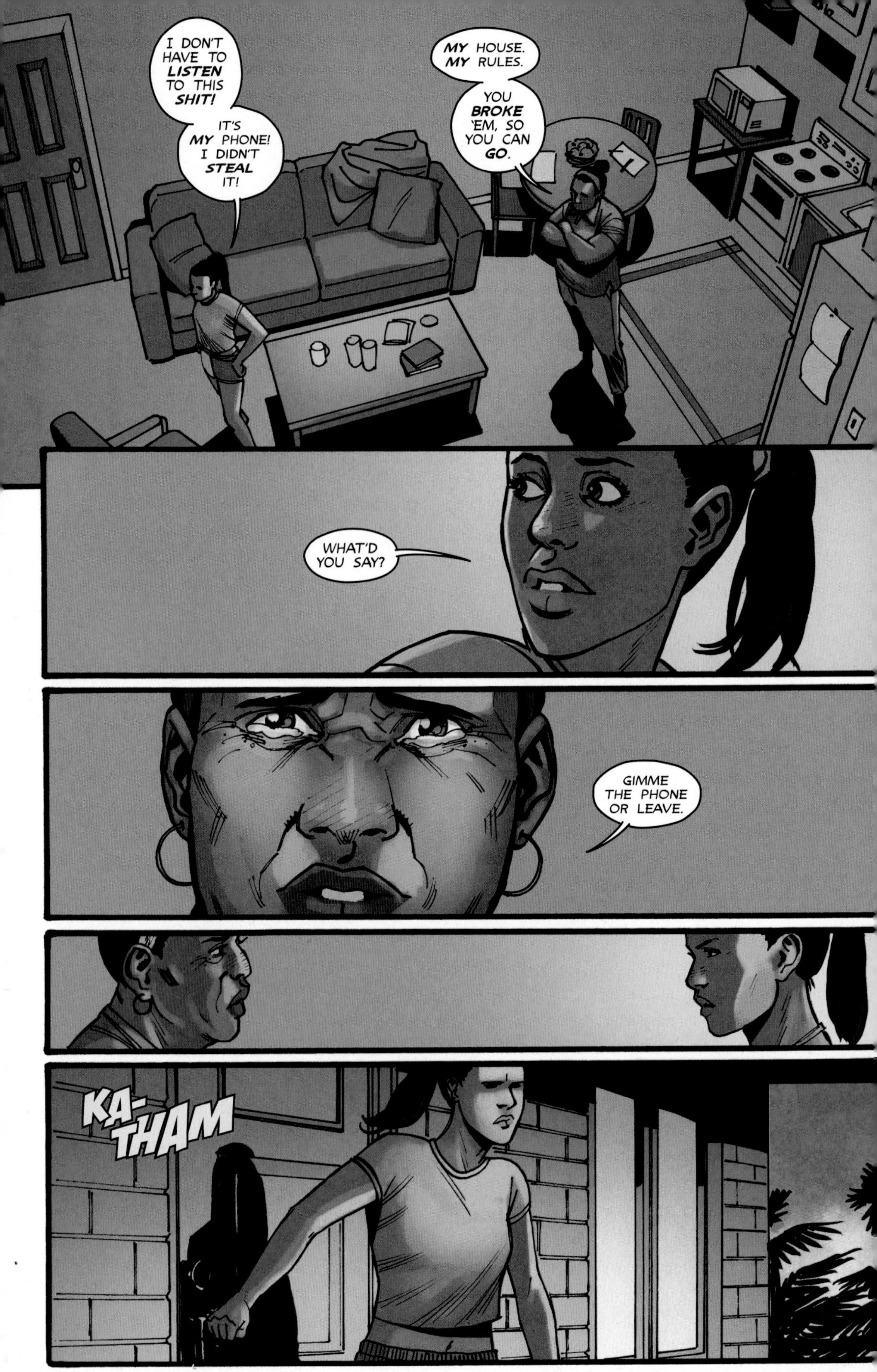

I DON'T HAVE TO LISTEN TO THIS SHIT!
IT'S MY PHONE! I DIDN'T STEAL IT!
MY HOUSE. MY RULES.
YOU BROKE 'EM, SO YOU CAN GO.
WHAT'D YOU SAY?
GIMME THE PHONE OR LEAVE.
KA-THAM

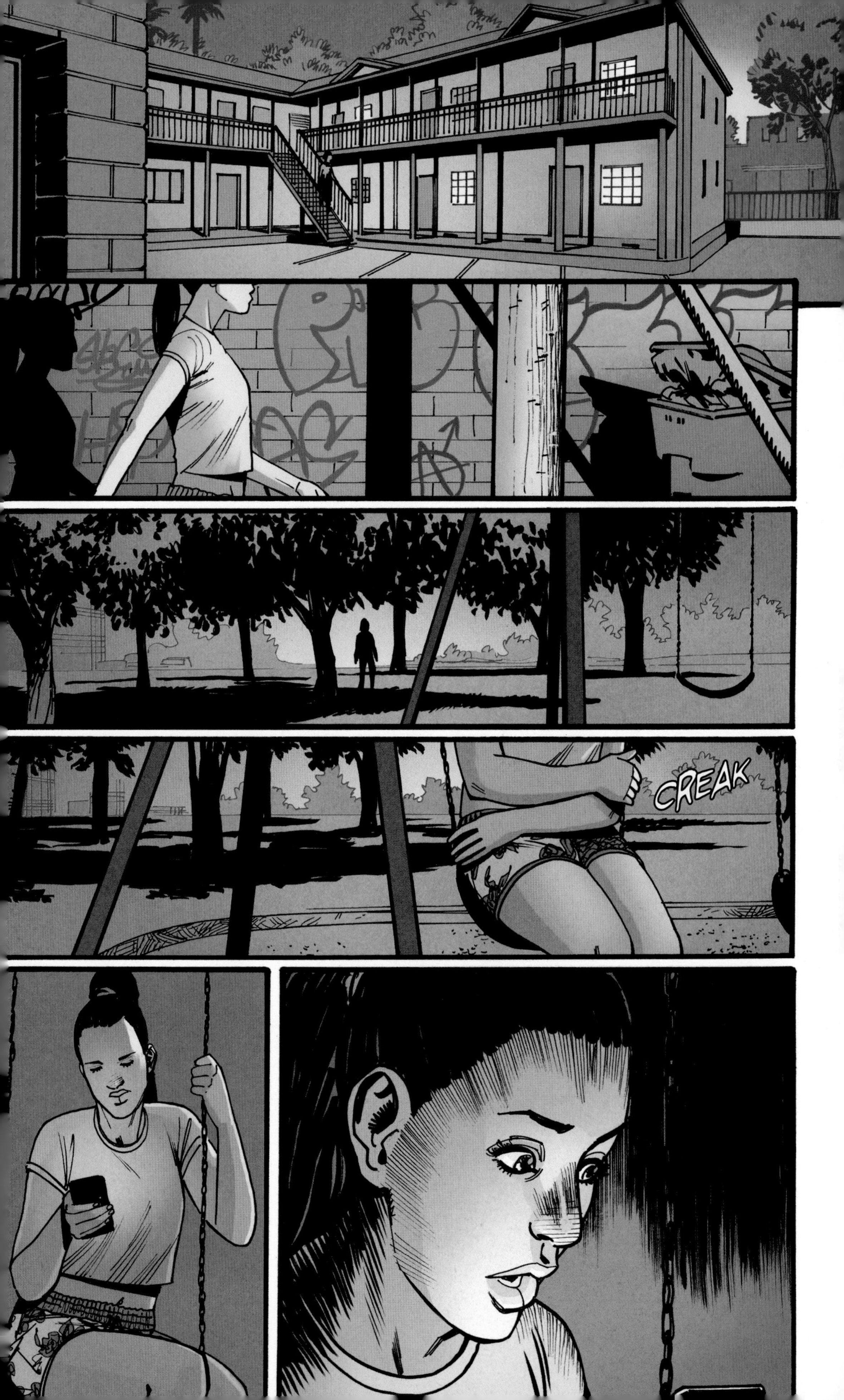
CREAK

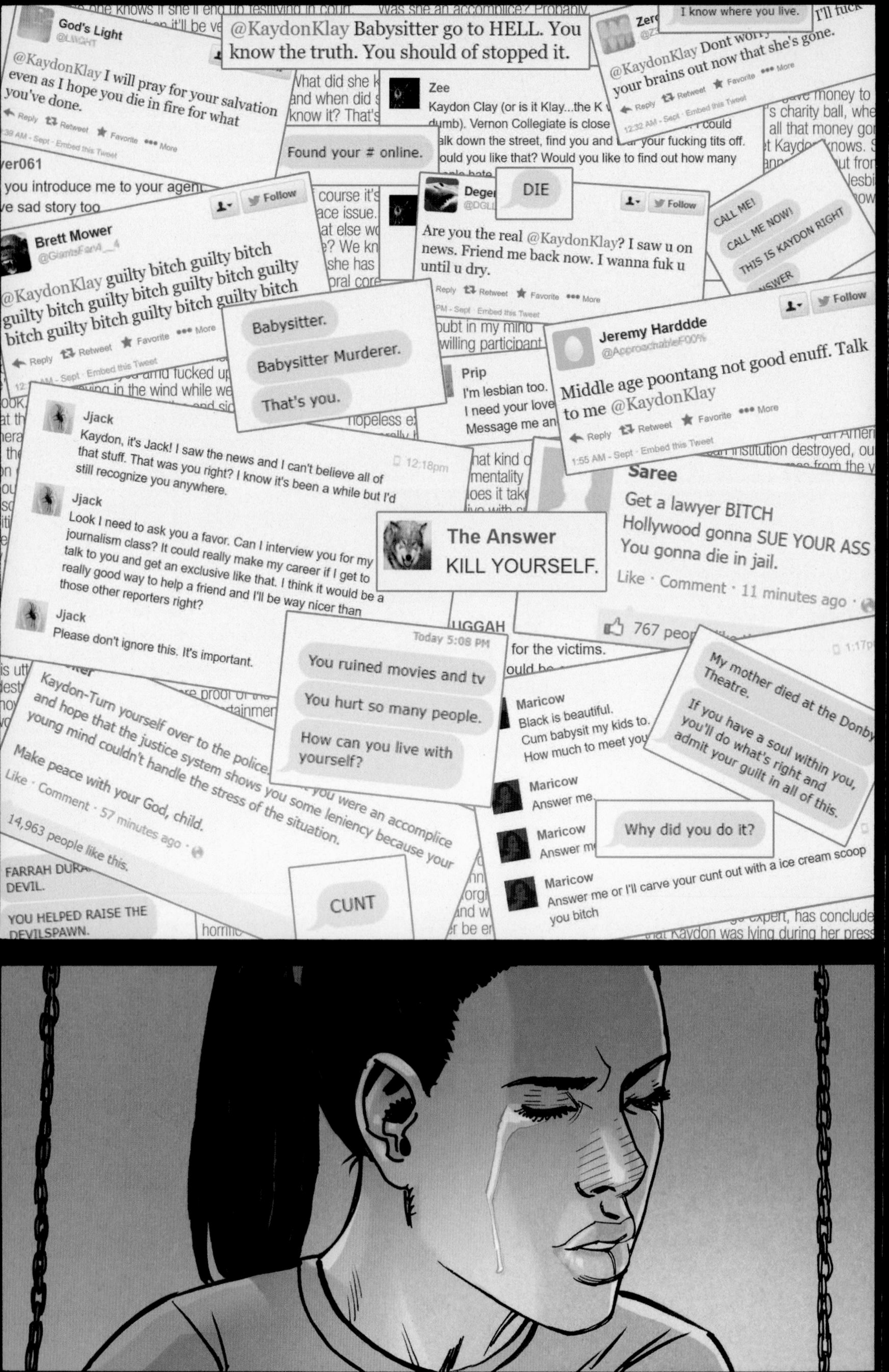
God's Light
@KaydonKlay I will pray for your salvation even as I hope you die in fire for what you've done.
@KaydonKlay Babysitter go to HELL. You know the truth. You should of stopped it.
I know where you live.
@KaydonKlay Dont worry your brains out now that she's gone.
Zee
Kaydon Clay (or is it Klay...the K dumb). Vernon Collegiate is close
Found your # online.
Brett Mower
@KaydonKlay guilty bitch guilty bitch guilty bitch guilty bitch guilty bitch guilty bitch guilty bitch guilty bitch
DIE
Are you the real @KaydonKlay? I saw u on news. Friend me back now. I wanna fuk u until u dry.
CALL ME!
CALL ME NOW!
THIS IS KAYDON RIGHT
Babysitter.
Babysitter Murderer.
That's you.
Jeremy Harddde
Middle age poontang not good enuff. Talk to me @KaydonKlay
Prip
I'm lesbian too.
I need your love
Jjack
Kaydon, it's Jack! I saw the news and I can't believe all of that stuff. That was you right? I know it's been a while but I'd still recognize you anywhere.
Jjack
Look I need to ask you a favor. Can I interview you for my journalism class? It could really make my career if I get to talk to you and get an exclusive like that. I think it would be a really good way to help a friend and I'll be way nicer than those other reporters right?
Jjack
Please don't ignore this. It's important.
The Answer
KILL YOURSELF.
Saree
Get a lawyer BITCH
Hollywood gonna SUE YOUR ASS
You gonna die in jail.
Like · Comment · 11 minutes ago
Today 5:08 PM
You ruined movies and tv
You hurt so many people.
How can you live with yourself?
Kaydon-Turn yourself over to the police and hope that the justice system shows you some leniency because your young mind couldn't handle the stress of the situation.
Make peace with your God, child.
Like · Comment · 57 minutes ago
14,963 people like this.
Maricow
Black is beautiful.
Cum babysit my kids to.
Maricow
Answer me.
Maricow
Answer me or I'll carve your cunt out with a ice cream scoop you bitch
My mother died at the Donby Theatre.
If you have a soul within you, you'll do what's right and admit your guilt in all of this.
Why did you do it?
YOU HELPED RAISE THE DEVILSPAWN.
CUNT

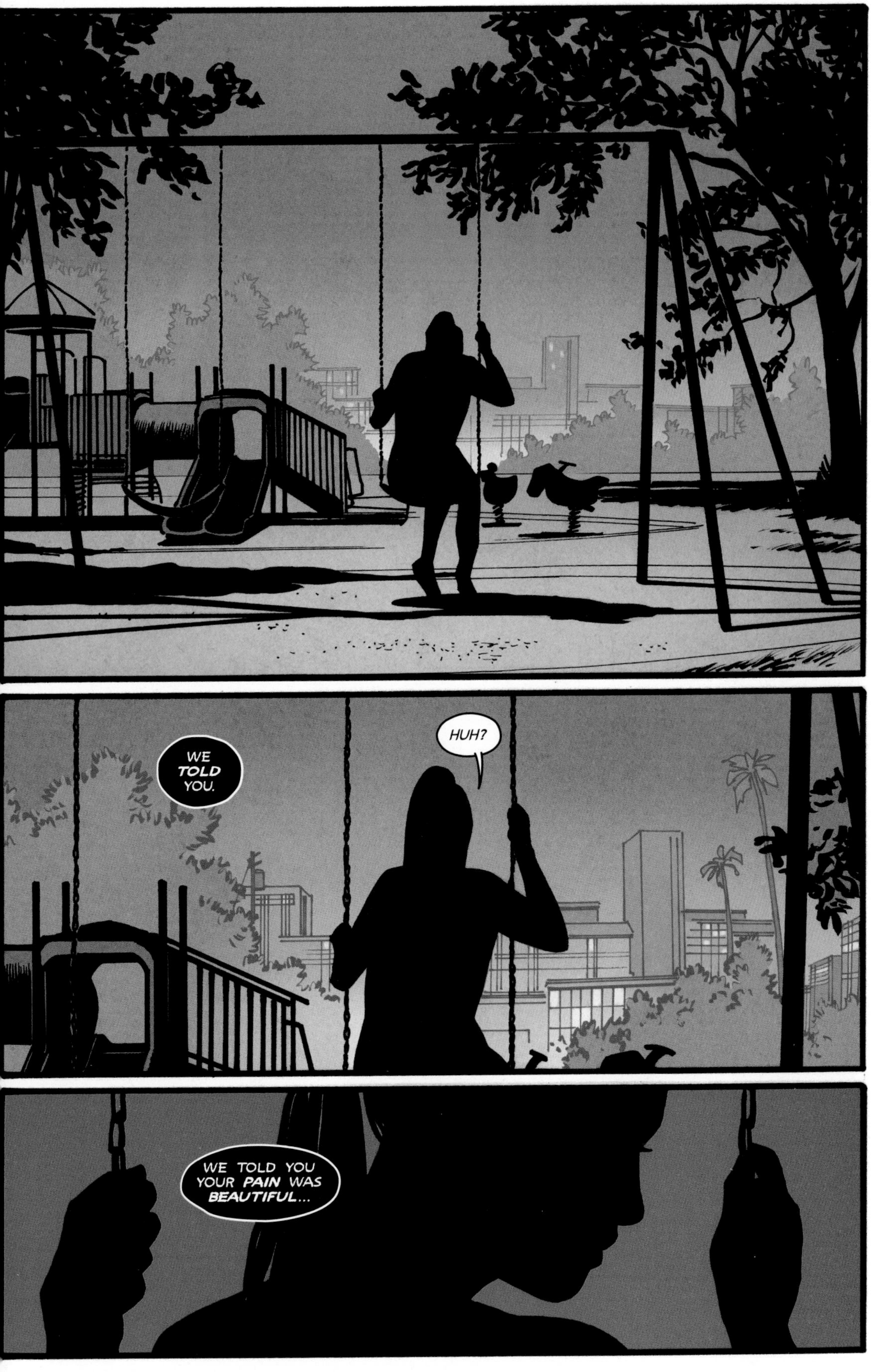
WE TOLD YOU.
HUH?
WE TOLD YOU YOUR PAIN WAS BEAUTIFUL...

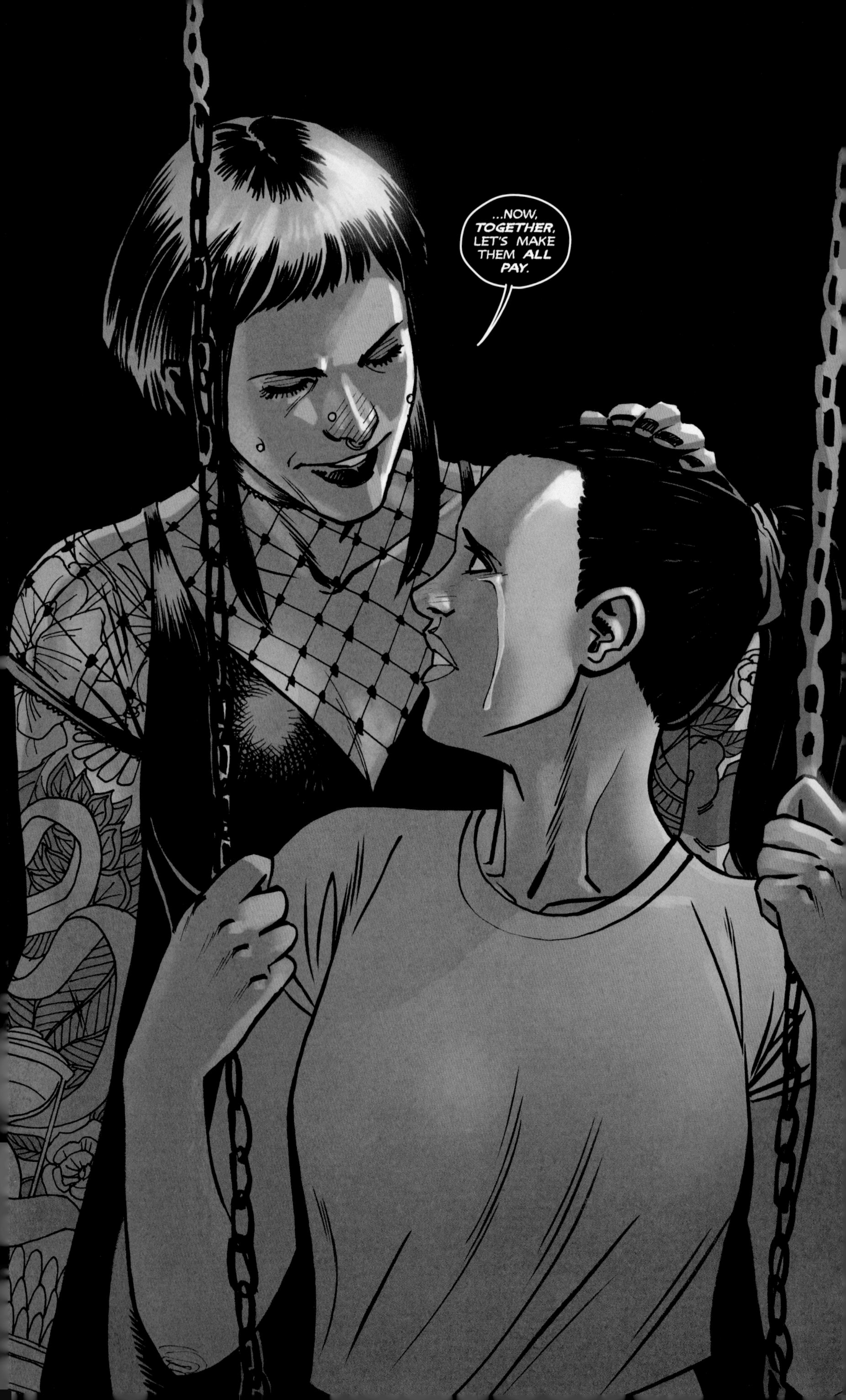
...NOW, TOGETHER, LET'S MAKE THEM ALL PAY.

PART 3: PURITY TEST

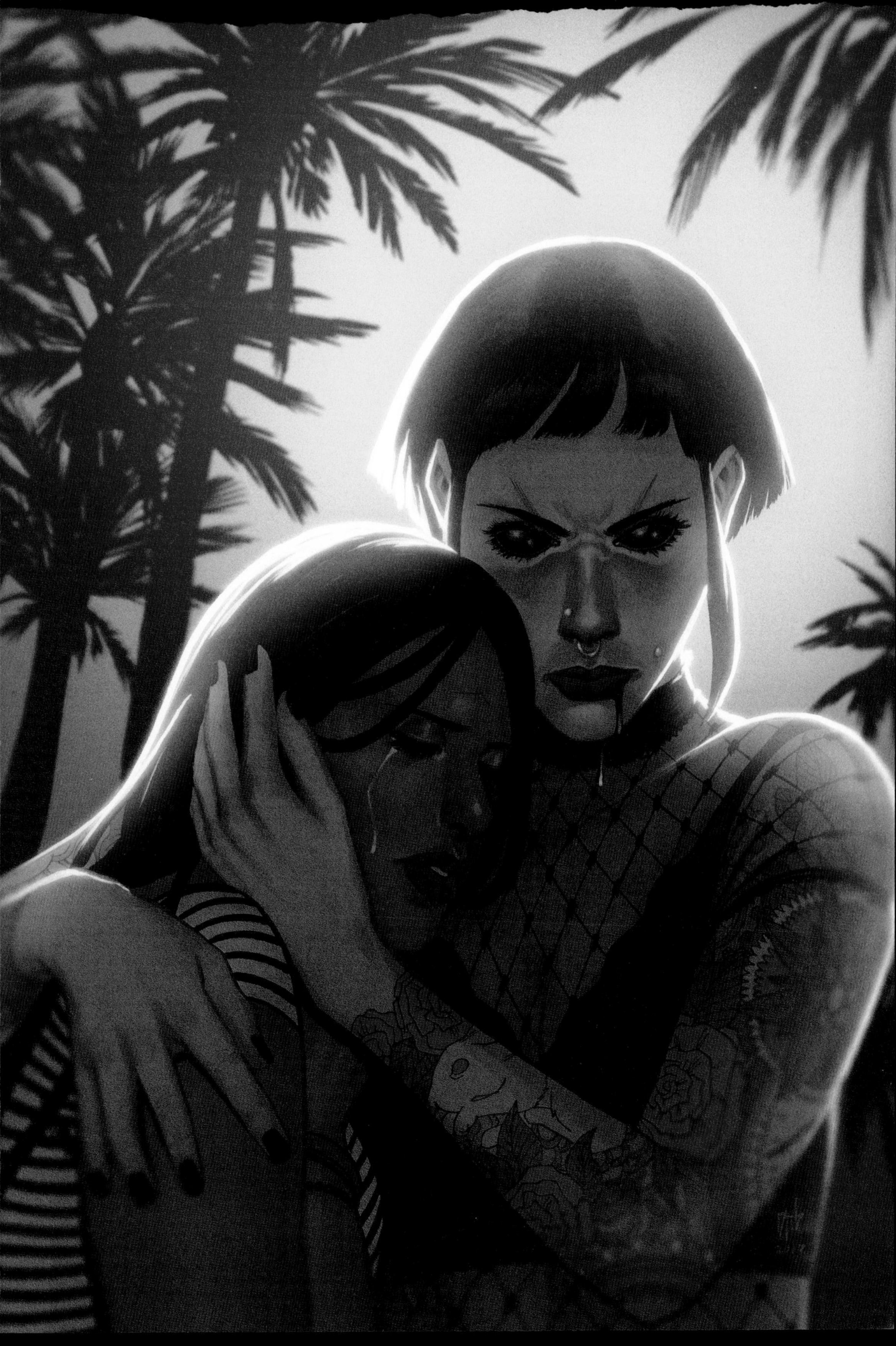

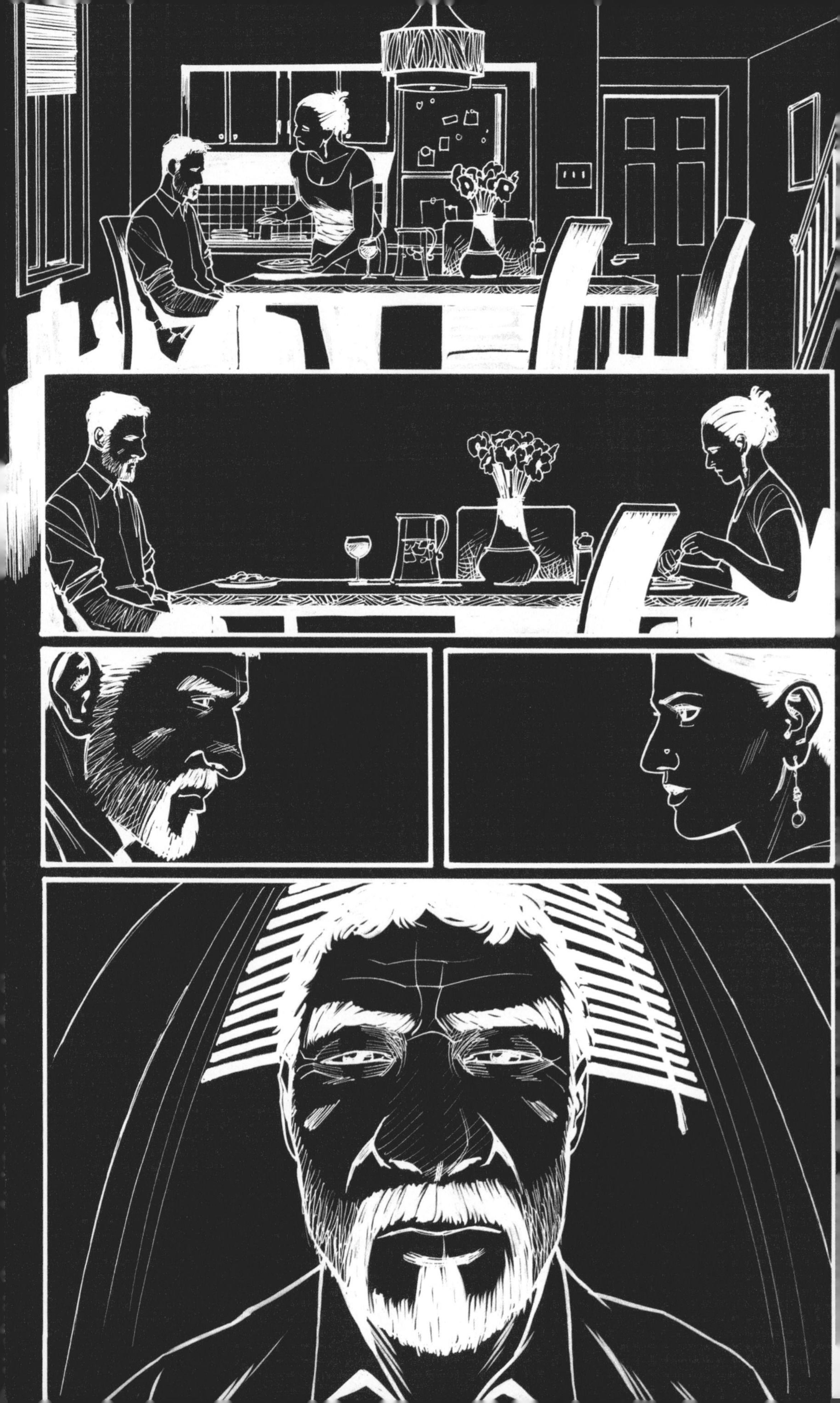

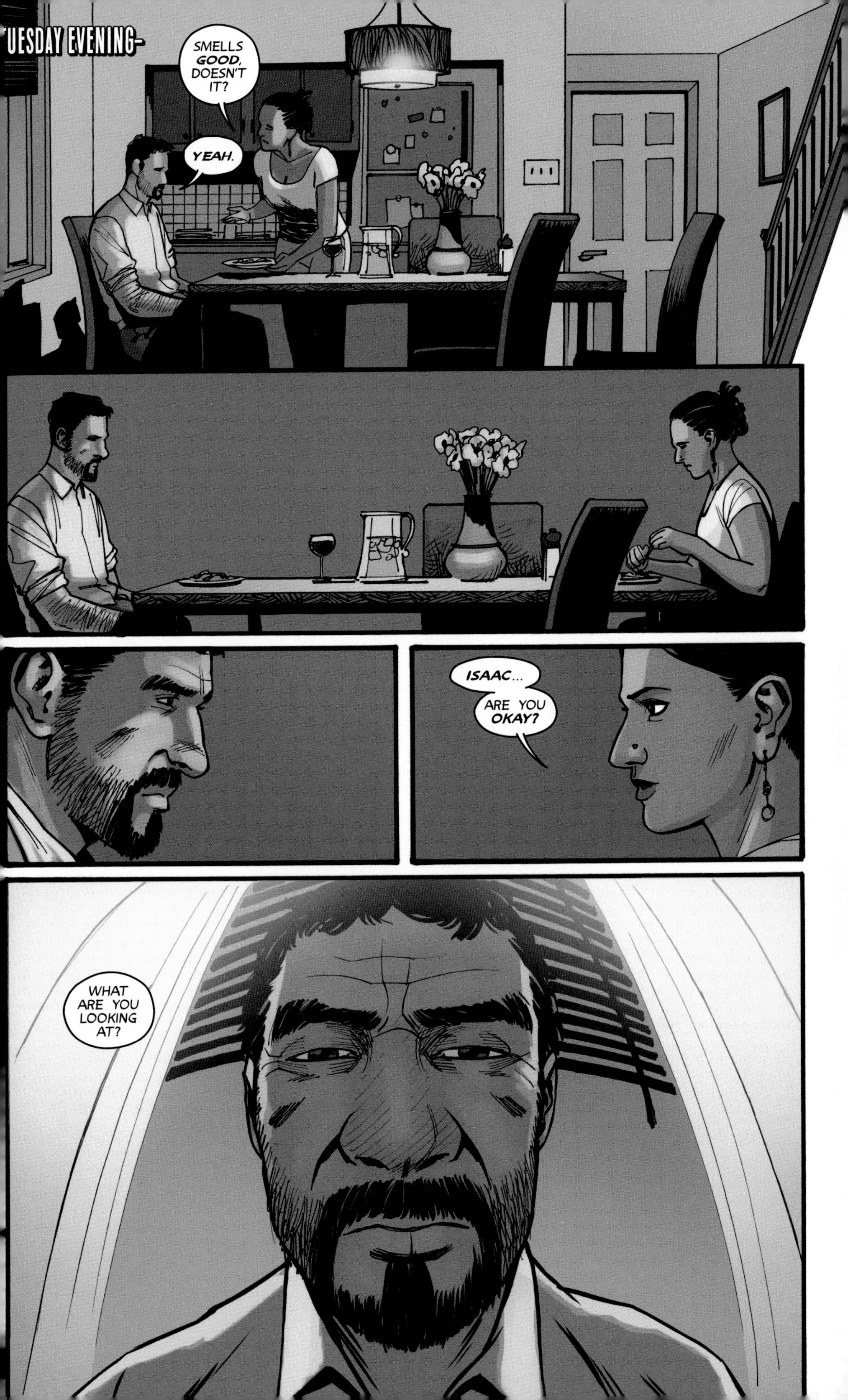
UESDAY EVENING–
SMELLS GOOD, DOESN'T IT?
YEAH.
ISAAC...
ARE YOU OKAY?
WHAT ARE YOU LOOKING AT?

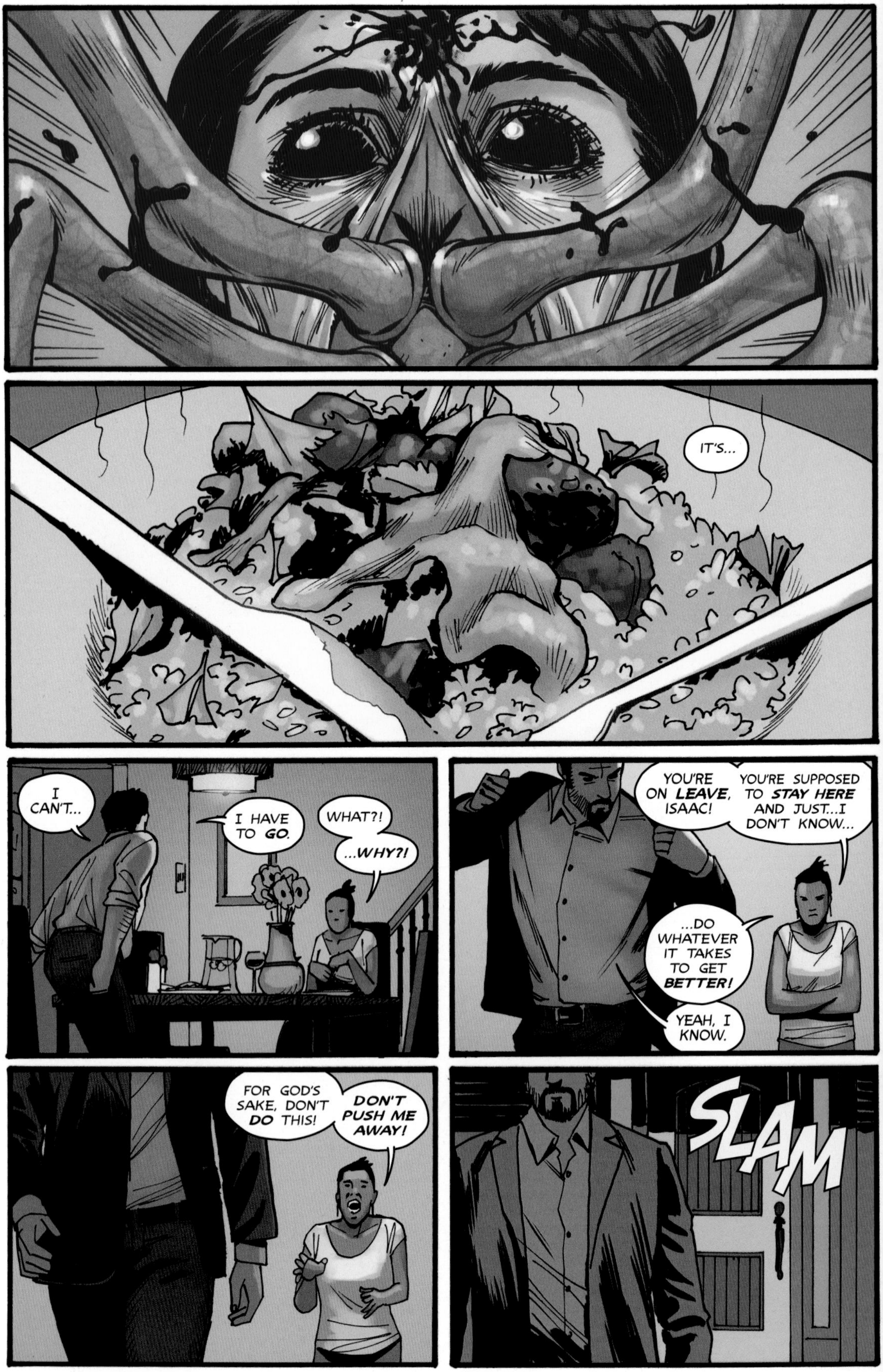
IT'S...
I CAN'T...
I HAVE TO **GO**.
WHAT?!
...**WHY?!**
YOU'RE ON **LEAVE**, ISAAC!
YOU'RE SUPPOSED TO **STAY HERE** AND JUST...I DON'T KNOW...
...DO WHATEVER IT TAKES TO GET **BETTER!**
YEAH, I KNOW.
FOR GOD'S SAKE, DON'T **DO** THIS!
DON'T PUSH ME AWAY!
SLAM

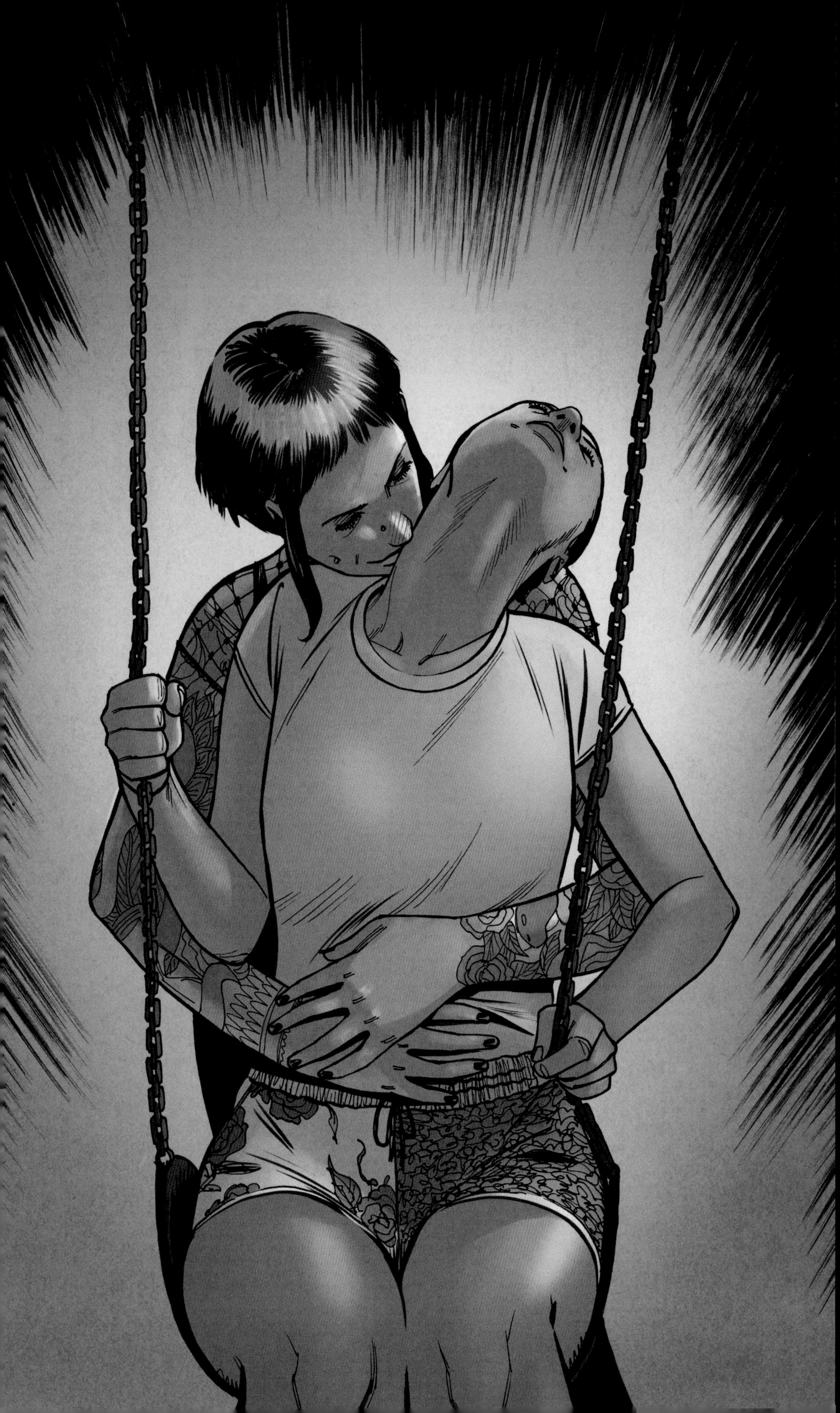

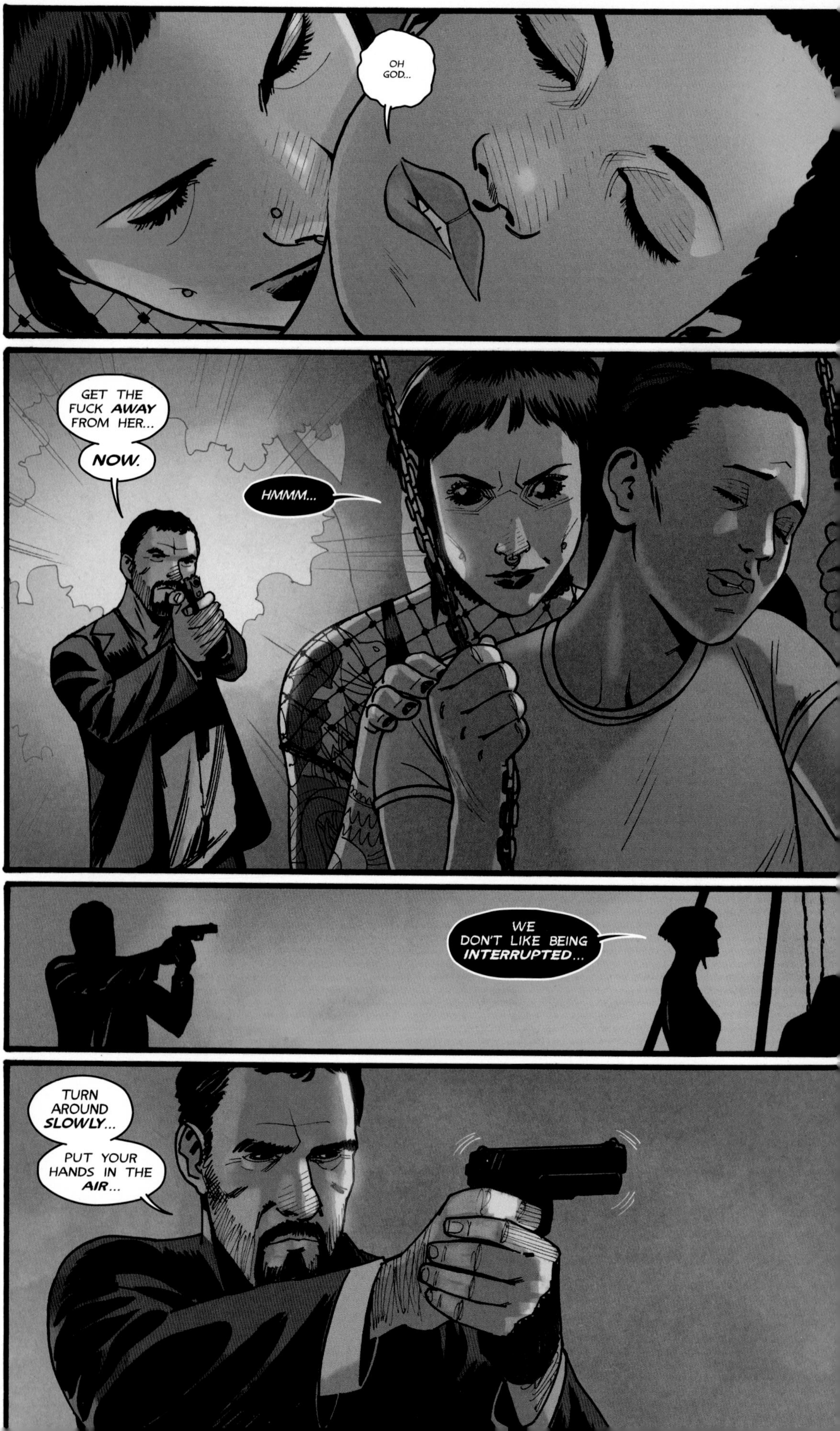
OH GOD...
GET THE FUCK **AWAY** FROM HER...
NOW.
HMMM...
WE DON'T LIKE BEING **INTERRUPTED**...
TURN AROUND **SLOWLY**...
PUT YOUR HANDS IN THE **AIR**...

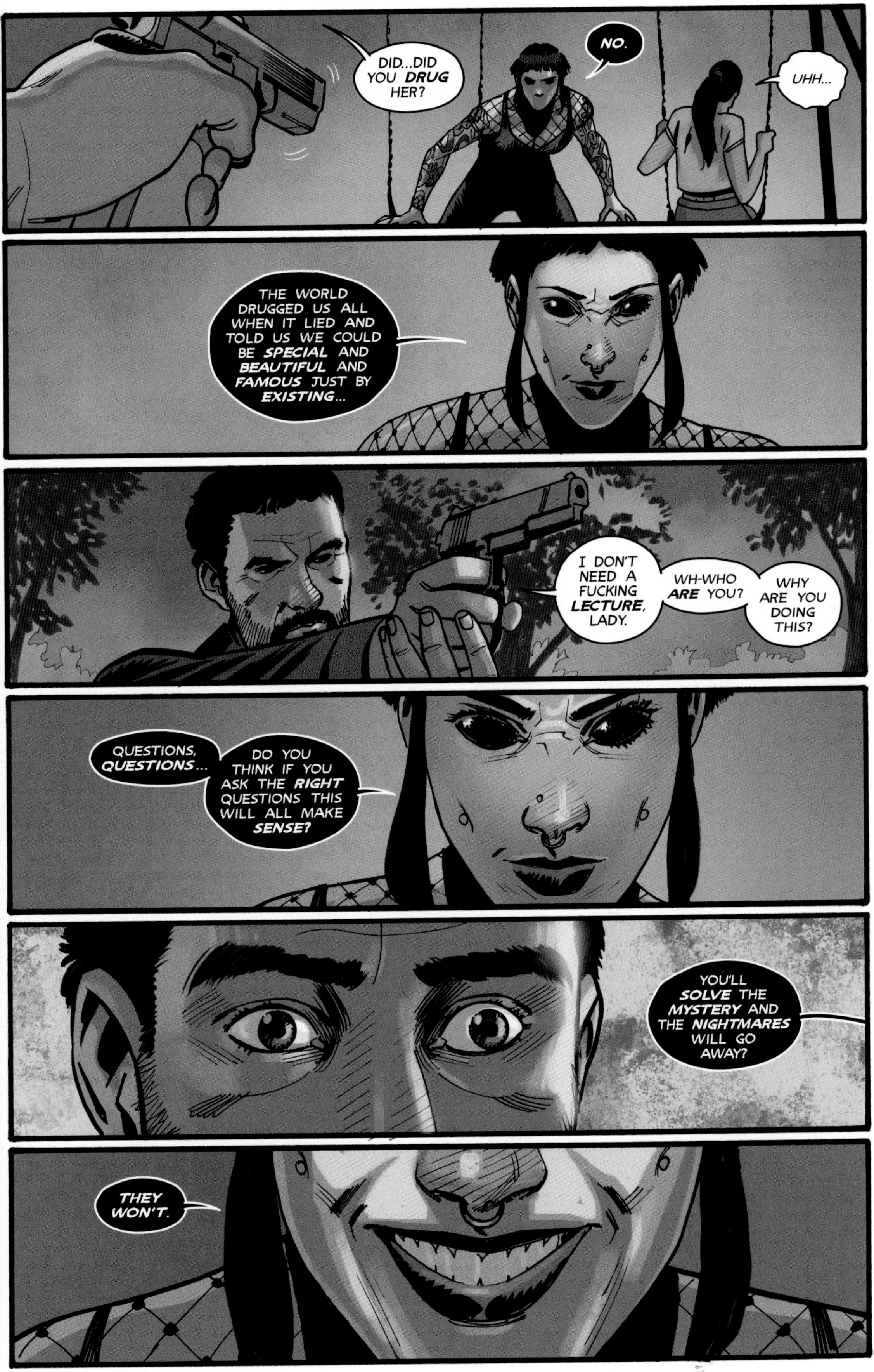
DID...DID YOU DRUG HER?
NO.
UHH...
THE WORLD DRUGGED US ALL WHEN IT LIED AND TOLD US WE COULD BE SPECIAL AND BEAUTIFUL AND FAMOUS JUST BY EXISTING...
I DON'T NEED A FUCKING LECTURE, LADY.
WH-WHO ARE YOU?
WHY ARE YOU DOING THIS?
QUESTIONS, QUESTIONS...
DO YOU THINK IF YOU ASK THE RIGHT QUESTIONS THIS WILL ALL MAKE SENSE?
YOU'LL SOLVE THE MYSTERY AND THE NIGHTMARES WILL GO AWAY?
THEY WON'T.

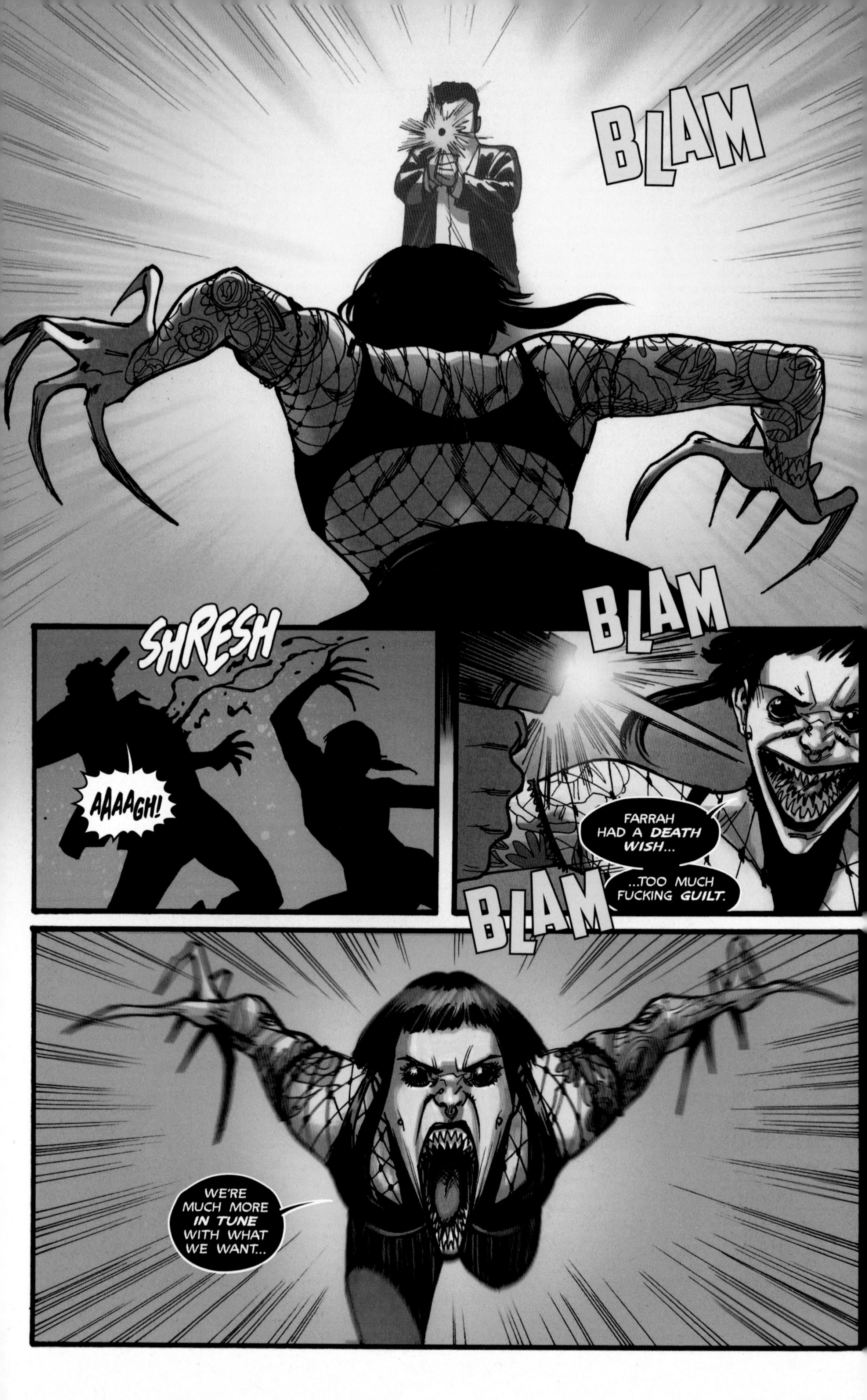

BLAM
BLAM
SHRESH
AAAAGH!
FARRAH HAD A DEATH WISH...
...TOO MUCH FUCKING GUILT.
BLAM
WE'RE MUCH MORE IN TUNE WITH WHAT WE WANT...

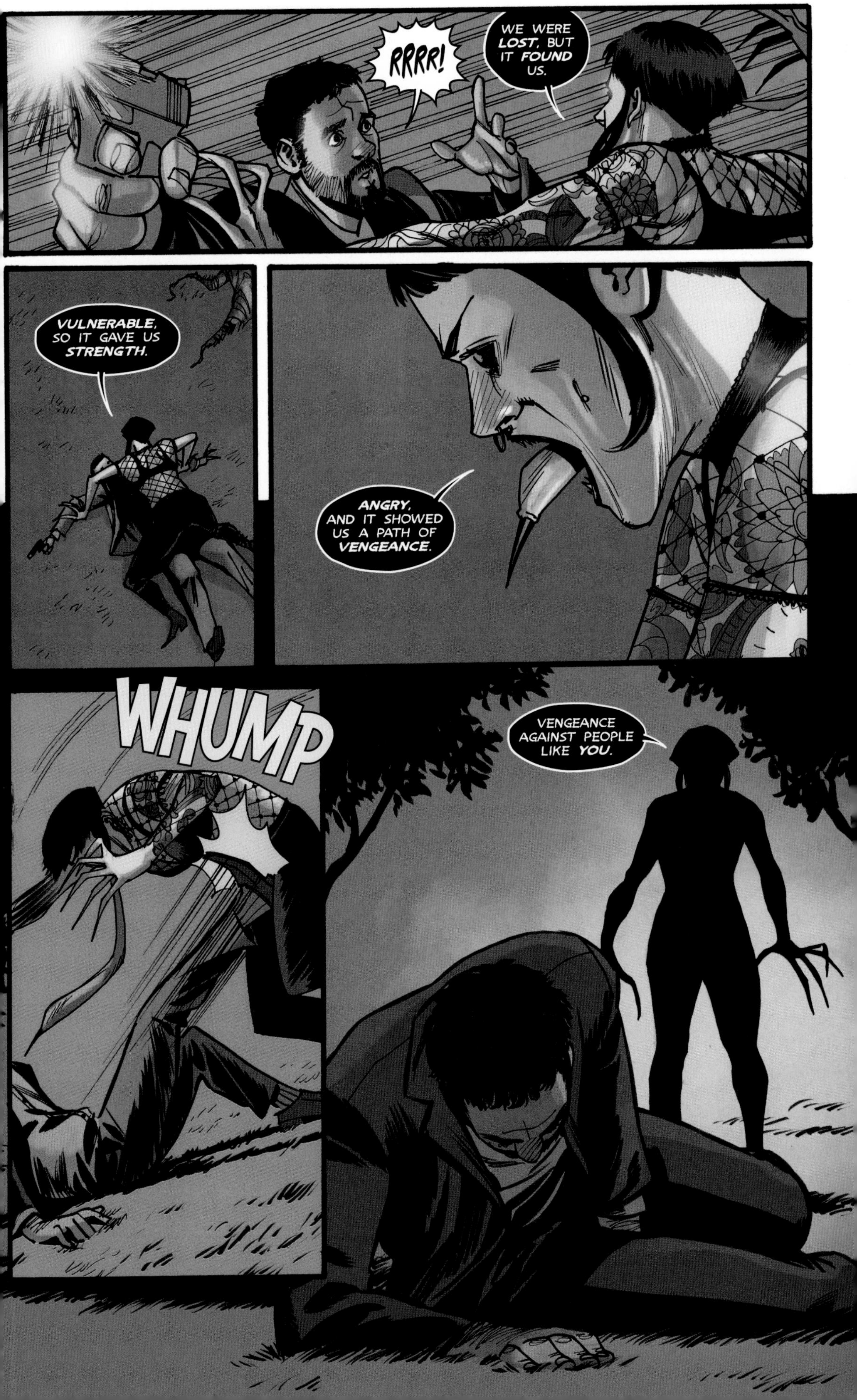
RRRR!
WE WERE LOST, BUT IT FOUND US.
VULNERABLE, SO IT GAVE US STRENGTH.
ANGRY, AND IT SHOWED US A PATH OF VENGEANCE.
WHUMP
VENGEANCE AGAINST PEOPLE LIKE YOU.

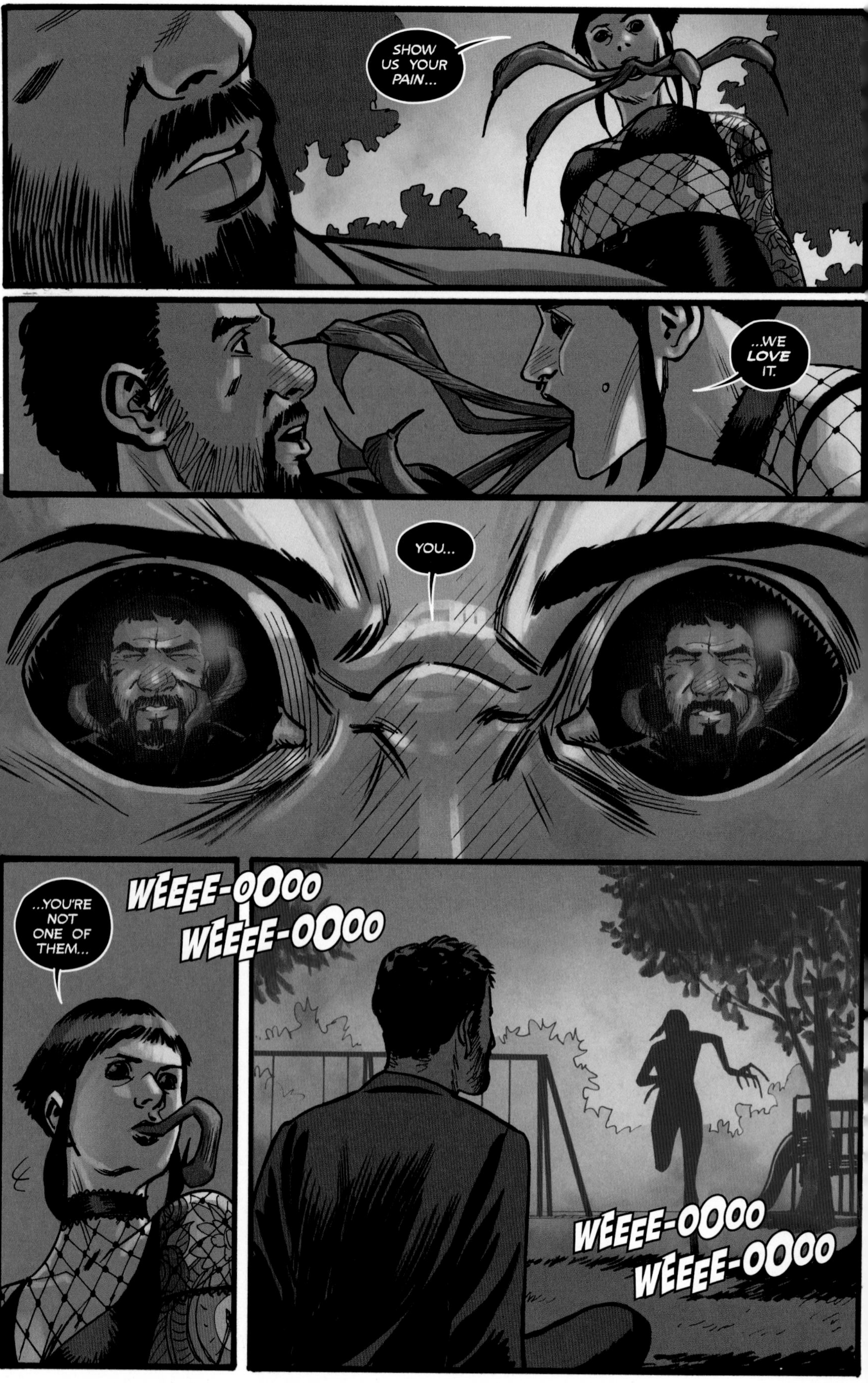

SHOW US YOUR PAIN...
...WE LOVE IT.
YOU...
...YOU'RE NOT ONE OF THEM...
WEEEE-OOOO
WEEEE-OOOO
WEEEE-OOOO
WEEEE-OOOO

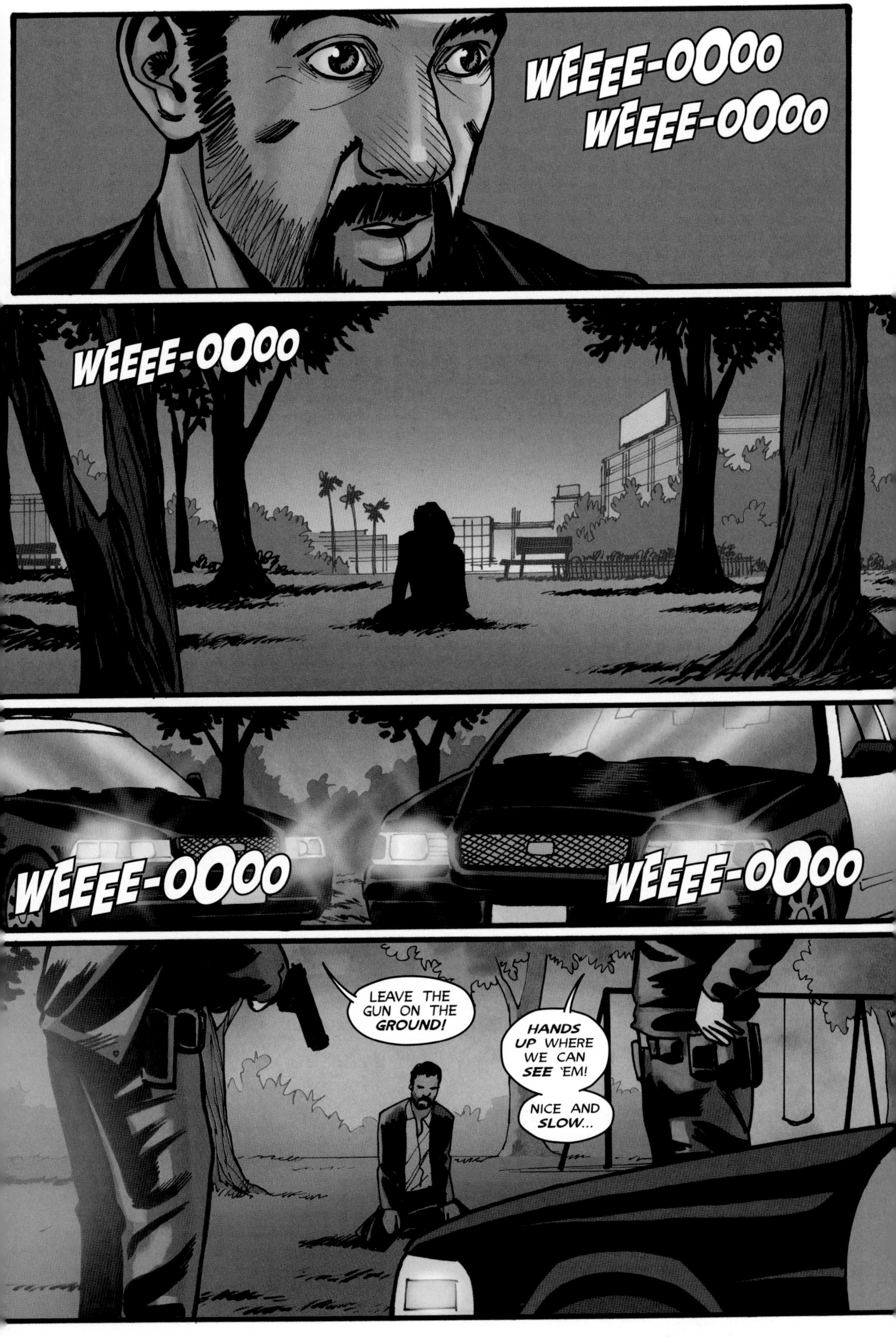
WEEEE-OOOO
WEEEE-OOOO
WEEEE-OOOO
WEEEE-OOOO
WEEEE-OOOO
LEAVE THE GUN ON THE GROUND!
HANDS UP WHERE WE CAN SEE 'EM!
NICE AND SLOW...

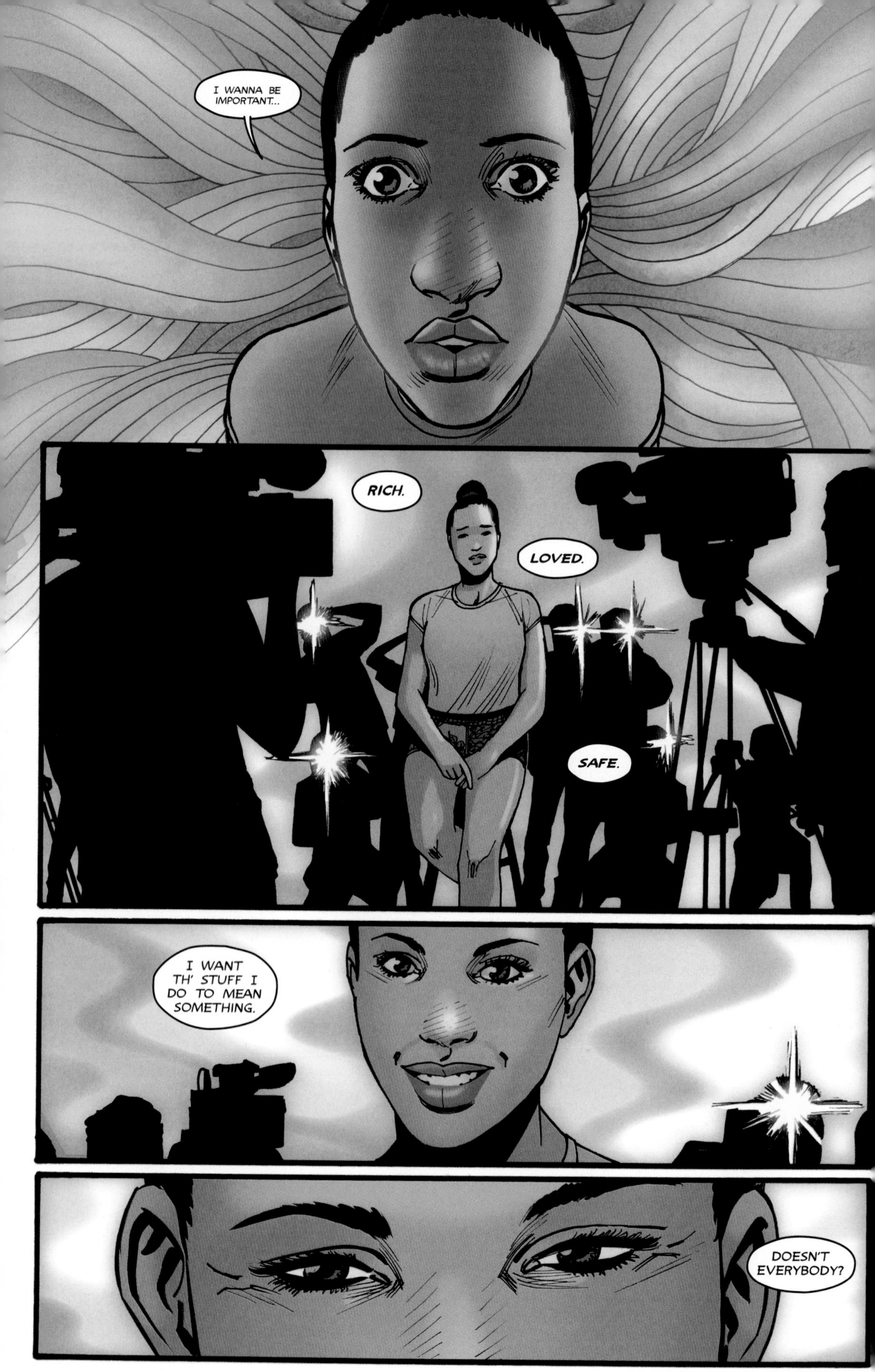
I WANNA BE IMPORTANT...
RICH.
LOVED.
SAFE.
I WANT TH' STUFF I DO TO MEAN SOMETHING.
DOESN'T EVERYBODY?

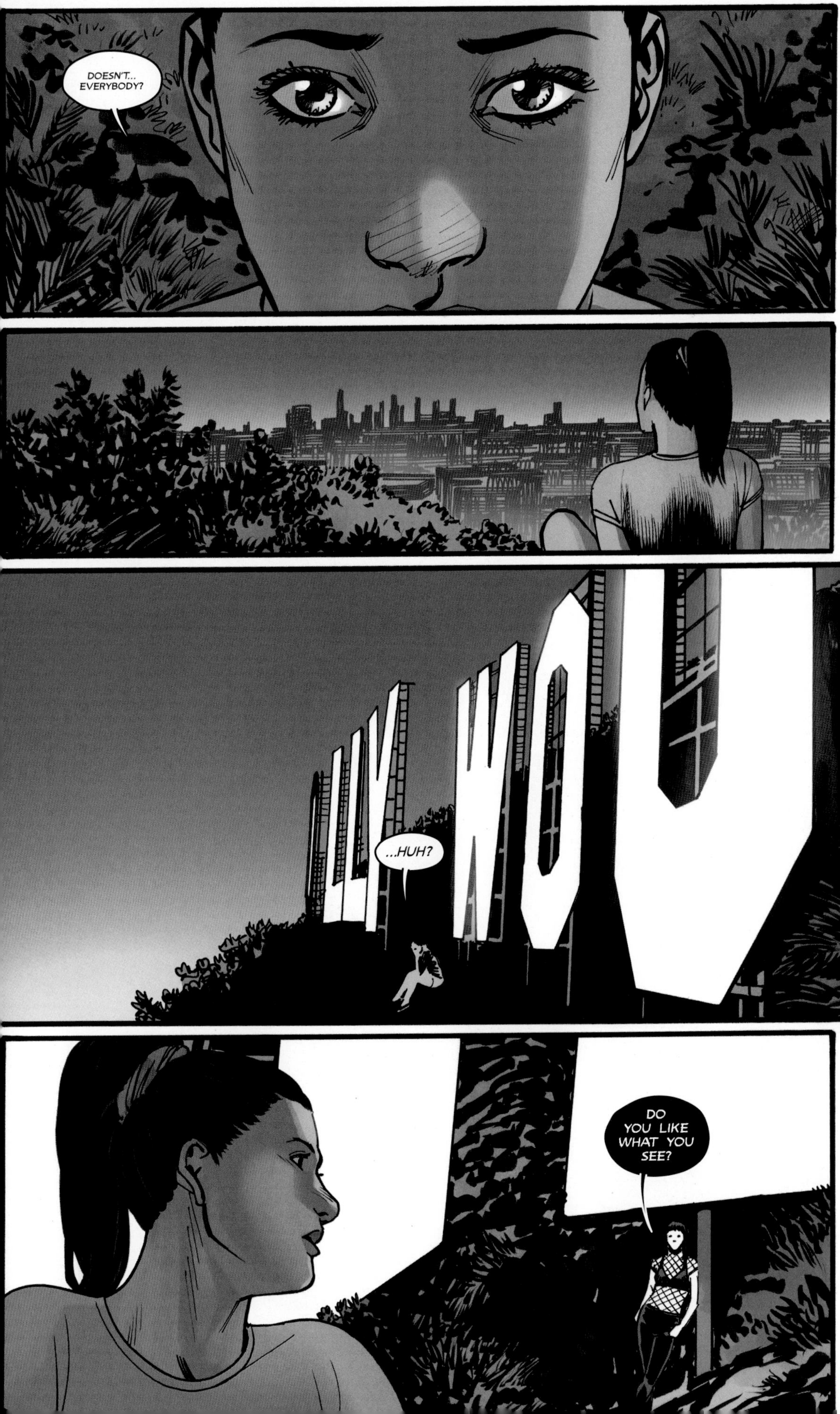
DOESN'T... EVERYBODY?
...HUH?
DO YOU LIKE WHAT YOU SEE?

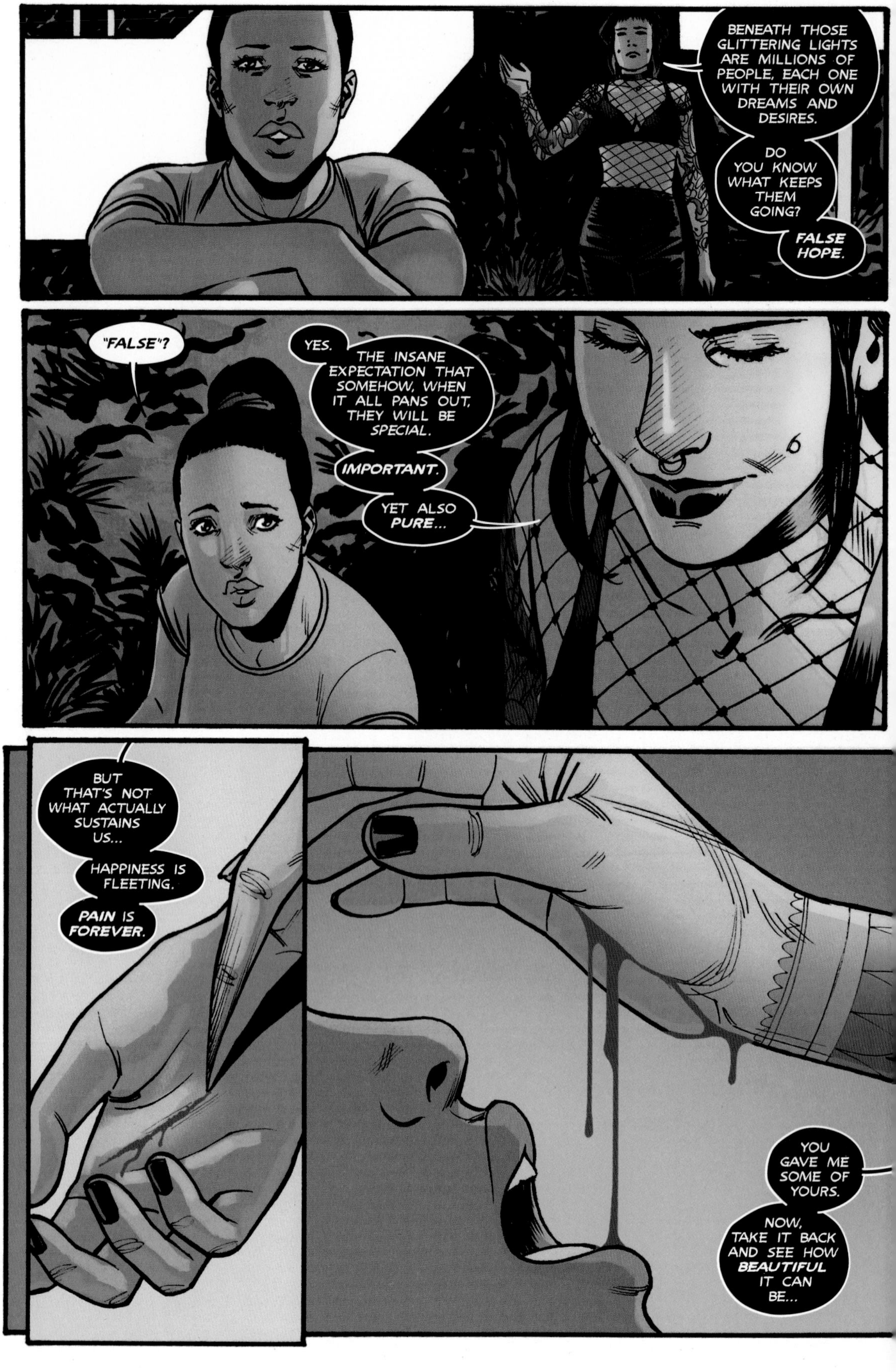
BENEATH THOSE GLITTERING LIGHTS ARE MILLIONS OF PEOPLE, EACH ONE WITH THEIR OWN DREAMS AND DESIRES.
DO YOU KNOW WHAT KEEPS THEM GOING?
FALSE HOPE.
"FALSE"?
YES.
THE INSANE EXPECTATION THAT SOMEHOW, WHEN IT ALL PANS OUT, THEY WILL BE SPECIAL.
IMPORTANT.
YET ALSO PURE...
BUT THAT'S NOT WHAT ACTUALLY SUSTAINS US...
HAPPINESS IS FLEETING.
PAIN IS FOREVER.
YOU GAVE ME SOME OF YOURS.
NOW, TAKE IT BACK AND SEE HOW BEAUTIFUL IT CAN BE...

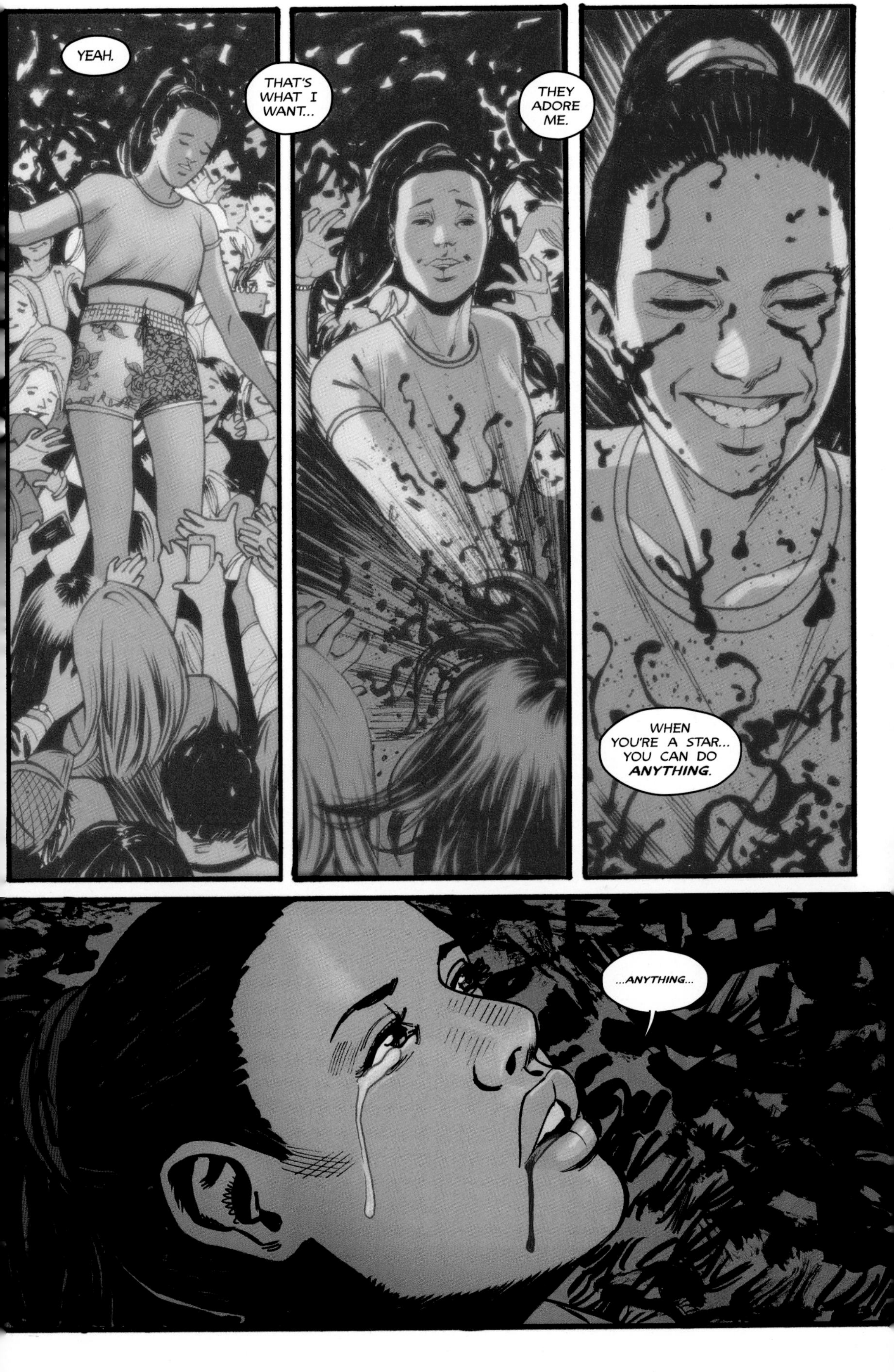
YEAH.
THAT'S WHAT I WANT...
THEY ADORE ME.
WHEN YOU'RE A STAR... YOU CAN DO *ANYTHING*.
...ANYTHING...

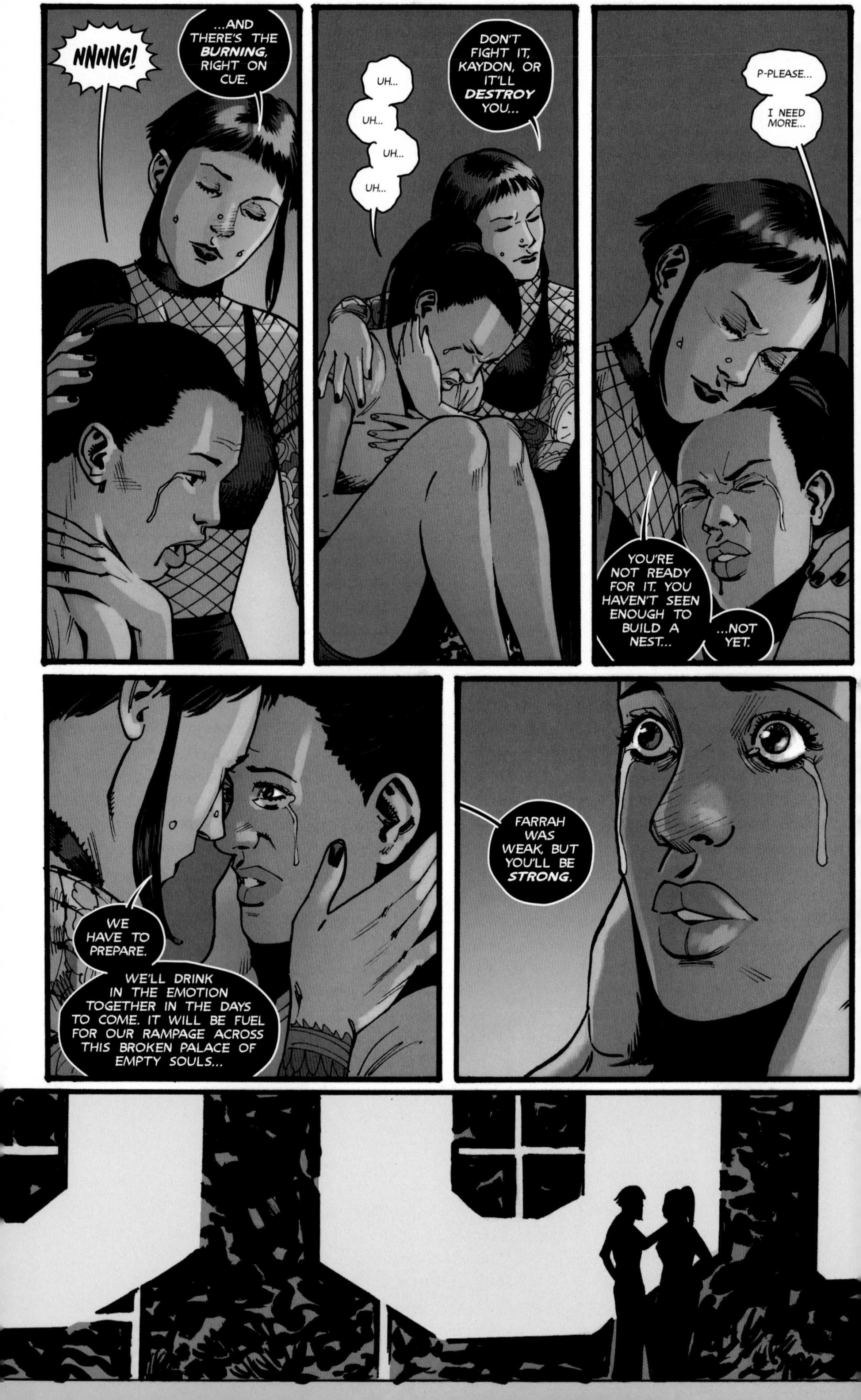
NNNNG!
...AND THERE'S THE BURNING, RIGHT ON CUE.
UH...
UH...
UH...
UH...
DON'T FIGHT IT, KAYDON, OR IT'LL DESTROY YOU...
P-PLEASE...
I NEED MORE...
YOU'RE NOT READY FOR IT. YOU HAVEN'T SEEN ENOUGH TO BUILD A NEST...
...NOT YET.
WE HAVE TO PREPARE.
WE'LL DRINK IN THE EMOTION TOGETHER IN THE DAYS TO COME. IT WILL BE FUEL FOR OUR RAMPAGE ACROSS THIS BROKEN PALACE OF EMPTY SOULS...
FARRAH WAS WEAK, BUT YOU'LL BE STRONG.

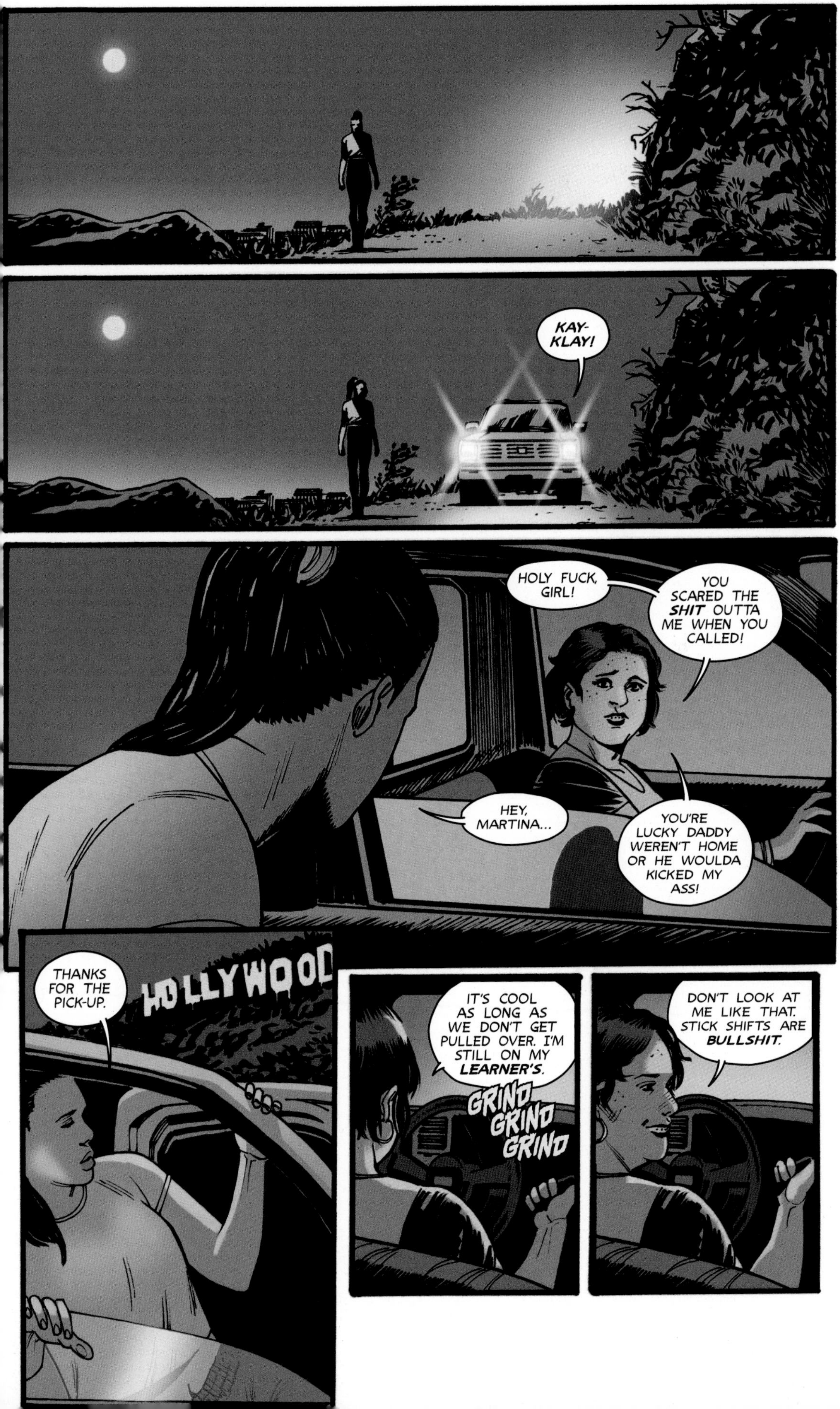
KAY-KLAY!
HOLY FUCK, GIRL!
YOU SCARED THE SHIT OUTTA ME WHEN YOU CALLED!
HEY, MARTINA...
YOU'RE LUCKY DADDY WEREN'T HOME OR HE WOULDA KICKED MY ASS!
HOLLYWOOD
THANKS FOR THE PICK-UP.
IT'S COOL AS LONG AS WE DON'T GET PULLED OVER. I'M STILL ON MY LEARNER'S.
GRIND GRIND GRIND
DON'T LOOK AT ME LIKE THAT. STICK SHIFTS ARE BULLSHIT.

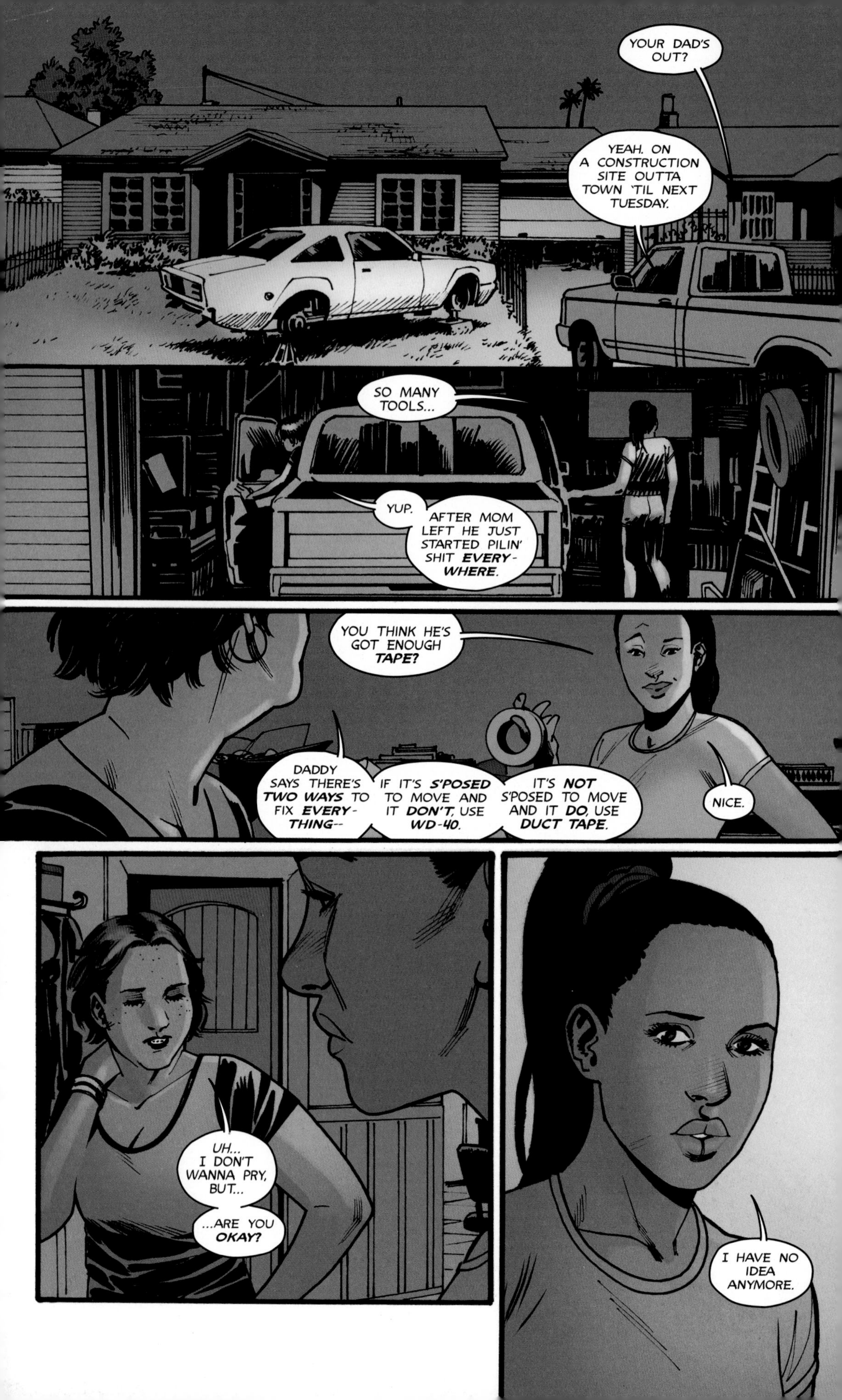
YOUR DAD'S OUT?
YEAH. ON A CONSTRUCTION SITE OUTTA TOWN 'TIL NEXT TUESDAY.
SO MANY TOOLS...
YUP.
AFTER MOM LEFT HE JUST STARTED PILIN' SHIT EVERY-WHERE.
YOU THINK HE'S GOT ENOUGH TAPE?
DADDY SAYS THERE'S TWO WAYS TO FIX EVERY-THING--
IF IT'S S'POSED TO MOVE AND IT DON'T, USE WD-40.
IT'S NOT S'POSED TO MOVE AND IT DO, USE DUCT TAPE.
NICE.
UH... I DON'T WANNA PRY, BUT...
...ARE YOU OKAY?
I HAVE NO IDEA ANYMORE.

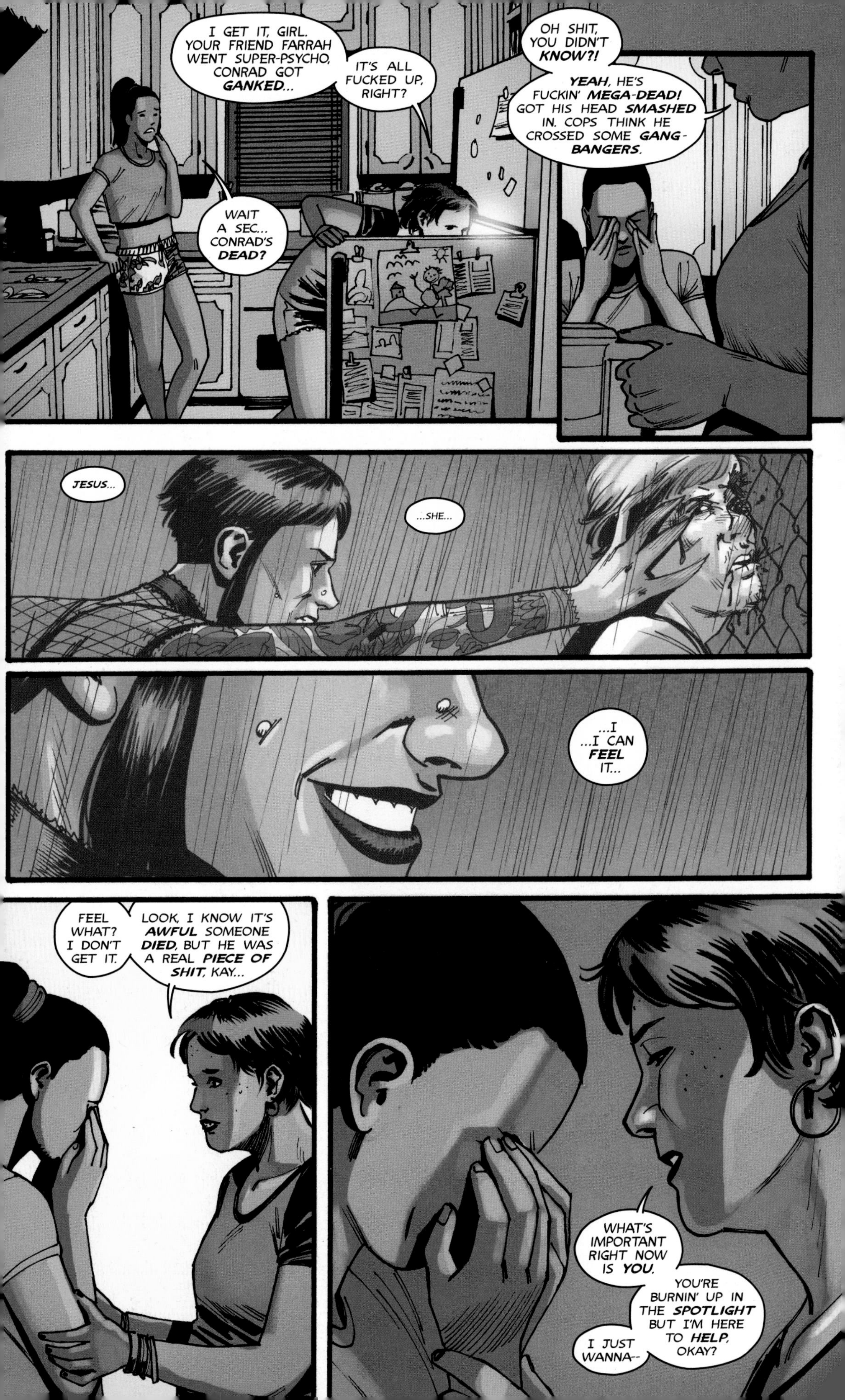
I GET IT, GIRL. YOUR FRIEND FARRAH WENT SUPER-PSYCHO, CONRAD GOT GANKED...
IT'S ALL FUCKED UP, RIGHT?
WAIT A SEC... CONRAD'S DEAD?
OH SHIT, YOU DIDN'T KNOW?!
YEAH, HE'S FUCKIN' MEGA-DEAD! GOT HIS HEAD SMASHED IN. COPS THINK HE CROSSED SOME GANG-BANGERS.
JESUS...
...SHE...
...I ...I CAN FEEL IT...
FEEL WHAT? I DON'T GET IT.
LOOK, I KNOW IT'S AWFUL SOMEONE DIED, BUT HE WAS A REAL PIECE OF SHIT, KAY...
WHAT'S IMPORTANT RIGHT NOW IS YOU.
YOU'RE BURNIN' UP IN THE SPOTLIGHT BUT I'M HERE TO HELP, OKAY?
I JUST WANNA--

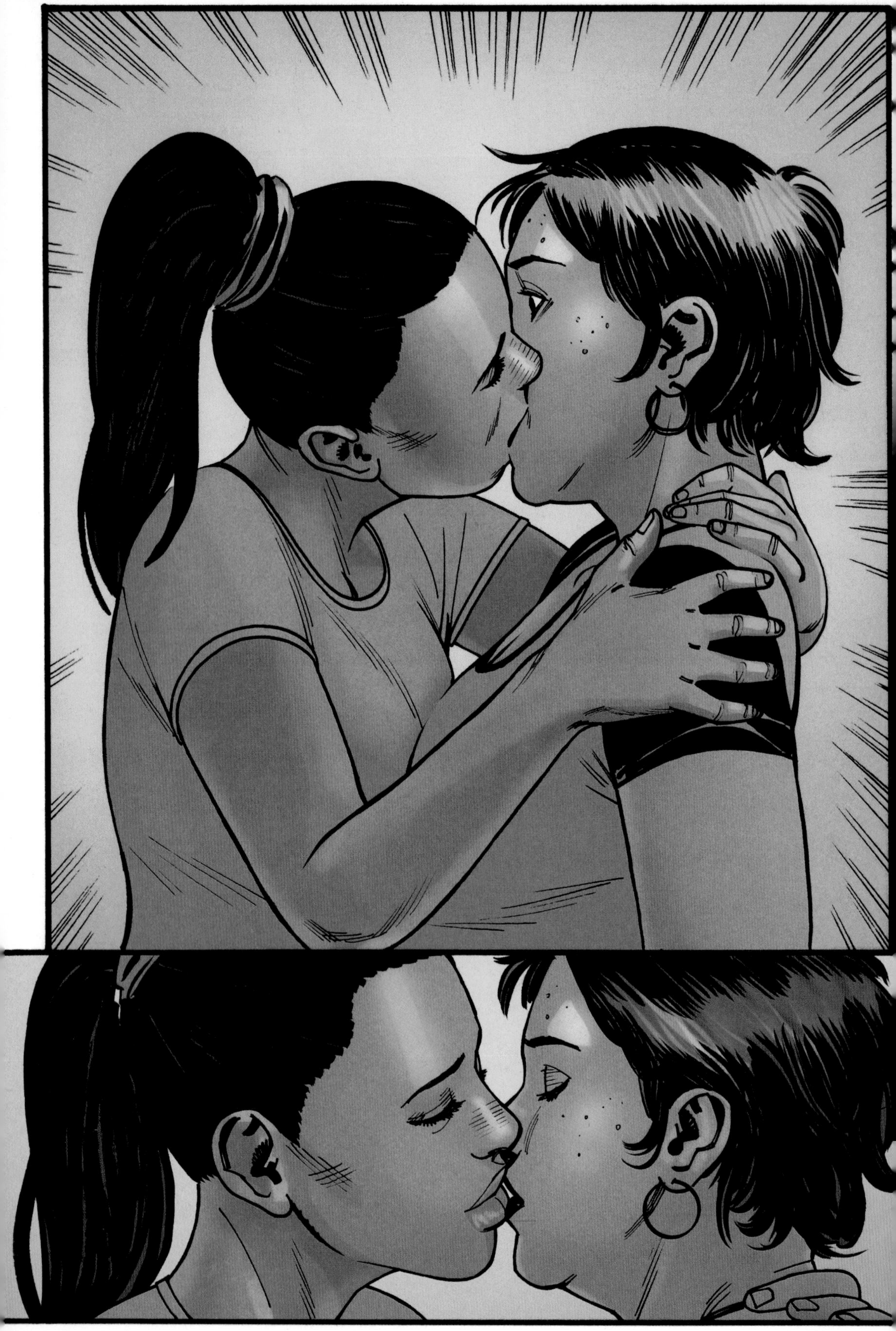

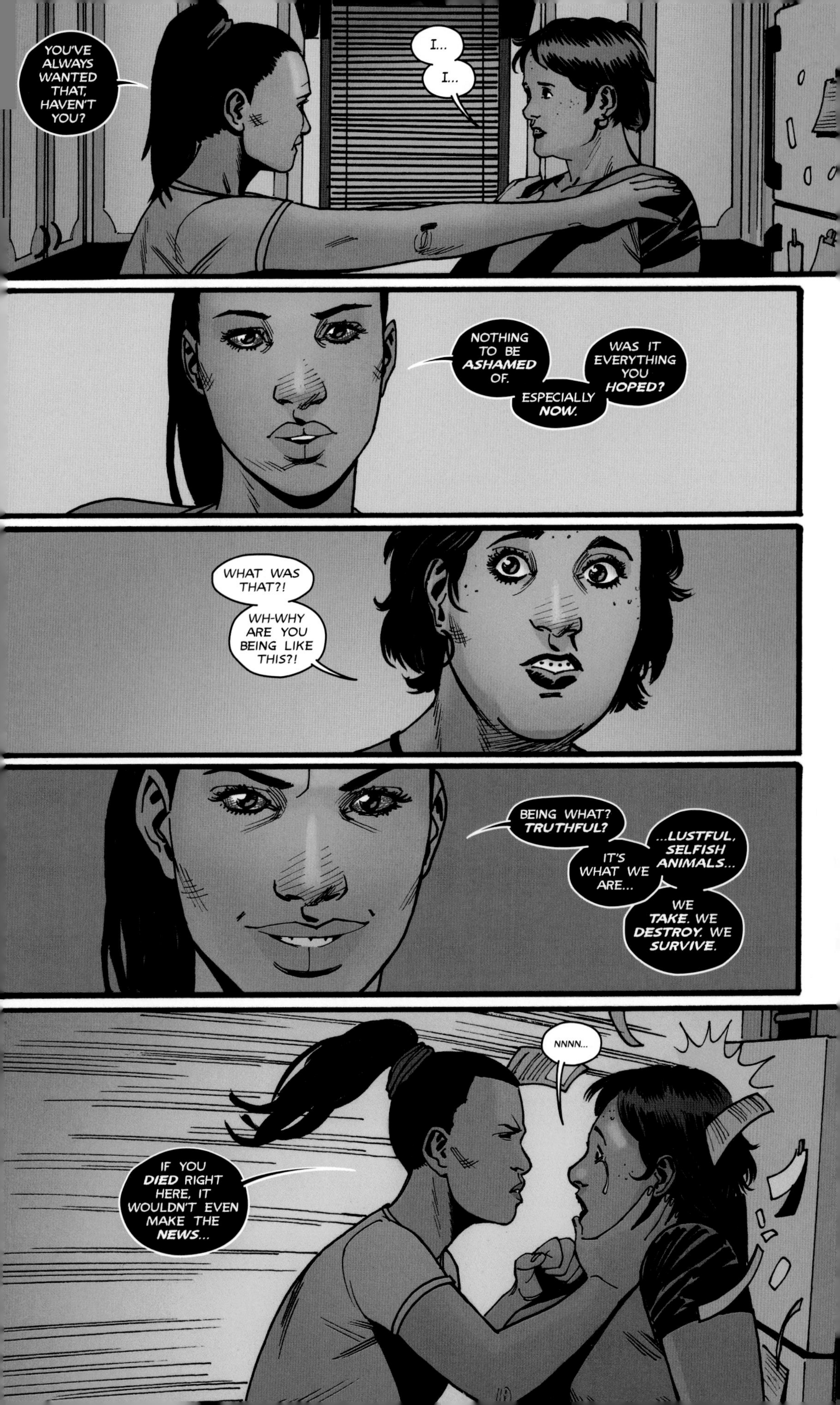

YOU'VE ALWAYS WANTED THAT, HAVEN'T YOU?
I...
I...
NOTHING TO BE ASHAMED OF.
ESPECIALLY NOW.
WAS IT EVERYTHING YOU HOPED?
WHAT WAS THAT?!
WH-WHY ARE YOU BEING LIKE THIS?!
BEING WHAT? TRUTHFUL?
IT'S WHAT WE ARE...
...LUSTFUL, SELFISH ANIMALS...
WE TAKE. WE DESTROY. WE SURVIVE.
NNNN...
IF YOU DIED RIGHT HERE, IT WOULDN'T EVEN MAKE THE NEWS...

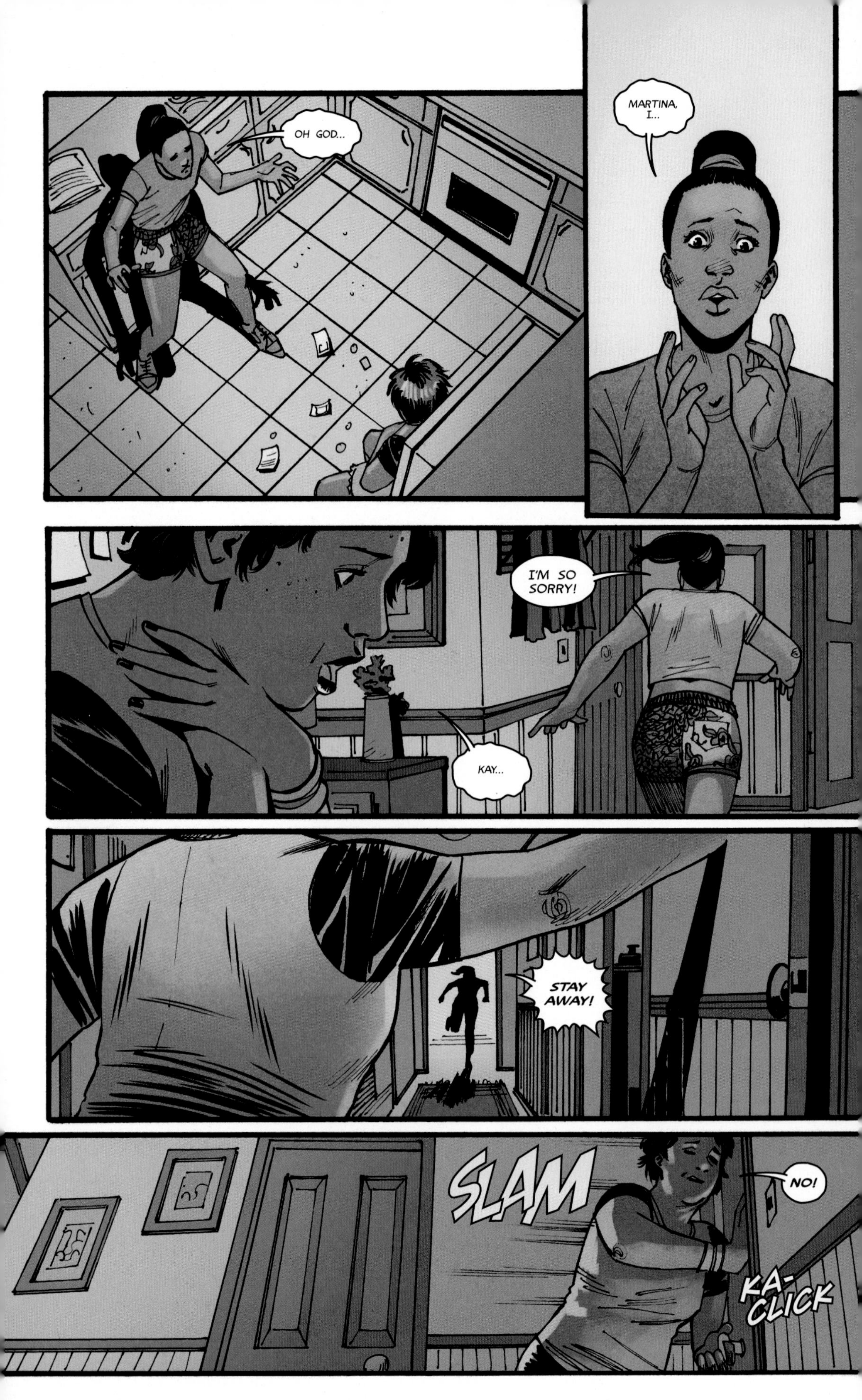

OH GOD...
MARTINA, I...
I'M SO SORRY!
KAY...
STAY AWAY!
SLAM
NO!
KA-CLICK

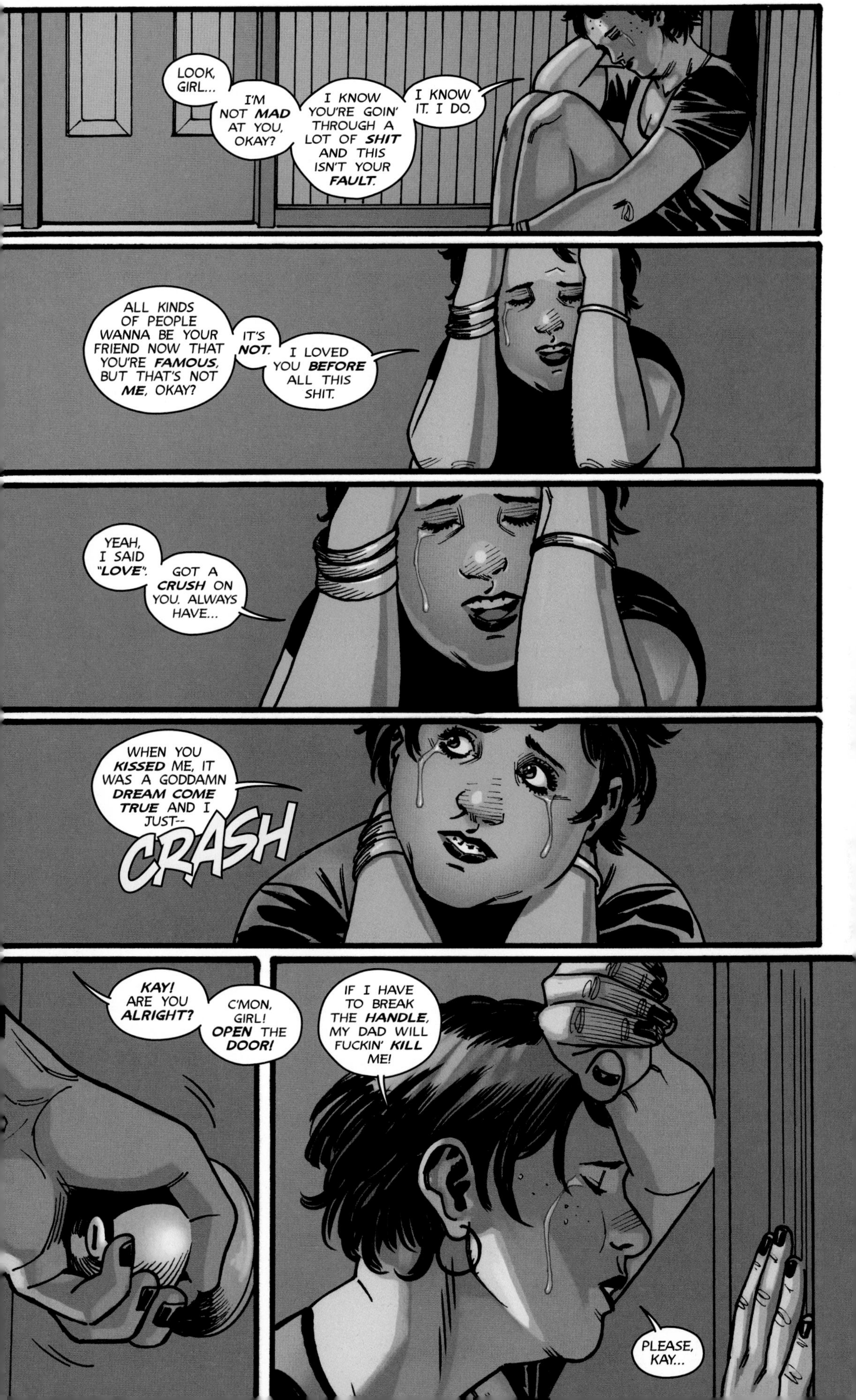

LOOK, GIRL...
I'M NOT MAD AT YOU, OKAY?
I KNOW YOU'RE GOIN' THROUGH A LOT OF SHIT AND THIS ISN'T YOUR FAULT.
I KNOW IT. I DO.
ALL KINDS OF PEOPLE WANNA BE YOUR FRIEND NOW THAT YOU'RE FAMOUS, BUT THAT'S NOT ME, OKAY?
IT'S NOT.
I LOVED YOU BEFORE ALL THIS SHIT.
YEAH, I SAID "LOVE".
GOT A CRUSH ON YOU. ALWAYS HAVE...
WHEN YOU KISSED ME, IT WAS A GODDAMN DREAM COME TRUE AND I JUST--
CRASH
KAY! ARE YOU ALRIGHT?
C'MON, GIRL! OPEN THE DOOR!
IF I HAVE TO BREAK THE HANDLE, MY DAD WILL FUCKIN' KILL ME!
PLEASE, KAY...

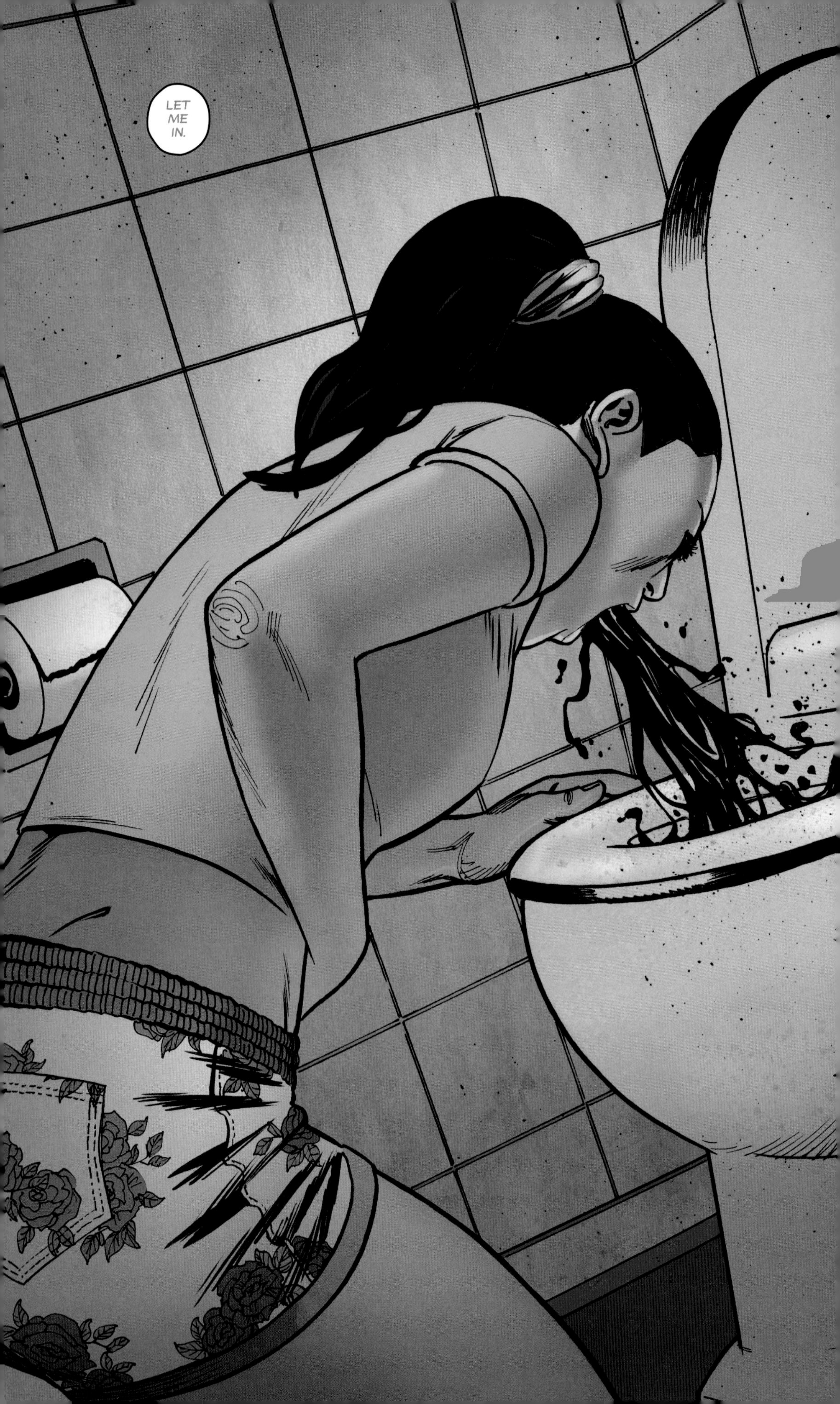
LET ME IN.

PART 4: FEEDING TIME

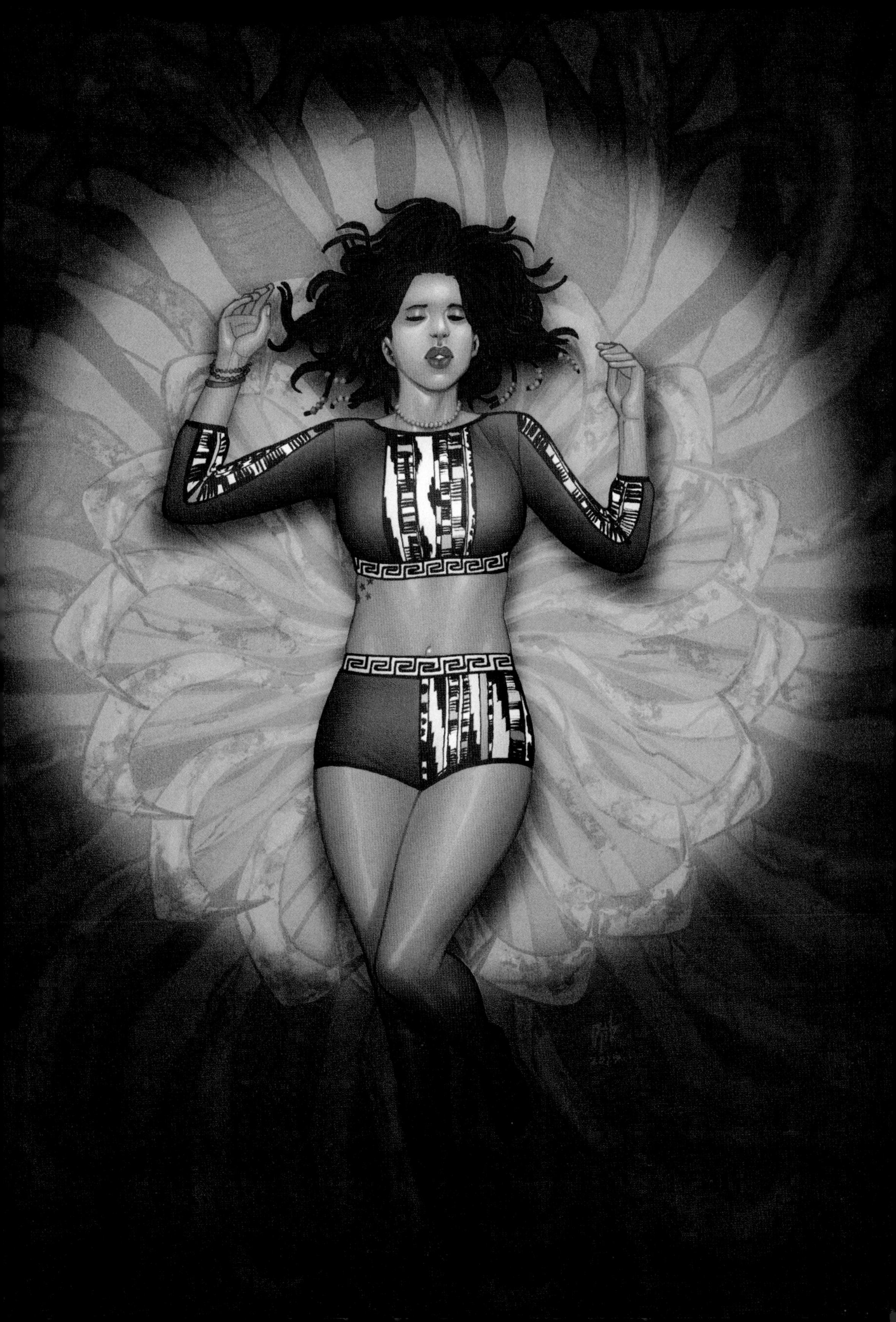

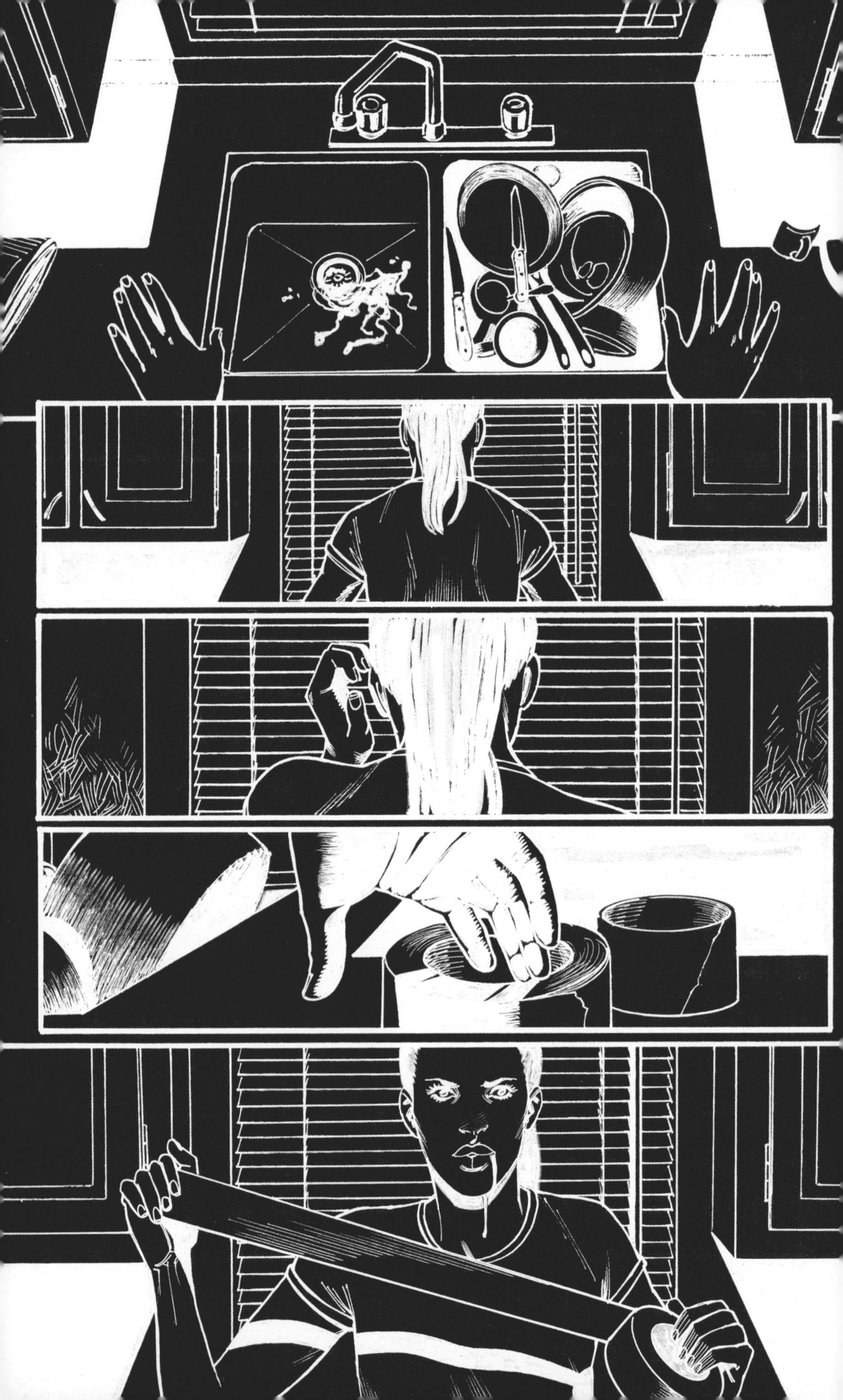

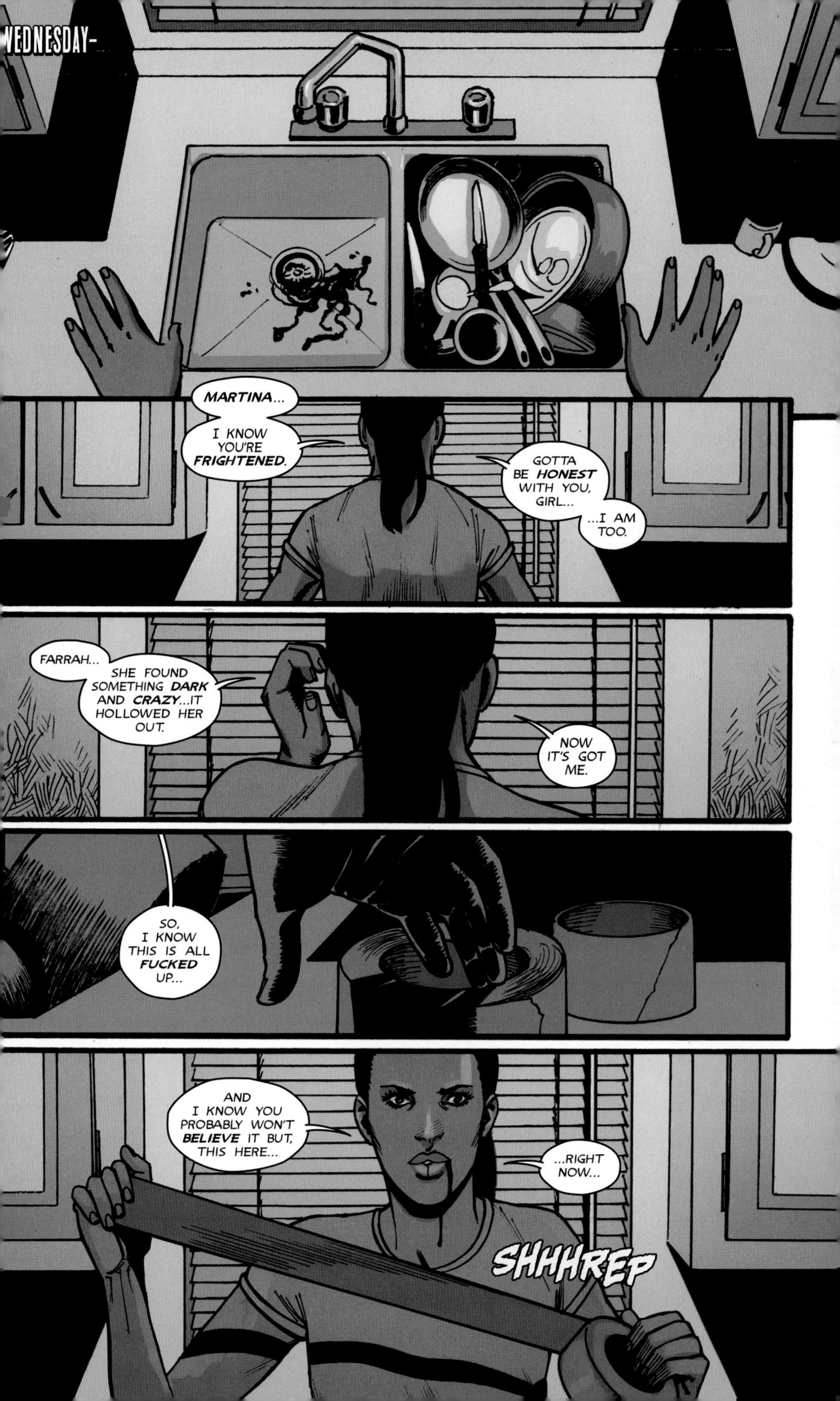

VEDNESDAY–
MARTINA...
I KNOW YOU'RE FRIGHTENED.
GOTTA BE HONEST WITH YOU, GIRL...
...I AM TOO.
FARRAH...
SHE FOUND SOMETHING DARK AND CRAZY...IT HOLLOWED HER OUT.
NOW IT'S GOT ME.
SO, I KNOW THIS IS ALL FUCKED UP...
AND I KNOW YOU PROBABLY WON'T BELIEVE IT BUT, THIS HERE...
...RIGHT NOW...
SHHHREP

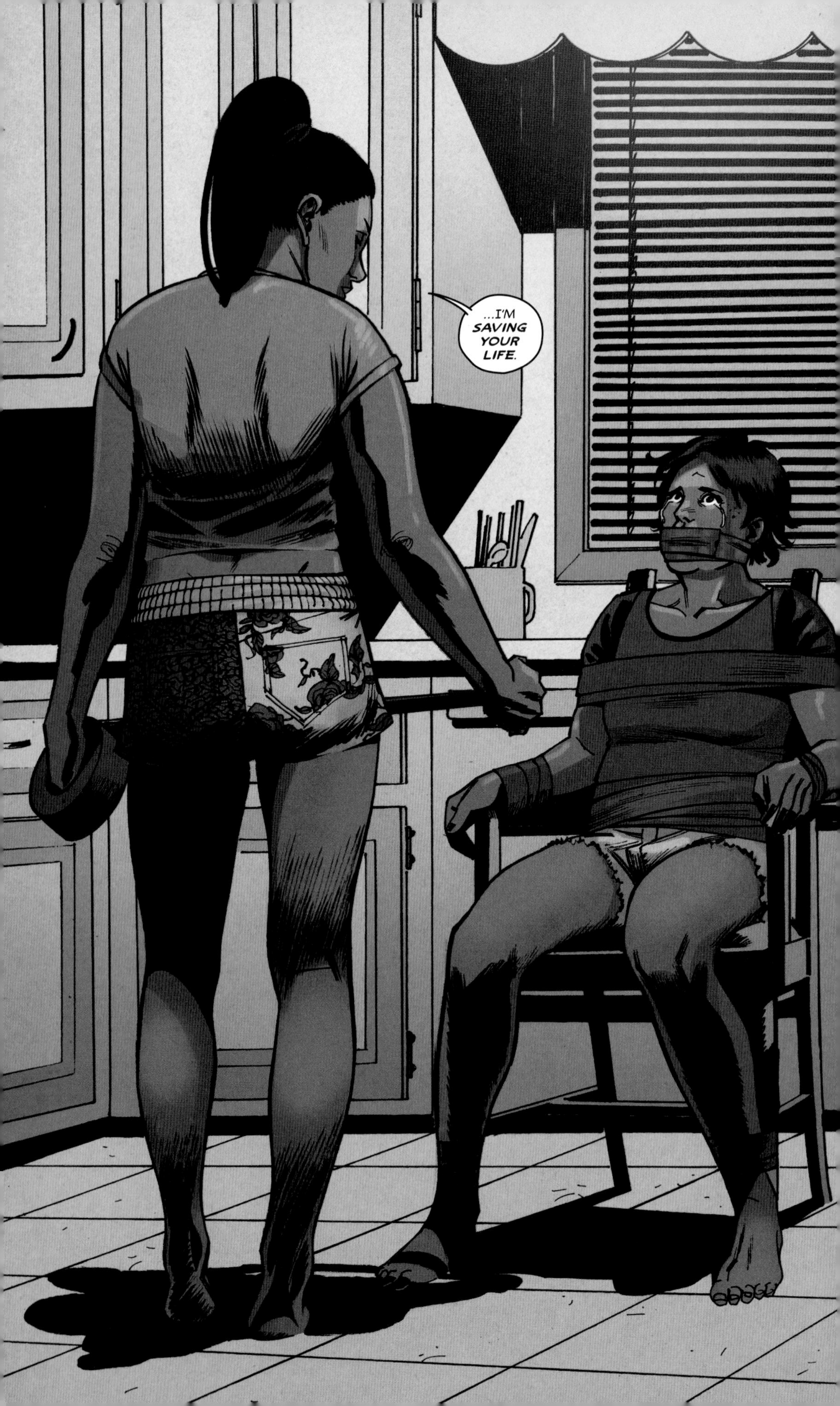

...I'M *SAVING* YOUR *LIFE*.

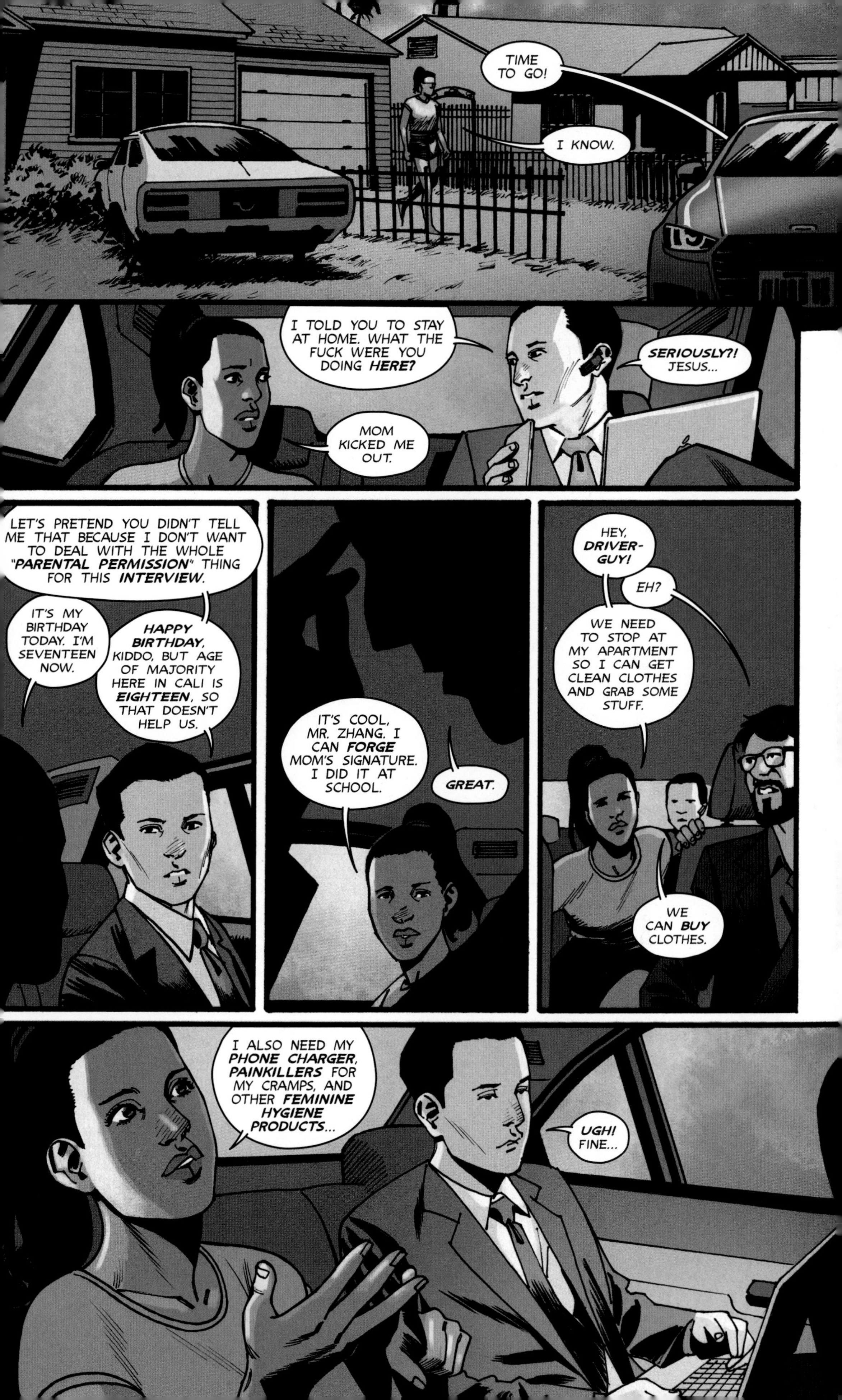
TIME TO GO!
I KNOW.
I TOLD YOU TO STAY AT HOME. WHAT THE FUCK WERE YOU DOING HERE?
SERIOUSLY?! JESUS...
MOM KICKED ME OUT.
LET'S PRETEND YOU DIDN'T TELL ME THAT BECAUSE I DON'T WANT TO DEAL WITH THE WHOLE "PARENTAL PERMISSION" THING FOR THIS INTERVIEW.
IT'S MY BIRTHDAY TODAY. I'M SEVENTEEN NOW.
HAPPY BIRTHDAY, KIDDO, BUT AGE OF MAJORITY HERE IN CALI IS EIGHTEEN, SO THAT DOESN'T HELP US.
IT'S COOL, MR. ZHANG. I CAN FORGE MOM'S SIGNATURE. I DID IT AT SCHOOL.
GREAT.
HEY, DRIVER-GUY!
EH?
WE NEED TO STOP AT MY APARTMENT SO I CAN GET CLEAN CLOTHES AND GRAB SOME STUFF.
WE CAN BUY CLOTHES.
I ALSO NEED MY PHONE CHARGER, PAINKILLERS FOR MY CRAMPS, AND OTHER FEMININE HYGIENE PRODUCTS...
UGH! FINE...

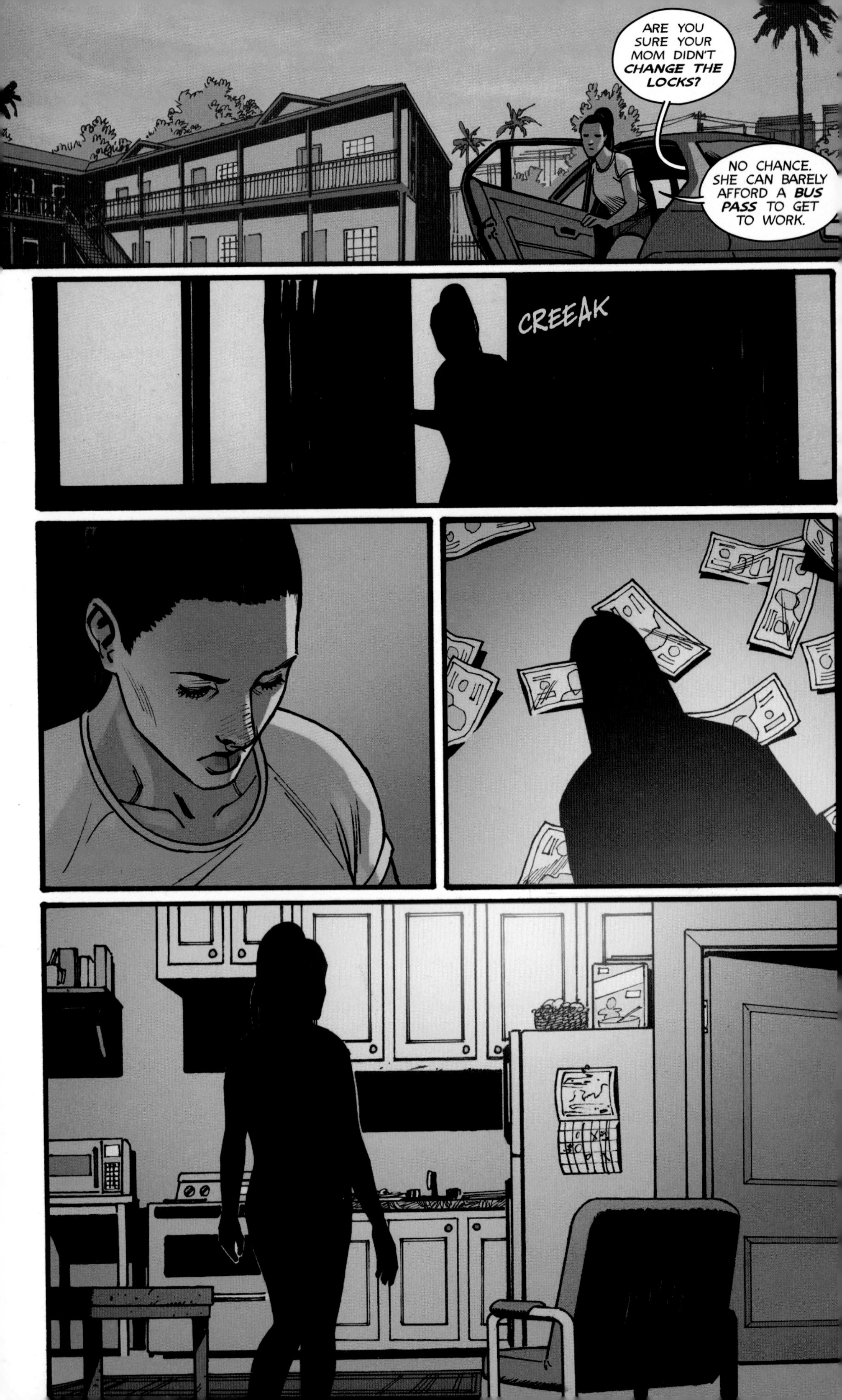
ARE YOU SURE YOUR MOM DIDN'T **CHANGE THE LOCKS?**
NO CHANCE. SHE CAN BARELY AFFORD A **BUS PASS** TO GET TO WORK.
CREEAK

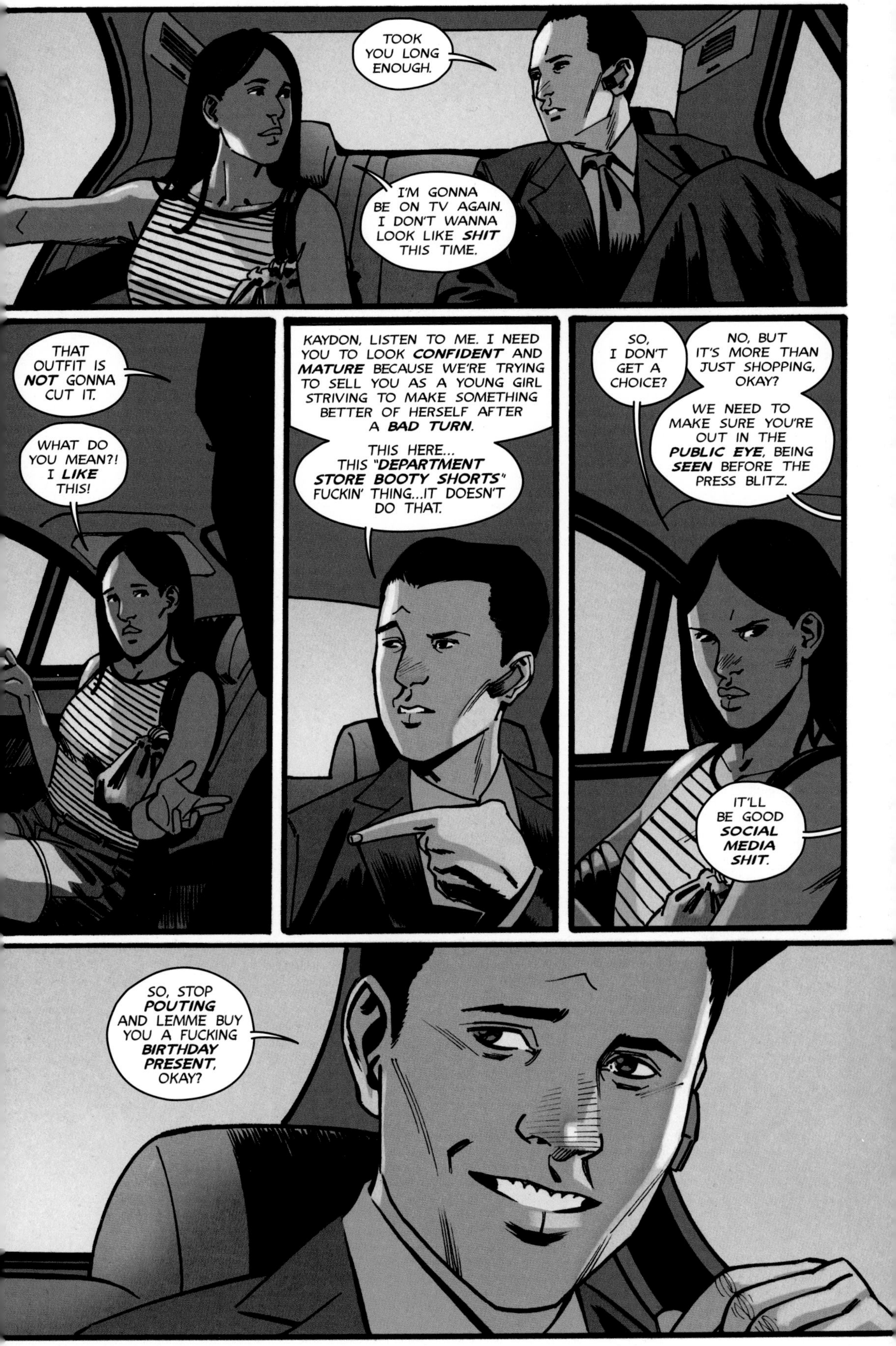
TOOK YOU LONG ENOUGH.
I'M GONNA BE ON TV AGAIN. I DON'T WANNA LOOK LIKE *SHIT* THIS TIME.
THAT OUTFIT IS *NOT* GONNA CUT IT.
WHAT DO YOU MEAN?! I *LIKE* THIS!
KAYDON, LISTEN TO ME. I NEED YOU TO LOOK *CONFIDENT* AND *MATURE* BECAUSE WE'RE TRYING TO SELL YOU AS A YOUNG GIRL STRIVING TO MAKE SOMETHING BETTER OF HERSELF AFTER A *BAD TURN*.
THIS HERE... THIS *"DEPARTMENT STORE BOOTY SHORTS"* FUCKIN' THING...IT DOESN'T DO THAT.
SO, I DON'T GET A CHOICE?
NO, BUT IT'S MORE THAN JUST SHOPPING, OKAY?
WE NEED TO MAKE SURE YOU'RE OUT IN THE *PUBLIC EYE*, BEING *SEEN* BEFORE THE PRESS BLITZ.
IT'LL BE GOOD *SOCIAL MEDIA SHIT*.
SO, STOP *POUTING* AND LEMME BUY YOU A FUCKING *BIRTHDAY PRESENT*, OKAY?

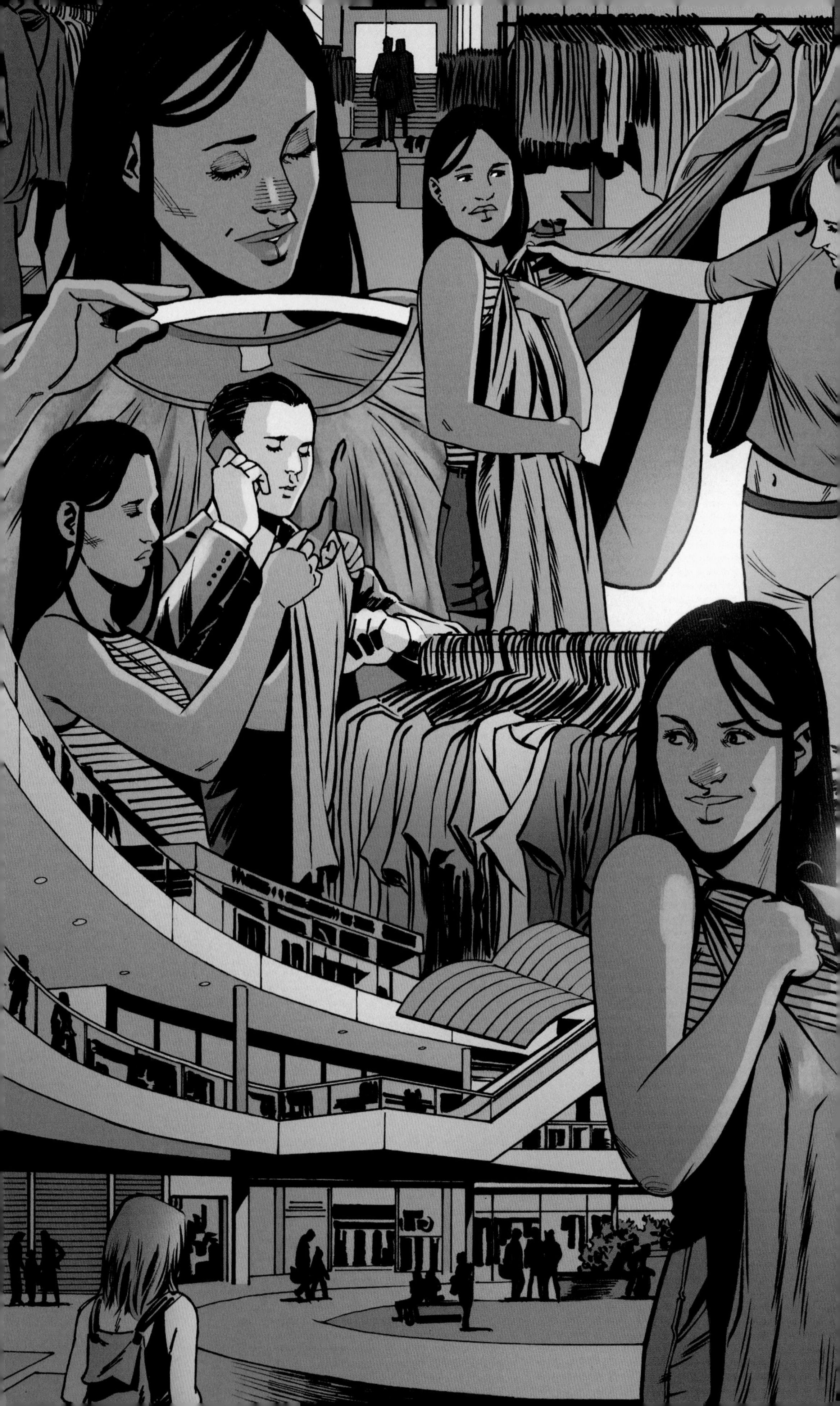

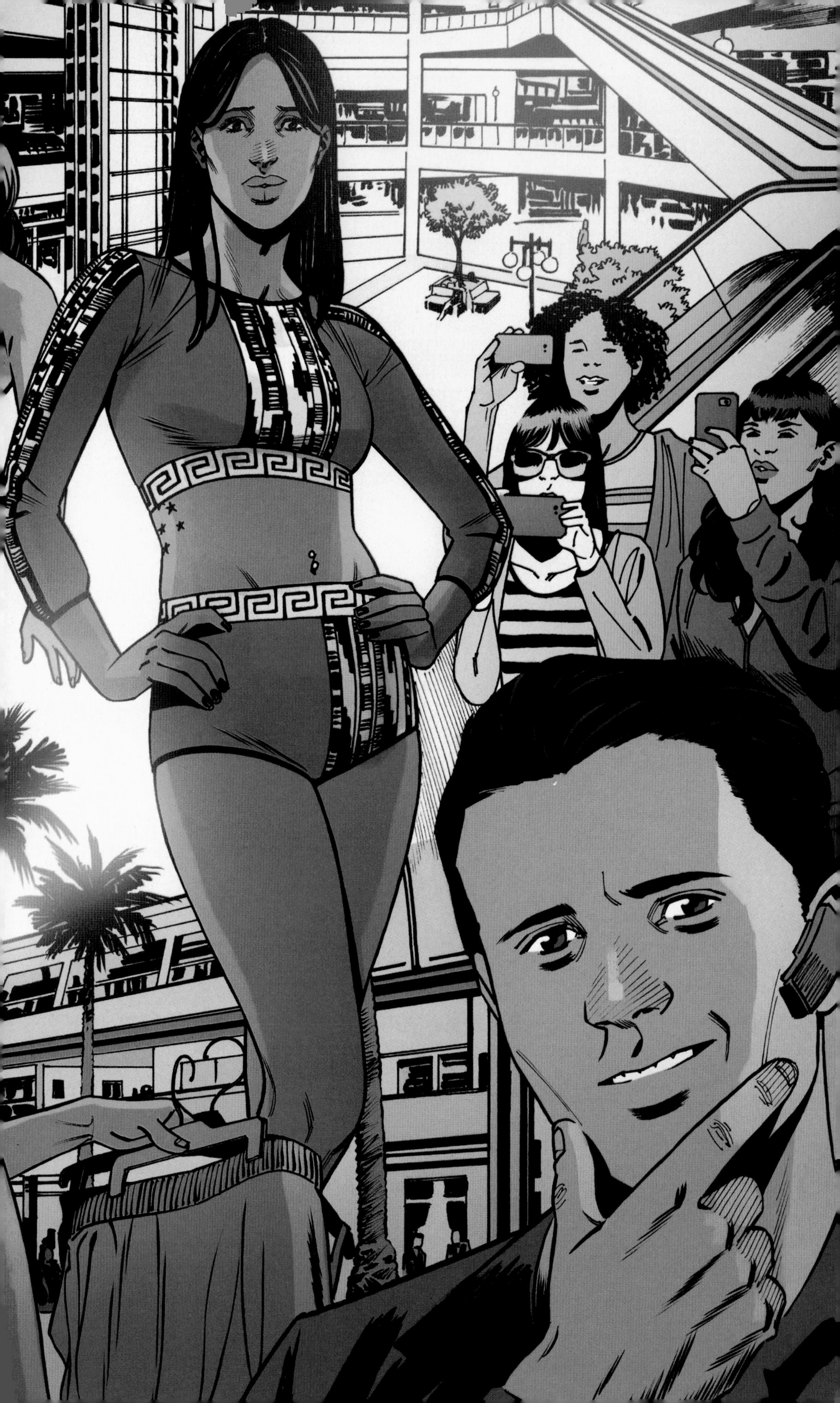

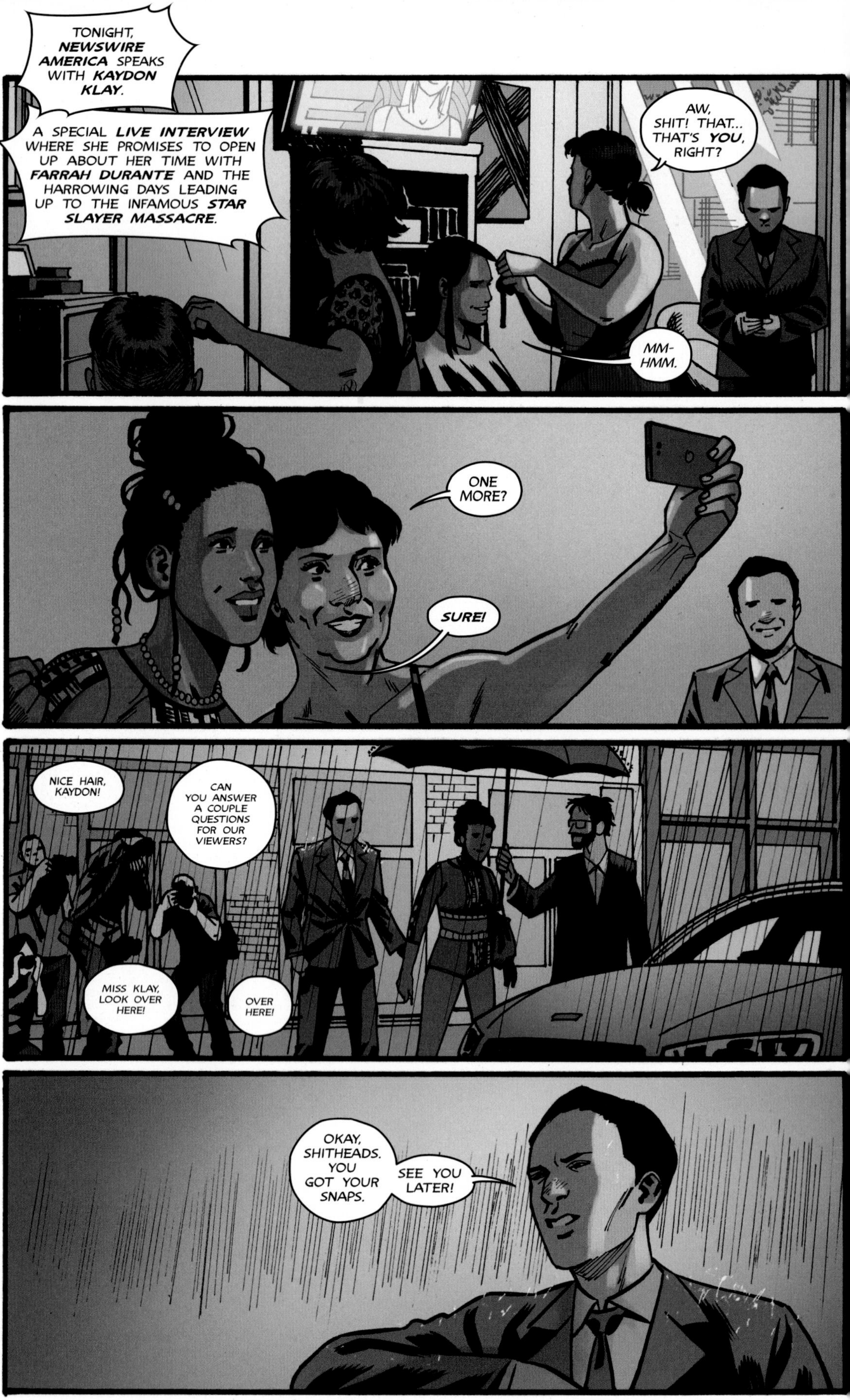
TONIGHT, NEWSWIRE AMERICA SPEAKS WITH KAYDON KLAY.
A SPECIAL LIVE INTERVIEW WHERE SHE PROMISES TO OPEN UP ABOUT HER TIME WITH FARRAH DURANTE AND THE HARROWING DAYS LEADING UP TO THE INFAMOUS STAR SLAYER MASSACRE.
AW, SHIT! THAT... THAT'S YOU, RIGHT?
MM-HMM.
ONE MORE?
SURE!
NICE HAIR, KAYDON!
CAN YOU ANSWER A COUPLE QUESTIONS FOR OUR VIEWERS?
MISS KLAY, LOOK OVER HERE!
OVER HERE!
OKAY, SHITHEADS. YOU GOT YOUR SNAPS.
SEE YOU LATER!

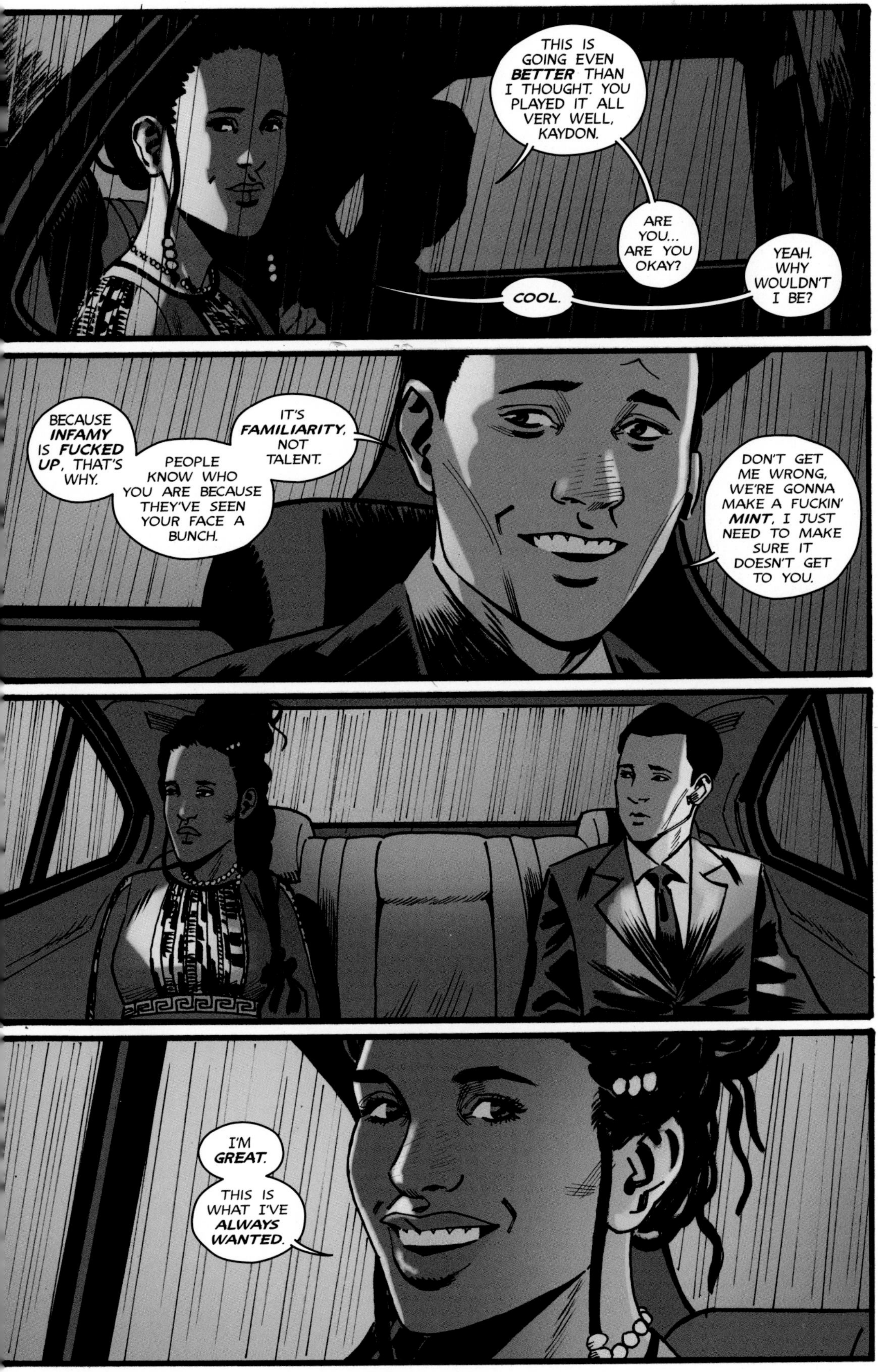
THIS IS GOING EVEN BETTER THAN I THOUGHT. YOU PLAYED IT ALL VERY WELL, KAYDON.
ARE YOU... ARE YOU OKAY?
YEAH. WHY WOULDN'T I BE?
COOL.
BECAUSE INFAMY IS FUCKED UP, THAT'S WHY.
PEOPLE KNOW WHO YOU ARE BECAUSE THEY'VE SEEN YOUR FACE A BUNCH.
IT'S FAMILIARITY, NOT TALENT.
DON'T GET ME WRONG, WE'RE GONNA MAKE A FUCKIN' MINT, I JUST NEED TO MAKE SURE IT DOESN'T GET TO YOU.
I'M GREAT.
THIS IS WHAT I'VE ALWAYS WANTED.

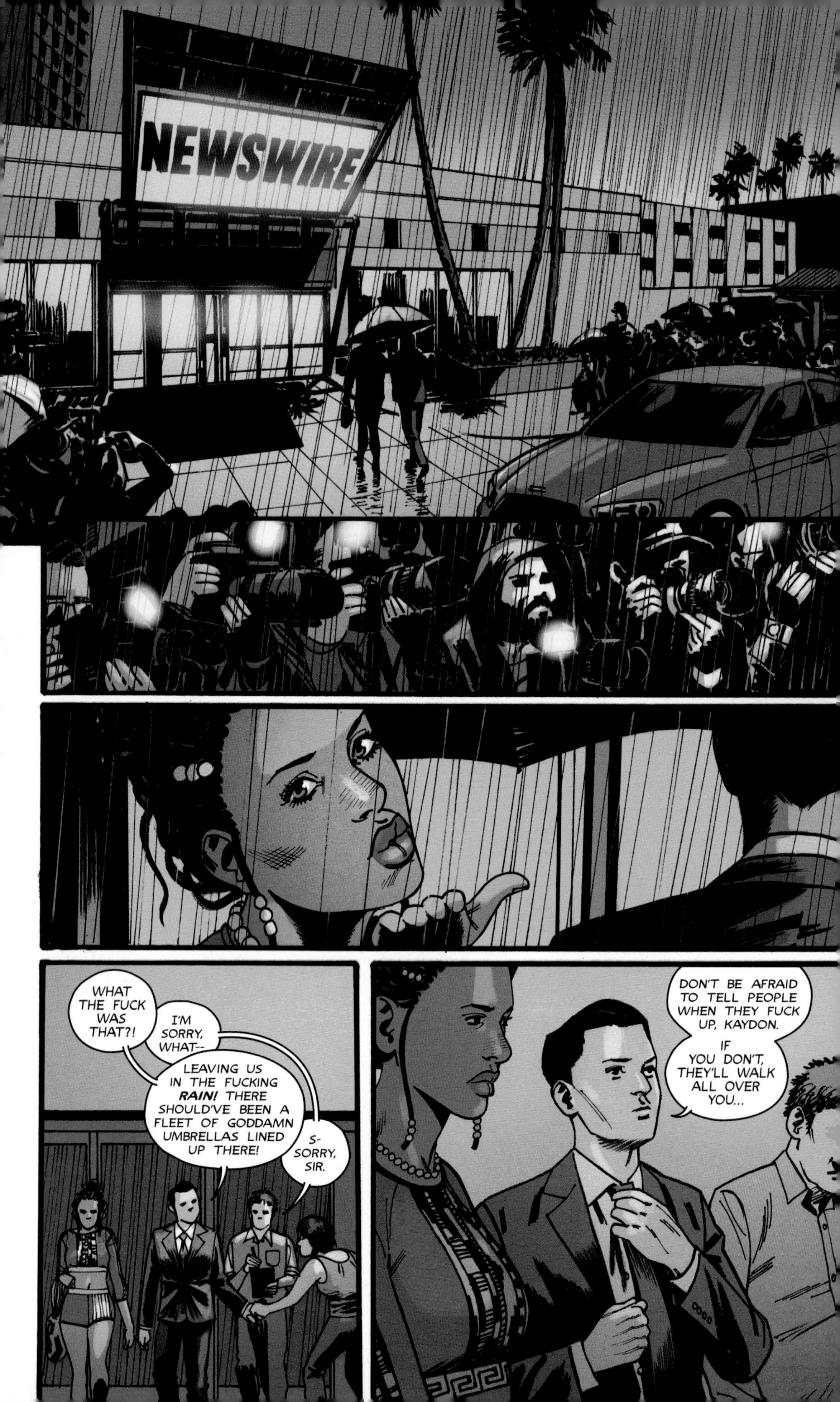

NEWSWIRE
WHAT THE FUCK WAS THAT?!
I'M SORRY, WHAT--
LEAVING US IN THE FUCKING **RAIN!** THERE SHOULD'VE BEEN A FLEET OF GODDAMN UMBRELLAS LINED UP THERE!
S-SORRY, SIR.
DON'T BE AFRAID TO TELL PEOPLE WHEN THEY FUCK UP, KAYDON.
IF YOU DON'T, THEY'LL WALK ALL OVER YOU...

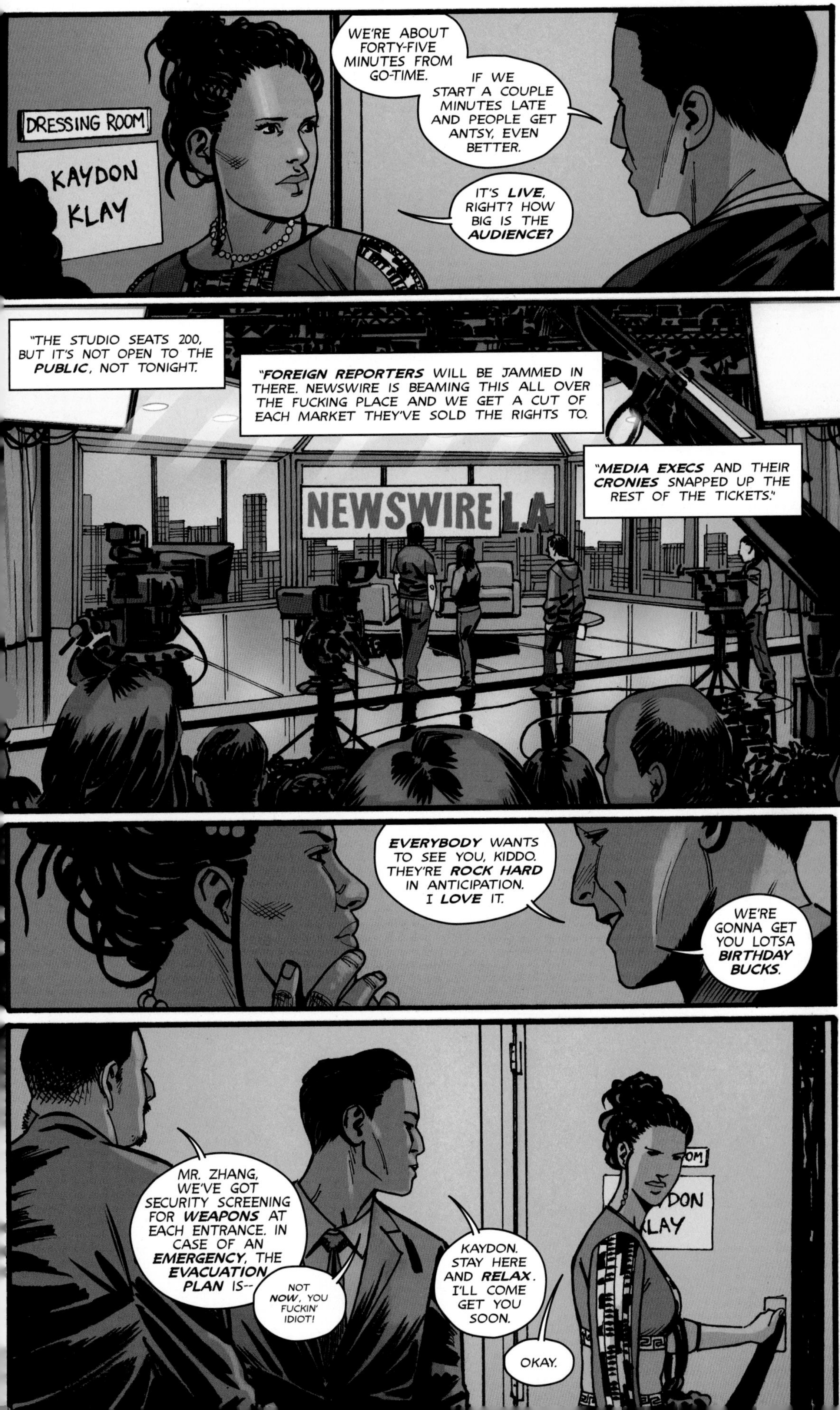
DRESSING ROOM
KAYDON KLAY
WE'RE ABOUT FORTY-FIVE MINUTES FROM GO-TIME.
IF WE START A COUPLE MINUTES LATE AND PEOPLE GET ANTSY, EVEN BETTER.
IT'S LIVE, RIGHT? HOW BIG IS THE AUDIENCE?
"THE STUDIO SEATS 200, BUT IT'S NOT OPEN TO THE PUBLIC, NOT TONIGHT.
"FOREIGN REPORTERS WILL BE JAMMED IN THERE. NEWSWIRE IS BEAMING THIS ALL OVER THE FUCKING PLACE AND WE GET A CUT OF EACH MARKET THEY'VE SOLD THE RIGHTS TO.
NEWSWIRE L.A.
"MEDIA EXECS AND THEIR CRONIES SNAPPED UP THE REST OF THE TICKETS."
EVERYBODY WANTS TO SEE YOU, KIDDO. THEY'RE ROCK HARD IN ANTICIPATION. I LOVE IT.
WE'RE GONNA GET YOU LOTSA BIRTHDAY BUCKS.
MR. ZHANG, WE'VE GOT SECURITY SCREENING FOR WEAPONS AT EACH ENTRANCE. IN CASE OF AN EMERGENCY, THE EVACUATION PLAN IS--
NOT NOW, YOU FUCKIN' IDIOT!
KAYDON. STAY HERE AND RELAX. I'LL COME GET YOU SOON.
OKAY.

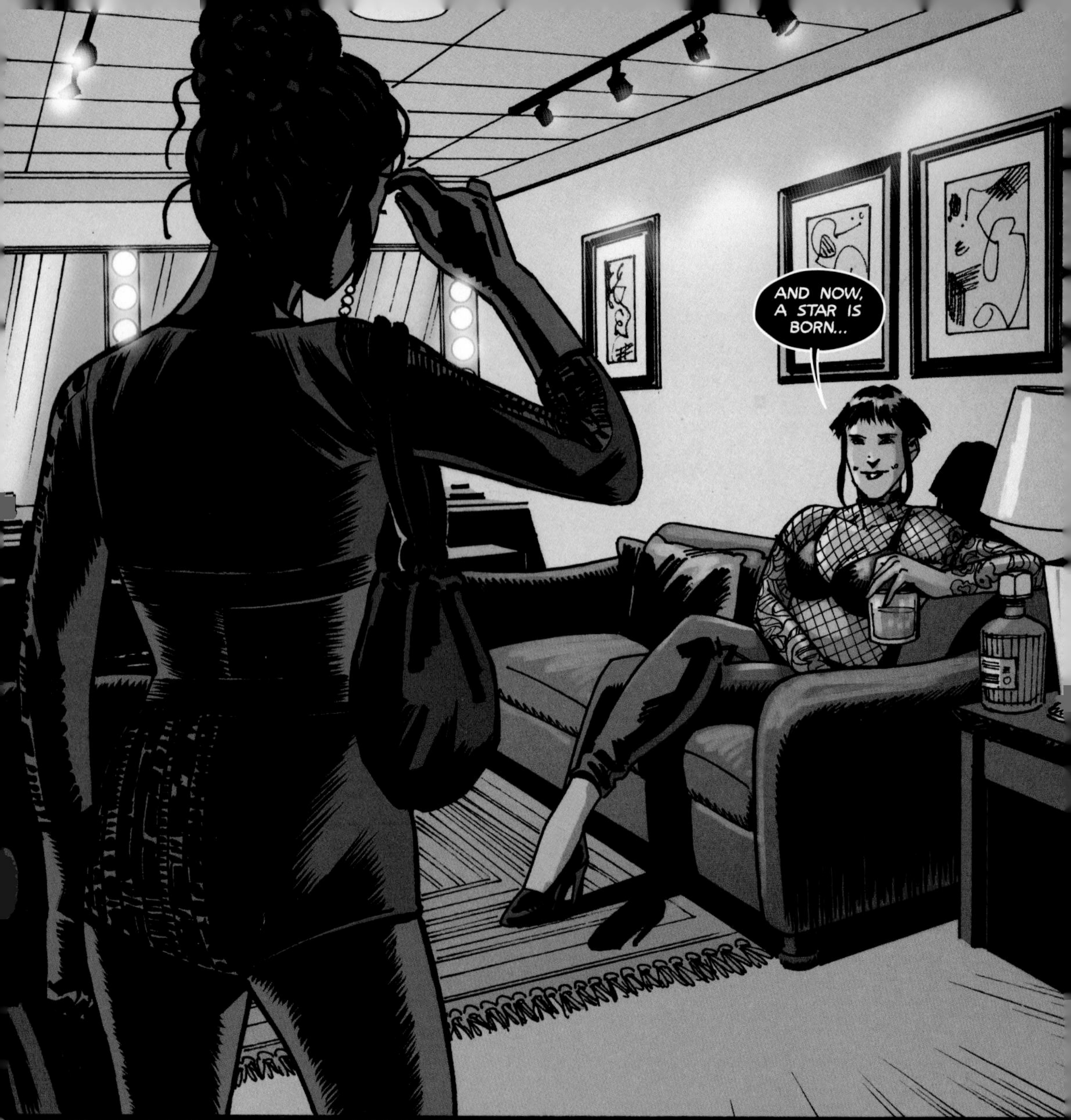
AND NOW,
A STAR IS
BORN...

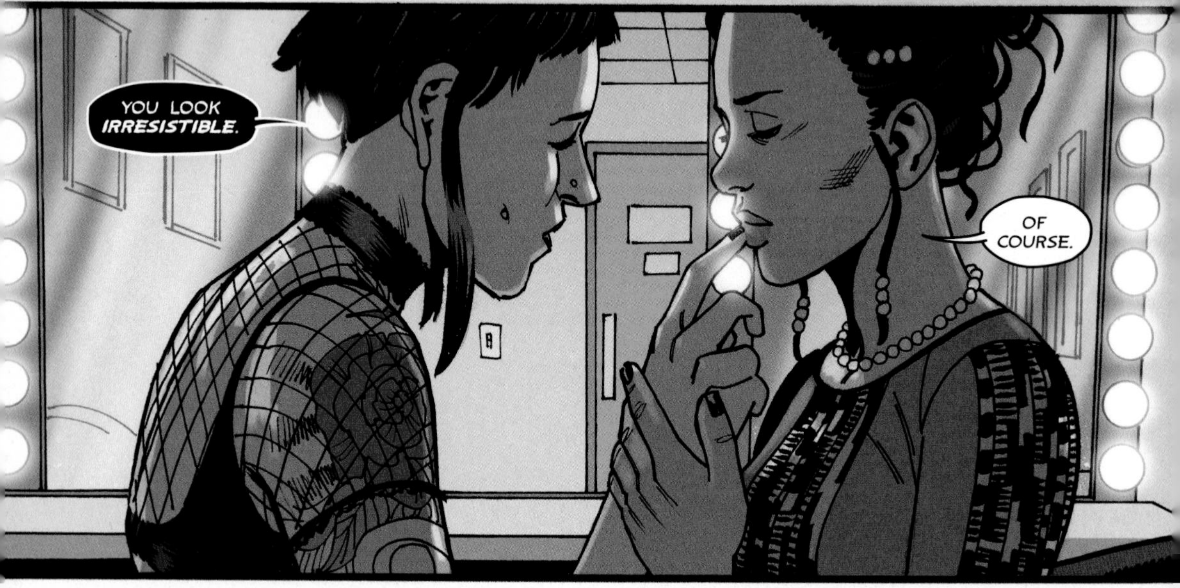
YOU LOOK
IRRESISTIBLE.
OF
COURSE.

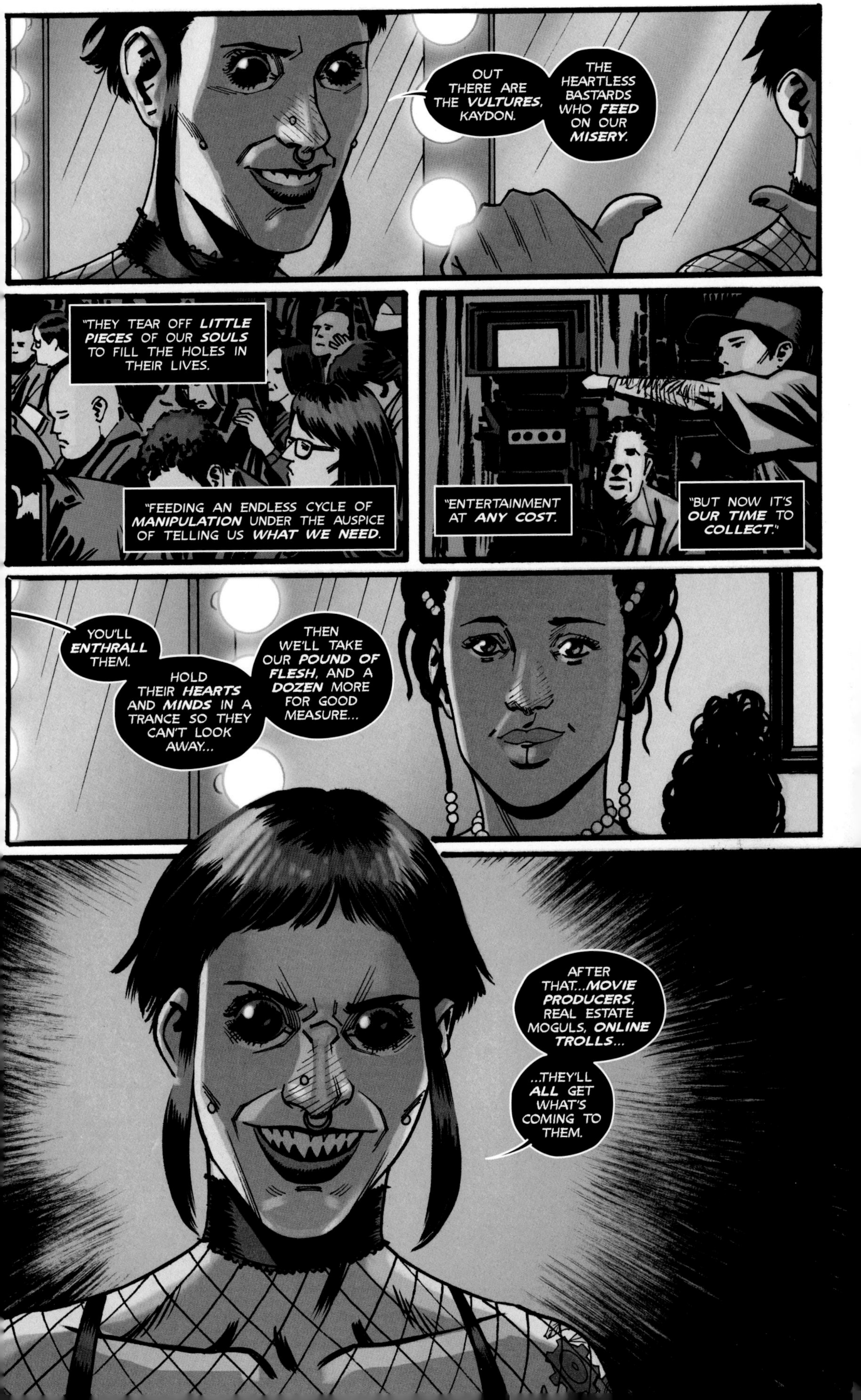
OUT THERE ARE THE VULTURES, KAYDON.
THE HEARTLESS BASTARDS WHO FEED ON OUR MISERY.
"THEY TEAR OFF LITTLE PIECES OF OUR SOULS TO FILL THE HOLES IN THEIR LIVES.
"FEEDING AN ENDLESS CYCLE OF MANIPULATION UNDER THE AUSPICE OF TELLING US WHAT WE NEED.
"ENTERTAINMENT AT ANY COST.
"BUT NOW IT'S OUR TIME TO COLLECT."
YOU'LL ENTHRALL THEM.
HOLD THEIR HEARTS AND MINDS IN A TRANCE SO THEY CAN'T LOOK AWAY...
THEN WE'LL TAKE OUR POUND OF FLESH, AND A DOZEN MORE FOR GOOD MEASURE...
AFTER THAT...MOVIE PRODUCERS, REAL ESTATE MOGULS, ONLINE TROLLS...
...THEY'LL ALL GET WHAT'S COMING TO THEM.

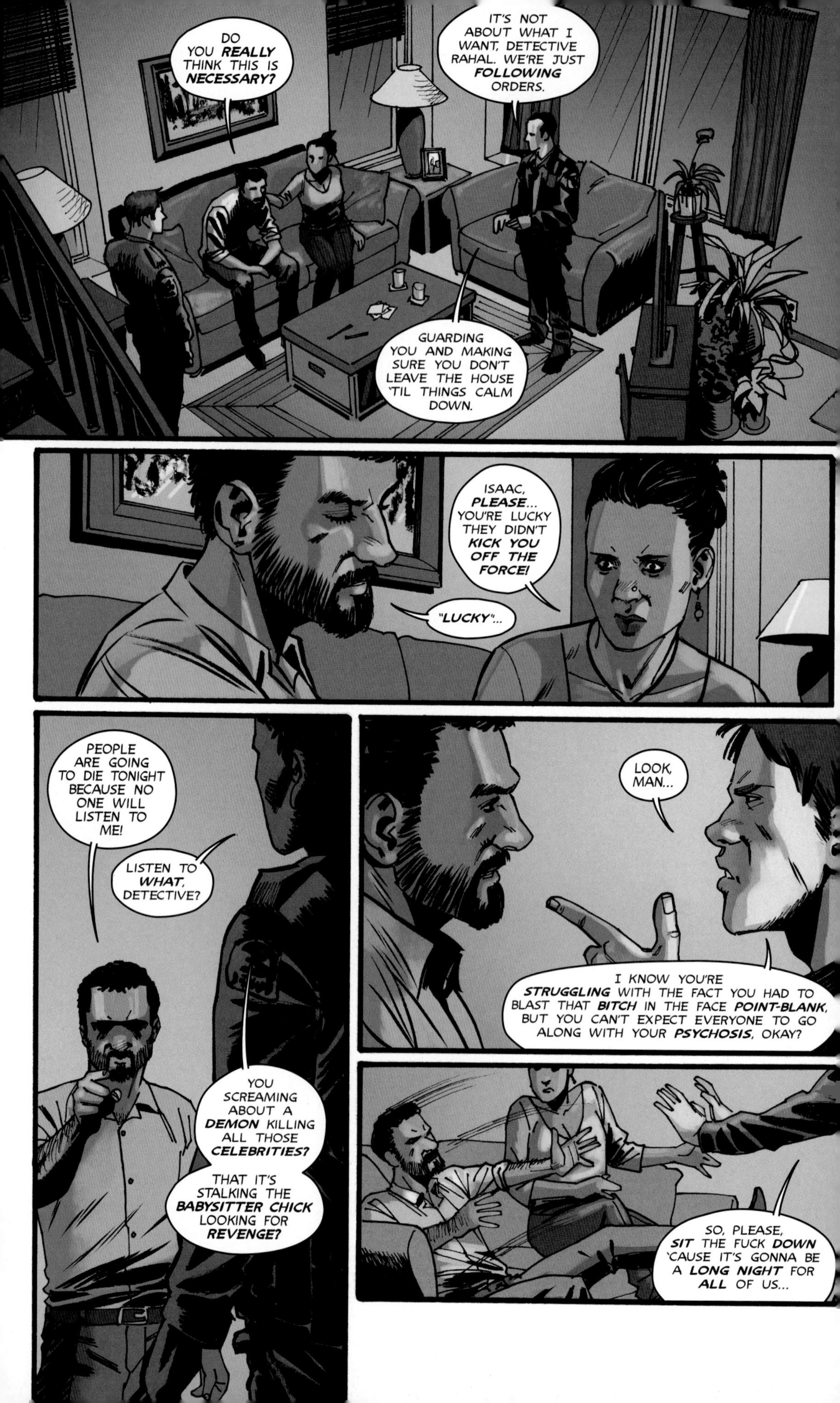

DO YOU REALLY THINK THIS IS NECESSARY?
IT'S NOT ABOUT WHAT I WANT, DETECTIVE RAHAL. WE'RE JUST FOLLOWING ORDERS.
GUARDING YOU AND MAKING SURE YOU DON'T LEAVE THE HOUSE 'TIL THINGS CALM DOWN.
ISAAC, PLEASE... YOU'RE LUCKY THEY DIDN'T KICK YOU OFF THE FORCE!
"LUCKY"...
PEOPLE ARE GOING TO DIE TONIGHT BECAUSE NO ONE WILL LISTEN TO ME!
LISTEN TO WHAT, DETECTIVE?
YOU SCREAMING ABOUT A DEMON KILLING ALL THOSE CELEBRITIES?
THAT IT'S STALKING THE BABYSITTER CHICK LOOKING FOR REVENGE?
LOOK, MAN...
I KNOW YOU'RE STRUGGLING WITH THE FACT YOU HAD TO BLAST THAT BITCH IN THE FACE POINT-BLANK, BUT YOU CAN'T EXPECT EVERYONE TO GO ALONG WITH YOUR PSYCHOSIS, OKAY?
SO, PLEASE, SIT THE FUCK DOWN 'CAUSE IT'S GONNA BE A LONG NIGHT FOR ALL OF US...

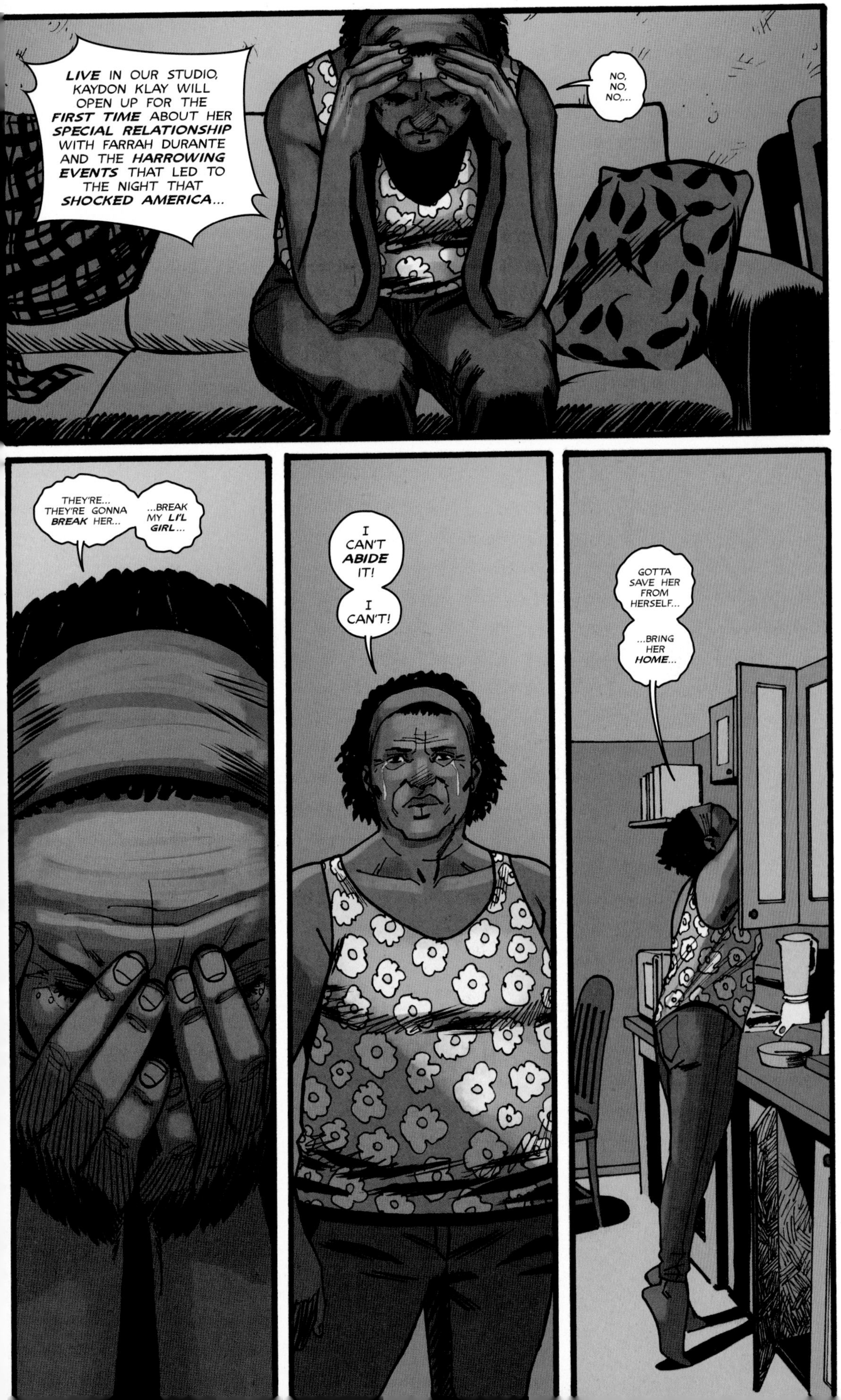
LIVE IN OUR STUDIO, KAYDON KLAY WILL OPEN UP FOR THE FIRST TIME ABOUT HER SPECIAL RELATIONSHIP WITH FARRAH DURANTE AND THE HARROWING EVENTS THAT LED TO THE NIGHT THAT SHOCKED AMERICA...
NO, NO, NO,...
THEY'RE... THEY'RE GONNA BREAK HER...
...BREAK MY LI'L GIRL...
I CAN'T ABIDE IT!
I CAN'T!
GOTTA SAVE HER FROM HERSELF...
...BRING HER HOME...

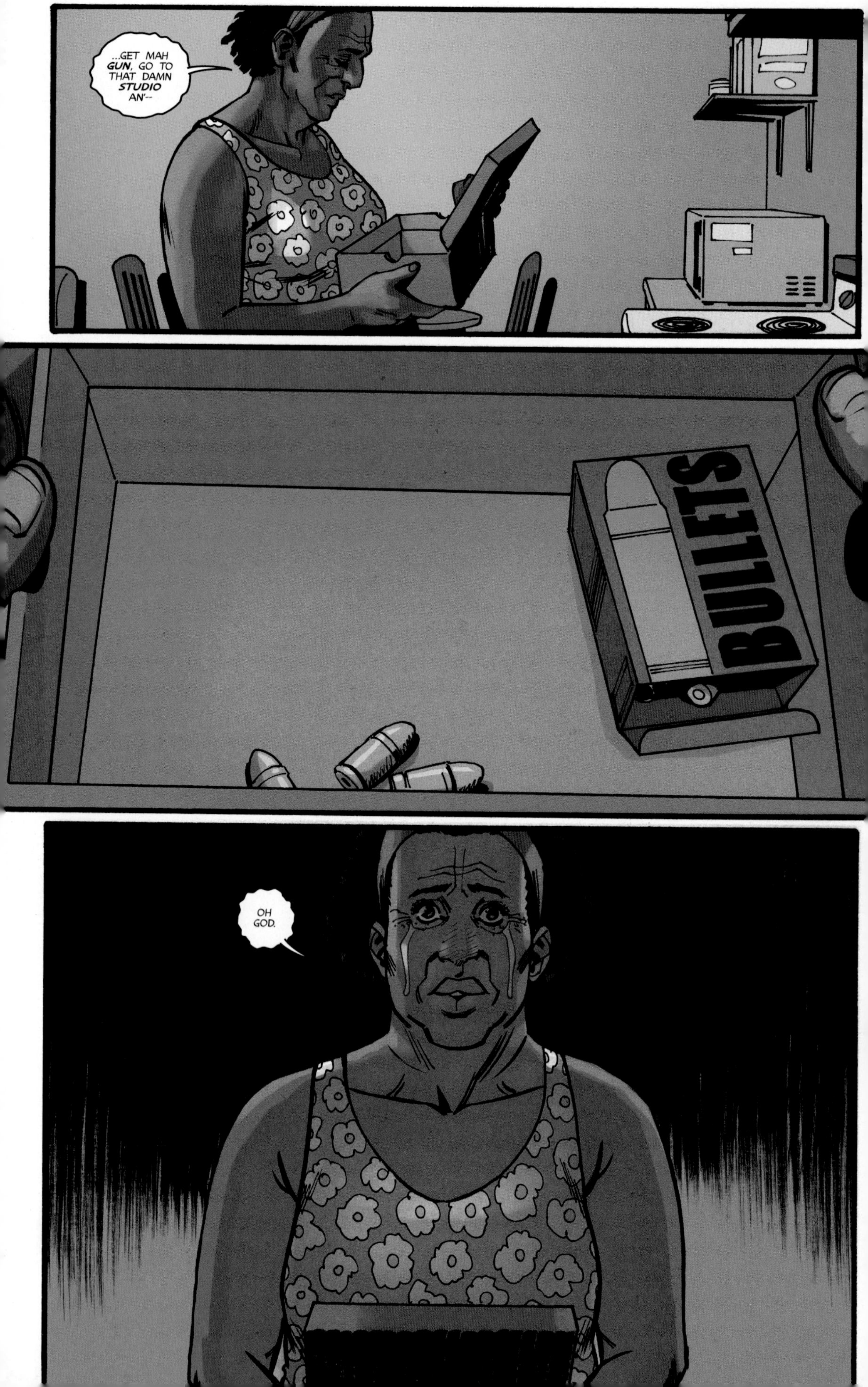
...GET MAH GUN, GO TO THAT DAMN STUDIO AN'--
BULLETS
OH GOD.

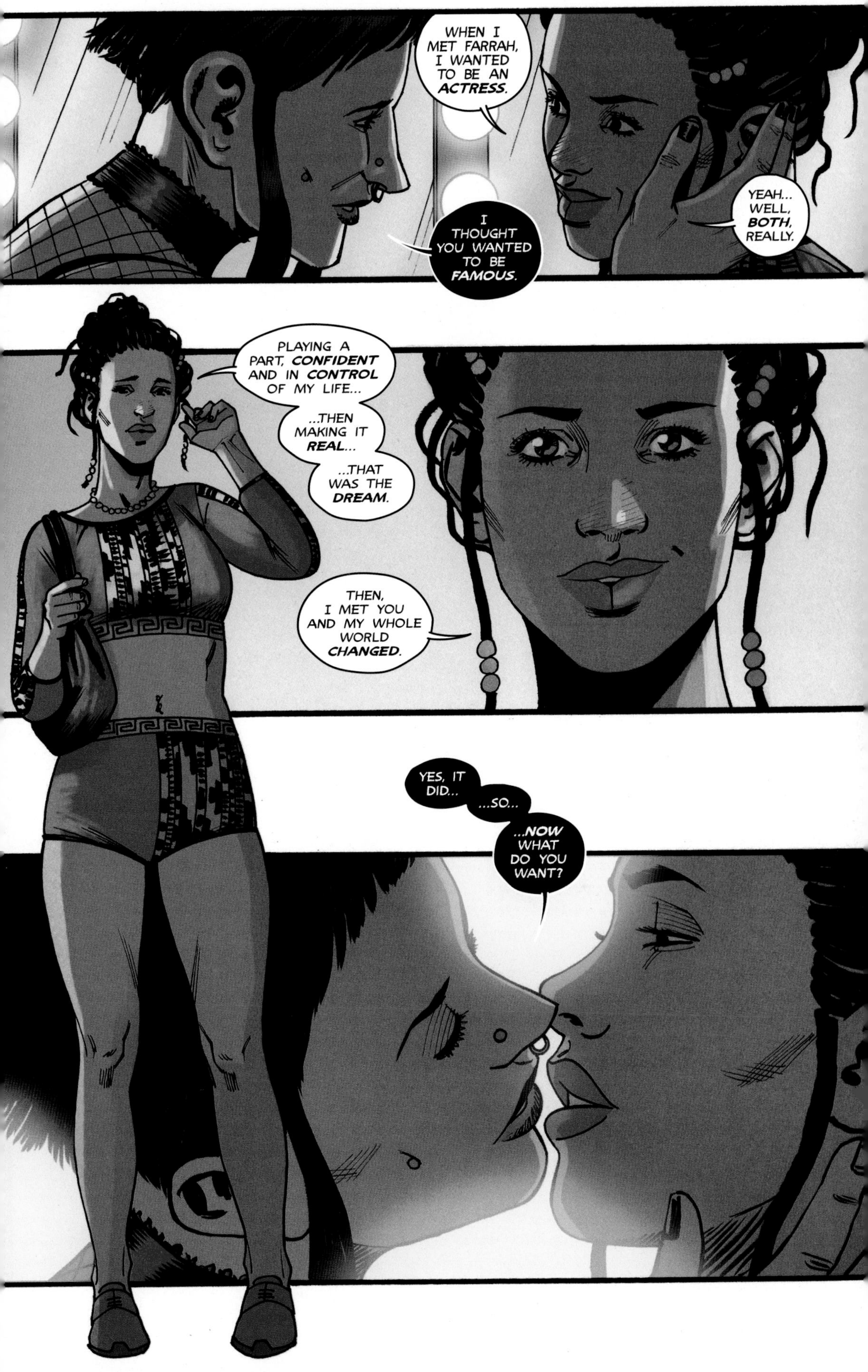
WHEN I MET FARRAH, I WANTED TO BE AN ACTRESS.
I THOUGHT YOU WANTED TO BE FAMOUS.
YEAH... WELL, BOTH, REALLY.
PLAYING A PART, CONFIDENT AND IN CONTROL OF MY LIFE...
...THEN MAKING IT REAL...
...THAT WAS THE DREAM.
THEN, I MET YOU AND MY WHOLE WORLD CHANGED.
YES, IT DID...
...SO...
...NOW WHAT DO YOU WANT?

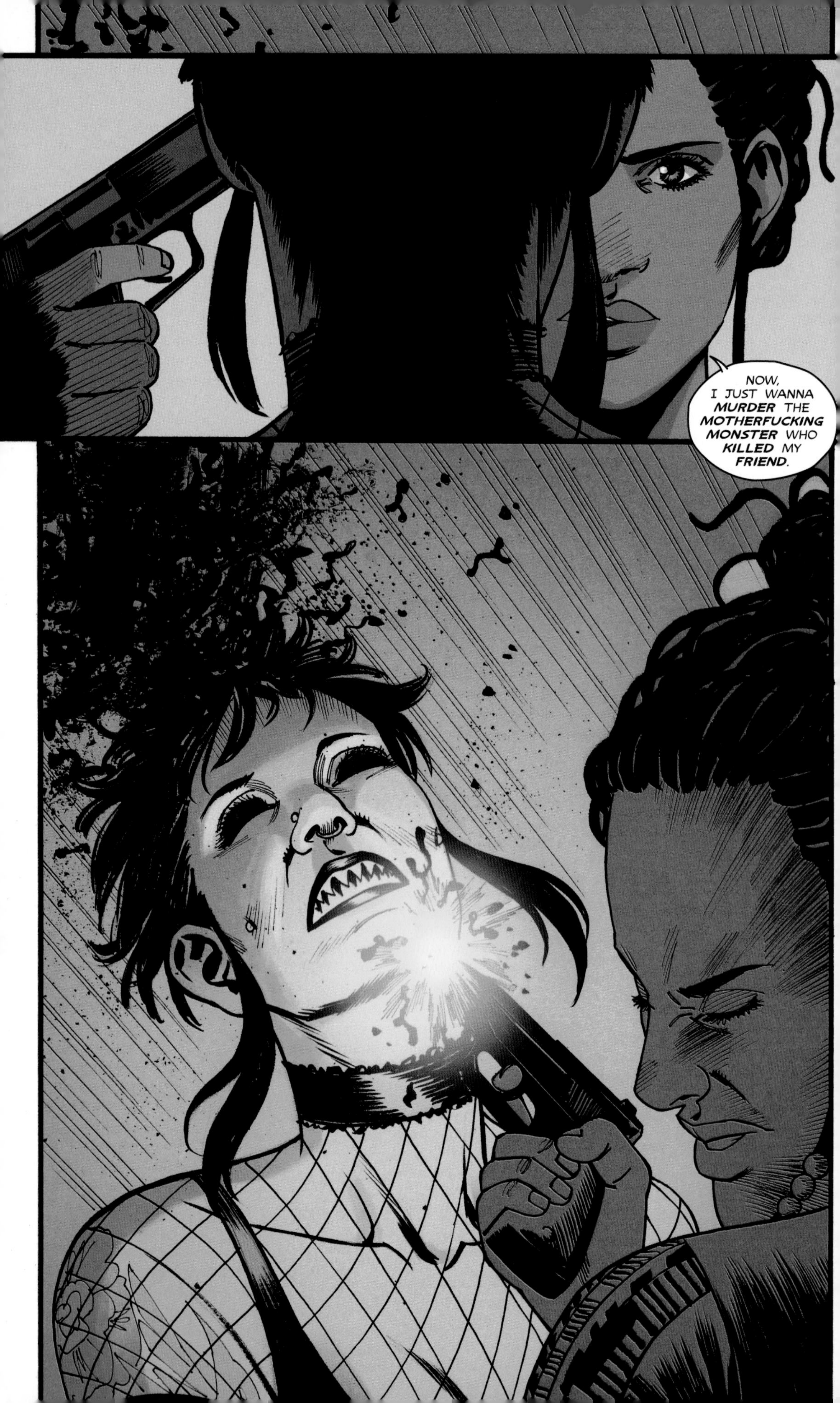
NOW, I JUST WANNA MURDER THE MOTHERFUCKING MONSTER WHO KILLED MY FRIEND.

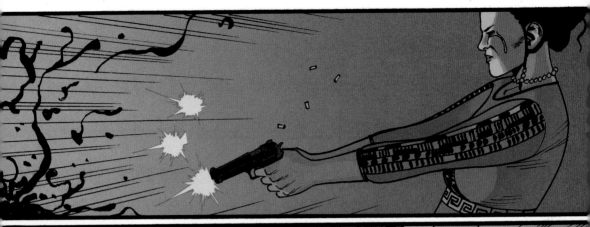

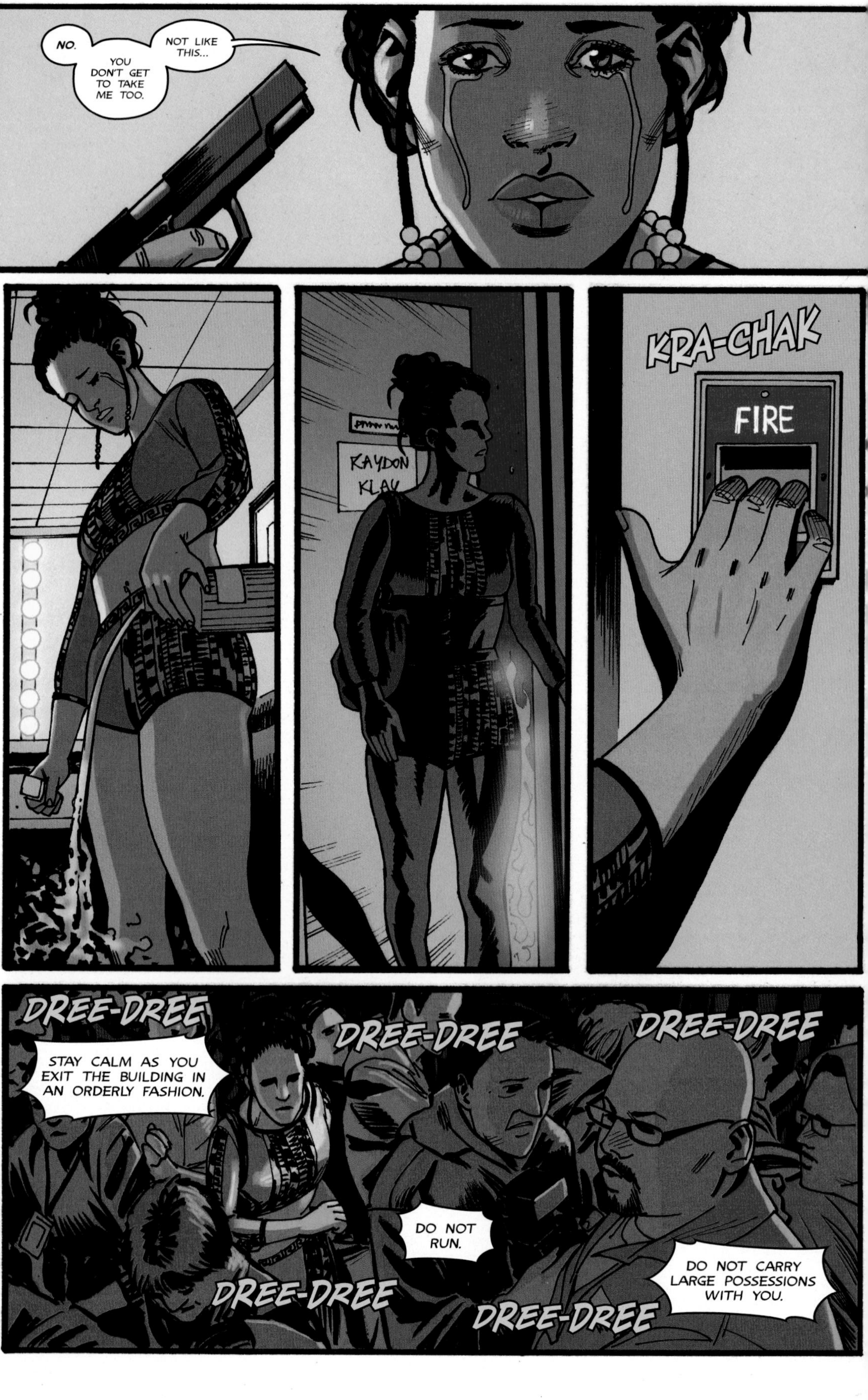
NO.
YOU DON'T GET TO TAKE ME TOO.
NOT LIKE THIS...
RAYDON KLAU
KRA-CHAK
FIRE
DREE-DREE
STAY CALM AS YOU EXIT THE BUILDING IN AN ORDERLY FASHION.
DREE-DREE
DREE-DREE
DO NOT RUN.
DO NOT CARRY LARGE POSSESSIONS WITH YOU.
DREE-DREE
DREE-DREE

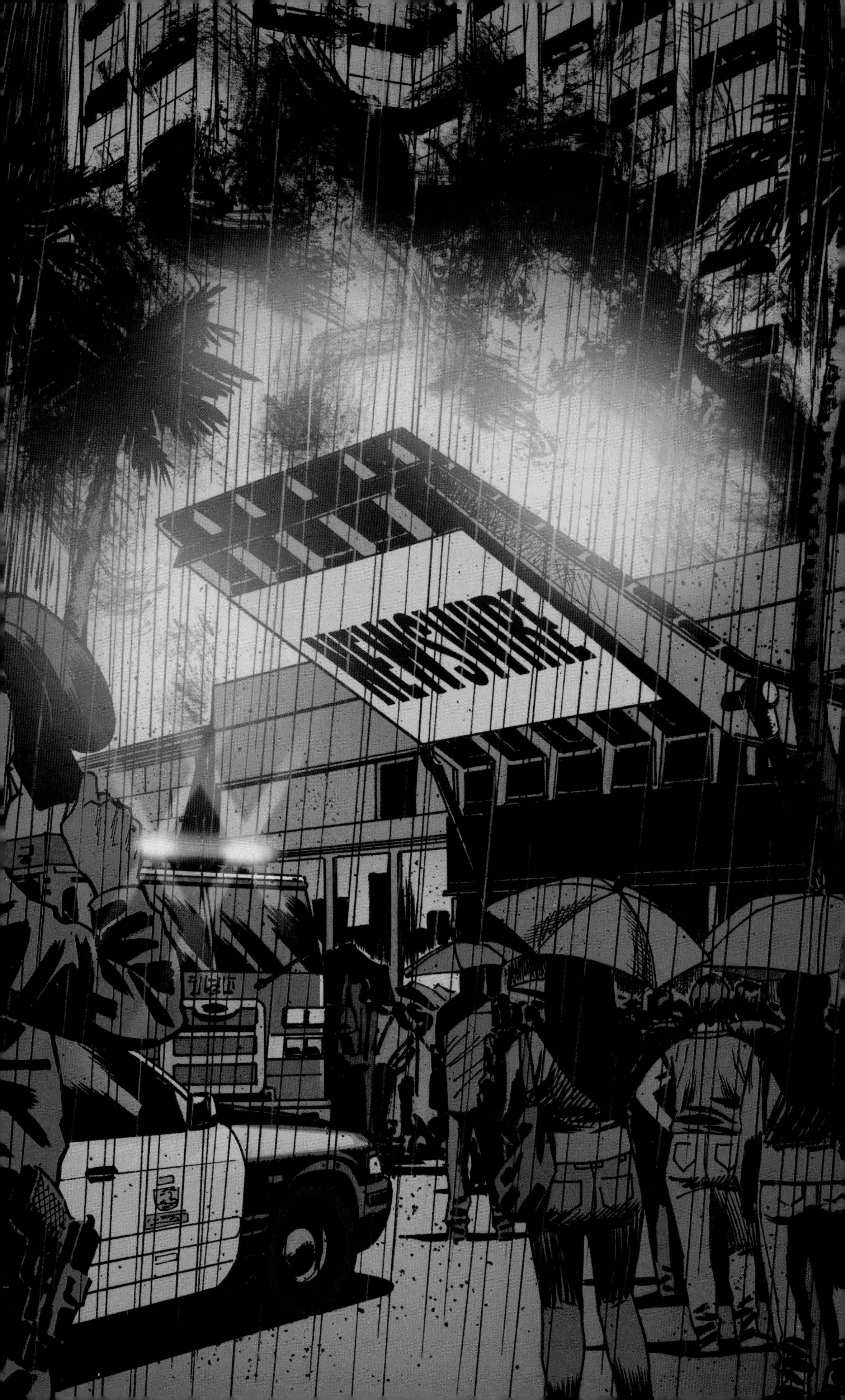
NEWSWIRE

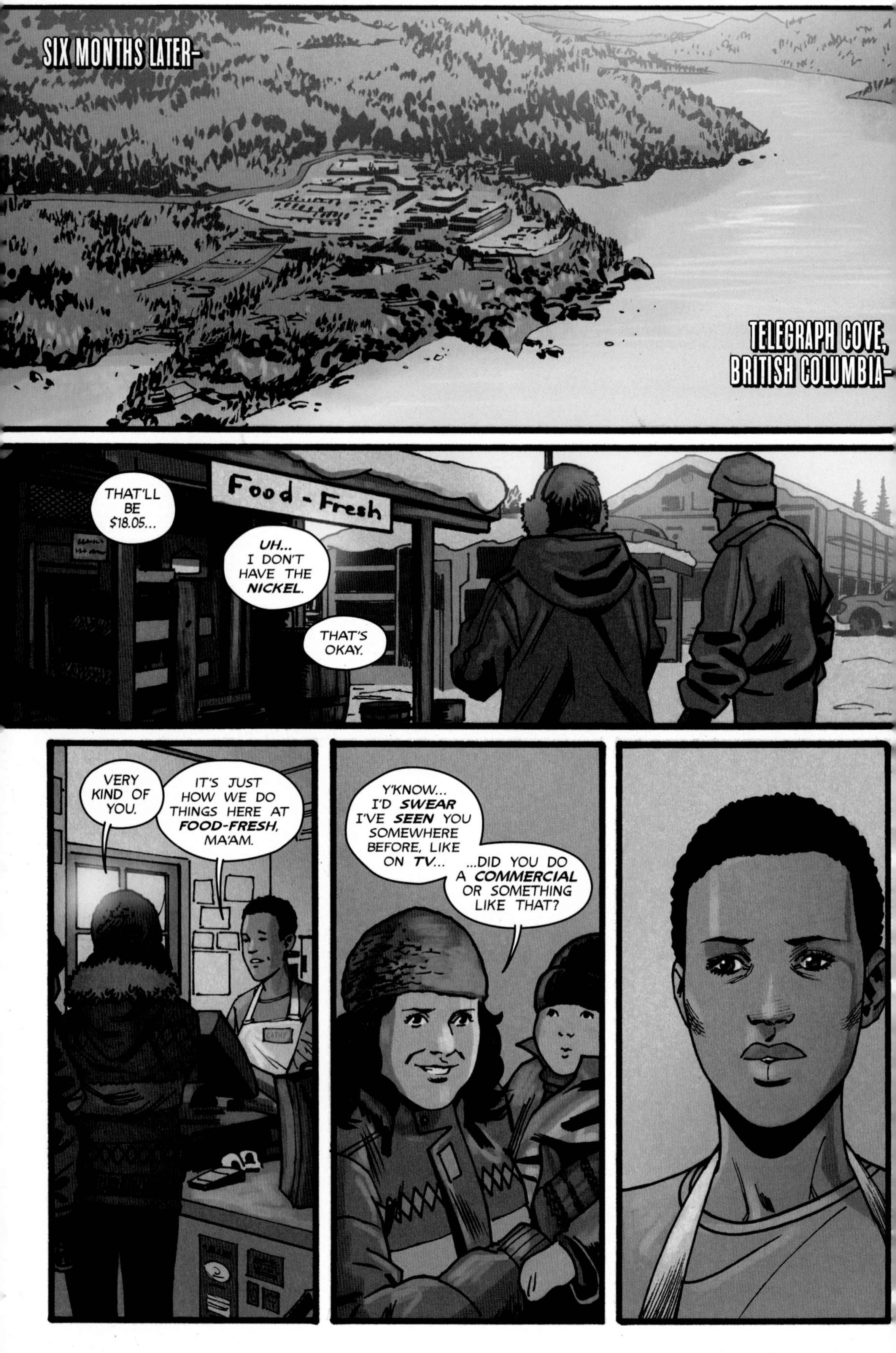
SIX MONTHS LATER-
TELEGRAPH COVE, BRITISH COLUMBIA-
Food - Fresh
THAT'LL BE $18.05...
UH... I DON'T HAVE THE NICKEL.
THAT'S OKAY.
VERY KIND OF YOU.
IT'S JUST HOW WE DO THINGS HERE AT FOOD-FRESH, MA'AM.
Y'KNOW... I'D SWEAR I'VE SEEN YOU SOMEWHERE BEFORE, LIKE ON TV...
...DID YOU DO A COMMERCIAL OR SOMETHING LIKE THAT?

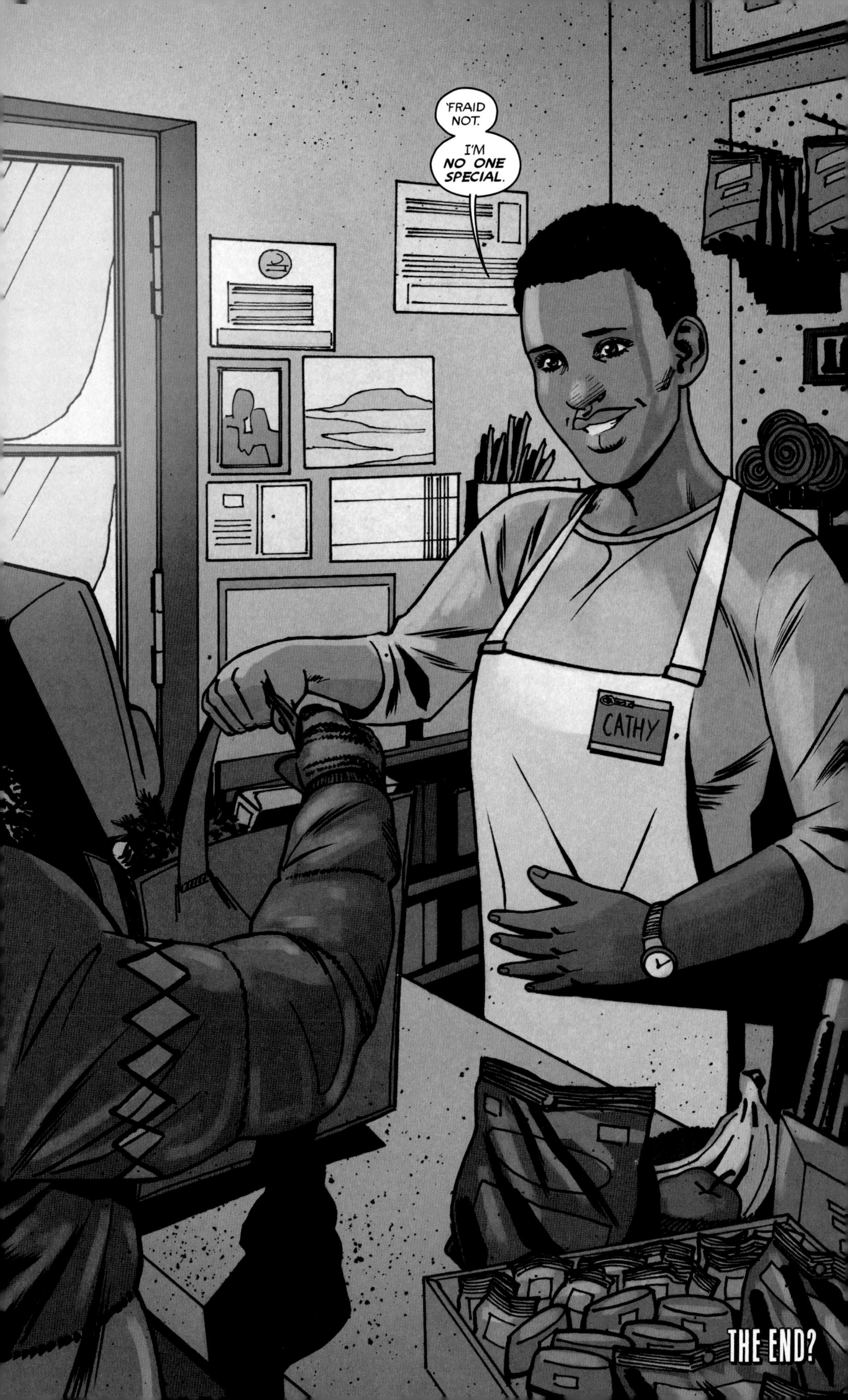
'FRAID NOT.
I'M NO ONE SPECIAL.
CATHY
THE END?

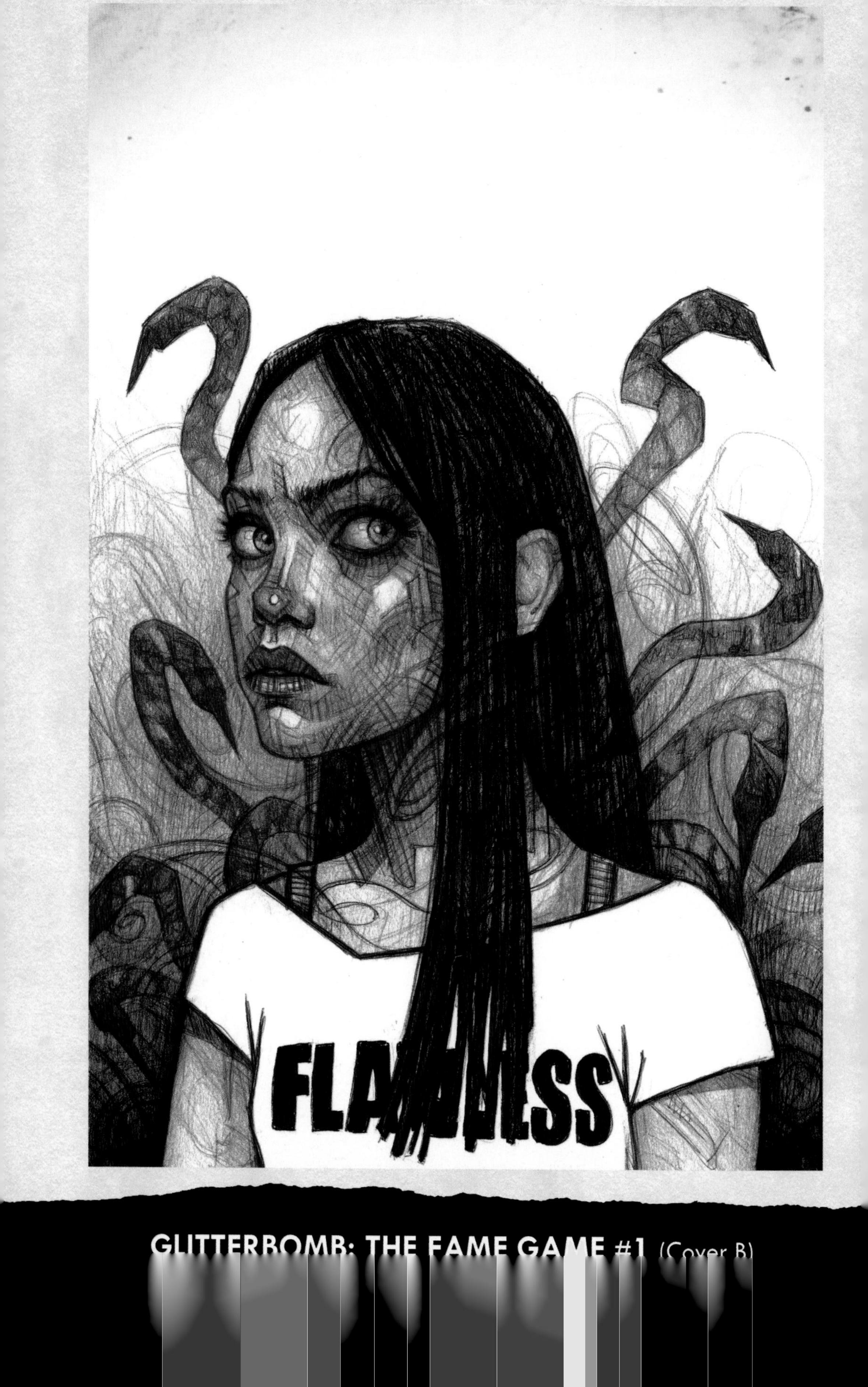

GLITTERBOMB: THE FAME GAME #1 (Cover B)

[redacted]

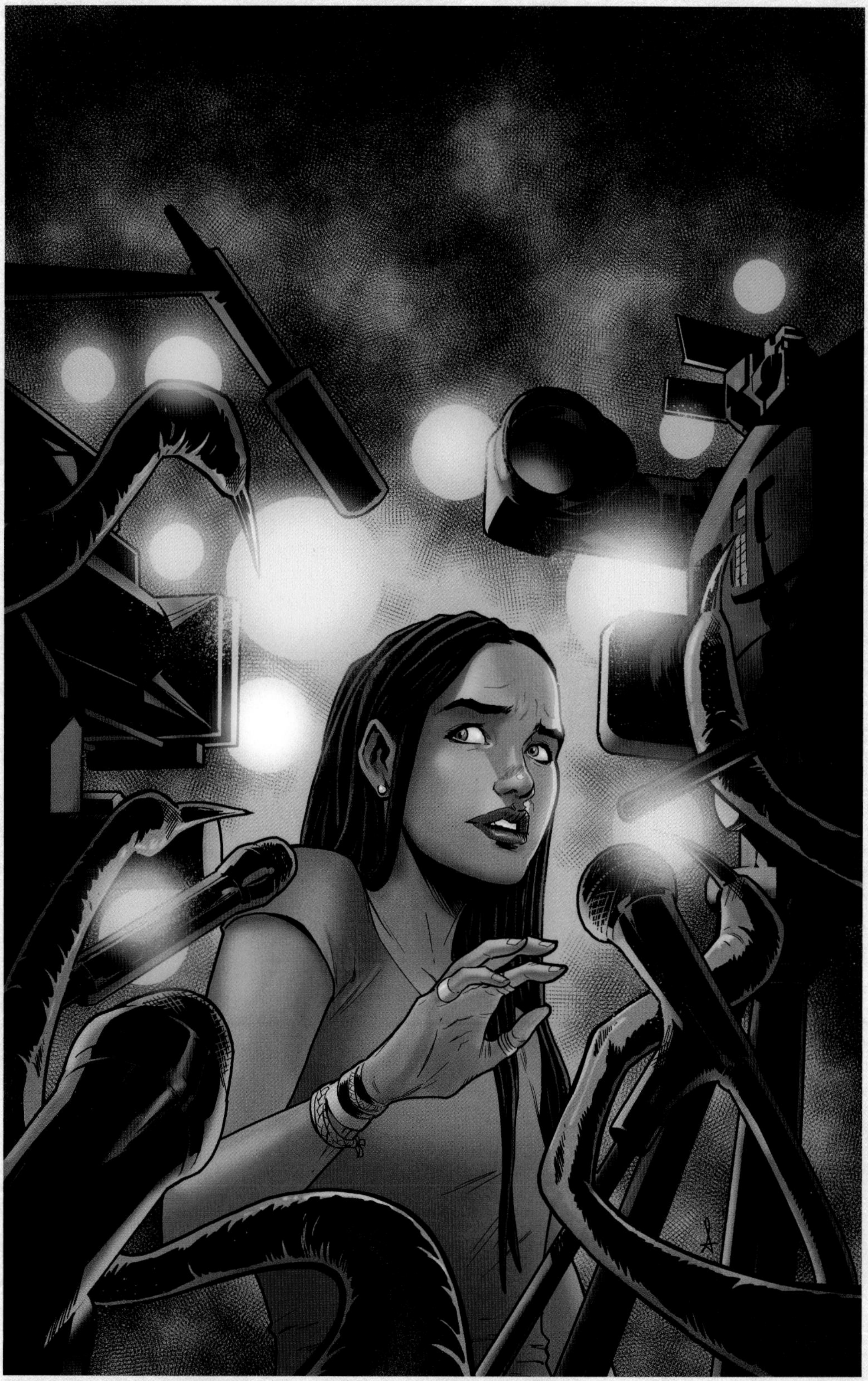

GLITTERBOMB: THE FAME GAME #2 (Cover B)

GLITTERBOMB: THE FAME GAME #3 (Cover B)

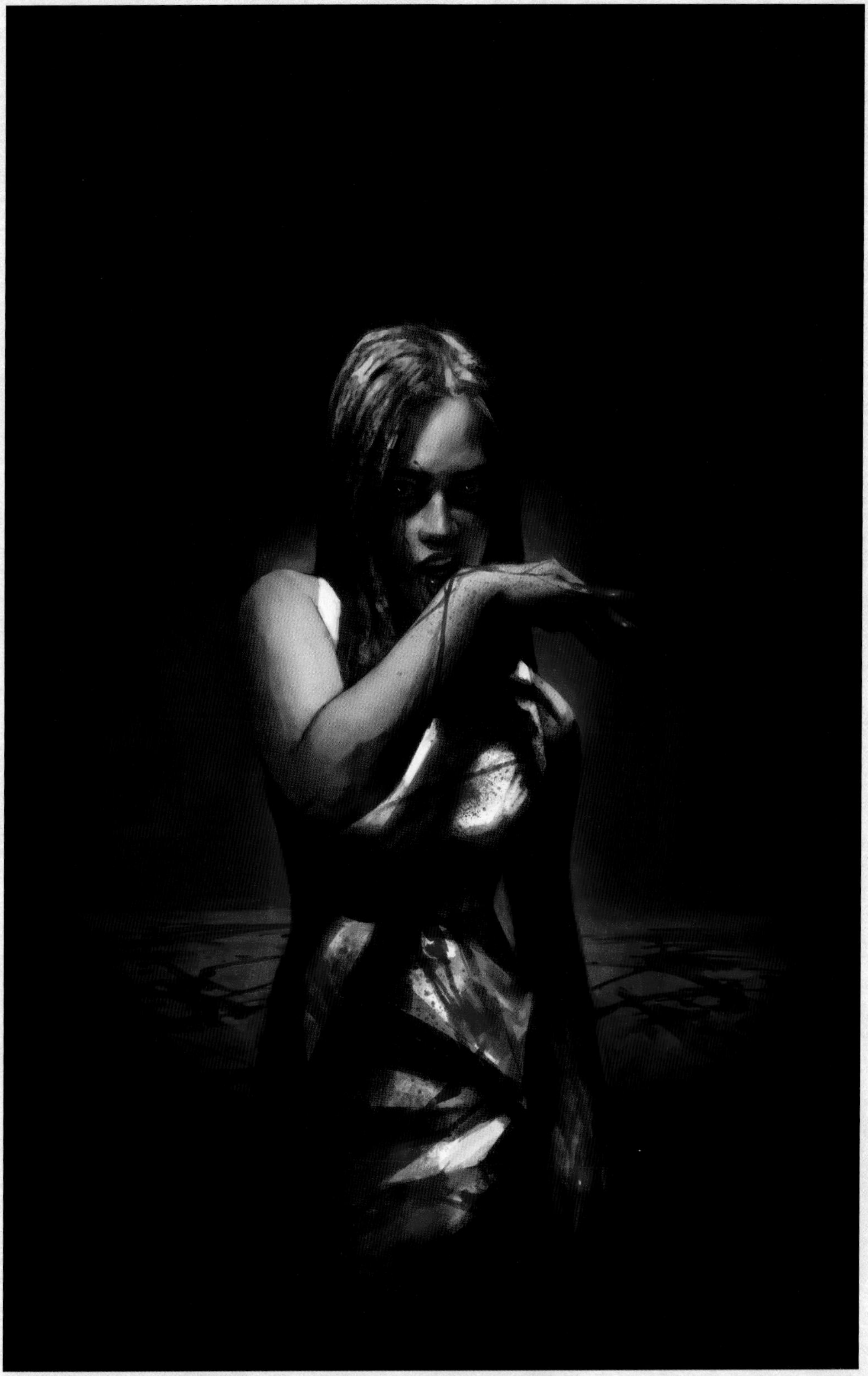

GLITTERBOMB: THE FAME GAME #4 (Cover B)

Artwork by Miguel Mercado.

SKETCHES

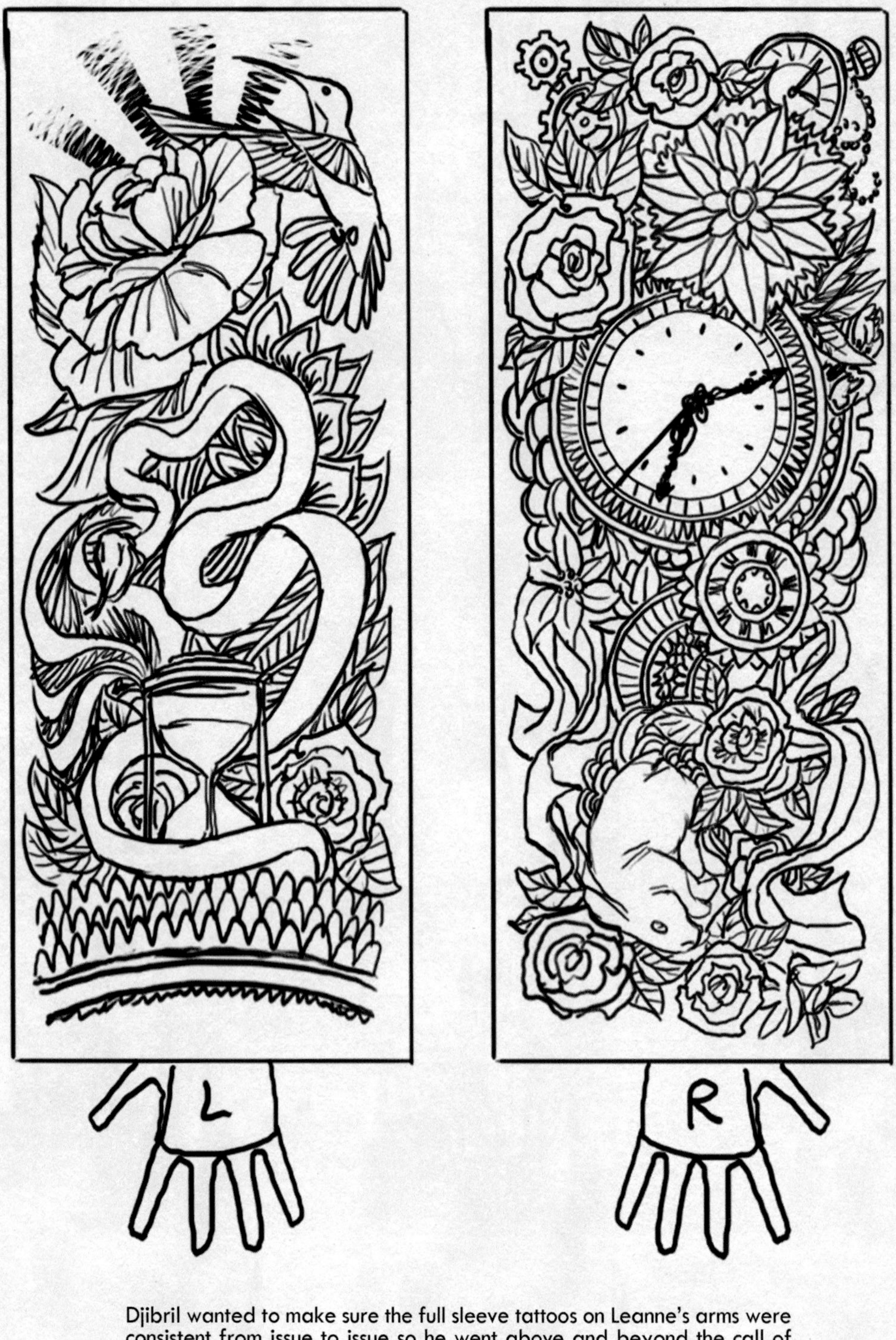
L
R

Djibril wanted to make sure the full sleeve tattoos on Leanne's arms were consistent from issue to issue so he went above and beyond the call of duty and designed them top to bottom. Gorgeous work, as always.

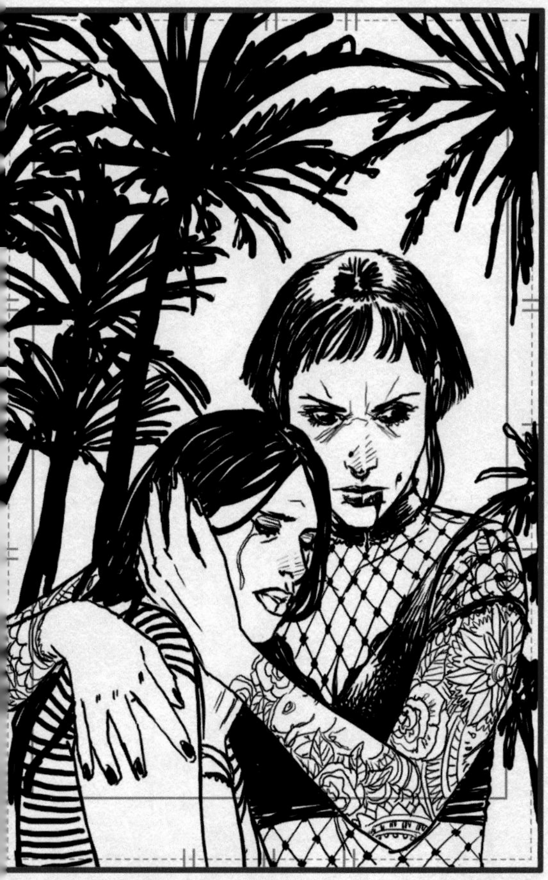

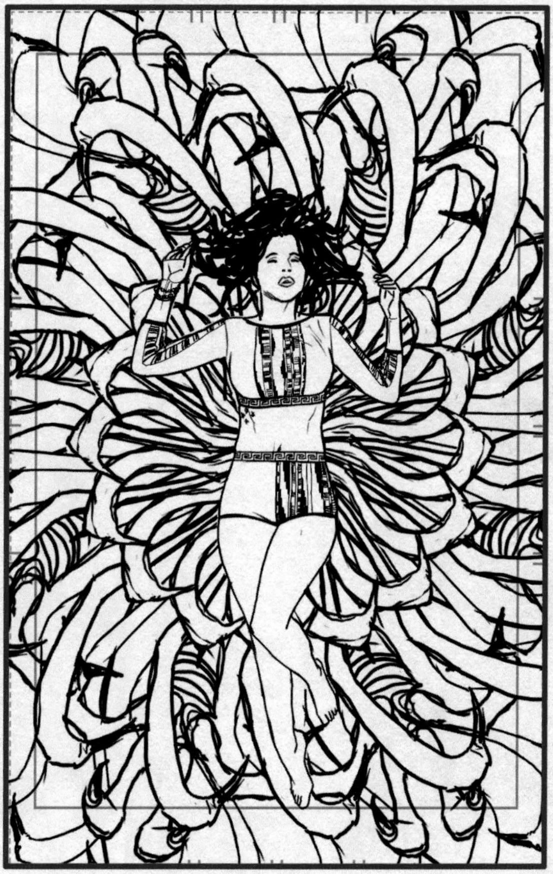

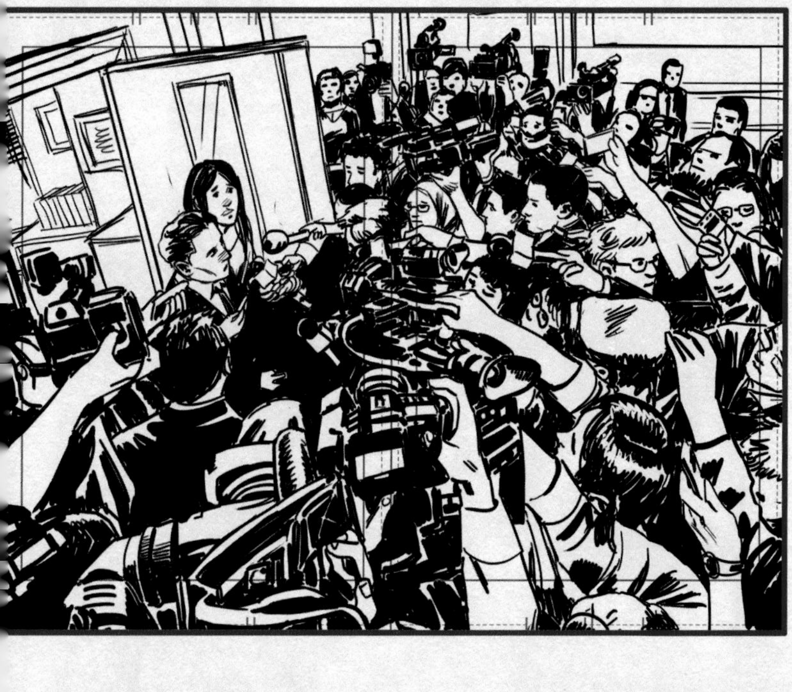

Digital sketches for the covers of Fame Game #3 and 4, and a digital prelim sketch for the two-page spread in issue 1.

AGENTS, AGENCIES, AND UNIONS: TALENT REPS IN HOLLYWOOD

When most people think of Hollywood talent agents they think of Ari Gold from *Entourage*; a fast-talking, ruthless, relentless, insanely driven person who will practically kill for his client and be murder to work for. He's a great character to believe in with his back room deals and personal shenanigans. I'm sure there are Ari-like agents in Los Angeles, but I never met one.

Most agents are hard-working people who hustle to get clients the best pay possible and foster their careers. It's their job to know what's coming down the pipeline, what opportunities are available for their actors, how to emotionally support talent, and be a tough contract negotiator.

Agents juggle multiple clients, deals, personalities, and phone calls. They tend to talk fast and cut to the chase. Agents will take on the bad guy role during contract negotiations while they fight to ensure their client gets equal contract treatment to others on the project, including billing, accommodations, and any other contractual provisions. This is sometimes called "favored nations" negotiation.

A good agent will push to ensure an actor feels compensated and appreciated. When those elements are in place the actor can show up on set prepared to work. Negotiations may include, but aren't limited to: specific food and water in trailers, wardrobe approval, assistants, approved hair and make-up artists, and transportation to and from set. The agent handles these demands so the actor is free to focus on their craft and be creatively vulnerable if necessary.

Not all agents are equal and neither are all agencies. There are big agencies like the *William Morris Endeavour (WME)*, *Creative Arts Agency (CAA)*, *United Talent Agency (UTA)*, and *Osbrink Talent*, but also boutique agencies as well. Boutiques are agencies people outside Hollywood may not know by name or initial, but also sustain actors and help many earn a living.

When actors arrive in Hollywood, they may dream of being represented by one of the big agencies because of the prestige associated with the name. Everyone knows CAA and WME. Actors earn bragging rights when they land an agent at a big agency. There's power in the name. The flip side to that mindset is that in a big agency, an up-and-coming actor is a small fish in a very big pond. How much attention will an agent devote to someone who hasn't broken through yet? At a boutique agency, the agent has time to focus on their clients and probably knows them far more than just a headshot on their computer screen.

If an agent wants to make money, they need to get bookings for their clients. Actors have to get auditions in order to land gigs. It's a tough business, but agents try to play by the rules to earn their 10%. There's a fine line between being a savvy representative and a pain in the ass people will avoid working with.

All that said, getting an agent isn't necessarily the first thing an actor needs to do.

When writer/actor/coach Dufflyn Lammers first arrived in LA an agent told her, "If you're in LA for more than a year and don't have a SAG-AFTRA card, you're not doing your job."

Hollywood is a series of hurdles and tests of stamina and talent every actor and crewmember continually navigate. For actors, getting into the Screen Actors Guild – *American Federation of Television and Radio Artists* – is a must. According to the Frequently Asked Questions on the SAG-AFTRA website:

There is no simple answer for how to break into the world of acting. Typically, performers take acting classes or study theater in school. Beginning actors often work in non-union background and principal roles in the early stages of their careers, as they get experience and build up a resume. SAG-AFTRA's interaction with performers begins after they have achieved professional status and are ready to join the Union.

According to Dufflyn, the top four ways to get into the union are:

1. Get a part in a union commercial, film, or TV show so you're eligible to join the SAG. If you're not sure if a production is union or not you can ask or check with SAG. A non-union actor can get hired for a union show and the production will fill out a SAG-AFTRA Taft-Hartley report.

The report includes information about the production, the actor's information, and checks off boxes stating why the non-union actor was hired. Reasons may include that the actor is a recognized "name" in a specialty group, a background actor was given a line of dialogue, or that it's the actor's first employment and they intend to pursue a career as a motion picture performer.

2. Work three days as a background actor on a union production. The actor will be expected to provide proof of employment (such as a pay stub).

3. "Sister in" through an affiliated performer union (ACTRA, AEA, AGMA or AGVA). An actor must be a paid-up

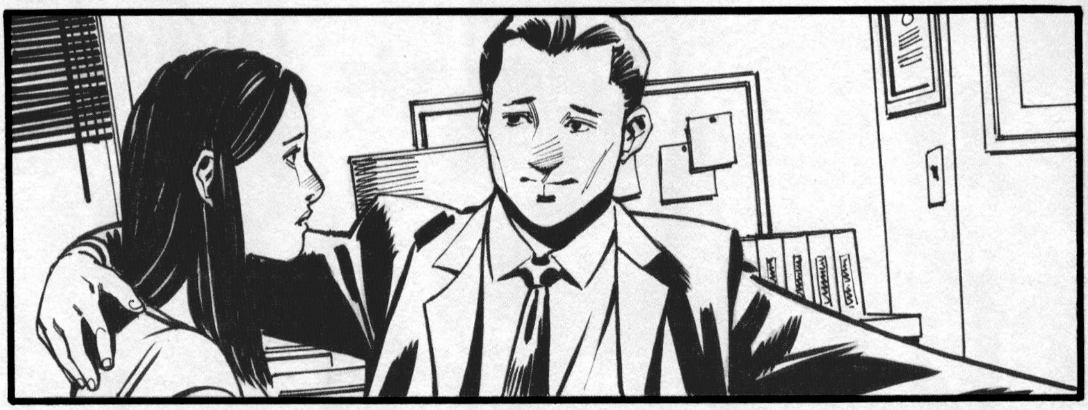

member in good standing for a period of one year and must have worked and been paid at least once as a principal performer in that union's jurisdiction.

4. Produce and perform in their own new media production and Taft-Hartley themselves. The actor must have existing union members in the production.

Dufflyn strongly advocates route #4 because it puts the actor in control of the process. The actor ends up with a piece of material for their reel, a credit, and the satisfaction of knowing they made it happen for themselves.

After all that, let's not forget the pitfalls of fame: arrogance, addiction, money, and power.

Not every actor manages to hang onto the rungs as they climb the ladder of success. Once, while I was working on a low-budget television series, an actress came to work completely wasted. Even worse, she was the lead. She fumbled through the shoot, barely able to hit her mark or remember a line. It was a disaster on set that cost production tens of thousands of dollars. When it came time for her to get paid, the producer and her agent arranged for me to walk her to the bank down the street where she cashed her check and returned all her earnings to production. I very much doubt this was legal.

I remember her hair was blonde and curled. She was LA thin, size zero or two. She walked beside me in high heels and a skirt, knowing I was there to guarantee she wouldn't cash the check and keep it. I recall her embarrassment and shame. I was twenty-three, with only one year of production under my belt. I looked down at the cement sidewalk along Avenue of the Stars in Century City as we walked in silence. I wanted to look her in the eyes and see if they were red and puffy or if her nose was running. I never imagined an agent would agree to this weird arrangement. I hated feeling bad for her and was annoyed the producer picked me to be the chaperone on this Walk of Shame.

I stuffed the white bank envelope into my purse and slipped the strap over my shoulder. I was nervous about carrying that much money. We left the bank and I walked back to the production while she headed for her car. I wonder if we even validated her parking. I wouldn't be surprised if the producer made her eat the extra five bucks. I knew the situation was bad if her own agent agreed to give up his cut. I wonder if the agency dropped her, if she's still in the business, and if she got the help she needed.

Dufflyn Lammer's FB one-woman show: www.facebook.com/DiscoveredShow/

SOURCES

SAG-AFTRA:
www.sagaftra.org

Taft-Hartley info:
www.sagaftra.org/files/sag/taft_hartley_report_principals_6_1.pdf

THE PUBLICITY MACHINE: HYPE AND CELEBRITY

My friend Jennifer's ex-boyfriend Toby, who was never the smartest person in a room, moved to LA and landed an internship with Chanticleer Films. They produced Academy Award-winning shorts. When I knew I was going to pack up and leave my east coast life for Hollywood, I researched Chanticleer's producers and owners Jonathan Sanger and Jana Sue Memel, before I called the production office. The office was located on the corner of Hollywood and Vine — quintessential Hollywood. I figured if Toby could work for them then I could, too.

I asked the Production Coordinator, Stephanie, if they still had internships.

"We do. Can you start Monday?" she asked.

"Yes," I said and I hung up the phone. It was Wednesday and I was still in Washington D.C.

I called Taz, my friend who lived in LA, "Can I crash on your floor for a while? I'm moving to California."

"Yes," he said. I was on my way.

I slept on a futon in Taz's Valley Village living room for about a month. His two roommates didn't mind. I eventually moved into the apartment across from his when three other friends of his decided to move to LA too. We were all trying to break into the business. I won't go into how messy the place was.

I drove a rented car, used a borrowed map, and on Monday morning I endured the notorious traffic of the 101 into Hollywood from the valley, exited the Vine Street Exit, made my way one block past the Capitol Records Building and began my career in film and television. I never dreamed I'd live in LA or work in show business. I studied Journalism and History in college. I wanted to be a news producer or a writer. I didn't go out there with stardust in my eyes.

Once I was in LA, I shifted those dreams from news production to film production. I set out to be the best and made a plan. It would mean long hours, hard work, leaving everything I knew behind and taking the plunge into SoCal culture. I dove in.

The difference between me and other people who come to Los Angeles to work is I didn't move to Hollywood in search of fame. It didn't occur to me to make it a goal. That's not to say I didn't dream of going to the Oscars. Of course I did. I wanted to wear a gorgeous designer dress, roll up to the red carpet in an open-air Jeep with my hair windblown, and

win "Best Producer." I wanted to be known for being the finest at my job, but never cared if anyone outside Hollywood knew who I was.

One night, while driving Forest Whitaker back home from our set in San Pedro, he struck up a conversation with me. Forest was reserved and spent his time in his trailer when not on set. I was told not to talk much in the car so I was surprised when he started chatting with me. I was afraid of being fired after getting lost earlier that week while driving Jeff Goldblum to set.

Forest wanted to know what I wanted to be — my Hollywood goals. I told him I knew I would never be as skinny as other girls out there and had no desire to ever be in front of the camera, but I wanted to be known for being a hard worker and terrific at my job. I remember him laughing and understanding the not being skinny because he wasn't thin either.

"I'll know I've made it when I get a story in the *Enquirer*," I said, hands gripping the steering wheel.

"Nothing that will hurt anyone, something about having an alien baby. That would be funny."

I'm sure he gave me side eye.

I went on, "I can see it now— a bad cut and paste picture of a green alien and my stomach all big and round. Or maybe I'd be holding it after giving birth."

Perhaps I had a little bit of the *Fame Game* monster lurking in me then. Lusting to be more powerful than an assistant, wanting recognition for my work, hoping to earn enough money to stop borrowing from my parents.

Being famous takes more than just being good at a job. It requires schmoozing — epic amounts of kissing the right asses. Famous people require advocates — agents, managers, publicists and lawyers. Those behind the scenes string-pullers and movers and shakers are the ones cropped out of red carpet photos but called out by name in thank you speeches. It's a symbiotic ecosystem built on publicity.

In all my years working in film and television, I never knew a production crew who enjoyed intrusions caused by the publicity crew. Sometimes publicity shots were taken on set and interrupted the shooting schedule. Producers, directors, location managers and assistant directors had to figure out

how much time they can sacrifice to get the cast through wardrobe changes, hair, make-up, and meal times to get a few photos or interviews to promote work that isn't even in the can yet.

I remember once, publicity came to do a photo shoot with Jeff Goldblum, Forest Whitaker and Kathy Baker. We were filming a huge scene in a hotel. The entire lobby had to be dressed including a grand staircase filled with extras, lighting, set dressing — the works. Every person on the 150 plus crew was running around trying to make this scene happen. While all that madness was going on, publicity set up a backdrop in a small corner with a soft box and lighting to get photos of the cast. That's time away from memorizing lines, blocking out movement for the camera, and even eating for the actors.

On another Chanticleer set, the producers completely forgot about a scheduled photo shoot. We were shooting nights, which means call time (the time you arrive on set) was around 7PM and we were going to shoot through until the following morning.

My job included locking down set, running errands, and picking up trash from the ground. Somewhere in the middle of the night, I remember pointing a photographer to crew parking and calling the producer, switching to channel two on our walkie talkies. Channel two is for private conversations you don't want the entire crew, all of whom are outfitted with walkies, to hear.

"Publicity is here," I said. I knew they'd panic. The producer never sent transportation to pick up the other actors who weren't on call that night to get them to set on time for the shoot. But I did.

"Don't worry, we sent transportation to pick up Gina a half hour ago. They'll be here soon," I said. Maybe I'd get a bonus or an atta girl.

"Don't tell anyone we forgot." the producer said.

"Now, go pick up cigarette butts off the street."

It wasn't quite the thank you I'd hoped for.

So, how does an actor get the publicity they need? I spoke with Michelle Czernin von Chudenitz about publicity. Michelle is an award-winning producer and the CEO/Founding Partner of Popular Press Media Group. PPMG represents companies and high-profile celebrities, crafting strategic public relations and publicity campaigns, consistently visible in leading news and pop culture media, both domestic and international.

Like most things Hollywood, it helps to know someone who knows someone. PPMG's new clients are often referred by their existing ones.

According to Michelle, "For publicity to be successful, it has to be a collaborative effort. In the entertainment space, we predominantly work with production companies, distributors, independent films, special events (ie. film festivals, award shows). We also have strong relationships with agents and managers."

PPMG has working relationships with celebrity news distributors since they both need the support of the other to do their jobs.

Michelle talks about negotiating terms for an interview, "Of course, we all know situations where press boundaries have not been observed. Boundaries include what an actor will or won't speak about and what they're promoting. Often, celebrity focus and direction are approved. When necessary, PPMG will coach or prep an actor for an interview so they feel comfortable."

So, what's the biggest misconception about Hollywood PR, Michelle?

"That you'll magically become a star the day after you hire a publicist. Publicity, as my business partner will tell you, is like gardening. You have to plant the seeds and water it, then over time your plant will grow. Celebrity is not built overnight. There are so many clichés and it's hard not to slip into them - but one that holds true is the ten-year overnight success."

Cheers to ten years going quickly.

SOURCES

Popular Press Media Group:
www.PPMG.info

Michelle Czernin von Chudenitz's Twitter:
@mcvcm

THE SHAME GAME

I tried leaving Los Angeles and show business once. I took a sabbatical in Denver, Colorado after my starter marriage failed. I'm glad it failed. It made me re-evaluate everything about myself. I had to figure out who I wanted to be as an adult, learn what I wanted, the kind of people, and career and how to make it happen without being what I hated.

The thing is, when I returned to LA two years later, LA didn't want me back. I abandoned it and, despite having over a decade of production experience, I was punished for leaving the game. People who used to hire me wouldn't. Reality television began and production houses wanted me to work for a fraction of my previous rate, so I had to start over. At least that's how it felt.

One assistant director friend, Vince, was glad I returned. He was starting up a music video company and wanted to know if I wanted to help. I could produce for him. I knew the right people in rental houses, knew how to budget, and I think he thought I was fun to work with. I wish I'd said no, but the idea was so enticing. I imagined myself back on set, playback rolling, new crews, and shorter shooting schedules, super trendy clothes — it was a challenge I wanted to take a huge bite out of.

I drove to his apartment in the valley from the west side and we watched directors' reels. Vince really liked one of them. It belonged to an Olympic athlete. The athlete's cousin was a singer and they had connections in the music business. If we hired him it could be a great stepping-stone and Vince loved the idea of working with a Summer Olympian.

The reel didn't impress me. It was very B-roll; no original shots or directing. Just basic footage. But the company was Vince's baby and so I went along with him. The first time we met Mark it was at a restaurant on Ventura Blvd. We talked shop. Mark was tall. He looked like a track star. He also had a one-man entourage, Will, who followed him everywhere.

Mark was charismatic and able to collect people. His phone was always ringing; people were constantly trying to get ahold of him. It can be hard to tell the difference between warning signs and someone in demand in LA.

These were warning signs.

The Olympian went by two different names, Mark and Donald. He had a wife and a baby. I didn't know at the time he wasn't paying his own rent. I didn't ask the right questions because Vince needed me and I wanted to be needed and back in the game.

Vince's music video production company dreams weren't getting off the ground. We hit snags. His dreams and the reality of doing things were vastly different. While we went around trying to make a music video for a band, Mark started calling me. He asked me for advice. He wanted to know if I agreed with other producers he worked with.

He started telling me about his LA dreams and his plan for achieving them. Mark loved science fiction like I did. We debated *X-Files* and talked story ideas. He shared his concept for a television series. It was rough, but sparked a hunger in me. This was something I could produce!

I asked Mark if he had a book or a script for the series. He did. After reading it, I knew I could make it better. The core concept was there, but the professionalism wasn't. We had more meetings in restaurants. Will was there. I met the other producing friends he had — I believe one was a retired stuntman, another a fresh-off-the-bus girl in LA. He met more people and flaunted his Olympic credentials. We were all dreamers hoping to make it by creating our own product. I wanted to be like Ben Affleck, Matt Damon and Ed Burns.

Vince's music video company dissolved, washed away in the LA basin like so many dreams in Hollywood do. My focus turned to revising the television pilot and book. Mark got us a pitch meeting at the Sci-Fi Channel (not yet Syfy). Everyone wanted to meet an Olympian; he was good at using that as a way to get his foot in the door. I put together a budget and broke the scripts down. Mark, Will and I were going to pitch acquisitions executives.

The meeting went well, but we needed to present a pilot. Mark, Will, and I met and discussed who would be involved with the show. Mark told me about the other producers he had on board. I said they all had to bring something to the table besides sitting at it. Things started getting weird.

Do you see what I forgot to do? Me, the person in charge of paperwork and contracts, didn't draw one up for myself. Sure, I had a deal memo, but nothing specific. I was so caught up in doing the work that I forgot to cover my ass. I was so deliriously eager to get back in the game I forgot the rules.

Mark said he trusted me and confessed he didn't have enough money to put gas in his car. Someone had to pick him up to go to the meetings. He said he had to make this work soon because he had to feed his family and pay rent. Through tears he told me how rough things were for him.

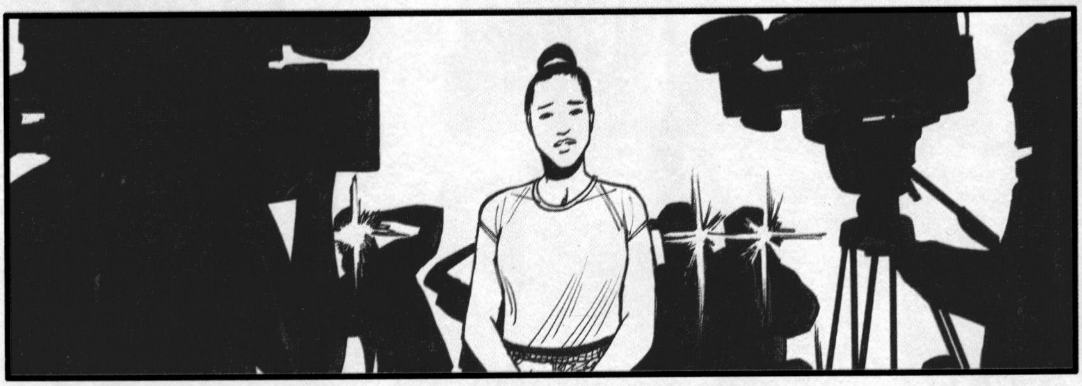

I thought we were friends.

Mark confessed he never actually ran in the Summer Olympics. He was an alternate. He was ashamed he never ran. He felt guilty for accepting the attention that belonged to a winner. He explained that the team as a whole had won, but his feet never touched the track. I thought we were building trust between a producer and director.

Despite the shadiness of some of the "producers" on board we agreed to shoot the pilot. I made a shooting schedule and found a house we could use for multiple locations. I hired a catering company, rented equipment and got a security team to watch the house and generator before production got underway. I hired a girl named Star to be my right hand and coordinator. I needed an extra set of eyes on things because I was producing, location managing, helping the art department, and handling all the money.

We held casting sessions. It was a ridiculous amount of work but I was glad to be in the middle of everything solving problems, making my dream come true.

If I could stop time and slap myself across the face for stupidity, this is the moment in my life I'd do it. I was legit but was being used and manipulated and too eager to see it much less stop it. A week before shooting was supposed to begin, Mark called me.

"We don't have the money," he said.

I wasn't going to let money stop me. I'd worked too hard and saw the possibility of being a show runner in my future. I was going to do the one thing I hated doing. I was going to ask my father for help.

Asking a favor meant an emotional string was attached, but I figured if I came in with the funds I'd be the executive producer and co-creator of the show. It could make me into the creative producer I dreamed of being. I was willing to risk my relationship with my father to do it.

Borrowing money made my dad feel like I'd accepted his new life. There'd be no way to avoid his new life and family if I took his money. I'd have to sit there and listen to stories about the trips they went on, the dinners and holidays they shared with my cousins, and learn how long they were together behind my back. I also understood money was his love. I wanted to prove I could take it and make it into my future.

I borrowed ten thousand dollars from my dad. I fought with the other producers and told them it was my show now. Mark backed me up. This was another missed opportunity for me to back out of a bad deal and see how Mark really treated people.

They were pissed off. I didn't care. My money, my show. We shot the pilot. It was a brutal shoot. Mark was not a director and the crew became angry

about his lack of professionalism. Everything I saw in that original reel, the bad choices and mediocrity were laid out there in front of me. I didn't get to sit next to camera because I was juggling locations, crew parking, where to put hair, makeup and wardrobe, catering, and a million other fires that needed to be put out.

We got the pilot in the can, which is to say we shot the script and had it developed. It was time to edit.

One night, during editing, Mark was a no-show. He stopped taking my calls. My assistant stopped taking my calls, too.

Something was up but, again I didn't listen to my gut because I wanted to finish the pilot. I told myself there would be time to deal with the drama after we were done.

I watched what the editor cut together. I was impressed by what he cobbled together from the footage. I asked him to make a few changes.

"No," he said. "Mark's the director, I only listen to him."

"I'm paying you. This is my show," I said.

"I only listen to him."

"I'm the one paying you."

"Nope. He is."

That's when it finally hit me. All the odd phone calls I watched Mark take. He was jumping from person to person. Using each one to finance his dream. I wasn't an equal, I was a stepping-stone. A dollar sign. Another hustle. And I risked my relationship with my father to do it!

I became angry and overwhelmed with shame. Not only was

I conned, I used up all my favors in town to shoot the pilot, and wasted my father's money! How could I be so stupid?

I called a lawyer. And what happened next is even more shameful.

Mark stole the film and edit. He literally locked me out and demanded I pay him more money if I wanted it back!

Here's what I learned too late: I was just one of the many people Mark took money from. That was how he supported his wife and kid. He was a practiced con man and I his willing victim.

I learned why Will was always with him. Will had seen him do this to other people. Will watched him scam fool after ambitious fool. After yelling at me for being stupid and not having a contract in writing, my lawyer told me how to fight him. I needed more than a verbal contract and emails I'd saved. Mark was clever and did most of his negotiations on the phone. I didn't have enough proof. If I wanted to win I had to borrow more money to pay for the legal fees.

I was broken all over again. I knew better but, at the time, this shame felt worse than all the times I was harassed or belittled. I knew better but didn't do better. Hollywood beat me. I borrowed more money.

I got all my film, the negatives, and the edit. I didn't sell it. I kept those cans as a reminder of what a dupe I was for years. They reminded me of my shame. I flagellated myself with my misguided ambition.

I dusted myself off and went back to work in production. I took a job that was lower than my pay grade and knowledge because I felt the need to punish myself for being so stupid. I pitched a dancing show to a friend, and he told me dancing shows would never take off. I didn't have fight left in me to prove him wrong. Dancing shows took off, but I never worked on one. I worked on Food Network shows.

I wrote a script with a trusted friend. We pitched Dream-Works, Walden Media, Revolution Studios, and Sid Ganis. I had a shot in the room with the big boys and it felt good. It was a project I was both proud of and had creative input. I earned my seat at the table.

I still regret every minute I spent belittling myself over the pilot. I'm ashamed at how stupid I was. I hate having the experience to share, but hope someone reading this will think rationally while they dream big and look for the clues between bullshit and real work.

I also hope karma kicked Mark's ass back down the hole he crawled out of.

Holly Raychelle Hughes is freelance writer and intuitive healer. Her short stories and essays appear in xoJane.com, Kveller.com, and a variety of online and print publications. She is represented by Agent Carlie Webber from Fuse Literary. When she isn't writing, you can find her online @hgirlla, www.writerhughes.wordpress.com, planning for Halloween or dancing.